BLOOD AND DESTINY

APRIL 2017

BLOOD AND DESTINY

CHRIS BISHOP

RedDoor

Published by RedDoor
www.reddoorpublishing.com

The right of Chris Bishop to be identified as author of this Work
has been asserted by him in accordance with sections 77 and 78 of
the Copyright, Designs and Patents Act 1988

ISBN 978-1-910453-33-9

A CIP catalogue record for this book is available
from the British Library

Cover design: Patrick Knowles
www.patrickknowlesdesign.com

Map design: Joey Everett
Typesetting: Medlar Publishing Solutions Pvt Ltd, India

Printed and bound in Great Britain by Clays Ltd, St Ives plc.

FOR LEONA
with love and thanks for all her support and encouragement

'Never before has such terror appeared in Britain as we have now suffered from a pagan race'

Alcuin, a monk of York, 793

Prelude

"Who are you who dares disturb my grave? Who is it that scrapes back the soil from my bones to leave me naked to the eyes of strangers? Surely only the lowest of God's creatures would pick at a carcass so long dead that even the maggots and the worms go hungry!

You say you seek only the knowledge of who I was and how I came to rest in such a lonely grave as this. Well know then that I am Edward, third born son of Edwulf who was both Ealdorman and counsellor to kings. As to how I ended here is a story worth the telling but it's not for the ears of those who would grub in the earth with their bare hands and sift the soil with their fingers!

Yet I see some profit here. You have clearly wandered so far from the righteous path of your forebears that your hearts are now as cold as stones and your souls withered like fruits in winter. Have you forgotten that your past is as much a part of you as is the blood which courses through your veins? Therefore I will speak of my time if you will listen; but you must first know that I had then but sixteen years of age and cannot tell of that which was beyond my wit or understanding. My dear brother Edwin could tell you more for he had older eyes than mine and a wiser head, but his memory now is not near as sharp as the sword which he once wielded.

Know then that he and I lived at a troubled time when the shores of this land were ravaged by fierce, blood-crazed raiders who feared nothing, not even death itself. Having secured a small victory against these heathen hordes, our King, Lord Alfred, retreated to Chippenham to rest his weary army for the winter knowing that, come spring, war would begin in earnest. It was whilst Edwin and I were wont to join him there that we came upon the news which, had we but learned of it in time, might well have changed the course of all our lives – and yours.

Thus it was on the tenth day after Christmas in the year of our Lord 878 that we—

But there, I go too quick. To loose a knot you must needs find an end and so it is with my tangled tale that I must find a thread which may be pulled and then, with patience, all may be unravelled…

Chapter One

I had never smelled death before that day – at least, not like that. Even as a novice monk I was familiar with the acrid smell of burning thatch and timber as were we all at that time, but the smell which was carried to us on the cold north wind reeked of something more. It was as though the smoke had become tainted with the putrid stench of wasted blood and cloying flesh, an odour I would come to know all too well in my short life. My brother Edwin would have known it readily enough but he chose to say nothing at the time, perhaps hoping all was not as it appeared. In fact he kept his silence until we crested the next ridge where the sight which confronted us meant that the terrible truth could no longer be denied; for there, within a fold of the hill, were perhaps a half a dozen homes, all of which were burning fiercely.

I prayed that Edwin would not see fit to go down to what was left of the small settlement, though I knew he would; for what warrior could ever resist the lure of battle and the prospect of booty? Thus he scanned the scene of so much carnage, searching for even the slightest sign of life. Unlike me it was not the dead or the dying who concerned him, for they were beyond any help he could render. It was the living who troubled him, particularly if their number included any of the Viking warriors who had inflicted such needless slaughter. With his hand rested on the hilt of his still sheathed sword he coldly assessed the risks. From where we stood on the ridge the land sloped away steeply, levelling out only when it reached a stout wicker fence, albeit that had been trampled flat. In between all had been purposely cleared by those who lived there so as not to provide cover for any who approached, creating an area that was now both treacherous and exposed. 'Here, take this,' he said grimly as he turned and passed me his spear.

As befitted my calling as a novice monk I carried no weapon of any kind – unless you count the cross of Christ I wore about my neck. Thus I held the weapon awkwardly, grasping it as though the shaft were edged with thorns. 'But I've no skill with this!' I argued, half pleadingly.

'Then pray you have no cause to use it,' he answered simply, reaching across and roughly moving my hands along the shaft. 'If you hold it thus and look as though you mean to use it we may yet survive this place. If attacked, we try for the cover of those trees.' He pointed to a sparse line of scrub and thorn that looked a long way off. 'If we can't reach them we turn and fight back to back and we sell our lives as dearly as we can.'

With that Edwin slid his shield into position and undid the peace tie on his sword. Then, drawing the fearful weapon from its scabbard, he started off down the slope. Half running, half walking, he moved quickly without seeming to hurry, his eyes fixed always on the burning buildings.

I followed and tried to stay close to my brother but, hampered by the hem of my habit, I found the slope too steep. Even using the spear as a staff I stumbled and struggled noisily to keep my feet until Edwin grabbed me by the arm to steady my uncertain steps.

2

'He who hurries to the fray dies soonest!' he hissed, then made me walk at his side so that we could press forward our advance together sharing the cover of his shield.

The first thing we came to was the dogs. Two of them lay a few paces apart, their bodies bloodied and broken having no doubt been killed when they rushed out as the raiders attacked. Edwin knelt briefly to feel the coat of the one nearest him. Even finding it stiff and cold he was not reassured knowing that on such a cold morning their blood would have chilled within an hour, perhaps less. Instinctively he checked behind him, his eyes following the trail of our own footprints in the frosted grass until he found the ridge from where we had first seen the burning settlement. With no sign of any Vikings there, he was certain that whatever danger there was lay ahead of us, not behind.

The first of the Saxon casualties was sprawled on the ground just beyond the broken fence. Only as we reached the man did I realise to my horror that he was still alive, his entire body convulsing as each spasm of pain passed through it. I knelt beside him to offer what comfort I could whilst trying not to look too closely at his wound. The poor soul had been disembowelled and his viscera placed in his open hands. His innards had slithered through his shaking fingers and lay on the ground in a heap, the sight and stench of which made me retch.

Edwin raised his sword but I moved to stay his hand. 'Surely he cannot be long for this world now,' I reasoned. 'Let the sin of his death burden the souls of those who slew him, not yours!'

My brother frowned. His instinct was to end the man's misery and be done with it. Yet my plea suited his purpose for he knew that if any of the Vikings were still waiting, what remained of the settlement would be no place for a pious boy. 'Tend him then,' he agreed. 'Stay with him and offer prayers. Wait for my signal before you follow.'

He turned to leave but then stopped abruptly. 'If I'm taken,' he added, 'stay long enough to count their numbers if you can, then run. Go north until you reach Chippenham and there find Lord Alfred. Tell him all you've seen.' With that he pulled a small knife from his belt and quickly tested the blade with his thumb before offering it to me.

I looked at it disdainfully. 'But you know I can't take this man's life,' I reasoned. 'My calling forbids it even if...'

'The knife is not for him,' said Edwin quietly, his eyes fixed hard upon me. 'If it comes to it, lay the blade across your wrist and cut deep. Death will be slow but painless.'

'But that would be...'

'Square that with God when you meet him. You can see before you what happens if you let yourself be taken.'

* * * * *

As my father's third born son a life in Holy Orders had been my destiny since birth. With Edwin serving as a warrior and our older brother, Edmund, managing our father's lands, it was a natural choice. Yet even after so many years at the Abbey near Winchester I knew I still had much to learn. Hardest to endure had been accepting my new name. Like all noble Saxons that which I was given at birth was derived from the name of my father – thus I was christened Edward. This spoke to my lineage and my blood and for much the same reasons the Church had renamed me for one of the Apostles in the hope that I might emulate the spirit of such a Holy personage. I therefore came to be known as Matthew.

Holy name or not, when I looked at the dying man Edwin had left in my charge I was not sure what was expected of me. As I was not ordained I could not offer absolution so, instead, I spoke to the man softly, choosing words I hoped might be of some comfort. In the end I took off the simple wooden cross I wore about my neck and gave it to the man to hold as I prayed for him. At the Abbey I had been taught that the art of prayer lay in clearing the mind of all save that for which you prayed and in adopting the correct stance – kneeling with eyes closed and hands pressed earnestly together. But prayer in the hallowed halls at the Abbey had come easily. Now, with a man dying in agony before my very eyes, the state of serenity I sought was harder to achieve and, try as I might, I could not keep my gaze from following Edwin's progress towards the burning buildings.

Mercifully, the dying Saxon had passed well beyond pain. His body still shook but the spasms had become more like shivers that rippled through him, all of which he endured by closing his eyes and clutching the wooden cross ever tighter. When at last the time came for his passing it was all quite sudden. He gave a deep gasp then stiffened. As the life left his body he relaxed and his head lolled backwards so that his eyes, still wide open, were staring straight upwards. I took this as a good sign for which I at once gave thanks. Surely as the man had spent his last moments on this earth looking towards heaven he was assured of salvation?

Hurriedly I made the sign of the cross and closed the man's eyes before retrieving my precious crucifix. Then, with nothing more than a glance at the body of the poor soul I had tended so ineptly, I hurried to join my brother.

* * * * *

As soon as I reached him, Edwin began to advance the last few paces towards the settlement. He was not to be hurried; instead, he moved stealthily with each step carefully measured against the last, thereby hoping to tempt anyone who was waiting for us to make their move too soon. Not that he would have expected the ambush to be there, so near the entrance. He knew they would wait until we were both fully inside the settlement where they could then come at us from all sides at once.

He stopped as soon as he reached the first of the burning buildings. Having seen no sign of the raiders, we both wrapped our cloaks across our faces as proof against the smoke, then began carefully stepping over the debris of the raid – household goods seized and then discarded; broken tools, pots and clothes, all of which were littered on the ground.

All around us the flames crackled and heaved sending up great showers of sparks as the burning timbers broke and fell into the glowing embers. The intense heat from those fires was almost as much as we could bear and the smoke stung our eyes, yet we pressed forward as best we could. And there were bodies too. The first we came to was that of a man whose head had been flattened against a grinding stone with the broad blade of a battle axe. The second, a few paces further off, was that of a woman. She had been stripped naked and I fear had been taken many times before they slit her throat.

Having seen death so often and in so many guises, Edwin barely glanced at the bodies. Instead, he led the way directly to the centre of the settlement where he stopped and turned slowly, his eyes still searching every shadow. Finding nothing, he voiced his challenge.

'Who has done this evil?' he bellowed loud enough to be heard above the roar of the flames. 'Which cowards have spilled Saxon blood upon this soil?'

He waited, but when there came no reply he half turned to face the forest which was to the rear of the settlement.

'What, do you cower behind trees and tremble rather than try the hand of one who would defend himself?'

Still there was no response so he turned again. 'Know then that I am Edwin, second born son of the noble Saxon Edwulf. Hear that name and mark it well, for though you lack the courage even to show yourselves you shall hear of it again.'

Although there was no response Edwin had fought Vikings often enough to know their cunning, certainly well enough not to relax his guard even for a moment.

Then something moved to our right. He spun round to confront whatever it was then stepped back to give himself more room. Through the smoke we could just make out the shape of a large dog as it heaved itself into view. The poor beast had taken the blow of an axe or a sword across its back yet somehow still survived. It struggled towards us, whining as it gamely dragged its hind legs, smearing a trail of blood on the ground behind it. It seemed too weak to reach us, so I went across and petted it, kneeling beside it and smoothing back its long grey coat with my hand. It seemed much soothed by this and yelped pitifully as it tried to lick my arm

7

but there was nothing to be done save to end its pain. Thus Edwin came across and despatched it with a single thrust of his sword, then wiped the blade clean upon its coat.

* * * * *

'Are any of them still here?' I asked anxiously as I stood beside my brother amid the still burning ruins.

He shook his head. 'No, but they left not long before we arrived,' he said, seeming worried. 'So keep your wits about you.'

Together we worked our way through the settlement looking for more victims. As the fires began to die down we could peer inside what was left of the buildings and there found the charred remains of three people who it seemed had been cast into the flames, though whether dead or still alive at the time we could not say.

Just beyond the buildings, near the edge of the forest, were the bodies of two men who had clearly fought their way back towards the shelter of the trees. One had had his eyes gouged out and his throat cut; the other had been butchered with a spear and lay curled upon the ground. A third man lay close by. He had sought to die within the sanctity of what served the Saxons for a church – a simple altar covered with a canopy of thatch – but he had been dragged back before being slain, for the marks could be seen where his fingers had clawed at the frosted ground as he struggled to resist. Edwin said the Vikings had taken him for a chief for they had cut off his head and hands to mark him out, then impaled the severed parts on sticks beside his ruined corpse.

In all we counted nine dead – five men, one woman and the rest too badly burned for us to tell for certain. There was nothing to be done save to scrape shallow graves in which to bury them, laying them alongside each other with the dogs close by. Then, though we had no names to call them by, I offered prayers for their eternal souls.

Although cremations were forbidden by the Church, we could not move the remains of those who had been burned. We therefore had no choice but to rekindle the fire and let the flames consume them fully. It was whilst gathering more wood for this from the forest that I found blood smeared against the bark of a tree.

'Whoever left this is badly harmed,' observed Edwin dabbing at the sticky mess with his finger. 'See how he leaned here for support? And there's more blood on the ground over there.'

'He can't be long for this world if he bleeds so much,' I suggested, though Edwin only frowned.

We followed the bloody trail for some distance. Sometimes it was little more than a few drops spilled upon the still frosted leaves, but wherever the man had stopped to rest there was a pool of it to show that his wound was indeed bleeding freely. It appeared he had half crawled, half staggered from the settlement, following the line of a stream before turning northwards to push his way through the forest. From there he had managed to drag himself but a few paces more, for we could see him lying on his back with his cloak wrapped around him like a shroud.

Fearing a trap, Edwin approached the figure with caution. That he was one of the raiders was obvious but he was older than I expected, with a face so lined and creased it looked like leather. And I had been right about the wound as the man seemed so badly hurt that he could scarcely move. His breathing was quick and shallow and his head was tipped back with his eyes closed tight. Even so he seemed to ooze defiance, as though he waited for death but was not yet ready to succumb to its embrace.

'Is he alone?' I asked, gripping the spear tightly.

'Well if he isn't we'll know about it soon enough,' warned Edwin. He clearly had no qualms on that account and ventured closer. He didn't even look back as he did so, preferring to keep his eyes on the Viking instead.

When he was satisfied that the man offered no threat, Edwin set down his shield and pushed the point of his sword into the ground so he could retrieve it quickly if it were needed. That done, he reached back for the spear he had given me. Using the point of it, he lifted the hem of the Viking's cloak so carefully that the old warrior seemed not to notice as his hand and the sword he gripped within it were revealed.

Edwin used the spear to lift back even more of the man's clothing, this time enough to reveal his tunic. We could see blood had soaked through, staining the garment with a large red crescent beneath the left arm. Some threads from the sheepskin jerkin he wore over the tunic had become matted in the wound and the Viking gave a stifled moan when they were lifted. As he shifted his body slightly we could see that he was, by then, watching us through half-closed eyes.

'So why have they left him?' I asked thinking the Vikings should have put a man so badly injured to the sword rather than let him suffer a slow death from such a dreadful wound.

'To die as best he can,' explained Edwin. 'We're his chance to gain a seat in Valhalla.'

Such was the Vikings' creed that to die in combat was the only way to be assured of a place in the Great Hall of Dead Warriors.

'You mean they left him to fight us alone even when so sorely maimed?'

Edwin shook his head. 'No, they meant only that he should die trying. See how they've stripped him of everything of any value save that sword? They didn't expect him to survive our coming.'

It was true that the man had no other weapons nor did he seem to possess any amulets or jewellery, not even a ring. 'So will you finish him or leave him here to perish from his wound?' I asked, not sure whether my Christian compassion should extend to Vikings.

Edwin smiled then moved closer to the old warrior, staring straight down into his eyes. 'No, we'll see him safe from this world to the next,' he said ruefully. 'But he must pay for his passage. Whether bound for the fires of hell or for the hall of Valhalla there's something I would ask him first.'

With that the Viking tried to move. He mustered all his strength and lifted his sword a little but Edwin quickly placed his foot on the blade then kicked it out of reach. The Viking lolled sideways and patted the ground feebly as though trying to recover it, but Edwin would have none of that. He used his foot again, this time to roll the man over onto his back once more. In so doing he revealed the true horror of the man's wound. His left arm had been all but severed from the shoulder and, although he had wrapped pieces of cloth and hide around it as binding, the dressing gaped to expose the raw and livid flesh beneath.

'Their beliefs are not so strange,' mused Edwin sensing my disdain. 'You've seen how men die when wounds like that fester and refuse to heal. Better to die fighting than to suffer that. Besides, what does your Holy Church offer us if our blood is spilled to provident its cause?'

'That you shall receive your place in Heaven,' I answered quickly.

'Well I'll warrant this warrior would find Valhalla paradise enough. And who are we to deny him that?' So saying he laid the point of the spear directly onto the man's wound and prodded viciously. As the Viking flinched Edwin peered directly into his eyes. 'Where's Guthrum?' he demanded.

The Viking said nothing.

'Guthrum!' repeated Edwin applying more pressure to the spear. 'Where's Guthrum and his army?'

The old warrior shook his head, then reached again for his sword but managed only to crush his shoulder as he did so. He screamed something which sounded like an oath, then spat at us.

Again Edwin pressed with the tip of the spear but this time even harder. 'Guthrum!' he demanded, twisting the shaft so that fresh blood welled up from the wound. 'Tell me where the bastard's hiding!'

The Viking closed his eyes and hissed through clenched teeth as he struggled to endure the pain.

'Guthrum!' screamed Edwin angrily, following every word with a brutal stab. 'Where...is...Lord...Guthrum!'

The Viking moaned miserably then began to drift from consciousness. Fearing his prisoner would die too soon,

Edwin kicked his legs to rouse him. Then, as the man's eyes opened again, he readied himself to resume the torture.

Already the Viking had endured more than any man should suffer. Taking a deep breath, he raised his right arm and pointed vaguely to the south. 'G...Guthrum,' he said pointing and nodding weakly. 'G...Guthrum.'

For a moment Edwin and the old warrior looked at each other as though sharing something which went beyond the need for words. Then, still without speaking, Edwin raised the spear and thrust it hard into the man's belly. The Viking moaned as it was driven home but otherwise made no complaint. Instead, he grasped the spear with his hand as if trying to pull it even deeper into his own body. Only as Edwin twisted the shaft did the old man cry out, but even then it was not from pain – it was a cry of triumph.

Chapter Two

Although my career in the Church had been chosen for me by my father, I had found that a routine of prayer and contemplation suited me well enough albeit the work in between was hard. I had shaved the crown of my head as a sign of my humility and acceptance of my 'calling' and, even though I was used to finer clothes, had donned the roughly woven habit of a novice monk without complaint. But this shallow root to my conviction allowed many doubts, not least of which was the unanswered question of why a merciful God would permit so much slaughter to be visited upon a pious land.

This question posed itself again as I looked down at the bloodied corpse of the Viking whom Edwin had so cruelly tortured and then slain. Not for the first time that day I saw all the slaughter for what it was – a pointless waste of blood. 'May God forgive us,' I muttered to myself, then made the sign of the cross.

Edwin looked at me strangely. 'What, have you pity for this heathen bastard whose kind slaughtered your own dear parents and took your brother and your sister to be slaves?'

I couldn't answer that. I knew I should say something about 'God' and 'forgiveness' but couldn't find it in myself to even speak the words. Instead, I kept my eyes firmly on the body on the ground. 'You do know he was lying?' I managed at last, as if that should make a difference.

Edwin looked down at the corpse and pressed the lifeless body with his foot. 'Of course he was lying,' he agreed. 'But you'll find there's sometimes truth in a lie just as there's a seed hidden in the soft flesh of a fruit.' Seeing that I didn't understand his point, he put his hand on my shoulder. 'Look Matthew, was this Guthrum's man or not?'

'Of course he was. That's why he lied; to protect his Lord.'

'Then those who raided this settlement were part of Guthrum's army?'

'Yes. As like as not,' I agreed.

'And with the winter now upon us what would you do if you were one of his band?'

'Return to his camp if I had food enough,' I suggested weakly, not quite sure what he was asking.

'Exactly. So having taken all they could from here, which way are they headed?'

I looked about me. Their trail led north through the forest, so I pointed in that direction.

'Then that's where you'll find Guthrum and his horde,' announced my brother. 'For they were surely returning to join him there; not in the south as this wretch would have had us believe.'

Such logic was as much a part of Edwin's way as was his skill with the sword. He stood tall and straight with long yellow hair that hung in loose Saxon curls but with many braids that marked him out as a seasoned warrior. His eyes were of such a vivid blue that our dear mother used to say they were mirrors of the summer sky, yet there were few men who could look into them without feeling his strength of mind.

He was scarce ten years older than me but had already earned a formidable reputation fighting at Alfred's side.

Like all warriors, Edwin regarded the spoils of war as his for the taking. Thus he was quick to search the Viking's body, rolling it over in order to remove the sword-scabbard which the man still wore about his waist.

Reluctantly I helped him but, as we had already noted, the Viking had been stripped of everything of value. Everything that is save his sword and Edwin already had that and was busy testing the weight and 'feel' of it in his hand as he tried a few short strokes. It was indeed a very fine weapon with a well-forged blade and two good edges. The grip had been gilded with a silver pattern of a serpent with the pommel shaped to form its head. There were also runes etched into the blade which we knew would be the name of the sword, though neither Edwin nor I could read them.

'Should we not bury him?' I asked.

Edwin looked at the body. 'No, let his own Gods take care of him,' he said sourly. Then, perhaps out of respect for one who had at least died bravely, he thought better of leaving the corpse to be ravaged by wolves. 'We'll drag him back to the settlement and add his carcass to the flames.' He then handed me the sword and scabbard, having first secured the peace tie to keep it safe. 'Here, you had best put this on.'

I looked at the weapon with contempt.

'What, are you afraid your abbot would disapprove?' mocked Edwin. 'Put it on lad, for 'twill be easier to carry if you do. And think no shame in it for I've fought beside more priests than I can count and some of them had a thirst for blood which sickened even our most hardened warriors.'

Although it troubled me I did as I was told. Then, half dragging, half carrying the corpse between us, we made our way back to the settlement where we rolled it into the still eager flames.

As the fire raged I watched and wondered about what happened to a man's soul when his body was committed to the fire. Would it rise up within the smoke and thus find its way to Heaven or would it be trapped for ever in the ashes? As I pondered this my brother was set on more earthly matters for, as a warrior, he needed to know more about the raid.

'How many people lived in this place?' he asked.

I turned away from the fire and looked at the line of freshly dug graves. I knew there would have been others at the settlement as well. Those we had found were all ceorls, although probably freemen working land they held in tenure from their Lord. Some might have made it to the safety of the forest but most of those who were not killed would have been taken to be sold as slaves. 'Perhaps twenty,' I said guessing at their number from the size of the settlement.

'And they were of good heart,' observed Edwin. 'For they didn't die without a fight. So the raiders would have been what, at least that number and maybe more?'

I shrugged for it hardly seemed to matter now.

'So,' continued Edwin, 'why would a score of Viking warriors trouble to attack a lowly settlement in the midst of winter?' As he spoke I looked back towards the ridge and tried to visualise what had happened. There were signs to show that some of the Vikings were on horseback, so they would have been forced to come in as we had done rather than use the cover of the forest. Therefore they would have attacked at dawn, coming over the ridge and trying to get as close as they could without being seen. It looked as though they made it as far as the wicker fence before they woke the dogs. From that point on they would have rushed forward, screaming and howling like wild beasts as the Saxons were still stirring from their sleep, then spread out through the settlement to secure it. The raid would have lasted little more than half an hour and perhaps as long again for them to complete their slaughter and scavenge all that might be of use to them before destroying what remained.

'They left in haste,' mused Edwin. 'So much so they were prepared to forgo the chance to kill two more Saxons, for they surely knew of our coming or why else would they have left the one we found in the forest?' With that he noticed a careless footprint pressed into some soft ground and crouched down to look at it more closely. 'They're not so far ahead of us,' he reasoned. 'Driving any stock they stole from here will slow them down, but even if we leave at once we'll be lucky to find them before dark.'

'But surely even you wouldn't think to take on twenty Viking warriors?' I said, astonished that he would even consider such a thing.

'No, but I must discover what I can of their numbers and their purpose here if I'm to make my report to Lord Alfred,' explained Edwin. 'That's my sworn duty as a warrior and I'm bound to it just as you are bound to serve your abbot.'

* * * * *

With nothing more to be done at the settlement, we set about trailing the Vikings through the forest. They seemed to have followed an old drover's path which continued northwards, making little or no attempt to conceal the tracks left by the stock they were driving. They had also rigged some form of litter which was being dragged behind a horse, the marks where it had scored the ground leaving two distinct lines.

'Perhaps they've other wounded,' I suggested as we stopped to rest.

Edwin shook his head. 'No, they would have left any who couldn't walk to fight alongside the one we've already found. The litter is for that which they've looted, not their wounded.' He stood up straight and stretched himself. The light was fading fast and he knew it would be dangerous to continue once it got dark, so decided we should make our camp there for the night.

Although we had no food, Edwin allowed me to risk lighting a fire as without it we would surely freeze. Even so it was still too cold to sleep and I huddled beneath my cloak watching the flames as they flickered and set the shadows dancing on the trees around us. I fancied those were the souls of all those so newly slain and was afraid of them. Worse still, thoughts of the slaughter at the settlement reminded me of the fate of our own dear parents. They had been killed in a Viking raid six weeks earlier whilst we had been away – me taking instruction at the Abbey and Edwin fighting at Alfred's side. We knew little of what had happened except that our father and mother had been murdered and our brother and sister, Edmund and Edwina, both taken, together with their respective spouses and their children.

When the news of this had eventually reached Edwin he had gone at once to our family Vill but found nothing there but the charred ruins of what had once been our home. He then collected me and together we tended our parents' grave and I offered prayers for their immortal souls. There was little else to be done, so we appointed a trusted Reeve to oversee our lands thereby enabling us to return to our respective lives.

Although brothers, there was no real bond between us then. In fact because Edwin had been sent away to become a warrior soon after I was born we scarce knew each other at all. Having been briefly reunited in the loss of our parents who were the only common tie between us, we expected soon to part once more, possibly never to see each other again.

As I pondered this strange quirk of fate, Edwin was troubled with less weighty matters. He was deep in thought wrestling with some small detail which still played upon his mind. I am not sure what it was that troubled him but all his instincts kept him from his sleep.

'Why did they attack the settlement?' he asked aloud without bothering to check if I was still awake. 'It was nothing but a few poor homes with scarce enough food for those who lived there.'

I sat up and pulled my hood over my head for warmth. I was hopeful this conversation might distract me from thinking about whatever lurked within the shadows, but it still seemed pointless to worry about what was so obvious. 'They came upon it by chance and took what they could,' I reasoned. 'Now, as you've said, they're hurrying back to Guthrum's camp.' Shivering, I put some more wood on the fire and warmed my hands against the flames. 'Surely that's what any man would do with the weather closing in. Already the air feels cold enough for snow and no sane man would, by choice, stay in the open.'

Edwin was not so easily satisfied. 'Twenty warriors risk a winter raid for a few cattle and a couple of pigs?' he continued. 'That can't be right. And then they made off before we arrived missing the chance for an easy kill. Why would they do that? My sword alone would be worth fifty times as much as whatever they stole from the settlement.'

'They're just a raiding party,' I shrugged. 'Now they've been discovered Lord Alfred will send men to see them off. Surely you need do nothing more than to make your report...'

'There's more to it than that,' he said, then picked up a stone and placed it on the ground between us. 'Look, this is Chippenham with Alfred's Vill.' Then he placed another stone beneath it. 'And we're here, to the south of it as are the raiding party.'

I was too busy warming myself to take much notice of the crude map, but Edwin continued.

'If Guthrum went north after Alfred paid him tribute to leave Exeter he should be somewhere here,' he reasoned, placing a third stone in position above that of Chippenham. 'So if the raiding party are now travelling north to rejoin Guthrum their path will take them right past Alfred's Vill.'

'Perhaps they're going there to join Alfred for the feasts of Epiphany,' I suggested weakly. 'Which is where we should be if—'

Edwin reacted at once. 'That's it!' he stormed.

'What, Guthrum's men are going to join Alfred?'

'Not join him, Matthew. They mean to attack him! Look, with Guthrum's main force to the north and these men to the south Alfred is all but surrounded.' With his finger Edwin scratched a circle in the dirt to make his point.

I looked at him in amazement. 'But they're so few! What could twenty men do against Alfred's army?'

'Alfred has no army at Chippenham. He has what, his personal retinue plus barely a few hundred men still with him? And these Vikings are not alone,' he added. 'They'll join with others. Don't you see? Guthrum dares not move his whole army at once lest it be seen. Instead he's moving them into position in smaller groups so the trap is set before Alfred knows anything about it.'

It was all speculation but it did make sense. It also explained why the raiding party had attacked the settlement and ignored the chance of slaying us. They were not looking for booty; they were foraging for supplies needed to feed themselves before joining an army that was gathering for a major offensive. The riches they might reap from that would far outstrip anything they could expect to take from one warrior and a novice monk.

'But surely they'll not attack at this time of year?' I argued. 'The winter is but halfway through. In the spring perhaps, but not mid winter...'

Edwin said nothing.

'But if Guthrum were to attack him now in force Lord Alfred would be taken by surprise! Every man in Chippenham would be slaughtered!'

'Aye,' agreed Edwin. 'Including Lord Alfred. And there's the real prize, for with our King slain the whole of Wessex would be laid wide open to Guthrum's blood-crazed horde!'

* * * * *

We knew then that we had to make as much haste as possible to warn Lord Alfred. His fortified Vill at Chippenham was still the best part of a day's march from there, much of it across difficult and dangerous terrain. To reach it we would need to continue directly north, crossing the edge of the high moor before entering the forests to the south of the settlement. Many of the trees closest to Chippenham had long ago been felled to provide timber to build the houses and defences, which meant there would be little in the way of cover as we approached the Vill.

Worse still, the raiders we were following were also travelling north and because they would be hampered by the beasts they were driving, there was a real risk of us catching them up along the way. If so we could not think to engage them for, if captured or slain, we would forfeit not just our own lives but those of every man at Chippenham – including our King.

But Edwin had already formed his plan. 'Tomorrow we shall leave at first light,' he announced. 'We'll travel west for a while and then turn north until we strike the banks of the river Avon. Once across it, we can follow it back to the Vill keeping the water between us and the raiders. But we shall need to take great care, for if Guthrum has gathered an army he'll have posted pickets.'

Edwin chose not to enlighten me further. To pass pickets we would need to split up and each take our chances alone under the cover of night in the hope that one of us might get through. It would be dangerous work, but there was something else Edwin had not told me, something of much more immediate concern.

* * * * *

Ever since leaving the settlement Edwin had had the distinct feeling we were being followed. Several times he had tried to see who it was but, whilst in the forest, it had been all too easy for our pursuers to conceal themselves. Now as we sat beside the fire every instinct he had told him that someone's eyes were indeed upon us.

He put his hand on my arm. 'We're not alone,' he whispered.

'Vikings?' I asked, starting to get up.

Edwin gripped my arm to restrain me. 'Don't move!' he ordered. 'Stay where you are and keep talking as though I'm still here with you.' With that, he pulled his knife from his belt, checked the blade then eased himself away from the fire, gradually withdrawing into the darkness.

I waited anxiously, careful not to check Edwin's progress lest I give away his position. I could think of nothing to talk about and so instead began reciting the Lord's Prayer which I had learned by rote.

'Our Father who art in Heaven, hallowed be thy name...'

With neither sign nor sound from Edwin, I clung to the words of the prayer for comfort but uttered them too quickly for them to be of much help. Out of habit, I also put my hands together and raised them up to God.

'Thy Kingdom come, thy will be done on earth as it is in Heaven...'

Prayer was not comfort enough as my mind raced to imagine what it would be like if the Vikings came for me. I tried to contain my fear by reassuring myself that if my brother were taken he would not go without a fight and thereby give me warning. But what then? Looking around, I recalled the Viking's sword I had been given to carry and without a second thought, undid the peace tie and pulled it from its scabbard.

'Lord, forgive us our trespasses as we forgive those who trespass against us...'

It was then I realised that my eyes were wide open and that my hands, which should have been clasped in prayer, gripped the Viking's sword instead.

'...lead us not into temptation but deliver us from evil, for thine is the kingdom, the power and the glory...'

I was shocked to find that when my need was most I had turned not to God for comfort but to the tools of the Devil. I stared at the brutal weapon as I held it in my hands, now frightened as much by this sudden lapse of faith as by the prospect of meeting any Vikings. I was brought to my senses only by the sound of something moving to my right. Still clutching the sword, I rose quickly to my feet and held my breath as I peered desperately into the darkness. But I could see nothing.

The moments which followed seemed like an age with every sound, whether real or imagined, feasting upon my fear. I turned first one way then the other, brandishing the sword in the forlorn hope that the very sight of it would somehow be enough to deter a band of blood-crazed Vikings!

Then, as two figures emerged from the darkness, I prepared myself for the worst. Only as they drew nearer did I realise it was Edwin dragging a young boy by the arm. The brat was kicking and wriggling as Edwin hauled him forward then thrust him to the ground in front of the fire.

I tossed the sword aside in shame. 'A boy!' I exclaimed, unable to hide my relief. 'It was just a boy!'

The lad was up in a moment and looking defiantly at the gap between us.

'Watch him!' warned Edwin sensing he was about to bolt.

I reached out and gently took hold of the lad. 'We won't hurt you,' I assured him, but the boy seemed not to hear. Instead he shook himself free and tried to dodge past me in order to make off into the night.

Edwin grabbed him roughly and pulled him back, this time keeping hold of his wrist.

'As like as not he's from the settlement,' I suggested. 'Perhaps he hid in the forest then followed us when he realised that none of his folk had survived.'

'Which would explain why he's frightened half to death,' agreed Edwin. 'For if he's seen his family slain or carried off as slaves he must— Aaargh!'

The boy had bitten deep into Edwin's hand and was free again but had not reckoned on one closer to his own age and agility. As he tried to weave past me I tripped him up then caught him by the arm.

'He's more like an eel than a boy!' said Edwin, nursing his hand.

'He has little enough to say for himself,' I noted.

Edwin nodded. 'So what's the matter boy, lost your tongue?' he asked. Then he gripped the boy by the chin and forced his mouth open. 'No he still has one,' he said peering inside. 'So why don't you speak, lad? Tell us who you are?'

'Has he lost his wits?' I suggested. 'There was a boy at the Abbey who saw his parents slain and uttered not a single word for weeks, not even in prayer.'

Edwin considered the possibility. 'Well, if he is from the settlement he'll have seen some dreadful things right enough. We'll take him with us to Chippenham; perhaps he has family there who'll recognise him and take him in.'

Though mute, he seemed a spirited lad, some years younger than me but with yellow hair and bright blue eyes which meant he could have been mistaken for our kin. Because of this we determined to call him Edmund after the brother we had lost. He was dressed plainly with a belted sheepskin tunic and woollen leggings but wore a cloak secured with a brooch of whalebone inlaid with silver. It was a costly piece to be worn by one so young but was probably a treasured heirloom passed to him by his father's father, grabbed as he fled the carnage of the raid. We hoped it might suffice for someone to recognise him as kin.

As we huddled around the fire, Edmund no longer seemed inclined to bolt but still kept his distance, sitting alone in the darkness. In fact only when I retrieved the Viking's sword did the boy show any sign of interest. He crawled across to where I sat and tried to inspect it, stroking the blade with his fingers with an almost curious reverence.

'Keep that sword away from him!' warned Edwin sternly. 'My hand bears the marks to show what his teeth can do; if we allow him a sword he may cut us both to pieces. Remember, he's seen things which may have turned his mind. With sleep will come all manner of torments and he'll dream of vengeance, as might anyone who's seen their family slain. Either that or he'll seek an end in death at his own hand and I wouldn't have that upon your soul, or mine.'

Although I could tell that my brother was in earnest, I wondered what a mere boy could do with a sword almost too heavy for him to lift. Nonetheless, when I re-secured the peace tie and tucked the weapon beneath me, the boy moved back to the far side of the fire. In truth, I was pleased to put the sword away. It still troubled me that I'd turned to it so readily whilst

27

waiting for Edwin and I felt my faith had been tested and found wanting. It was not something I was ready to dwell upon too deeply. Instead I applied my mind to the welfare of the boy, certain he would freeze to death if he slept so far from the fire. 'Perhaps his young blood doesn't feel the cold,' I suggested.

'No, he needs his own company for now,' said Edwin. 'He'll come to us in time.'

In the distance a lone wolf howled against the cold. This seemed to unsettle Edmund.

'At least now he'll be less inclined to wander off,' teased Edwin.

I patted the ground beside me to show Edmund he could sleep there if he wished, but still the boy wouldn't join us. Even when the wolf cried out again he simply pulled his cloak up tighter beneath his chin and huddled in the darkness on his own.

'It's just a wolf,' I offered, trying to reassure him. 'You needn't be afraid for they're shy of us when we're together and won't come closer to the fire.'

'Exactly. So get some rest, both of you,' added Edwin. 'We've a hard day's march ahead of us and must be gone at first light if we're to be in time to warn Alfred.'

'But the raiders can scarce reach Chippenham before us,' I reasoned. 'And if they're to join the attack it must mean that it's yet some days off.'

'Only if they're part of the assault and not men sent to gather food and provisions. Remember, Guthrum's men must eat like any others.'

'Then Lord Alfred's Vill may have already fallen?' I had not meant to speak the words aloud as the prospect was almost too terrible to think of.

'Aye,' replied Edwin, his voice heavy with concern. 'And if so may God have mercy upon the souls of all who shelter with our King, for we'll be too late to do more than offer prayers for their salvation. That and dig their graves and I for one have done enough of that this day already.'

Chapter Three

That morning as the dawn chased the shadows from our dreams and stirred us with its icy fingers, I couldn't help but notice that the sun had broached the darkness long before the moon was gone. It was an omen so powerful that I called to mind an ancient saying:

> *'When sun and moon both share the same sky*
> *So the plans of men shall go awry.'*

If Edwin also saw the portent he chose to ignore it. Instead he got up and tried to warm his hands over what remained of the fire, thereby prompting me to begin my chores. Reluctantly I roused myself and went to fetch more wood, returning quickly with a small pile of dry logs. Although still hungry, I thought we might at least start our journey warm.

'Did you not see the sky this morning?' I asked as I blew on the embers trying to coax the flames to rise. 'Surely such signs don't bode well for us or for Lord Alfred?'

Edwin got up and stretched himself. 'What will be will be,' he said simply. 'We can't change that which fate has set in store for us.'

'But if it was an omen...' I protested.

'Matthew, you of all people should know better than to heed such nonsense,' warned Edwin. 'Or has your religious training taught you nothing? For my part, I've seen enough so-called "omens" to know they're nothing more than foolish superstition. If Alfred is to be saved it'll be because we acted with speed and with courage, not because some sign in the sky decreed it would be so.' With that he made his way towards the stream.

I watched for a few moments then called after him. 'Should I at least wake the boy?'

Edwin turned as if considering it. 'No, leave him be. He can have slept little as it is and we'll need to rouse him soon enough.'

I joined my brother at the stream where we knelt together to scoop up handfuls of the icy water. It was too cold to wash so we simply drank our fill before returning to the fire. Edmund was awake by this time and was seated beside the fire holding the Viking's sword which he had found and drawn from its scabbard.

Edwin rushed across and seized the weapon, snatching it roughly from the boy's hands. 'This is not yours to hold!' he scowled. Then he turned to me. 'And you should take better care of that which is given to your charge!'

'But he was only—'

'I don't care what he was doing,' he barked angrily. 'You were told to keep that sword away from him!'

I was shocked at his sudden temper which had come so quick it had taken me by surprise. I knew I was at fault, but no harm had come of it and thus I felt that it hardly warranted such a harsh rebuke.

Edwin sheathed the sword and secured it, then almost threw at me. 'Put it on!' he barked. 'And next time do as you're ordered!' Then he stormed off and began to gather up his things in silence.

31

Hurriedly we broke camp, kicking out the fire and pissing on the embers before gathering up the last of our belongings. As we left, Edwin seemed much calmer. It was as though losing his temper was like drawing his sword: swift and deadly but then, once the weapon was sheathed, the quarrel was quickly forgotten.

I recall that it was a bitter morning that day, with the frost set hard on the ground and the wind so sharp it seemed to bite any flesh left uncovered. Edwin led the way with his shield strapped across his back, leaving the forest to turn westwards and then following a shepherd's trail which kept to the high ground close to the line of the trees. After marching in silence for nearly an hour we then turned northwards again and continued until we reached the edge of the moor.

It looked a lonely and desolate place which stretched as far as our eyes could see. Thankfully we had only to cross the corner of it and reckoned to be in the forests to the south of Chippenham by that same afternoon. However, that was not to be for no sooner had we started across than the weather worsened still further. Snow began to fall, not thick enough to coat the ground but blown in wild flurries by the wind so that we could scarce see a hand in front of us. That same wind tore into us so that we walked hunched like old men as we struggled against it. Even with my hood pulled low across my face and my hands tucked deep into the sleeves of my habit the icy wind seemed to cut right through me. Thus our progress was pitifully slow and it was growing dark by the time we reached the shelter of the forest on the far side. There we rested briefly, cold, wet and hungry, knowing there were still several desperate hours ahead of us if we were to reach Chippenham in time to warn Lord Alfred.

As we set off again we hoped to strike the banks of the river within the hour. Not that it was far, but the winter forest was bleak and bare and with no trails to follow we were obliged to cut our way through some parts of it, which was a noisy and laborious task. It was also dangerous work and we needed to keep well apart for fear of striking one another in the dark as we hacked and slashed with the swords. Edwin and I both took turns to lead, leaving Edmund to follow behind. Every so often we stopped to listen and to check for any sign of the Vikings, knowing that the closer we got to Chippenham the more likely it was we would encounter whatever forces Guthrum had mustered. Yet even as we reached the banks of the river we had seen or heard nothing.

That night the river looked black and flowed as thick as cream. Small slivers of ice had formed near the bank; so thin that when swept against the reeds they broke and were carried away downstream. Yet there were places where the ice was beginning to thicken.

'With the stock they're driving and all their booty they'll not cross until they find a bridge,' declared Edwin. 'Thus we should be safer on the other side.'

In order to cross a river Edwin might normally have formed a makeshift bridge by felling a tree or hauling one which had already fallen into position. Without ropes or an axe that wasn't possible and, in any event, we could ill afford the time it would take, especially in the dark. The only other option was for us to wade across. Even that was not easy for, in the darkness, we could scarce see the far bank. Also the water flowed between the trees at that point and their roots, which seemed to grow in a tangled web from the riverbed itself, were slippery with moss and slime.

We walked upstream until we found a gap safe enough to try. There Edwin began to strip off his clothes until he stood naked and shivering as the flakes of snow touched his already pale skin. I was surprised to see the scars that marred my brother's body. One looked raw and livid and ran all the way across his back. The other was less obvious but suggested a spear wound to his shoulder.

Suddenly conscious of my gaze, Edwin seemed strangely ill at ease. 'Hurry!' he ordered, his voice shaking with the cold. 'We'll work our way across together. Place all the clothes on my shield and carry it above your head. Whatever you do keep them from getting wet or we'll all freeze to death long before we reach Chippenham.'

I removed my clothes and urged Edmund to do the same. The young boy seemed reluctant at first but when he saw we were determined, did as he was told. I left the Viking sword fastened securely around my waist, for it was too heavy to carry any other way, then bundled all our clothes together and used the belt from my habit to tie them as securely as I could to the upturned shield.

Edwin worked his way down into the icy waters and began to wade across. He also wore his sword about his waist but kept his spear to hand, using it to probe the river in order to know its depth.

Although wide, the river was seldom more than waist deep, so Edmund was sent in next, followed closely by me. As I entered the water it felt so cold it drew the breath from my body, numbing the flesh wherever it touched my skin. Beneath my feet the riverbed was soft mud so that I sank into it with every step, stirring up rotting leaves that smelled foul as they floated to the surface.

Edwin and the young boy seemed to make good progress and were almost on the other side whilst I, struggling to keep the shield above my head, was still but halfway across. Twice I nearly soured our fate by slipping so that Edwin had to return in order to help me with the precious bundle. In the end we carried the shield between us.

Once safely on the other side we hurried into a small clearing where we stamped our feet and shivered, our bodies bent and curled against the cold. My fingers were so numb that I could scarce unbend them, thus I struggled to untie the bundle of clothes.

'Be quick,' urged Edwin clasping his hands together and blowing on them for warmth. Then, seeing the knot set fast, he pushed me aside and used his sword to cut through my belt. We dried ourselves on Edwin's cloak then began to dress as hurriedly as we could. I was able to repair my belt by retying the two halves together, but all our clothes were by then so damp from the snow that the chill wind seemed to cut us to the very core. In fact we were so cold we could scarce feel our hands and feet at all.

'We'll have to risk a fire,' I pleaded, but Edwin would have none of it.

'W-what, would you have us invite Guthrum and his whole army to join us?' he asked shivering. 'Besides, there's no time. If we walk quickly we'll soon be warm.'

He was right. Once we started moving it became easier except that as our fingers and toes warmed it was as though they were on fire.

I grumbled with every painful step but Edmund, being of younger blood, seemed to cope more easily with the cold. At one point he stumbled in the dark and both Edwin and

I heard him cry out what sounded like an oath. Surprised, we both looked at the boy but could not see him clearly. In the end we said nothing but took his new-found voice as a sign that his anguish was melting.

As we marched, Edwin set his discomfort aside and planned how best to approach Chippenham. Lord Alfred had good cause to winter there, for being set within the loop of the river it was protected by water on three sides. The open end to the south had been newly fortified with a deep ditch; the soil which had been taken from it heaped up along one edge to form a rampart. A low palisade of split timbers had then been set into the rampart, their ends sharpened to form a defensive wall. This fortification stretched the entire length of the southern boundary, the only gap being where the old Roman road entered Chippenham and that was protected by a timber gatehouse.

Despite the fortifications, Edwin was certain that the Vikings would launch themselves at these southern defences knowing that the guards there would be more thinly spread. The alternative would have been to attack the western gatehouse via the bridge, but as that formed part of the Vill itself it would be heavily defended. Surprise being their favourite tactic, they would almost certainly attack at dawn hoping to breach the ramparts with an all-out assault and then open the gates before Alfred's main force could be deployed.

Whilst it therefore followed that Guthrum's main army would be mustered on the far side of the river, there would almost certainly be a smaller detachment detailed to attack the western gates as well if only to serve as a diversion.

All this made perfect sense to Edwin's logic as a warrior. What he could not account for was why we had seen no signs of such a large army as we approached. We had passed no pickets nor seen anything that might suggest the movement of so many men. I was starting to think he had been mistaken; that the men who had attacked the settlement were just a raiding party and that Guthrum was somewhere far to the north of Chippenham, warming himself by his fire with his men boasting of their battles and counting their spoils. With these thoughts we slackened our pace and, to our eternal shame, even rested until it was light, certain we would still be in time to tell Lord Alfred all we had learned.

But we were wrong. Edwin should have heeded the omens I had seen in the sky the previous morning, for even as we drew nearer to Chippenham we could hear the dreadful din of battle.

* * * * *

With thick smoke drifting towards us through the trees, we covered our faces and pushed on as best we could. The noise of men shouting and fighting filled our ears, but at that point we could tell very little about what was going on.

As we drew closer it became obvious that, as Edwin had predicted, much of the fighting was centred on the southern defences where the ramparts had been breached in several places. Already the Vikings had broken through and with many of the buildings on that side of the river ablaze, the battle there was all but lost. Armed with nothing but their everyday tools – scythes, pitchforks, hammers and axes – the people of Chippenham could not hope to match the full thrust of a Viking army.

There seemed no point in us crossing the river to join a hopeless cause, particularly as it would mean Edwin attacking the rear of Guthrum's army single-handed. So instead we worked our way towards the western gates where Edwin thought to join those defending the Vill. Even there we could see heavy fighting as Alfred's diminished army fought back against impossible odds. Edwin knew he had no option but to join the fray.

'Stay close!' he ordered. 'And keep the boy beside you.'

He led the way, following the river so as to keep his bearings amid the smoke and confusion. From there we could see the Saxons who lived in Chippenham – men, women and children – wading across to escape the carnage as the Vikings ransacked their homes. Many carried a few precious possessions but most had simply abandoned all they owned and were fleeing for their lives. Some called out for help, screaming as they were caught and cut down even before they could reach the river, others crying out with sheer terror.

Edwin ignored them. Already he could see that the western gates were flung wide open and that part of the Vill was also on fire. He wanted to reinforce whatever was left of Alfred's army but it was a futile gesture; the bridge was already crowded with men hacking and fighting like demons, all locked in desperate hand-to-hand combat. One group of Saxons had fought their way out and across the bridge presumably intending to work their way around to attack the rear of Guthrum's main force. Having not managed to form themselves into proper rank they had been forced to split up and were being mercilessly slain.

With so many men surrounding us Edwin was not sure where to begin. In the end providence made the decision for him. Two Viking warriors rushed towards him screaming wildly, the closest of them wielding a heavy axe above his head. Without a moment's hesitation Edwin turned to face the man, the warrior's axe making a deafening 'thud' as my brother blocked it with his shield. Then, as the Viking struggled to wrench it free, Edwin drove his sword up into the man's throat. That done he turned to face the other Viking but he had sunk back into the gloom and was gone.

'Quickly,' shouted Edwin, his eyes everywhere at once. 'Take the boy and wait over there!' He pointed to a large willow that grew by the water's edge, its long trailing leaves offering at least some measure of cover.

'But...' I protested.

'Just do it!' bellowed Edwin. 'And keep out of sight.' Then even though he had neither helmet nor mail vest, he rushed towards the melee of fighting men.

* * * * *

As a novice monk I knew nothing about fighting but as Edmund and I sheltered beneath that tree I feared all that was about to change. There was no time for me to think about the morality of it; I simply drew the sword I had been given to carry and readied myself to defend my life and that of my charge as best I could.

At that point all I felt was fear. A sickening fear that churned in my guts and etched at my bowels until all I wanted to do was run. I looked at Edmund and tried to reassure the boy, holding up the sword and shaking it defiantly. Then I saw someone moving towards us.

At first I assumed the man was wounded as he stumbled forward looking shaken and confused. Then I realised he had seen the sword and meant to take it; that having lost his own weapon in the fray he was desperate to rejoin the battle and thereby slake whatever lust for blood still stirred within him. There was no mistaking the manic look in his eyes as he lumbered forward roaring like a wild beast.

Instinctively I was on my feet in a moment. I meant to shout my defiance, but my heart beat so fast that I could scarce catch my breath. Instead of a mighty roar, my voice sounded weak and shrill.

The warrior stopped for a moment, laughed at me, then lunged forward to seize the sword. He grabbed my arm and gripped it between his like the jaws of a mad dog, pulling and twisting as he tried to wrest the weapon from my grasp. I half turned away and, free for an instant, lashed out wildly. I felt the blade grind against something hard then heard a scream. When I looked again the warrior was reeling backwards, clutching his side with blood welling out from between his fingers.

I was stunned and not sure what to do. The man was staring at me, his eyes blazing fiercely but he now had a look of sheer terror on his face. Then he sank to his knees, cursing and moaning, clawing at the gaping wound with his hands.

That he was dying was plain enough. I knew I should finish it but could not bring myself to do it. In fact could scarcely summon the courage even to look at him, never mind take the sword to him again. In panic, I turned away and tried to block the sound of his pain from my ears.

When I dared to look again I found that the man was still on his knees, one hand clutching his side the other held out imploring me to end his agony. Weeping like a child, I raised the sword and, with my eyes closed, swung the blade wildly at the man's head.

It was a clumsy blow that glanced across the top of his helmet. He moaned pitifully, blood now pouring down his face as well. In a blind panic, I struck again; then again and again in a mad frenzy, raining blow after blow upon the helpless warrior, desperate to end the nightmare. I stopped only when I was certain he was dead.

For a moment I stared at the bloody, tangled body. Then I turned away from it, staggered towards the tree and vomited. Only then did I realise that Edmund was gone.

* * * * *

I felt sickened and ashamed by what I'd done. Not only had I butchered an unarmed man whilst failing to observe even the rudiments of Christian mercy, I had also been charged with nothing more than to look after a small boy whilst others fought for their lives, yet I had failed in that as well.

Frantically I called out for Edmund. I kept shouting as I left the sanctuary of my hiding place and began to wander across the battlefield, sword in hand. I must have looked a bizarre sight as I went: a monk carrying a sword with blood dripping from the blade whilst calling a name that could scarce be heard above the frantic noise of battle. All around me others were locked in combat, their weapons and shields crashing together. Men were screaming – some from pain, some from the sheer madness they find in war, so that the noise was deafening. I blundered on through all of this turning only to wield the sword and strike out at anyone and everything that crossed my path. Then it was as though I were in a dream. I simply walked right through the frenzied battle and everyone who saw me let me pass. I floated through the carnage like a spirit that was beyond the sight of human eyes, oblivious to it all.

Eventually I came to a small group of men crowded together, their axes rising and falling on each other like hammers, their spear points busy with the business of probing any unguarded flesh. I could see Edwin among them, cutting and slashing with his sword as he drove them back, but he had not seen a man creeping around to his rear with a spear raised, both hands gripping the shaft ready to strike.

I remember shouting to my brother to warn him but my words were lost to the noise of the battle. I shouted again and again, screaming till my lungs hurt and my chest was ready to explode, but it was all to no avail for Edwin could not possibly hear me.

In a desperate panic I rushed headlong towards the group, but even before I could reach it someone turned and swung an axe at my head. I ducked the blow but felt instead something strike me across the face. As my vision exploded in a crimson mist, I went down hard upon the ground.

Chapter Four

B y the time I recovered the battle was done. I found myself lying opposite Edwin in a small hollow some distance from where the fighting had taken place. 'How long have I…?' I asked, confused and still not sure what had happened.

Edwin looked almost too tired to answer. He sat with his head in his hands, his face, hair and clothes soiled with blood. 'A few hours,' he managed at last.

I started to sit up but stopped when I found it pained me just to move. My neck had stiffened and the side of my face was throbbing. Also my head ached dreadfully.

Edwin got up and offered some water, which I drank gratefully.

'So what happened?' I asked, gingerly touching the top of my cheek.

'I would ask you as much,' said Edwin sternly. 'I ordered you to stay under cover and end up carrying you from the thickest part of the fray!'

'You carried me?' I said still struggling to recall anything.

'Aye, I carried you. T'was that or leave you to perish where you lay.'

For that I was thankful. I knew full well that had I been left unconscious on the field I would have been put to the sword by one side or the other.

'I gave you that sword to carry not to wield in battle,' continued Edwin, still angry. 'You said yourself that you lacked the skill to use it, so what in God's name prompted you to try?'

'I did kill a Viking,' I boasted without mentioning that the man had been unarmed.

'And near got killed yourself!' scoffed Edwin reaching across to touch my cheek as if to examine the wound.

I flinched from his touch. I could recall the almost mystical feeling of walking through the battle unscathed and wanted to ask Edwin about it but knew it was neither the time nor the place. 'Well at least I'm alive,' was all I could manage. 'Thanks be to God.'

'Thanks be to Wilfred's quick thinking!' corrected Edwin. 'It was he who struck you when you bore down upon us.'

Hardly able to believe what I was hearing, I looked at Edwin in horror. 'I attacked you?' I stammered.

'You were like a madman fighting everyone, friend and foe alike,' he explained. 'You were lucky to be recognised for Wilfred might just as easily have stopped you with the point of his spear, not the boss of his shield.'

I reached up and touched my face again, recalling the blow. I certainly didn't feel very lucky; the side of my face was numb and my left cheek raw where the skin had been flayed. Dried blood had crusted beneath my nose and my head was still pounding. 'I'm sorry,' I said weakly, knowing I had made a fool of myself.

'And what of the boy?' asked Edwin.

'I lost him and was looking for him,' I confessed.

Edwin shook his head in disbelief. 'So are you yet well enough to stand?'

I tried to get up but felt so dizzy that Edwin had to support me. When it was clear that I could not manage even a few steps he helped me to sit down again.

Edwin sat opposite and resumed cleaning and sharpening his sword. 'We must look to our wits if we're to survive this field,' he said gravely. 'Already the Viking warriors are out to bloody their hands on anything left living. For now they're busy thieving what they can from the dead and the dying so, with luck, we may be safe here for a while. We can rest until dark then use the cover of the night to go south. If we then cross the river we can be safely away from here come morning.'

I said nothing, still feeling too ashamed. 'So is the battle over?' I asked at last, suddenly aware how quiet it had become. In the distance there were screams as the Vikings found some poor wretch with yet enough life to be worth wringing from his body, but the dreadful din of the battle had gone.

'Aye, it's done,' said Edwin mournfully. 'And Guthrum has the Vill. Most of our men are dead or have fled the field and Chippenham itself has been taken, or what's left of it.'

Feebly I turned to look behind me and saw that the sky glowed red from the flames of the many buildings which were still on fire. 'Then what news of Lord Alfred?' I asked.

Edwin could not bring himself to meet my eyes as he answered. 'Who knows?' he said. 'There's so much confusion that no man can be sure of anything least of all who lived or died in that bloody fray. We can only pray that God saw fit to spare him.'

* * * * *

Although still in pain, I regained my balance sufficiently to stand and walk unaided. Therefore as soon as it was dark we started to make our way from the battlefield.

'We should try to find Edmund,' I suggested, knowing that to do so would mean retracing our steps to the willow tree beside the river where I was supposed to have waited.

Edwin would have no truck with that. 'The boy's gone,' he said firmly. 'Whether lost, killed or taken there's nothing we can do for him now.'

'But he was in my charge,' I protested.

Edwin rounded on me sharply. 'Then you should have taken better care of him!' he snapped.

The sharp edge of his tongue reminded me how quickly he could be roused, so I said nothing. There followed a silence between the two of us which could not be filled with words until Edwin seemed to regret being so harsh. 'On the way we may learn news of the boy,' he offered. 'But we've no time to spare or we'll be taken and our bodies fed to the crows.'

There was no denying the truth of that. The night was filled with the cries and moans of the wounded and along the way our path was strewn with the bodies of wasted men and women, many butchered beyond recognition. The lucky ones had been killed quickly and cleanly but many had been cruelly tortured, for the Vikings prided themselves on how inventive they could be when it came to slaughter. Some had been hanged or disembowelled but there were many others too, all brutally killed in a myriad of ways. Yet as we wandered that bloody field it did not do to dwell upon the agony those poor souls endured for we were ourselves but one step away from sharing their dreadful fate.

Along the way we also came across a few men, both Vikings and Saxons, too badly wounded to be moved. We left the Vikings to wait in misery for the ministrations of their comrades but as for the Saxons, Edwin knelt beside each one to comfort them and, whilst I uttered a brief prayer, he mercifully slit their throats.

It was a grisly night but we were not alone. Under the cover of darkness others were also desperately seeking to escape the carnage. News was hurriedly exchanged at every such meeting and a little food or water shared. Edwin always asked after both Edmund and Lord Alfred but learned very little. Not surprisingly, no one had noticed a boy either during or after the battle and, as for Lord Alfred, there were some who said he had retreated and planned to flee abroad, others who were certain they had seen him slain. One rumour had it that his personal guard had heaped themselves upon him to protect him but had been hauled off one by one and made to watch as their liege was put to the sword. There was even talk of his head having been impaled on a spear and mounted on the west bridge, but the truth was that no one knew what had or had not happened. The only thing that all seemed to agree upon was that the ranks of the dead would outnumber those of the living and among them would be the names of many great Saxons. The day was lost and we knew we had to get as far away as possible from the site of so much slaughter;

for we had not just lost a battle, we had lost our cause – and probably our King.

* * * * *

Not all the Saxons were ready to accept defeat. We met one group of just three men who seemed intent on fighting to the very death.

'We must fight on,' said the one who seemed to have taken command, a bearded giant of a man dressed in a long fur cloak and carrying a huge two-handed broadaxe on his shoulder. It was hard not to mistake him for a Viking except that his head had been shaved and an elaborate blue ring drawn on his scalp like a crown. From the design of this we took him to be from Northumbria, not Wessex, but we had no idea as to why he should be among us on that fateful day. Not that it mattered; he seemed to have an intense hatred of the Vikings and was intent upon finishing the battle single-handed. 'We'll regroup and catch them unaware in the dark!' he roared, urging us to join him.

Edwin indulged him. 'We'll fight again right enough, but not this day. Tend to your men and we'll gather others as we go so that Lord Alfred may lead us all to victory.'

The giant seemed unsure of this. 'What, are you beaten so soon? Would you leave this field whilst there's still blood in your veins?'

Edwin did not rise to the challenge. 'The day is lost,' he reasoned. 'We best serve our cause if we live to fight again.'

The giant spat at the ground in disgust then turned to his two companions. 'Is there no fight left in any of you?' When it was clear they too had had enough he swung the axe from his shoulder and leaned on the shaft for support. Drawing a knife from his belt, he offered it to Edwin. 'There's a man over there who's wounded beyond hope and needs a friend. Or have you not the stomach even for that?'

Edwin nodded but drew his own knife then crossed to where the man lay. Only when he was closer did he realise it was an old family friend called Aelwyn. 'You're too old for this,' he said as he knelt beside him.

Although barely conscious, Aelwyn seemed to recognise him.

Edwin lifted the old man's head so he could sip some water. 'So, are you badly hurt?' he asked.

Aelwyn swallowed hard as though choking back the pain then raised his right arm slightly to show that his hand had been severed. He had wrapped cloths around the end of his wrist but it still bled profusely.

'Help me to get him to his feet,' said Edwin turning to the others. 'We can't leave an old man to die on the battlefield like this.'

The giant looked at him in amazement. 'You'll not take him with you! Have you not seen the wound? It'll be festered and rotten by morning. If he's your friend you know what's needed. Put an end to his misery and be done with it!'

Edwin would not listen. Instead he started to help Aelwyn to his feet.

'In the name of God man let him be!' pleaded the giant. 'If it pains you let me attend to him.' He still had his knife drawn and motioned with it, graphically drawing a line in the air.

All there knew the giant was right but Edwin would not see it.

'Then go alone,' said the giant. 'I'll not come to watch an old man die in agony.' With that he sheathed the blade and led his men away into the night.

* * * * *

Edwin and I carried Aelwyn as far as the river where we hoped we would be safe till dawn. We laid him down a few paces from the water's edge then went to quench our thirst. The river flowed slowly as though choked with cold and the edges were already part frozen from the night before. Although the ice had stiffened, it was still brittle enough for us to break – or we could reach out past it in order to scoop up handfuls of water to drink.

Edwin began to wash the blood from his face and hands, then tried to remove the worst of it from his clothes. 'We'll stay here till morning to give Aelwyn a chance to rest,' he said. 'Gather some wood for a fire; I'll take him back some water.'

I protested, worried that a fire would draw the Vikings to us, but Edwin seemed unperturbed. 'There are fires enough this night so they'll not pay any mind to ours. We must keep Aelwyn warm, for you saw how his old body shakes and shivers.'

It was indeed clear that Aelwyn's health was failing. He was already pale from having lost so much blood and we needed to staunch the wound to stop him losing more. As soon as the fire was established, Edwin began heating the blade of his knife in the flames. As he waited for it to become hot enough, he began to unwrap the cloths used to bind the old man's wound, peeling them off slowly so as not to cause more pain than could be helped. Even this seemed more than Aelwyn could bear. Wincing, he gripped Edwin's shoulder so tightly with his one remaining hand that his knuckles were almost white.

'Easy old friend,' said Edwin trying to comfort him. Then, with the cloths removed, he examined the wound. The hand had been severed cleanly enough but the end of the bone was shattered and exposed. It needed to be trimmed back so that the skin could then be folded across to form a seal, but there was not enough time for that. 'All we can do for now is sear the wound. That should keep out the fever,' he said. Then he looked at Aelwyn. 'You know what I must do?'

Aelwyn nodded weakly.

As I knelt beside him Aelwyn began to mutter a prayer in which he asked the good Lord to give him strength to bear the pain of what would follow. He prayed for his dear wife and then for forgiveness for his sins. That done, he gripped Edwin's shoulder tightly. 'If the Lord should take me know that I'm ready,' he said, his voice feeble. 'Tell my wife I died by a warm fire in the company of friends and in the service of my liege. Bury me as befits a Christian soul if you will and lay my sword beside me for my sons are both dead. There's no one left to honour me by carrying it to battle now and I would not have it taken as a trophy by some heathen Viking.'

Edwin nodded. 'You're not dead yet,' he said simply. Then he cut a length of cloth from Aelwyn's cloak and twisted it to form a thick strop which he gave to Aelwyn to set between his teeth. As I made the sign of the cross he reached back for the knife and laid the red-hot blade directly to the wound.

As the searing heat smouldered on his raw flesh Aelwyn tried to cry out, but his scream was muted by the strop.

He tried to twist violently from side to side, but we held him firmly until, mercifully, the old man lost consciousness.

Edwin finished the job in silence then pushed the blade back into the fire to cleanse it. 'And what of your wound?' he asked looking at my cheek which was, by then, bruised and swollen. 'Shall we tend to it whilst the blade is still hot?'

I was not sure whether he spoke in jest but feared to answer. Instead I took myself to the river where I bathed the wound with ice-cold water. It was then I noticed that my habit was stained with blood, though more likely this was from the man I had killed than from my own wound. The stains were a reminder of the many things that had happened during the previous few days which I knew I would need to repent. My brittle faith assured me it was never too late for that, but I also knew what my abbot would say; that if I truly desired absolution I would have to reinforce my conviction to God by suffering some personal trial or chastisement. I would like to have started by symbolically washing the blood stains from my habit but it was much too cold for that. Instead I washed my hands thoroughly, wishing I could cleanse my soul as easily. Then, taking a piece of the ice, I held it against my cheek to ease the swelling. That, with sleep and prayer, were all the medicine I was willing to endure.

* * * * *

The dawn found us still sleeping, exhausted after all we had been through. I was the first to stir and, feeling again a stiffness to my neck and shoulder, stretched myself. It was already light by then and I saw at once that the ground was coated with snow near ankle deep in places. The fire had gone out but I knew better than to relight it. Instead I went straight to get fresh water but found the river was frozen hard all the way across; as if by some strange magic it had been stopped in mid flow during the night. It was when I went back to fetch something with which to break the ice that I noticed that Aelwyn lay very still and that snow had settled on his face and beard.

Hurriedly I woke Edwin. The warrior grumbled at first but on hearing what had happened, responded readily enough. Even as he leaned across to look at Aelwyn we both knew that the old man had not survived the night.

'The giant was right,' said Edwin mournfully. 'I should have had the courage to finish him myself. Who knows what torments this old man suffered in his final hours; what pain he endured because of my weakness.'

I stood over them both looking down at the body. 'He looks at peace to me,' I said consolingly. 'Perhaps his old bones could not survive so cold a night. Whether wounded or not his blood would still have frozen in his veins. Besides, did you not hear him say that he was content to die beside a warm fire in the company of friends? There'll be many from yesterday's battle who'll envy that when he stands in line with them outside St Peter's gate and waits to be admitted.'

Edwin seemed to accept this. 'We'll bury him as best we can,' he announced. 'But not here, for we dare not stay too long. Already the day is well on and we're much at risk.'

'Are we not to search for Edmund?' I asked.

Edwin struggled to his feet. Once up, he leaned his hand on my shoulder. 'Matthew, you see before you what happens when you let your heart rule your head. The boy is gone, as like as not perished, and there's nothing we can do to help him now. My duty is to find Alfred and, with him, avenge the death of so many friends. And you must come with me until we can find a way of returning you safely to your abbot.'

Although I said nothing, I dreaded the prospect of returning to the Abbey. Once there I would have to do penance for my sins and omissions, and thus anything which delayed my return was to be welcomed, though I knew that even that thought was, in itself, a sin.

'We'll take Aelwyn's body across the river and bury him on the other bank,' announced Edwin. 'There'll be time then to give proper weight to the proceedings for we shall be safe enough.'

'You're not thinking to cross on the ice!' I exclaimed.

Edwin walked down to stand at the water's edge. 'All the bridges will be in Viking hands by now so we can't think of using them,' he explained.

'But with the ice so newly formed it will scarce hold one of us never mind three,' I protested.

'Then it's for you to find the strongest parts,' said Edwin as though that were a simple matter.

We had to cross, that much was certain. And being the lightest it was fitting that I should be the one to test the ice. Thus I stepped gingerly from the bank and, using the sword as a probe, began to edge my way across the frozen river. There were areas where the ice still looked too thin to support my weight, but much of it was firm enough to hold. I found a path to a point some twenty paces from the edge and then returned to help Edwin, certain we could cross safely provided we took great care.

In the meantime, Edwin had removed Aelwyn's sword and was examining it. Although once a fine weapon, it was now old like its owner, the blade having been sharpened so often it was worn thin; for in the days when Aelwyn was a warrior he had always kept it honed to perfection.

I took the sword and held it as I had done many times before. Aelwyn had often shown it to me, allowing me to marvel at the delicate design traced onto the pommel. Originally it had depicted a dragon breathing fire, but that had worn away. Even the bone which formed the main part of the grip had split and been braced with bands of brass to hold it together so that it was beyond the point where it might be considered fit for battle. It seemed only right that such a fine old weapon should rest with the man who had once wielded it with such pride. In a way it seemed to have died with him and both Edwin and I were sorry for the passing of both.

As I returned the sword to its scabbard and secured it, Edwin reached down and removed a brooch which the old man had used to pin his cloak. It was an ornament carved from ivory which Aelwyn claimed had come from a walrus, though neither he nor anyone else we knew had ever seen such a beast. Traders spoke of them as being like huge quarrelsome seals with teeth like horns hanging from their jaw. They lived in the frozen seas of the north where they had to be hunted on the huge islands of floating ice which were to be found there. The thin slivers of ivory were cut from the tusks and were thus very precious, for it took a brave hunter to venture far enough to even find such a beast, never mind kill one with a spear.

'We shall keep this for his widow,' said Edwin knowing it might be worth enough to feed her in times of need. With that we set about moving the body. Although his frail old bones weighed little enough, his flesh had stiffened making it awkward to shift. In the end we decided to lay him on the ice and gently drag him across between us so as not to impose too much weight on any single point. Even so it was not an easy task and needed great care, for several times the ice grumbled and seemed to flex beneath our feet. Then, when we were but halfway across, Edwin seemed to change his mind.

'We'll leave him here,' he said firmly, then stood up straight to stare at something on the bank where we had spent the night.

When I followed his gaze I could see at once what troubled him.

Chapter Five

We had been so intent on getting Aelwyn's body safely across the river that we had failed to notice half a dozen Viking warriors searching through the remnants of the camp where we had spent the night, even kicking through the ashes of our fire. Having found nothing of use to them, they lined up along the bank of the frozen river curious to know why two Saxons were bothering to drag the corpse of an old man across the ice. The obvious explanation was that Aelwyn was of high birth or perhaps very rich. Either way that meant only one thing to them: the prospect of booty.

As soon as they realised we had seen them the Vikings began to shout abuse at us across the frozen divide, trying to goad us to return and fight.

'Make for the far bank,' urged Edwin, his voice calm and low.

'But...but what about them?' I protested, unable to believe that he, a warrior, could ignore their taunts.

'We can't fight them here,' he insisted. 'So move quickly. We must make it to the other side before they reach us.'

Leaving Aelwyn's body where it lay, we worked our way slowly towards the far bank, me finding the safest path and Edwin following several paces behind. Looking back,

I could see that one of the Vikings had already started out across the ice, no doubt meaning to search Aelwyn's body.

'Look where you're walking, not at him!' warned Edwin as, step by slippery step, we made our way across, the water sometimes seeping up through the surface as the ice flexed beneath our feet. It was a treacherous journey, not made easier by the taunts of the Vikings ringing in our ears. 'Pay them no mind,' urged Edwin. 'Just keep moving for if the ice fails we shall perish just as surely as if we wait for those heathen bastards to reach us.' Through all this he would not so much as glance back at the Vikings until we had gained the safety of the far side. Once there it was a different matter. He turned and stared directly at them, quickly assessing the situation.

A second Viking had also chanced the ice, the first being all but halfway across. Seeing this, Edwin drew his sword and raised it high above his head. Standing there, tall and proud with the breath steaming from his mouth, he let out a chilling cry which sounded in the still air like a beast in pain. Then using the point of his sword he drew a line in the snow. 'I shall perish before you move me from this mark,' he said loudly. 'And if you dare to try my hand you shall pay dearly for your taunts.'

By this time the first of the Vikings had reached Aelwyn's body and was busy searching it. He stopped when he heard Edwin's challenge and responded by shaking his fist in the air, clearly thinking that anything more could wait until he'd claimed his prize. He removed Aelwyn's sword quickly enough and held it up for his comrades to see but, when he looked at it more closely and saw that it was so old and worn, he tossed it aside.

The second Viking stopped when he saw that the prize had been claimed, such as it was. All that remained for him was the prospect of fighting two Saxons and he was in no rush for that. Realising there were places where the ice was dangerously thin he heaved his battle axe into the air to answer Edwin's challenge, clearly hoping we would go to him.

Meanwhile the first Viking had done with Aelwyn's corpse. Finding nothing of value, he kicked it in disgust then, fearing his comrade might reach the Saxons first, drew his own sword and started towards us. He quickly paid the price for his greed. No sooner had he moved than his feet slid from under him. His arms went up as he fought for balance, then down he went, hard upon the ice. At first he seemed frozen to the spot as if afraid to make even the slightest movement lest it cause the ice to fracture. Then, when he heard Edwin roar with laughter, he shook his fist at us and scrambled quickly to his feet. Recovering his sword, he started out again but his luck had run its course. He managed no more than three steps before the ice gave way with a loud crack.

'Aaaagh...!' The Viking's scream was muffled as he disappeared beneath the ice. He surfaced once, his arms thrashing and flailing in the icy water as he tried desperately to claw his way out, but the edge of the ice was too frail and broke away as he tried to grasp it. Then he seemed to give up. As his body stiffened he slid beneath the surface to be carried away by the flow.

Now silent, the Vikings who had remained on the bank realised the true danger. The second warrior looked back at them then at the hole in the ice and must have known then that his own fate was sealed. Ahead of him lay death, if not from the ice-cold water then at the hands of two defiant Saxons. Having answered Edwin's challenge his honour would not allow him to turn back so it came down to a simple choice – death by combat or death by drowning in the icy depths of the river.

It was surprising how far he got given that the ice was already weakened. He managed to skirt around the fracture to stand within ten paces of the bank before his gods deserted him. There the ice cracked again, pitching him forward into the freezing water. He was lucky the river was no more than waist deep at that point so he surfaced quickly, rearing up from the water with a roar. He struggled to find his footing in the soft mud and slipped under several times more before, at last, he was able to wade ashore.

His comrades on the other side of the river sent up a great cheer as he dragged himself up onto the bank. He half turned to acknowledge them, weakly lifting the axe which he still gripped, but his movements were slow and laboured where the cold water had chilled him to the very core. He managed to get to his feet, swaying and shivering, his sodden clothes hanging heavily from his shoulders. Then, with his axe raised, he chanced a few uncertain steps and lumbered towards where Edwin waited.

When it came his blow was powerful enough but delivered so slowly that all Edwin had to do was step aside and let the axe sweep past. As he did so he scythed the edge of his own sword across the man's chest. Though probably too cold to feel the pain, the Viking groaned and dropped to his knees.

Gripping his sword in both hands, Edwin levelled it at the man's neck. Then, without so much as a word, he sliced the man's head cleanly from his body.

I watched in awe and horror as the headless corpse slumped to the ground like a sack of grain, a fountain of blood spurting from the neck and spraying out onto the snow. It was a clean, efficient kill; so unlike my own clumsy efforts when confronted by the man during the battle. Where I had hacked and cut like a madman, Edwin had used just two strokes, each delivered with an almost effortless power that ensured his man was killed outright.

The snow all about him was stained with blood as Edwin picked up the severed head by the hair and held it aloft like a trophy. With the head in one hand and his sword in the other he let out another chilling war cry. This time there was no reply from those on the opposite bank.

* * * * *

In contempt, Edwin tossed the Viking's head out onto the ice where it rolled until it settled looking like a man buried up to his neck in the frozen river. On the far bank the other Vikings watched in silence then simply turned and left. There was none among them who craved vengeance and with no spoils worth having they saw no point in braving the ice as well.

Edwin cleared the snow from a fallen log then sat and rested as he watched them leave.

'They were all afraid of you!' I said as I sat down beside him, very much in awe of my brother's skill.

'Never mistake good sense for fear,' advised Edwin. 'Had they placed even one foot upon the ice honour would have demanded they see it through. But they resisted my challenge and so were free to walk away.'

'But I thought you said they welcome death,' I reasoned. 'Isn't that how they gain their seat in Valhalla?'

Edwin laughed. 'No, it's never that simple. If they're to die they seek a glorious end with their sword soaked in blood and the bodies of their foes heaped at their feet.'

'Not freezing in the icy river?' I suggested.

He shook his head. 'Exactly, for that's no way to die; but if there comes a point where death is the only option a good warrior will embrace it like a brother and meet his end in glory. But only a fool would throw his life away.'

'Like you walking away when first they challenged us?' I said.

'Aye. I wasn't afraid of them. I simply chose my ground as I wasn't prepared to meet them on the ice where my skill would be hampered as I struggled to keep my feet.'

'So why were we able to cross, yet the ice wouldn't hold for them?'

Edwin shrugged. 'Perhaps they were careless of it. Having watched us cross safely they saw no need for caution. Also, when newly frozen ice will take so much before it breaks but once it does…'

'Then we were lucky,' I observed.

'Luck has no part in it,' said Edwin sounding very serious. 'We each live or die according to fate. But that's where your creed and mine would differ,' he added. 'You Holy men think you can mould fate's path with prayer whereas we warriors simply make the best of what unfolds.'

'But I've seen warriors pray! What about before a battle, surely all warriors kneel in homage then?'

'Ah, but we pray not for God to change our fate but for the courage to meet it as we should. That and for him to receive our souls if we should fall.' I was surprised by what he said. I had not thought of Edwin as a religious man yet he seemed to have come to terms with his faith. There were many at the Abbey who, for all their pious ways, had not managed as much. 'Then how do you square your faith with so much slaughter?' I asked, looking again at the headless corpse of the Viking.

Edwin seemed to find that amusing. He wiped some blood from his face with the back of his hand and looked at it. 'You mean how do I sleep at night with so much blood upon my hands? Well, as I see it, we each of us go to hell in our own way. I've sworn to do so in the service of my King. Thus my conscience is clear enough.'

'Which is more than I can say of mine,' I admitted. 'I've killed but one man, yet even that troubles me; particularly as he wasn't armed.'

Without getting up, Edwin put a consoling hand on my shoulder. 'He attacked you, so you had no choice.'

'Still it was a brutal end for I lacked the skill to kill him cleanly. Not like you just now...'

'He chose the manner of his own death when he confronted you,' Edwin assured me. 'He saw his chance and took it. It was his fate to die thus and there was nothing you could do to change that. Besides, if he'd taken the sword from you and cut you down, whatever path God has in mind for you would now be denied.'

'True, but how can I serve God when my soul is stained with blood? And in these past few days I've surely sinned so often that...' I shook my head sorrowfully, unable to finish what I was trying to say.

Edwin did not seem inclined to console me. 'You'll have to square all that with your abbot,' he said simply. 'But it's good we should talk. Although we share the blood our father gave us we've seen little of each other since your birth. With him gone we must look out for each other for there's no one else to guide us now. Yet perhaps we make a good pair, you and I; you with the ways of God and me with the ways of war. If we can but find a path that suits us both—'

He suddenly stopped what he was saying and rose quickly to his feet having noticed a group of men coming towards us. I realised at once that Lord Alfred himself was among them for though I had only seen him a few times before, there was no mistaking the long chin and fierce blue eyes, even at a distance. There were others there who Edwin knew as well, though they looked a sorry lot as they approached wearily, all on foot apart from Alfred who sat astride a small grey mare.

As he dismounted, Alfred let one of the men take the reins of his horse then came across to where Edwin and I waited. He still wore a vest of chain mail but his helmet was missing so that his hair, which was the colour of the earth, hung loose about his shoulders. He walked with heavy steps, slow and dejected, his face unusually sallow and his demeanour somehow diminished. Both Edwin and I dropped to one knee as he approached.

'Sire, I thank God you're safe,' said Edwin. 'We've heard so many rumours...'

The King motioned for us both to rise then clasped Edwin warmly by the hand. Two others had come with him. One was Osric, chief of Alfred's personal guard, and the other was the giant we had met the night before who went straight to the headless corpse of the Viking and began prodding it with his foot.

'There's another like him beneath the ice,' boasted Edwin, watching the giant carefully.

Alfred spoke loud enough for all to hear. 'A fitting place for a dead Viking,' he said. 'For I'm told they come from a cold land where it ever snows and where huge islands of ice, some bigger even than twenty longships, float freely in the sea.' He gazed across the river towards Chippenham. 'But why do they come?' he asked wistfully. 'To seize our lands only to destroy them? Or is it blood they crave?' He spread his arms to show he did not know the answer to his own questions. 'Do you think Guthrum has now taken enough Saxon blood? Will his appetite now be sated?'

Edwin shook his head. 'Not till he's taken yours, sire. For only then will he control all of Wessex. I fear you are what he's come here for.'

Alfred then noticed Aelwyn's body resting on the ice. 'Who's that?' he asked.

'Sire, its Lord Aelwyn. You remember him, he was—'

Alfred raised his hand. 'I well remember all who serve me,' he said. 'Did he die well?'

Edwin bowed his head with shame.

The giant, who had finished poking and prodding the Viking's corpse then joined us. 'He could have died well enough had you let me do what was needed.'

'You two have met?' asked Alfred looking first at one then the other.

'Our paths have crossed,' said Edwin curtly.

'And no doubt you are the wiser for the encounter,' scowled the giant.

Alfred could not help but sense some hostility between the two men. 'Cedric is an Ealdorman from Northumbria,' he explained. 'He lost his lands to the Vikings and is come to help us in our struggle.'

Edwin sneered. 'Do we need the help of one whose King has already yielded to the Viking sword and whose people cower beneath the shadow of the raven banner?' he retorted sourly.

Alfred looked at him sternly. 'We need help from whatever quarter we can find it,' he said. 'And Cedric has served us well at a time when that need was most.'

'Then it's a pity he didn't serve his own King near so well. Had he fought as hard for him perhaps the Vikings would have been halted long before they reached our bounds.'

Alfred spoke flatly. 'I would know what's transpired between you two to cause this quarrel. We've enemies enough without fighting those who come to help us.'

Considering his position, Edwin spoke more softly. 'Sire, the fault is mine,' he admitted. 'Aelwyn suffered for my weakness. He was sorely wounded with no hope of life and I should have put him to the knife to relieve his pain but lacked the stomach for it. Instead he died last night as the blood froze within his veins.'

I could see then how much Edwin regretted having tried to heal the old man's wounds. It was true that Aelwyn had suffered, but when I looked at the body it had an air of quiet reverence about it; like an island with the river frozen all around it. I felt it was a fitting end for such a grand old warrior, certainly better than many who had died in the battle would have been granted. Yet I also knew it was something for which Edwin would do penance at his next confession.

Alfred did not press the point. 'We shall bury the faithful Aelwyn as befits his rank and then offer prayers for his eternal soul,' he announced. 'And Edwin, I will not have it that you carry any blame in this. Compassion is not a weakness in one as bold as you.'

Although much comforted by this Edwin knew that to bury Aelwyn was now out of the question. 'Sire, the ice is broken. To send any man out upon it now is much too dangerous. Besides, Aelwyn is at peace and his body will not be troubled by scavengers, be they men or beasts. Why not let him rest where he lies? The waters will take him and his sword when the ice thaws.'

Alfred considered this for a moment. 'So be it,' he said at last and, with that, knelt to offer a short prayer entreating all those present to join him. When it was done he clutched Osric's arm and with some difficulty, heaved himself up.

'Sire, you're wounded?' observed Edwin.

'It's nothing,' said Alfred dismissing his concern. 'My back pains me that's all. Others have suffered far worse. Now Edwin I would speak with you in private.' With that he led my brother to one side but, curiously, spoke loud enough for all of us to hear. 'I have need of you, Edwin son of Edwulf. I need your courage and your skill. Look about you and you'll see all that yet remains of my army.' He turned and let the sweep of his arm take in the ragged band of near twenty men waiting a few paces off. They looked more like a group of weary travellers than an army, some too tired even to stand, others slouched against spears for support or waiting with heads bowed as they nursed their wounds. 'There's not a man here who's not lost kin in this bloody fray and we are resolved on vengeance. I would have you join us for one last charge.'

Edwin looked very surprised. 'But, sire, you cannot think to...'

Alfred held up his hand to silence Edwin's protest. 'There's nothing else left to us now. I've sent the women and children to a place of safety. All that remains is for us to die as Saxons should. Cedric is certain the west bridge to the Vill is still intact and I mean to make one last charge across it. Guthrum will not be expecting that and even if we can't retake it, with God's good grace we may at least die in glory.'

Edwin turned to Osric, who stood closest to Alfred. 'Osric, what say you in this?' he asked.

He had known Osric for many years and regarded him well, having fought beside him many times. He was a stout man with a slow demeanour but also a fearsome warrior who carried his sword strapped across his back in a leather sheath. It was a weapon with a short blade especially forged for use whilst serving in the shield wall. It therefore suited Osric's particular skill, which was combat at such close quarters that there was scarce room to wield a normal sword. Although only the same age as Edwin, Osric had been appointed chief of Lord Alfred's personal guard, an elite force of perhaps twenty men who shadowed the King's every move. To be selected for such a duty was an honour bestowed only on the most trusted warriors. This was evidenced by the fact that just three other members of the guard had survived the battle, the rest having given their lives to enable Alfred to escape from Chippenham. Thus Edwin had turned to Osric for support knowing that he whose loyalty was beyond question would be heeded above all others. But Osric was slow to answer.

'I am sworn to follow my liege wherever he takes me,' said Osric at last.

'What, to certain death?' asked Edwin.

Osric smiled but spoke very seriously. 'Death is always certain, Edwin,' he answered. 'You and I know nothing could be more so. It's just a question of how and when we meet our fate. For my part I would as soon die in honour rather than live in fear. Thus I would willingly make one last charge if my liege so commands it.'

It was not the answer Edwin wanted. 'Sire, I too would follow wherever you lead,' he protested. 'But to die on this field is foolish! There was but a fraction of your army here at Chippenham, the others having returned to their homes and farms for the winter and who could yet be summoned to follow you to victory. Would you deny them that?'

'Pah!' scowled Cedric. 'And what of these faithful souls?' asked the giant looking back at the ragged group who had survived the battle. 'Would you deny them vengeance for the friends they saw butchered yesterday?'

'Never!' replied Edwin rounding on him sharply. 'But I'd give them something to live for, not something to die for!'

Alfred seemed to feel a chill in the air and rubbed his hands together. 'A good king listens to wise words before he speaks any of his own,' he said at last. 'I say Edwin is right. We best serve our cause if we regroup, rally our forces and live to fight again. This day is lost, but whilst yet a single Saxon warrior survives the war is not yet over.'

Chapter Six

As we began our slow retreat, Alfred's band of survivors numbered little more than twenty men. Most were thanes who had served the King as part of their sworn duty and then remained with him, though some were of lower rank who had got caught up in the fighting and now had nowhere else to go. All were too tired even to talk and many carried wounds, yet they knew no other way than to follow their liege, as indeed they were sworn to do.

'So you came to warn us?' asked Alfred who had chosen not to ride, preferring instead to lead his horse by the reins. Edwin walked to one side of him and Cedric to the other. I followed close behind with Osric and his remaining guards who were anxious to stay close to their charge. 'But how then did you learn of Guthrum's plan, for we had no inkling of his coming?'

Edwin explained about the Viking warrior he had interrogated and I then showed him the sword he'd taken as a prize. It was indeed a fine and very valuable weapon, but not just in financial terms. A sword carried with it a history of all the men it had slain and the battles in which it had been used. When steeped in glory they became more than just weapons; they were treasured heirlooms, passed proudly from father to son. Unlike an axe or a spear, they were beyond price and could not be bought and sold but one taken in battle could be offered as a gift inferring respect and great honour on the man who received it. It followed that if tribute were to be paid to persuade the Vikings to plunder elsewhere, a sword could be an important part of that, its worth resting upon the reputation of the man who had used it – and that of those whose blood had soiled its blade.

'I see the handiwork of the Franks in this,' said Alfred as he admired it. 'But if you took it from a Viking warrior then I doubt the man who forged such a fine blade was ever paid for his craft.'

'There's an inscription on the blade,' said Edwin. 'Though neither Matthew nor I can read it.'

Alfred looked at it more closely. 'These are indeed runic symbols,' he announced, tracing them with his finger. 'They say this sword is called "Red Viper" and here, if you look, the smith has traced the pattern of a snake onto the handle with the pommel forming its head.' He passed it to Cedric.

''Tis surely a weapon made for war,' agreed Cedric as he too examined it. 'The man who carries this must know how to wield it or he'll lose it soon enough.'

'But why is it called Red Viper?' I asked. 'The blade is the same colour as any other.'

Cedric laughed. 'Look again when you've thrust it into some poor bastard's guts!' he said running his thumb along the blood channel which ran almost the full length of the blade.

'What will you do with it?' asked Alfred taking the sword from Cedric and returning it to Edwin. 'You already have your father's sword. Will you not give this one to young Matthew here?'

Edwin shook his head. 'First I shall have it blessed, for there's likely to be much Saxon blood upon the blade. As for my brother, he has no need of a weapon for he's answered a religious calling as was our dear father's wish, God rest his soul.'

Alfred looked doubtful. 'We're now so few that when the Vikings come again we shall each of us need to answer with whatever comes to hand. Much as we shall welcome Matthew's prayers he'll need to do more than that to stay alive. I say bless the sword and teach him how to use it.'

'Sire, I have fought with it,' I offered. 'And I killed a man during the battle yesterday, though I repent it with all my heart.'

It was Alfred who responded. 'We've all done things which may trouble our souls,' he said. 'But a clear conscience is for saints not mere mortals like ourselves. Teach him Edwin, for he could have no better master.'

Edwin looked displeased but had no choice but to agree. 'I will, sire, but tell me, how come the walls to Chippenham were breached and the gates thrown wide open? Did Guthrum take you by surprise?'

Alfred stopped and considered the question carefully. 'In truth he did,' he said, and then signalled the others to keep moving. 'We thought ourselves secure for the winter and were busy preparing our Mass for the feast of Epiphany.' He paused, looking at the thin line of survivors as they filed past. 'The attack came at dawn. The first we knew of it was when they poured through the southern gates. We rushed from the Vill to meet them and even managed to drive them back, but they spread out through the settlement and came at us from three sides at once. Though we fought hard we were hopelessly outnumbered so retreated into the Vill. We dared not close the inner gates for fear of leaving so many Saxons trapped outside. When the Vikings then attacked the western gates as well I knew the day was lost. We managed to force our way out and across the bridge by splitting into small units intending to then regroup but, in truth, it was a wasted effort. Guthrum had foreseen we might try to escape that way and concentrated his best men there to meet us as we fled. The bloodshed was terrible and as you can see, we were all but destroyed.'

'So they came through the southern gates first?' observed Edwin.

'Aye, God alone knows how they forced them open but once they did our fate was sealed. Guthrum had near a thousand men and I commanded barely a third of that number even if you count those from the settlement who were prepared to make a fight of it.'

'From what I saw the people fought hard to save their homes,' observed Edwin.

Alfred seemed reluctant to acknowledge the point. 'Some did,' he said at last. 'I fear most fled across the river to save themselves, but we mustn't think the worse of them for that for only a few had weapons with which to defend themselves.'

'But your warriors acquitted themselves with honour?'

'As you would expect,' he said sadly. 'And they paid for that courage with their lives.' He shook his head mournfully. 'So many killed; so many slain. My heart weeps for them all.'

'And what now, sire?' asked Edwin.

The whole band had stopped by this time and gathered round to listen. Seeing he had their attention, Alfred chose his words carefully. 'As I've said, our womenfolk are safe.

They journey ahead of us and I've arranged for Lord Ethelnorth to meet them on the road. He'll see them safe to the marshes at Athelney. I intend that we shall join them there and seek shelter for what remains of the winter. I don't claim to know the marshes well but I once hunted there with Ethelnorth and the good Bishop Eahlstan when I was a boy. There's a Vill which can be fortified and shall suffice as our quarters till the spring.'

'And then?' pressed Edwin.

'Then we shall gather our forces and drive Guthrum back into the sea,' said Alfred as though that were obvious. It was certainly a proud boast but one even he could not truly believe would ever be achieved.

One of the Saxons called out from the back and voiced the fears of many. 'I will follow you, sire, as I am sworn to. And I pray I shall serve you just as well if and when you do strike back. But I must ask why you would choose such a godforsaken place in which to spend the winter?'

A murmur arose from those around him. Most of us knew of the marshes at Athelney which lay amid the Somerset Levels, an area so vast a man might easily be lost there. They were also dank and desolate and apt to flood, but of more concern were the rumours of the demons said to lurk among the reeds; the spirits of men trapped between this world and the next.

Although these superstitions did not seem to trouble Alfred he understood and recognised the fear they impressed upon the rest of us. 'I'll tell you why we go there,' he said raising his voice so that all could hear clearly. 'We go there because the Vill can be fortified and defended. We go there because there's fish and game and fresh water. We also go

74

there because there's shelter from the cold. But most of all we go there because we can be sure of one thing. The Vikings will not.'

* * * * *

Alfred's plan was to join the old Roman road that led through the forests. This would take us south of Bath and avoid any large settlements where he might be recognised and betrayed. We would then follow the road until we reached the pass through the Mendip Hills from where we would strike out across country until we reached the marshes. With the snow and the weather closing in he knew it would take at least two or three days to reach Athelney but, given how weary we all were, his first thought was to find somewhere safe to spend the night. That would enable us all to rest and, for those who were injured, the chance to properly tend their wounds.

By mid-afternoon we chanced upon a travelling tinker who had set up a makeshift camp where a small stream crossed the road. As soon as he realised who we had among us the tinker fell to his knees and meekly bowed his head in homage. Alfred bade him stand then asked his name.

'I am called Goda, my Lord,' said the tinker. 'And this is my wife, Mildrith. We was bound for Bath when the weather turned against us. You and your men are most welcome to share what little we have.'

Looking around the camp it was clear that the tinker was right; he had precious little to share. He had formed a small clearing in the forest and built a meagre hovel woven from saplings which he had thatched with sticks and leaves. Opposite this was a cart on which he carried his wares plus a few tools and all his worldly belongings, such as they were. With the snow falling the cart had presumably proved too difficult to move, so he had stopped to wait out the weather.

Alfred gave Goda a small coin to pay for his hospitality and assured him that we required only food and to spend the night beside his fire.

Goda took the coin gratefully, tested it with his teeth and then slipped it into a small leather pouch he wore tied about his waist. 'So 'tis true then. Chippenham has fallen?' he said, though he didn't sound surprised. 'And a bloody fray by all accounts.'

'Bad news travels fast,' said Cedric looking at Goda suspiciously.

Goda nodded. 'Aye, as do those fleeing from the Vikings. There've been many ahead of you, I can tell you that. Most was too frightened even to stop for food and drink. We was in Chippenham ourselves but a few days past. 'Tis hard to believe so much has changed so sudden like.'

This talk of how quickly things could change prompted Osric to think about posting guards. Knowing there was a real risk of the Vikings following us, Alfred agreed at once. Two men were selected, leaving the rest of us to settle where we could.

There was no doubt that Goda was a Saxon, but as he had not mentioned his father's name when he introduced himself, we all knew he was of low birth. In those dark days such things were not always obvious from a person's appearance as there were many good men who had fallen on hard times. Yet he seemed an amiable fellow and was suitably respectful of his betters. Although both he and his wife were very thin they seemed contented enough. That said, I sensed they were keen to be gone from that place as quickly as they could, which I thought natural enough given they were but a day's march from Chippenham and the prospect of further Viking raids. Goda told us also that he had a daughter but had sent her to hide in the forest when he heard so many men approaching. Such was a normal precaution against which no one took offence, for he would have had no way of knowing our intent. I realised it might also explain the absence of a horse to pull the cart.

Edwin laughed when I mentioned this. 'What, are you surprised?' he said. 'Do you think we'd be content to stay hungry if the beast were standing here before us?'

It was a fair point. Goda could ill afford to lose his horse for, as a travelling tinker, he could not ply his trade without one. It was probably only an old nag but still the most precious thing he owned; certainly it was worth more to him than a night's supper for a band of strangers even if one of them was his King.

For all that, the tinker was hospitable enough, allowing the wounded to sleep in the hovel albeit packed in as tight as fleas in a blanket. The rest of us found a space on the cold ground, making the best of whatever shelter we could find.

Goda went off to get more firewood from a pile he had gathered, then returned with an axe which he used to split the logs with an easy skill. These he added to the fire, first moving the brazier with tongs so that it was set just outside the shelter. The men then gathered round, pressing in close to share the warmth.

Goda also fetched his daughter, Emelda, whom he set to work with his wife to prepare some food. She was a short girl of about thirteen or fourteen years of age, not pretty but with a full body for her age and hair that hung in two plaits. She wore no jewellery or ribbons, not even a birth ring or a pin, and her clothes were ragged and dirty.

'Not worth hiding,' remarked one of the men under his breath as she gave each of us a bowl of broth. It was thin and watery fare, three days in the pot but welcome just the same.

Osric then returned from having checked the guard. He seemed very ill at ease as he took his place beside Edwin. 'The man had swine,' he whispered. 'There's an empty pen back there in the trees.'

Overhearing the comment, I suggested that perhaps he hid them as well.

With that Cedric emerged from the forest with a face like thunder. He went straight to Goda, seized him roughly by the arm and dragged him before Alfred. 'This man's a traitor!' he accused loudly, hurling the tinker to the ground.

Goda cowered on his knees. 'No sire!' he pleaded. 'I am a loyal and honest man... I...'

Cedric tossed a silver armband onto the ground. It was the type worn by Vikings to serve as currency. If payment was to be made a piece of the silver would be hacked off and weighed to use as coin, otherwise it would be worn safely on the owner's arm. Although very thin, the armband was still worth a good deal of money, so much so that everyone there stared at it in amazement.

'I followed this knave into the forest when he went to fetch more wood. Whilst there he hid the coin you gave him, sire, placing it in the hollow trunk of a tree. When I looked inside I found this secreted there as well. A tinker could not earn half as much silver if he lived to be a hundred!'

'My Lord I can explain!' pleaded Goda, his voice filled with fear. 'I had some swine. I sold them before I left Chippenham and—'

'Why would you sell swine when winter is upon us?' demanded Cedric.

Goda looked up at Alfred, his hands clasped together as if begging for mercy. 'Sire, they was mine to sell,' he protested. 'I thought to take myself to Bath, there to find a husband for my daughter and so spend my last days in rest and…'

Some of the men laughed. It was a dream shared by many but achieved by few and certainly not by the likes of a wretched tinker.

'I couldn't take them with me,' continued Goda sounding ever more desperate. 'So I sold them. What else was I to do?'

Alfred looked at him sternly. 'How many pigs?' he asked.

'Five, sire. Good swine, fattened and ready for slaughter.'

'They must have been,' observed Alfred. 'It was a heavy price for just five pigs. So who was your buyer?'

Goda looked even more frightened but would not answer. Then Osric got to his feet. 'Whoever it was, sire, they were not in Chippenham. The pigs were sold when they were here. There's an empty pen in the forest yonder.'

'You don't need to ask any more!' stormed Cedric. 'He sold his swine to the Vikings. For that alone he must be punished!'

Alfred raised his hand to settle the men. 'To aid our foe is to be our foe,' he pronounced looking directly at Goda. 'That is our law and you must answer the charge.'

Goda looked terrified, as well he might. He was still on his knees, his head shaking sorrowfully from side to side. 'Sire, I cannot lie to my liege. I sold the Vikings that which they would have taken anyway. I had no choice. 'Twas all I owned... I...'

'I think you sold them more than swine,' said Cedric picking up the band and weighing it in his hand. 'You could buy a drove of pigs with this much silver! And as you say, they had no need to pay for that which they could have taken!'

'No sire! I would never betray you!'

Osric walked across to stand by Alfred. 'Remember, sire, by his own account he made a very timely departure from Chippenham getting out just before the attack.'

'If he was ever there!' added Cedric taking up the point. 'I say he was on his way there when he met the Vikings. He sold them swine and gave them information, then turned to get as far away as possible knowing his treachery would never be discovered for none would survive the bloodshed that would follow. But fate never favours the betrayer. He was caught when the snow began to fall and he couldn't move his cart. Now he must answer for his treachery!'

Alfred considered the matter carefully but the evidence was damning to say the least. 'Well man, speak up for yourself,' he demanded. 'You're charged now with more than aiding our enemies. You stand accused of betraying Saxon lives to the Vikings, including that of your King.'

'No! Never!' insisted Goda, shaking his head in despair. 'I wouldn't do such a thing, my Lord! Not a word of this is true! Sire, you must believe me!'

But Cedric would have none of it. 'Here's the proof of it!' he said throwing the armband back at Goda.

The tinker was white with fear. 'But sire,' he implored, 'I have explained...'

'Pah, you have explained nothing!' said Cedric. 'Every man here has lost friends and family whilst you profit from their blood. I say you must pay and we all know the price which must be set!'

'Wait!' commanded Alfred rising to his feet. 'He has the right to speak.'

Goda was almost beyond words. 'Sire,' he managed, 'I beg of you to show mercy. I'm naught but a poor tinker so what could I tell the Vikings that would be of use to them? Truly I'm no traitor. I admit I sold them swine. I admit I mended some weapons. I put an edge to their swords but I had no choice...'

'You sharpened the swords which spilled Saxon blood!' said Alfred, looking at him sternly. 'You sold food and gave shelter to those who would harm your King!'

'No sire, not willingly. They gave me no choice!'

Cedric roared. 'They gave you silver! You know the penalty; the hand which helped the enemy must be severed from his body. Your law demands it!'

Mildrith rushed forward and threw herself at Alfred's feet. 'Sire, show mercy!' she pleaded as she grovelled beside her husband.

I could see that Alfred was unhappy with the verdict he knew he was obliged to make, but the mood of the men was growing dark. Only the day before they had seen their friends slain, which was enough to ensure that Goda's fate was sealed. Although he kept protesting his innocence he must have known it would be to no avail. Three men stepped forward and dragged him back towards the tree stump he used as a block for chopping wood, whilst the rest gathered round, jeering and spitting on Goda as he was wrestled to his knees once more. Two of the men held him down whilst the third stretched out the tinker's left arm, gripping the fingers so that his hand was held flat on the makeshift block.

Taking up his own axe, Cedric waited for Alfred's order.

'For God's sake have mercy!' screamed Mildrith and then put her hands over her face in horror.

Cedric brought the axe down so hard that the hand was severed cleanly.

Those holding Goda released him as soon as it was done. Then everyone watched as, still kneeling by the block, he curled himself into a ball nursing the bleeding stump where his hand had been. He was silent as though he could find no words to express his horror. Not so Mildrith who screamed and ran to her husband, wrapping her cloak around his shoulders and weeping. She tore cloth from the hem of her skirts and bound the wound to staunch the flow of blood whilst Goda stared at Alfred, his eyes filled with hate. Finally he shook his head and sobbed woefully.

Mildrith rose to her feet and ran at Cedric, beating his chest with her fists. 'We'll starve!' she screamed. 'We'll all starve! God have mercy upon us! God have mercy...' Then she buried her head in his chest and wept.

She was right about their fate. A tinker with just one hand would indeed starve as would his entire family. His only option would be to become a beggar and thanks to the Vikings there were enough of those in Wessex as it was.

Alfred said nothing but went back to sit beside the fire, followed by others. Meanwhile Edwin, who had played no part in the proceedings, seemed equally ill at ease with what had transpired. He went to Mildrith and gently eased her away from Cedric. As he did so the two men exchanged a glance so harsh that no words were needed between them.

Mildrith turned to look at her husband. 'You're a fool,' she said accusingly, almost spitting the words through her tears. 'To trade with the Devil... I told you what would come of it. I warned you!' Then shaking her head and still sobbing she knelt beside him. Their daughter, Emelda, had been spared much of the spectacle by one of the men who had turned her away from the sight of the execution itself, but he could not restrain her long. Pushing past him, she ran to join her parents and the three of them huddled together on the ground where they were left alone to share their grief.

* * * * *

The next day Alfred roused us all long before dawn. He knew that if the Vikings had followed us they would attack at first light and he was not about to be caught unaware for the second time in as many days. When no attack came, he had us prepare to leave at once, anxious to put as much distance between us and Chippenham as he could.

As we readied ourselves to march out Goda sat watching us with contempt. Mildrith had bound the end of his arm with a poultice but there was no mistaking the misery of his plight. 'At least take my daughter with you!' he pleaded. 'She had no part in this and should not suffer for my crimes.'

Reluctantly Alfred agreed. 'She may come as my slave but I can promise nothing,' he warned. 'The road ahead will be hard and dangerous and she'll have to fend for herself along the way.'

It was not much of an offer and Goda knew only too well what 'fending for herself' would lead to. A young girl alone in a band of broken men would at first be needed to cook and tend their wounds. After that, as the men began to recover their strength, there would be other needs to satisfy. Still it was better than starving and he knew that many of the Saxon women who had been taken prisoner following the raid at Chippenham would suffer worse, so he nodded his agreement.

Alfred left them to say their farewells and led us from the camp.

We had not gone far when he called Edwin to his side. 'I have need of you,' he said without looking at him. 'Slip away on the pretext of covering our tracks. I would not leave a man to die thus, traitor or not.'

Without a word Edwin did as he was ordered, taking me with him. As we retraced our steps I was unsure about what it was we were to do. 'Surely the judgement was too harsh,' I reasoned, voicing the view many now shared in the cold light of day. 'I mean Goda had no choice...'

Edwin did not agree. 'Whatever information he was able to give the Vikings was worth a great deal to them. And that they paid for it means they think to use him again.'

'After the way he's been treated he'll tell them anything they want to know!'

'Aye,' said Edwin. 'And therein lies the true purpose of our mission. What would Guthrum give to know which way Alfred is headed and that he has but twenty weary men to guard him?'

I then realised what Edwin was implying. 'So you're going to kill Goda? Is that it? And not as an act of mercy!'

Edwin said nothing.

'No wonder he betrayed us. His friends treat him worse than his foes.'

'He treated his foes as his friends; that's the root of his trouble. And he could betray us again if he's allowed to live. Alfred has realised his mistake and I'm to put it right. I'll give Goda the chance to die well but if he refuses…'

'This is dark work!' I protested. 'What, are you reduced to being an assassin?'

'I serve a troubled King,' explained Edwin. 'He no more likes what must be done than do I but has no choice. My only regret is that Cedric was too quick to meddle in our affairs. He's a guest in this realm and it was not for him to accuse anyone. Alfred should have stopped him and tried to ensure Goda's silence.'

'Perhaps,' I agreed. 'But the crime was still the same. It's just the sentence that's changed.'

With that we arrived back at Goda's camp but found it deserted. The cart was still there along with most of Goda's belongings but there was no sign of either the tinker or his wife.

'Do we follow them?' I asked.

Edwin shook his head. 'No we must return to warn Alfred as quickly as we can for if Goda and Mildrith have taken the horse and gone straight to Chippenham they'll quickly tell Guthrum all they know.'

'Then all is lost. The Vikings could be upon us in a matter of hours!'

'Perhaps,' said Edwin thoughtfully. 'But finding us is one thing. Killing us will be another matter entirely.'

Chapter Seven

Given that they were making such slow progress, Edwin and I quickly caught up with Alfred and the remnants of the Saxon army.

'Sire, we were too late,' admitted Edwin breathlessly. 'I fear that even now the traitor is telling Guthrum which way we travel. What's more your tracks in the snow will lead the Vikings directly to us.'

'What, would you have us cover every footprint as we go?' asked Alfred. 'Already we travel much too slowly.'

'Why worry?' shrugged Cedric who had overheard the conversation. 'Fresh snow will soon cover our tracks.'

Edwin disagreed. 'Snow lies upon snow,' he argued. 'It doesn't fill the troughs and hollows. Our path will be plain enough to any who would find it.'

'Pah! They'll be too busy with all the plunder at the Vill!' declared Cedric.

Edwin took a contrary view. 'What does Guthrum care for what little can be wrested from the ruins at Chippenham?' he asked. 'You are the real prize, sire. For once you're taken all Wessex will be at his mercy and with it, more land, booty and slaves than his men ever dreamed of. What's more, only whilst you survive can we hope to rally enough men to stop them. Thus only through you can the Saxon cause survive.'

Alfred listened to both men carefully. 'It's true Guthrum will take us if he can,' he said at last. 'And I agree with Edwin, that's why he attacked Chippenham in the first place. But Cedric is also right; he'll struggle to prise his men away from such easy pickings. Their greed is thus our best hope and we must use whatever time it affords to get as far away as we can. Our best hope is to reach Athelney before they overtake us.'

'But the going's hard and the snow slows our progress,' moaned Osric who had listened to all that was said.

Alfred turned to his horse and stroked it. 'This good beast may help us there,' he said letting it nuzzle his hand. 'Have the men place all they can upon its back. That'll lighten their load and thereby speed our journey.'

'Still we shall travel no faster than the slowest man,' observed Osric. 'And there are many among us who are tired and still frail from their wounds. Sire, you must think to save yourself.'

'That's right, if they can't keep up we should leave them here,' said Cedric. 'Let them die as warriors should; fighting off any of Guthrum's men who dare to follow.'

'Or more likely they'll freeze to death as they wait,' replied Alfred. 'Their wounds will heal and we shall need every man we can muster when the time comes to strike back. No, if Guthrum finds us we shall stand as one. That's our best chance of survival.'

For once, Edwin agreed with Cedric. I think the memory of how by letting his heart rule his head he had prolonged Aelwyn's suffering was still fresh in his mind and he was not about to make the same mistake again. 'Sire, Cedric's right,' he reasoned. 'Osric and his men could see you safe to

Athelney. No one will pay much mind to a few men wending their way through the forest, thus you would have a better chance of reaching safety. The rest of us can wait here, tend our wounds and make ready to ambush Guthrum if he does try to follow. Even if we can't defeat him we could delay him long enough to—'

Alfred would not let him finish. 'I hear you, Edwin, but I'll not run and leave men to die here in my stead. On that my mind is set.'

The King having thus spoken so firmly, the matter was decided. Edwin ordered the men to tie whatever they could not carry to the horse's back although, when it came to it, that didn't amount to very much. Most had left Chippenham with little more than the clothes they stood up in. Those who had blankets had wrapped them about their shoulders as proof against the cold and any spare clothing had been put on. So the horse was left to carry just a few domestic items. Some of the wounded added their weapons, though with the prospect of an imminent Viking attack most men preferred to keep theirs to hand.

'That it should come to this,' mused Alfred as he watched the load being secured. 'The beast which once carried a King is now saddled with the baggage of his people.'

Cedric mistook Alfred's meaning and laughed. 'That beast of yours was destined to share our fate and so should share our burden,' he quipped. But no one shared his humour. Like Lord Alfred, all the men were genuinely distressed by what they saw as yet another sign of just how wretched we had all become. As King, Alfred knew his own burden was to bear responsibility for having allowed our fortunes to sink so low, something which he felt more keenly than he deserved.

As we prepared to move off again two men were sent to form a rear guard, travelling some 200 paces behind our main column; close enough to give warning if they were attacked yet far enough to allow time for the rest of us to muster a rudimentary defence. Both Edwin and Cedric knew it was a futile tactic, but it was a comfort to us all to know the guards were there. More importantly, it allowed us all to concentrate on what lay ahead rather than worry about the terror which followed at our heels.

Thus we journeyed, a silent line of broken men each lost in private thought. With hoods and cloaks pulled across our faces to shun not only the cold but also the company of each other, we must have looked like a funeral procession moving slowly through the bleak, snow-filled forest. And perhaps that is what it was; for each of us carried with him the burden of our dead, albeit hidden within our hearts.

* * * * *

We travelled thus for several hours before Alfred, seeing how tired and weak we all were, sought a place at which to spend the night. Eventually we found a cavern cut deep into the side of a steep bank which was therefore sheltered from the wind and snow. Easily defended, it was an odd place, dug originally for the mining of flints but still in use as a hide for hunting or possibly as a place of refuge from Viking attacks. Either way it made a good camp, so guards were posted to cover the road and three men sent to hunt for food.

Being young and without serious wounds I was an obvious choice as one member of the hunting party. It also included Wilfred who was the one who, with a blow from his shield, had saved my life during the battle. The third member of the party was a thane named Rufus who was a renowned hunter.

The lives of all the men rested on the three of us finding food, but we were ordered to stay close to the camp in case it was attacked. Both Wilfred and I were glad of this for the snow was so deep it was hard to wade through, especially for me as I was hampered by my habit. Rufus on the other hand seemed to find new legs. A tall, willowy man of near Edwin's age, he loved nothing better than to hunt and so readily took charge of the small party by suggesting we should look for deer or wild boar as one kill would then feed all. Because the forest was too dense to use the horse, we hunted on foot and, with no dogs or hawks to help us, had to stalk our prey in order to move close enough to make a kill with either a spear or bow. That was the true art of hunting. Many men could boast of excellent marksmanship even at some distance, but an arrow at long range was seldom fatal so the wounded prey might bolt into the forest only to die once it had gone to ground. The skilled hunter like Rufus could move close enough to ensure his prey was brought down and, as often as not, killed outright.

For this purpose Rufus carried a quiver strapped to a belt tied around his waist. It held several types of arrow each carefully crafted and fitted with a feathered flight and a head designed for a specific quarry. Most of his arrowheads had been carved from bone which, being cheap and plentiful, meant he could afford to lose them in the foliage if he missed his mark. Those with metal heads were costly and used only where he could be sure of recovering them to use again. Part of his art was in having the right type of arrow to hand. For game he had ones with small rounded heads which were heavy enough to knock a bird from the air, whereas for deer or boar he used ones which were pointed and barbed, designed to pierce deep into the flesh and remain hooked in until his prey fell. He also carried one arrow quite unlike the rest. It had a long, thin metal head – like a nail – specially shaped for piercing a vest of chain mail. This he always boasted was for 'special quarry', just in case he ever chanced upon a lone Viking warrior.

Using his skill, Rufus soon found the trail of a deer for us to follow. In pursuit of it, the three of us hurried between the trees but with me and Wilfred often tripping over roots hidden beneath the snow or cursing as thorns tore our flesh. On one occasion I breasted a drift so deep I almost disappeared beneath it, causing Wilfred to roar with laughter until Rufus told him to be quiet. Unlike us, Rufus seemed able to move through the forest with ease. He never stumbled or tripped, it was as though he copied his quarry, running with an easy grace which was a skill to behold. Having seen how clumsy Wilfred and I were I think he would have preferred to continue alone but it was growing late and all hopes of finding anything were fading with the light. In the end we had to be content with the carcass of a deer which we found by chance. Even this we might have missed but for three noisy ravens perched upon it, pulling at the stringy flesh and sinews. Not content with what they could draw with their beaks, the greedy birds squabbled over every morsel like three old hags at a market. The sight of the birds concerned Wilfred greatly for there was no mistaking it as an omen.

'They're the black messengers of doom,' Wilfred whispered as we watched them.

'Aye,' agreed Rufus. 'And they quarrel over what's left of the carcass of our land.'

I understood their qualms at once. The raven was a symbol depicted on Viking banners and was thus much feared and hated by all true Saxons. Being of younger blood, I took a spear and charged straight at the birds, yelling loudly. The ravens took flight but rose into the air with a lazy flapping of their great wings as if my assault barely troubled them at all. Grinning, I turned to my two wiser companions. 'See, they're gone!' I boasted. 'A good Saxon can drive them off as easily as that, just as we shall one day drive the Vikings from our shores!'

Wilfred crossed himself and spoke solemnly. 'I would it were so easy,' he said pointing to the sky where the ravens still circled. 'See how they wait to feast again? You may drive them off a hundred times, Matthew, but still they'll come again. Then again and again, be sure of that. No man may hold them off for ever.'

Meanwhile Rufus sniffed the carcass. 'Still fresh enough to eat,' he pronounced. 'We shall find no better supper before nightfall.'

It was probable the beast had been brought down by wolves for their tracks were all around it in the snow. It was a recent kill, perhaps no more than a day old given the amount of snow which had settled upon its hide. The wolves had ripped open its belly and eaten the soft entrails and also torn open the neck, but it was otherwise intact.

'No doubt it was wounded when they found it,' suggested Rufus. 'The greedy pack could not resist an easy kill but as like as not had already eaten their fill elsewhere last night.'

Whether true or not we were far too tired and hungry to pass up the chance of such a good feed. We strung the carcass to the shaft of a spear and, between us, lugged it back to the cavern.

There we found a camp had been hurriedly set up with a fire under the canopy of rock where all were seated eagerly awaiting our return. The carcass was quickly gutted, skinned then butchered. Whilst one of the haunches of meat was placed on a makeshift spit some men found large flat stones which they positioned around the edge of the fire on which to cook what remained of the offal.

The fire was a luxury Edwin argued we could ill afford lest the Vikings see the smoke, but the men were too cold and hungry to care. 'Then we shall at least die warm,' said one of them who seemed to speak for us all.

Osric had set himself apart, having become unpopular by insisting his guards should be excused menial camp chores such as digging the latrines as they had one overriding duty, which was to guard their King. With so few men fit enough to share the work, others had readily accepted the need to do tasks normally considered beneath them. Thus Osric's attitude was much resented by them all.

He was leaning against a fallen tree sharpening his knife on a stone when I took some meat across for him to eat. As he used the knife to cut slices of venison I asked him how he had managed to get Alfred out of Chippenham alive when every Viking warrior was intent on claiming the royal head.

At first Osric seemed disinterested in the question. 'We fought our way out,' he shrugged as though that was all there was to it.

'But Alfred said the Vikings had breached the gates and were swarming through,' I retorted. 'He spoke of men locked in combat and I've heard others say there were bodies heaped one upon the other. Yet you somehow managed to secure his escape.'

Osric stopped eating for a moment. 'I'll grant it was a bloody fray,' he conceded as though recalling the battle for the first time. 'As cruel as any I've ever seen. In truth we simply opened the western gates and charged across the bridge with our shields locked together concealing Alfred and his lady in our midst.'

'And lost many brave men,' I suggested.

'Aye,' agreed Osric, studying his knife as if to check its edge. 'And good men too, but they all knew their duty. There was not one among them who wasn't ready to die for his liege if called upon to do so.'

'So the traitor must have been one of the others?' I said.

For the first time I had Osric's full attention. 'Traitor? What traitor?' he demanded.

'The one who opened the southern gates in the first place,' I explained, surprised that I should need to.

'No one opened the gates,' snapped Osric. 'The Vikings forced their way in!'

I was taken aback. 'Surely not,' I stammered. 'I mean the cross beams used to secure them were huge. They must have been lifted from within!'

Osric looked as black as thunder. 'Who says this?' he demanded.

'No one says it. I just assumed that…' In fact that was not true. Edwin had earlier voiced his fear that someone had let the Vikings in, a view I knew was shared by others.

Nonetheless, Osric appeared stunned by the very suggestion and pointed at me with his knife. 'You mind your tongue boy! Speak only of matters of which you know!' he warned angrily. 'Had you been there you wouldn't doubt the loyalty of any man who was on guard that night.'

'I'm not accusing anyone!' I protested.

'Then mind you don't!' said Osric. 'Anyway, there could be no profit in such treachery. All those who manned the gates were slain.'

'What, all of them?' I asked.

'Aye, every man there was slaughtered when the Vikings broke through. I saw it for myself. Not one of them survived.'

'Then were the gates left open by mistake? Or perhaps opened to let someone in or out of the settlement?'

Osric glared at me. 'What? Were they fools that they would leave their homes open to attack? I'll hear no more of this, do you understand me? Stick to your prayers and leave matters of war to those who know the way of it.' With that he would say no more on the subject. 'I have my duties to attend to,' he said bluntly. Then taking the remainder of the meat with him, he strode away to check the guard.

Chapter Eight

Edwin was right about the smoke for it seemed to draw men from every corner of the night. Mostly they came alone, approaching warily and seeking shelter and a place of refuge. Alfred welcomed each of them personally once they had been recognised or their lineage established, inviting them to share our food and take their place around the fire.

As the company grew larger so the men began to relax. Comforted by the warmth and glow of the flames, they at last felt secure enough to speak of the battle. At first they grumbled about the hardships they had each endured, the wounds they had suffered and about those they had seen cruelly killed or maimed, but soon came tales of courage and daring. News was also shared, which meant that many at last learned the fate of friends and relatives they had not seen since that fateful day, albeit that news was seldom good. Although anxious we should strike out early the next day, Alfred saw how warmth, food and comradeship seemed to remedy our flagging spirits and so did nothing to discourage us from talking late into the night.

By morning the snow had ceased falling and the whole group set off in better spirits. All were fit to march save one, a man named Eadred who had suffered a cruel cut to his shoulder which had swollen so much that he could scarce move his left arm at all. The pain was spreading down his back, so there was no option but to let him ride. What remained of the venison was also draped across the horse before we set off again, still following the road through the forest.

For reasons of security our route had been chosen so as to avoid the major settlements as the Vikings had many spies and news of Alfred's position would be worth a great deal to anyone who, like Goda, was tempted to betray him. Alfred also decreed that for the safety of us all he would travel within the ranks where it was unlikely he would be recognised. As second in command, Edwin would lead the column in his stead. Thus to anyone curious enough to ask we were just a group of bedraggled warriors returning to their homes after the battle.

Initially the lands through which we passed had been part of Alfred's personal estates at Chippenham or were within the bounds of his Vill, but this would not always be so. It was the custom for men bearing arms to first send word to the local Ealdorman and seek his consent to pass, and whilst none would deny such permission to their King, it would mean disclosing that he was indeed travelling with us. Therefore Alfred decided that two men should be sent on ahead to announce our coming and thereby slake any idle curiosity should we be noticed, but he chose an unlikely combination.

Cedric was a diplomatic choice, for his rank entitled him to play such an important role. The danger was that being from Northumbria he would not be familiar with the ways and customs of the local Saxons. Also, with his shaven head and huge double-handed axe he might easily be mistaken for a Viking. With feelings running so high throughout the realm, there would be those who would strike first and ask questions afterwards – and an arrow loosed from the cover of the trees would kill just as readily whether shot by friend or by foe! Thus I was sent to accompany him. As a novice monk I would be an unlikely target and being of high birth it was felt I would know how to speak to anyone we might encounter, many of whom might even know or have heard of my family.

Few people lived within the forest itself so we did not expect to meet anyone at first, yet we very quickly came upon a narrow path leading from the road. At the end of this we could see a clearing with a small homestead which had been crudely fortified with a stout wicker fence. Those who lived there had surely heard us approaching, as indeed we intended they should, thus only the menfolk came out to greet us, the women and children having no doubt been sent to hide. The small family group comprised a father and two sons who scratched a living from the forest collecting bundles of firewood and burning them to make charcoal. Despite their lowly occupation, they were clearly thanes who had fallen on hard times. As such they were entitled to the respect afforded by our Saxon ways. That courtesy demanded that we speak first to the head of the family and explain our needs. He would be obliged to help his betters, although he could expect payment or perhaps a favour in return.

The three foresters had positioned themselves just inside their compound and were unarmed except that one of the sons held a stout wooden staff. Ignoring them, Cedric strode through the gates and without waiting to be invited, went to stand beside their brazier. As he warmed himself he seemed to expect the headman to come to him.

'These bastards should show me some respect!' he said curtly when I tried to explain the way of such meetings. 'They should be grateful to those who've risked their lives fighting for the freedom they'll enjoy.' Then he turned to the headman. 'We've come to demand victuals for the remainder of our band,' he insisted. 'Fresh meat and bread if you have it. And also mead.'

The headman nodded knowingly. 'You say you "demand" these things?' he queried. 'By what right do you demand anything of us?'

Cedric stepped away from the fire and shouldered his huge axe. 'This is my right,' he roared. 'And I make my demands in the name of the blood shed for your benefit and protection.'

The two younger men moved across to stand either side of their father.

'You must forgive us,' I explained sensing what was about to follow. 'This man is from Northumbria and knows nothing of our ways. He is—'

'Be silent boy!' stormed Cedric. 'These are men's ways not those of a pious monk.'

The headman looked at me. 'You are of Saxon blood?' he asked.

'I am. My name is Matthew, son of Lord Edwulf,' I replied. 'My brother is Edwin who is a warrior to the King and—'

He held up his hand. 'I have heard tell of your family and hold them in much esteem,' he said respectfully. 'I am called

Roland and although not as illustrious as your own family, all here are of good Saxon stock. But tell me, why do you keep such company as this?' he asked pointing disdainfully at Cedric.

Cedric erupted and bellowed his defiance. 'Hold your tongue or we shall settle this as best it pleases me! I've asked for food not for myself but for those who had the guts to stand with me against your foes, not hide in the forest collecting sticks until the danger was past!'

Roland nodded wisely. 'Had you asked for food I would willingly have shared what little we can spare but you've demanded it in the manner of a greedy and insolent pig. Therefore I shall give you nothing, though Matthew here shall take his due.'

'I'll teach you what's due!' roared Cedric turning towards the nearest of the two sons. He had scarcely moved before Roland put his fingers to his mouth and let out a shrill whistle. From behind one of the buildings three huge hounds loped forward and headed straight for the giant. Shocked, Cedric levelled his axe and tried to strike at them as they closed upon him but they were much too quick. These were hunting dogs, broad chested with jaws like wolves and well used to prey which could defend itself. Instinctively they went at him from all sides at once. As he lashed out at one dog another seized him from behind. As he spun round to deal with that the third was hard upon him, snarling and tearing at the hem of his long fur cloak. Within moments they were all over him – one at his feet, one at his back and the other with the shaft of his axe gripped within its huge jaws, ripping it from side to side. Between them the pack wheeled the giant round, pulling and snarling until they had him on the ground. The noise they made was terrifying as they sensed a kill, but when Roland whistled again they stopped at once. Although reluctant to give up their prey they sloped away at his command and settled a few paces off.

Cedric lay on his back with his fur cloak spread out upon the snow like wings, his legs splayed apart. He was so still I thought him killed. Then slowly he began to move, raising his head and looking back at the dogs with terror in his eyes. His body was shaking and his face as grey as ashes as he glanced first at the three hounds then at his axe which lay in the snow to his right. The question was could he reach it before they reached him? Even once he had it, was there room enough to wield it before he was torn to shreds?

'Well what say you now?' challenged Roland as he looked down at Cedric's pathetic figure.

'I say you fight like craven cowards!' scowled Cedric. 'You use your dogs to do what you've not the guts to do yourself!'

Roland put his hands on his hips and shrugged. 'You say you want our food so fight for it. Every scrap I give to you is food these poor hounds will have to do without. So it's their fight, not mine.'

Cedric looked to me for support. 'Draw that sword, boy!' he ordered. 'And when I give the word strike at the beast nearest you then come quickly to my side.'

He must have sensed my hesitation.

'What, are you afraid to fight as well?'

'I'm not afraid,' I said. 'But I've no quarrel with these good people. They've already promised to provide me with whatever they can spare.'

Cedric spat at the ground. 'Forget about the food! This is about our honour!'

Those were strong words to a Saxon and I knew I had to answer carefully. 'My honour is not in question,' I said at last. 'If you would have me fight for yours then I would answer that I have no cause. Besides, there's no honour in fighting three unarmed men. Or three hapless dogs.'

'Well said,' acknowledged Roland then looked down at Cedric who was still on the ground. 'So what's it to be? Will you die here grovelling in the snow? If so I shall feed your carcass to my dogs and give what would have been their supper to Matthew to carry back with him. Is that not fair?'

Cedric was fuming. 'Let me up and I'll show you what's fair!' he demanded.

Roland was not so foolish as to rise to such a feeble challenge. 'I'm minded to spare your miserable skin but only because you've served our cause,' he offered. 'But if I let you up, you must leave this place and swear never to return.'

In those brief moments Cedric assessed his chances. He knew his life hung by a thread and his eyes showed all the fear he felt within. The dogs were still waiting, whining and slavering at the prospect of a kill. Two of them were growling expectantly whilst the other had its cruel eyes fixed upon him. They would have him; that much was certain; years of breeding were not to be denied. Having got him to ground they would strike fast, going first for the throat and then the belly, ripping him apart before toying with his lifeless body as they gorged themselves on his innards. It was no way for a man to die but then few of us get the chance to choose. Slowly he began to get up but kept his eyes on the dogs the whole time.

'Not so fast,' warned Roland. 'You've yet to make your answer.'

'Pah!' said Cedric. 'What choice is that to give a man who serves your King: leave or be torn apart by your vicious dogs? So much for your so-called honour!'

Roland appeared not to hear the reference to Alfred or, if he did, he tactfully chose to ignore it. 'Make your choice!' he threatened. 'I've wasted enough time on you already and have more profitable work for my dogs than gnawing on your worthless corpse.'

'All right, I'll go,' said Cedric begrudgingly. 'There's nothing in this shit hole worth dying for anyway.'

To insult a man's home was normally a challenge in itself but Roland was wise enough to let it pass. 'Leave and never return,' he insisted. 'That was the bargain you were offered.'

'It's all the same to me,' said Cedric. 'Why should I want to return to—' He stopped himself from saying more, knowing he had already gone too far. 'All right you have my word,' he concluded. 'I'll leave and not come back.'

'Your word?' queried Roland. 'Your word's worth nothing here!' Then he noticed Cedric's axe in the snow and picked it up. 'I shall keep this in satisfaction of your pledge,' he said feeling the weight of it. 'If you ever set foot in this place again I'll use it to hack your wretched body into morsels and feed them to my dogs. Is that clear?'

Cedric glared at him but made no answer. Instead he scrambled to his feet and, nursing his arm, hobbled towards the gates. Even then he could not resist turning to make one last jibe but Roland did not respond.

I watched until Cedric had gone from view, then Roland turned to me. 'We shall spare all we can for your friends but the winter has been hard,' he said.

I knew this as well as anyone and acknowledged the point.

As his two sons went off to fetch supplies Roland seemed concerned about Cedric. After all, although not from Wessex the giant was still an Ealdorman and as such enjoyed a much higher status than the lowly forester. 'Will that bastard make things hard for us?' he asked.

'No, he won't dare tell anyone for fear it makes him look a fool,' I assured him. 'But his pride is hurt. I can't believe he let you treat him thus. I would have died a thousand times rather than endure such dishonour.'

'Perhaps that's why Wessex stands alone against the Vikings,' mused Roland. With that his two sons returned with a sack which they had filled with supplies. It was mostly salted meat but also some smoked fish, some apples and some nuts picked from the forest. 'Take these with our blessing,' he said. 'And may God go with you to aid your cause.' They had certainly been very generous, much more so than I expected, and I realised then that Roland had indeed picked up on Cedric's careless boast of serving Alfred. There was nothing to be done except to trust the forester to keep the secret for to have said more would have only made matters worse. Besides, I saw no reason not to trust him given all he had said and done.

As we parted Roland gave me Cedric's axe as well, saying that if the giant was indeed on the side of the Saxons it should be put to better use than chopping wood.

I was relieved for I had dreaded what would happen when Cedric returned to the band wounded and without his prized weapon. Doubtless he would conjure up some pretext for it all and I would be faced with the dilemma of whether or not to speak of what had really transpired, which might well have implicated Roland. As it turned out I need not have worried; Cedric emerged from the forest almost as soon as I reached the point where the path to the forester's camp met the road.

The giant was unusually quiet even when I gave him back the axe. 'I knew they wouldn't dare to keep this!' he boasted as he shouldered the weapon once more. 'They had no right to treat me as they did!' he reasoned. 'But what can one man do against a pack of dogs?'

I knew what Edwin would have done but said nothing. Instead I gave the giant some of the provisions to carry to help him save face.

'If Alfred were to learn of what transpired he'd send men to teach those bastards some respect...' persisted Cedric.

I knew that was not true either. Alfred would have sided with Roland for if anyone had shown a lack of respect it was surely Cedric.

'But Alfred has troubles enough,' continued Cedric. 'So we'll not speak of these matters to the others. Do you understand me?'

I nodded for I understood all too well. Or at least, I was beginning to.

Chapter Nine

When the rest of the men arrived they found Cedric cleansing his wounds with handfuls of snow. There were deep lacerations to his forearms where the flesh was still bleeding and, to his right leg, a series of small holes where one of the dogs had sunk its fangs into his thigh. 'These are nothing,' he lied when Edwin asked what had happened. 'We were attacked by a mad dog, that's all.'

'What!' teased Edwin. 'Did you steal his supper? Is that where all this food came from?'

Cedric scowled at him but limped off still nursing his arm.

Edwin sensed something was amiss but when he pressed me on the matter I quickly changed the subject, telling him instead about the foresters who had given so generously because they knew of Alfred's presence. He was concerned as to whether they could be trusted, but I said nothing about the dogs or about Cedric's rudeness.

I was prepared to keep my word to Cedric only because I wanted to ensure there were no repercussions for Roland and his family, who had struck me as being honest thanes who, having fallen on hard times, were striving to scratch a meagre living from the forest. Also, there was already enough bad blood between Edwin and the giant and I had no wish to make matters worse. Cedric, on the other hand, had no such qualms. I know that he complained bitterly to Alfred about my failure to support him when he was attacked by a vicious dog, but Alfred had more to worry about than some petty quarrel. He excused my behaviour on the grounds that I was a novice monk, not a warrior. To relieve the situation, he then ordered Wilfred to go with Cedric in my place.

The two men set off ahead of us leaving the main party to follow once we had sorted out the provisions which had been so generously provided. The threat of an imminent attack from Vikings seemed to have faded from everyone's mind as we took our time in preparing to leave which, as Edwin pointed out, was extremely foolish and very dangerous.

'I hear what you say,' replied Alfred when Edwin expressed his concern. 'But these men are weary. We've done much to lift their spirits and their wounds are starting to heal, but I dare not push them too hard. We shall make haste where we can but I must keep the group intact at all costs.'

Still, Edwin did what he could to rouse the men, but by the time they were ready to leave it was well past midday. To make matters worse we had barely started out when we rounded a bend to find a narrow bridge carrying the road across a river. On the far bank, just beyond the bridge, Wilfred and Cedric were brutally interrogating a prisoner. The poor wretch was lying flat on his back with the edge of Cedric's axe rested upon his chest.

'What crime has this man committed!' demanded Alfred as soon as we reached them.

Wilfred looked sheepish and stepped back leaving Cedric to explain.

'He's a Viking spy,' announced Cedric as though that were obvious.

Clearly terrified, the man let forth a stream of words no one could understand. Edwin tried to calm him but still the words meant nothing. His was such a strange dialect with much rolling of the tongue and spitting, every word sounding like an oath.

'You see!' claimed Cedric. 'He's a Viking! Now let me put an end to his miserable existence.'

Alfred could speak some Viking words and so tried asking the man his name. Even that was to no avail for he just looked back at us blankly seeming even more frightened and confused.

'Let me try some Latin,' I suggested. It was a language most people understood from having learned it for prayers and such like by rote, though only those who had been educated spoke it well. As a monk, my studies meant I was all but fluent.

The frightened wretch appeared to understand me at once but replied with such a harsh accent that it was still difficult for me to follow.

'He calls himself "Emelyn" or something like it,' I announced. 'And I think he's saying he's a traveller from across the water.'

'Well one thing's for certain, he's no Viking,' said Alfred looking at Cedric angrily. 'Would you kill a man simply because he speaks a different tongue?'

Full of remorse, Wilfred helped the man to his feet and offered him some water.

The stranger brushed the snow from his clothes then bowed to Alfred as if thanking him for sparing his life. He was a small man with a round belly and a ruddy face framed with a shock of black and thickly matted hair. From what

I'd gleaned, it seemed he had crossed the fierce waters of the Severn estuary some days before intent upon a pilgrimage to Rome. On his way through Wessex he had chanced upon something which seemed to excite him greatly. To explain this, he kept repeating himself and making the sign of the cross.

'He's warning us,' suggested Edwin. 'Maybe he's spotted a Viking trap.'

I listened carefully, syllable by syllable. 'No, I think he's saying there's a settlement ahead and he's urging us to see it for ourselves.'

'No, it's some sort of church,' insisted Alfred who was also fluent in Latin. He repeated the words *Domus Dei* and the man nodded vigorously.

'A new church? Is that what he's saying?' I asked.

'Edwin's right!' warned Cedric. 'It's a Viking trap! Can't you see that? This man's no pilgrim; he's a spy like I said. And he's luring us into an ambush!'

Unaware of the accusation, Emelyn kept nodding and smiling then grasped Alfred's hand and kissed the ring he wore on his finger before backing away, bowing as he went.

'Not so fast!' bellowed Cedric.

But Emelyn was much too quick for him. He dodged to one side then darted into the forest and quickly disappeared between the trees.

'Let him go,' said Alfred, fearing that the men would all give chase and in so doing become separated. 'He means no harm and even if the Vikings catch him they won't understand him any more than we did.'

With that Alfred called the men to gather round. 'I believe this man was a pilgrim and that he was trying to tell us about a new church founded alongside this very road,' he said. 'If so, it's surely a good omen not only because it heralds that our path is truly a righteous one, but because it's also a sure sign that some good may yet spring from so much evil, hope from our despair and order from this chaos. We must take the time to find this church and there give thanks to God.'

Edwin wanted to protest but could see it was a wasted effort. Heartened by what Alfred had said, all the men seemed intent on finding the new church, perhaps because it was the first good news they had heard in days.

'All right,' agreed Edwin reluctantly. 'But we have no more time to waste. Matthew can hurry on ahead to find it. Being a monk it's fitting he should be the one to go but I'll travel with him in case it is a trap.'

Alfred agreed and ordered that we should set off at once, praying that he was not sending his most trusted warrior to his death.

* * * * *

Edwin remained gravely suspicious of the stranger, all the more so for the fact that we had so mysteriously met him on the road as if by chance. Still fearing a trap, he kept me close beside him until we reached the edge of the forest. From there the road began to rise steeply towards a series of rounded hills, each capped by sparse open ground which was covered with snow. We knew this road would lead eventually to a narrow pass between those hills, one which had been used for longer than anyone could remember. According to legend it was once the site of a bloody ambush in which an entire Roman Legion had been slaughtered.

'You don't think Cedric was right, do you?' I ventured, recalling the stories I had been told about the massacre.

Edwin didn't reply. He was too busy scanning the horizon. In particular, his keen eyes had noticed a thin column of smoke rising from somewhere just beyond the next bend. 'What's that do you think?' he asked pointing it out.

It was impossible to say from there and Edwin knew better than to blunder in. 'We'll approach quietly and keep out of sight until we can assess things,' he announced, leading the way.

Once close enough to see, we found that the smoke was coming from a large walled building with a central courtyard. Being on the southern slopes of the hill it was probably built on the remains of what was once a Roman villa. As such it was a remnant of more settled times when homes could be sited for prestige rather than defence and concealment. The main building had been fortified and enclosed but what intrigued Edwin was that within the compound what had once been a small private temple now had a cross set above the two slender columns which framed the doorway. From what we could see, all the buildings were in poor repair. Many had roofs missing and the walls were scorched by fire. Also the gates were broken and flung wide open.

Apart from the cross there was no outward sign that it was a church, so Edwin could still not rule out the possibility of a trap, although he seemed satisfied that there was no immediate danger. Thus as we approached he called out aloud so as not to surprise and thereby alarm those within.

At first there was no reply, but at length a monk appeared and came forward to greet us. He was a broad-shouldered man built more like a warrior than a man of God but poorly dressed in a ragged and threadbare habit which was stretched tight across his belly and tied with a length of cord.

'And what, pray, is your business here?' asked the monk.

'We come in peace,' Edwin assured him, keeping his distance.

The monk looked at us both carefully. 'Peace you say? Then I'm right glad to hear it. For with so much blood upon your clothes I wouldn't care to meet you if you came here intent upon a quarrel.'

I realised with embarrassment that my own habit was even more dishevelled than his. 'I can explain…' I stammered.

'This boy is my brother, Matthew, and was granted leave from Holy Orders that he might attend to family matters, our folks having being murdered by the Vikings,' explained Edwin interrupting me. 'On our way back we became embroiled in the battle at Chippenham and even now are, with others, fleeing for our lives.'

The monk crossed himself but said nothing.

'We seek only shelter for the night,' added Edwin hurriedly.

'I'd not refuse you that. But how can I best be sure that you are truly Saxons?' asked the monk.

'Well it's a little late to ask,' mocked Edwin. 'If we were Vikings we'd have sacked this place by now! But see, I wear the cross of Christ about my neck not the hammer of Thor.'

'Any man might wear a cross. The question is can you live and die by its creed?' So saying he studied us for a moment then seemed satisfied we meant no harm. 'No matter. Any road, 'tis a question we must each answer for ourselves. Besides, we've little enough worth stealing as everything was taken in the last raid. All we have now is our lives and you're welcome to those, for 'tis a hard living and if truth be told we should all prefer to stand before our maker rather than shiver here in the cold and snow.'

With that he led the way into the courtyard which was lined on one side by a covered walkway. The place had indeed been ransacked for there was little that wasn't broken or damaged. The main gates had been roughly braced with timbers to keep them upright and even the door to the church itself was propped up against the wall. Two other monks stood together, warming their hands beside a brazier of glowing coals.

Edwin acknowledged them and asked after their abbot.

'He's gone where we would follow,' said the monk who had greeted us and he pointed to a line of freshly dug graves to one side of the church. 'He perished when the Vikings attacked this place not ten days since.'

'Were they all killed at one time?' I asked, counting the graves.

The monk nodded. 'Aye, all twelve,' he said wistfully, crossing himself again. 'Like the Apostles of Christ.'

'Yet you three survived,' observed Edwin, not meaning to imply anything by the remark.

'That was God's will,' replied the monk looking at him uneasily. 'We three were absent when the heathens came. We returned to find this Holy place as you see it now and with our abbot and our brothers slain. But it remains a house of God and we shall strive to restore it if we can.'

When we peered inside the church we saw it had been stripped of its Holy ornaments and books. All that remained was a table which served as an altar on which had been placed a casket and a simple wooden cross.

'The casket holds a Holy Relic,' explained the monk. 'A piece of the true cross of Christ.'

'And the Vikings didn't take it?' asked Edwin.

'Only because they didn't see it,' explained the monk. 'It fell to the floor when they upended the altar upon which it stands. Strange to say they took everything except the one thing we value most. It was a miracle of course, for surely the good Lord intended it should thus be saved. We're therefore intent upon founding a new church here on this very spot dedicated to this Holy Splinter. That's the work to which we set our hearts and our hands.'

Edwin was clearly impressed by their fortitude. 'Then you'd best be prepared,' he warned. 'The Vikings will come again, and soon, for we believe them to be in pursuit of us.'

The monk smiled broadly. 'If they come, we'll hide,' he said simply. 'As you can see there's nothing left now for them to destroy or steal which we cannot carry with us. But who are you that you would bring them down upon us?'

I was about to speak of Alfred and the others when Edwin stopped me. 'We're just weary warriors,' he said. 'Good Christians in need of shelter for the night.'

'Our Holy Orders could not deny you that,' admitted the monk. 'But as you see we've little enough to offer...'

'We have our own food,' added Edwin quickly. 'And enough to share. But there are others with us following behind. With your consent I'll fetch them here for there are some with wounds who would benefit from your ministrations.'

114

The monk was clearly impressed by the promise of food. 'Then you are indeed most welcome,' he said. 'My name is Brother Godwin. These two goodly brothers will look to your needs but you must forgive them if they seem to say little, for such is our way.'

Edwin then realised he had not introduced himself and so promptly did so, certain he had found the new church which had so excited Emelyn.

'Perhaps young Matthew here should stay to help us prepare for your friends,' said Brother Godwin, more contrite now that he knew of Edwin's status as a warrior from a noble family. 'Also I would speak with him, for I fear his devotions have been much neglected. Is it not my duty to search his faith and thereby restore him to grace?'

I suspect that Edwin had no idea what the monk intended, but it seemed only fair that I should help with whatever preparations were needed. Thus he went alone to fetch Alfred and the others.

As soon as Edwin had gone Brother Godwin led me into the church and told me to kneel before the makeshift altar. 'You wear the habit of a novice monk but it's stained with blood,' he observed harshly. 'You wear the cross of Christ yet you carry the sword of a warrior. I sense from this that your faith is much troubled and your soul divided. From what your brother has said the life you now lead was thrust upon you by circumstance but the road ahead of you offers two choices. Your friends will come tonight and tomorrow they'll leave. Will you go with them or will you stay here with us and fulfil your Holy Orders? The choice must be yours.'

At first I could not bring myself to speak. Brother Godwin had voiced what deep within my heart I already feared – that

I was shying away from the life of a monk and being drawn into my brother's world. 'What do you think I—?'

Brother Godwin put his fingers to his lips. 'Ask nothing of me on this matter for I cannot guide you. Pray to God and he'll show the way.' With that he left me to prayer and contemplation. Not that it was of much help for even after some time I was still unsure of my true feelings. There was no time for further counsel before Edwin then returned with the others.

The sight of such a large band must have surely alarmed Brother Godwin, yet he greeted them with good grace as they shuffled in, weary from the journey. Cedric was leading with Alfred safely hidden amid the ranks.

'This deception cannot be right,' I whispered to Wilfred as I stood beside him. 'These are Holy men who should be trusted.'

Alfred had edged close enough to overhear me. 'Matthew, they cannot speak of that which they do not know,' he said. 'Besides, if they recognise me they may be tempted to offer more than they can spare.'

Eadred was led directly into the church and helped to sit on the floor in front of the altar. One of the monks set about examining his wound, finding it much swollen and with the skin around it turning blue.

'We shall need to lance the wound to remove the pus,' announced Brother Godwin. 'A poultice of honey mixed with herbs should then draw the poison, but he'll need to rest for several days.'

Edwin looked at Alfred before replying on his behalf. 'We thank you for your kindness but if we stay we fear we may bring yet more destruction upon you. Therefore we ask you to keep this man and tend his wound. We shall leave some meat towards his keep if that will suffice.'

Brother Godwin seemed pleased with the prospect of venison and readily agreed. 'We'll disguise him as one of our own so that if the Vikings come they'll not take him for a warrior,' he offered.

Others also had their wounds tended whilst, outside the church, the monks had set up a cooking stand over the brazier and on it placed a large round pot. Emelda began cooking broth using some of the venison together with roots and herbs. It was served with a thick mead the monks had brewed and thus we all ate well that night and slept secure for the first time since the battle.

In the morning, Edwin assembled the men on Alfred's orders and Brother Godwin led us all in prayer. We gave thanks for what many saw as the first signs of something good growing from so much carnage – like the first shoots of spring. When we had finished we said our farewells to Eadred, Edwin charging him not to mention Alfred's name or our plans to go to Athelney. None doubted that he could be trusted.

Edwin then explained to Eadred that it might be hard to find us once we reached the marshes. 'Find Lord Ethelnorth instead,' he advised. 'He'll bring you to us. But wait until you're well for as much as we enjoy your company it's your sword arm we'll have need of.'

Eadred grinned. 'Then I'm ready now, for I can fight more Vikings with one arm than most men can fight with two!'

Edwin clasped Eadred's hand in friendship. 'I was wrong,' he said, laughing heartily. 'We also need the spirit of men such as you. Find us when you're well my friend and may God speed your recovery.' Edwin then bid farewell to Brother Godwin and thanked him for his help.

'And what of this novice?' asked the monk referring to me. 'Yesterday I offered him the choice to stay with us for I see his training has been much neglected.'

'That's for him to decide,' advised Edwin looking towards me.

All waited for me to answer. I was hesitant at first, not sure how I should respond, but then I found my voice. 'Had you asked me but a few days ago I would have stayed willingly to aid a venture such as this,' I replied. 'My calling applauds all you've done but my heart now questions whether I was ever truly meant for Holy Orders for I've seen and learned much that was not known to me before. In this I've taken inspiration from your relic which, though being just a small part of the Holy Cross, plays such an important part in your work. I'm just a small part of this group but sense I have my part to play and that God has set me on this path for a purpose. Thus these men have become my life, their cause has become my calling and I would stay with them even though I know I may well perish if I do.'

Edwin was surprised at the response. 'He's answered well,' he said proudly and for the first time seemed truly glad to keep me with him.

Brother Godwin agreed. 'He has indeed. And though I shall pray he returns to the Church, I wish him well. But I sense there are others among you who are troubled. I would offer to hear their confession but am not ordained to do so.'

Alfred whispered something to Edwin then gave him the armband they had seized from Goda. Edwin set it down on a block used for chopping wood then took a hatchet and sliced it into two equal halves, one of which he gave to Brother Godwin. 'This silver is tainted with Saxon blood,' he said solemnly. 'The lives of many men were bought and sold with it. We offer it now that it may help with the founding of your church and, in so doing, hope the metal will be cleansed.'

The monk looked wide eyed at the offering and did not know what to say.

Again Alfred prompted Edwin.

'Take it,' he insisted. 'In return we would ask only that you pray for us; for I fear with all that lies ahead of us we shall need your prayers far more than we shall ever need this silver.'

Chapter Ten

Our retreat from Chippenham had been long and hard, not helped by the severe weather or by the fact that we were already weary and fearful of being attacked at any time. All that we put behind us as we pushed on towards the Mendip Hills knowing that once safely through the pass we would be in staunch Saxon territory where at least there would be less risk of being betrayed.

From the high ground we would also be able to see the Somerset Levels stretched out before us with the marshes in the far distance. I am sure Alfred was gambling on the hope that once we could sight our objective everyone's spirits would be lifted. For once he was wrong; for no sooner had we broached the pass than men began to voice their concerns aloud, questioning again the logic of going to such a remote and desolate place as Athelney.

'The damp in the marshes will sap our strength so that our sword arms will grow weak,' complained Wilfred.

It was left to Edwin to counter these grumbles. He told them a Saxon warrior's strength lay in his heart, not his arm. 'If any grow weak it's because they're already weak,' he reasoned. 'The strong grow stronger in adversity.' Yet for all his fine words I knew he was no more anxious to enter the marshes than were the rest of us, for we all regarded the prospect of what lay ahead as being every bit as daunting as that which lay behind.

I know now that if Alfred seemed deaf to these complaints it was because he had more compelling reasons for choosing Athelney. Not only was it a secure place to see out the rest of the winter, it was also strategically important being part way between Exeter and Bath. He feared that either of those Saxon settlements might be Guthrum's next target and wanted to be close enough to defend them if he could. How he planned to do that with a handful of broken men he didn't say, but even at the head of a ragged and defeated army his spirit remained undimmed. When he confided these reasons to Edwin, the warrior could not help but marvel at a King who could share the deprivations we all endured yet, whilst others thought only of survival, was still intent on triumph.

* * * * *

As we marched down towards the Levels, Edwin took the chance to speak with me about my decision not to remain with Brother Godwin and thereby help to found the new church. 'Because of the years between us we've not been close,' he ventured, choosing his words carefully. 'But the cruel fate of our family has brought us together and, in terms of kin, we now have no one but each other. Thus I hope I've done nothing to sway you in your choice, for your life in the Church was something which our dear father wanted just as he wanted me to become a warrior.'

I welcomed the opportunity to speak about my decision for in many ways it had puzzled even me. 'I know,' I replied.

'And this may sound strange, but I hadn't decided what I was going to say until I started to answer Brother Godwin's question. When I did it was as though God had placed the words inside my mouth and all I had to do was open it to let them out. I'm not saying I'm ready to become a warrior like you, but I do believe that my destiny lies here, with my King.'

My brother didn't answer at first, as though still searching for the right words. 'There are times when your heart knows what's right,' he admitted at last.

I was unsure whether this helped or not, nor even whether Edwin approved of my decision: but at least the matter had been broached, which meant I could now discuss it openly if I wished.

Meanwhile the men's misgivings about Athelney were not helped when a solitary magpie swooped past us and settled on the road ahead. A number of the men hurriedly crossed themselves for, when seen alone, the bird was thought to beckon sorrow, and we had all seen enough of that to last a lifetime.

As if to affirm the point, a group of riders were sighted shortly afterwards approaching from the open ground to the west. They were spreading out in line abreast, their horses kicking up white clouds as they struggled in the snow.

'Vikings!' went up a cry from the man who saw them first.

'How many?' snapped Edwin.

They were still too far off to be seen easily but Wilfred's eyes were keen. 'Five, no more,' he announced.

Hurriedly Edwin looked about him. Noting a copse to our rear he knew at once where the true danger lay. 'Watch your backs!' he ordered. 'There may be more in the trees who wait for our retreat!'

Cedric looked astounded. 'Retreat! Retreat from what? Five men on horses yet still too far away to even see them!'

Ignoring him Edwin began to marshal the men into position. 'Fall in!' he urged whilst almost pushing them together to form a proper rank. Ultimately it would become a wall of warriors but in the snow they struggled to link up properly. Osric and his men ushered Alfred behind this makeshift line and crowded close about him.

'Be on your guard!' shouted Edwin moving along the line trying to close any gaps.

Cedric stood some paces off and mocked them. 'What are you afraid of? We've four good men at least to every one of them!'

Edwin still ignored him. To his warrior's mind it made no sense for five Viking warriors to ride headlong into a band of Saxons who were armed and ready; it therefore had to be a diversion. He turned two men to guard our rear. 'Keep your eyes on those trees,' he ordered sternly.

Meanwhile Rufus had trained his bow in that direction and was waiting for orders. 'Shoot only if you see a clear target,' Edwin told him. 'Shadows won't harm us and we've not enough arrows to waste.'

The riders still struggled against the snow which slowed their progress. Edwin doubted it was the main attack and by committing men to watch the trees knew he was splitting his force. Yet he had no choice; if the riders drove us back to where more Vikings waited we would all be slain like dogs. It was a typical Viking ruse to use the terrain as an integral part of their tactics, and forests and woods were a favourite. Whereas we Saxons tended to avoid them if we could or use them as a place to hide, a trained Viking force could enter a forest, split up so that every man would cut his own way through then emerge as a fighting force on the other side. It was a skill they used to devastating effect. 'Sire, we must send someone into the trees,' he announced. 'If the Vikings are there we should flush them out now before their horsemen reach us.'

Cedric, who still refused to join the line, considered this. 'He's right, my Lord. Why not send Matthew? He has no other part to play in this.'

Edwin spun round to confront the giant but was obliged to hold his tongue. Going into the copse would be extremely dangerous, for if the Vikings were indeed waiting, whoever was sent there would be slain at once. Having been first to suggest the idea Edwin could hardly now argue that his brother should be exempted.

'Matthew's the obvious choice,' pressed Cedric, clearly pleased with the dilemma he had given Edwin. 'He has no skill with any weapon and thus if he's slain it harms us less than if we lose a trained warrior.'

All waited expectantly for Edwin's response. In truth I think he would rather have gone himself than send me, but he had no option.

Realising this, I didn't wait for orders. Instead I drew the Viking sword I still carried and started towards the trees.

With every step I knew I was taking a fearful risk. Without a shield and unable to move freely in the snow I would be an easy target. Even if I reached the copse alive the chances were I would be cut down at once. I tried to shake these thoughts from my mind by concentrating instead on putting one foot in front of the other. Then, when I was still a few paces off, I stopped and scanned the trees searching for the slightest sign of the Vikings' presence. Glancing back, I saw that Rufus had moved across to one side and now waited with his bow drawn to provide cover for me if he could. Edwin was with him, though there was nothing he could do to help from there. Then I recalled something Edwin had said: *'If there comes a point where death is the only option a good warrior will embrace it like a brother'*. I intoned the last few words under my breath like a prayer, repeating them over and over: *'embrace it like a brother…embrace it like a brother…'* The words were easy to say but did nothing to quell the fear I felt inside. My stomach churned and my heart beat fast as I struggled to find the courage to go on. Then it occurred to me that perhaps this was a chance to test myself; a chance to put all my trust in God and thereby begin to restore my damaged faith. If so I dared not let it pass for in my heart I knew I'd been found wanting all too often. Drawing a few deep breaths, I prayed earnestly for God to give me strength, then crossed myself. That done, I straightened my back and, although my legs were weak with fear, I strode forward as boldly as I dared.

All who watched me held their breath as I moved towards my fate. None, save perhaps Edwin, would willingly have traded places with me but, buoyed by my faith, I did not allow myself to falter. I could think only that it would be a lonely place in which to die; a place where my grave would be quickly forgotten. Despite such despondent thoughts I forced myself to keep walking even though every instinct I had was willing me to turn and run. Such was my resolve that only once I reached the copse did I allow myself to stop. There, although hardly daring to turn my head, I glanced quickly from side to side. When nothing happened I looked around more carefully. There were no tracks in the snow, no whispered voices to be heard, no arrows flying through the air. Bolder now, I felt it might be safe after all; safe enough at least for me to raise my sword and signal that I was still alive. Then something moved to my right. I turned, instinctively dropping to one knee. Even as I did so I knew that was a mistake. By kneeling I had rendered myself defenceless as the ground would impede my sword stroke and I could not dodge one way or the other if I was attacked. But God had heard my prayers. Something scurried into the undergrowth and was quickly gone. I never saw what it was but it wasn't a Viking!

As soon as they saw it was safe Osric and his guards led Alfred and Emelda into the copse. The defensive line then re-formed in front of them, this time with those who had shields locking them together and the other warriors standing behind them, their weapons ready.

Rufus moved to stand further forward than the others so that he could loose his arrows then retreat to the safety of the rank. When Cedric saw this he heaved his great axe onto his shoulder. 'Hide in the woods if you're afraid,' he jeered. 'I'd as soon fight in the open where there's room to greet the bastards properly!' With that he strode forward to join Rufus.

When others started to follow Edwin grew angry. He could see the danger in confusion and so barked his orders. 'This line must hold!' he shouted. 'We stand our ground till we know what's against us!'

Cedric turned and sneered at him. 'Five men on horses, that's what's against you. Yet you cower like frightened girls!'

Men looked at each other not sure what to do. The riders still posed no immediate threat yet all there had cause to know how quickly that could change. Then Alfred made his choice. He stepped forward to stand beside Edwin thereby reinforcing my brother's authority.

Taking his cue from Alfred's support, Edwin addressed the men in line. 'Mounted they have the advantage in the snow,' he warned. 'Therefore Rufus will try to shoot their horses as soon as they come into range. He'll then retreat and as he does so you must be ready to advance at my command. If any are still mounted, spread out and let them pass between you leaving enough space for Rufus to shoot again without fear of hitting you. With God's grace we shall see them off with ease.'

Then Rufus raised his arm. 'Their swords are sheathed!' he called out as the riders drew close enough for him to see. They had regrouped by this time and rode together as a pack, their horses bucking and rearing through the drifts of snow.

Suddenly Alfred let out a great cry of surprise and rushed forward, pushing his way through the line of startled warriors. 'But these are friends, not Vikings!' he called. 'Good friends! Is this how we greet our fellow Saxons? With our swords drawn and our spears poised?'

The riders drew up their horses just short of where Rufus waited, their leader raising his arm in greeting whilst still struggling to control his mount. He was a big man, not a giant like Cedric but tall and lean with long silver hair and a ruddy complexion. He wore a leather jerkin with a black cloak and carried a small shield on his left arm.

Having remained within the trees I was suddenly aware of someone at my side.

'So who are these men?' asked Emelda, her voice shy and small.

'Why, Lord Ethelnorth's,' I said, and could see at once that she recognised the name. It was fitting she should for although of advancing years he still had a reputation as a fearsome warrior.

By this time Lord Ethelnorth had dismounted and was kneeling before Alfred in homage. The King accepted the gesture then almost hauled the old warrior to his feet and embraced him.

Edwin and Ethelnorth were old friends and greeted each other warmly. Cedric was introduced by Alfred who explained how the giant from the north came to be part of his band. During all this time Ethelnorth's men remained mounted. All, that is, save one, a monk who had travelled with them and who seemed glad for the chance to stretch his legs. With the introductions exhausted Alfred addressed the rest of us.

'I'm told that my queen and her two ladies have been taken in secret to Exeter where they should be safe till spring,' he announced. 'Some of the other women from Chippenham are already at the Vill in Athelney and await our coming. This monk will take us there to join them leaving Lord Ethelnorth and his men to watch the road and warn us if Guthrum moves to attack. He has patrols already posted and will keep us supplied with all we need.'

There was a general feeling of relief but most still dreaded the prospect of entering the marshes, even with the monk as our guide.

'Why is everyone so pleased to see Lord Ethelnorth?' asked Emelda. 'He brings just four men and one of those is not even a warrior. What difference can they make now?'

Edwin overheard her and answered in my stead. 'Mark my words, girl, these few men and those who ride with them will make all the difference in the world. And you'd best pray I'm right; for at the moment they are all that stands between us and the grave.'

* * * * *

'So this Holy Brother is to be our guide,' observed Osric.

'He is,' replied Ethelnorth. 'His abbot has assured me that he knows the marshes well for he gathers herbs and roots there. He's to show the way then remain with you to tend the good Bishop Eahlstan who fared poorly on the journey there and even now awaits you at the Vill.'

Bishop Eahlstan was a man known and loved by us all. He was so old and frail it was a miracle he had survived the journey at all and everyone was saddened to hear he was unwell.

However Osric's concern was for a different reason. 'Then does this monk's abbot know who we have among us?' he asked

Ethelnorth looked at him coldly. 'What, are we fools?' he snapped. 'No one knows of Alfred's presence save those I'd trust with my life.'

If Alfred said very little at this point I believe it was because he was disappointed not to be reunited with his wife and their children. Although he was assured they were safe, he had hoped to spend the winter with them even though the marshes were no place for a woman of such high status as the Lady Elswith.

Meanwhile the monk was introduced to us as Brother Felix. He was a thin wiry little man who, according to Ethelnorth, came originally from Rome and more lately was a refugee from a bloody massacre at an Abbey somewhere in the north. He now shunned the company of men and instead took solace from the scriptures. Having sworn a vow of silence which remained unbroken for three full years, he now spoke only in the service of the Lord. To that end he carried a magnificent Bible strapped to his back, so heavy he stooped a little beneath its weight. Yet despite this impediment he led the way on foot, setting a brisk pace and stopping only so that we could all keep up. Although he spoke no words he was a cheery soul who smiled often and seemed to take great joy from the task assigned to him. As to whether or not he knew that his King was among those he guided it was difficult to say. Edwin made the point that he would not have cared much one way or the other. He simply did God's work and his abbot's bidding, carrying his blessed Bible like a penance freely borne.

I should like to have spoken with Brother Felix about various spiritual matters but was obliged to respect the monk's vow of silence. In fact that same silence seemed infectious for the whole group was very quiet as we entered the marshes; a silence broken only by the booming call of the bitterns giving voice as we approached. They were shy birds living within the reeds, the hollow, haunting sound they made giving rise to many of the tales of demons and devils, for it had an eerie tone which chilled the heart.

The marshes were mostly swamps of brackish water bounded by tall reeds and rushes. These waters were so foul they were best avoided by keeping to the narrow path which Brother Felix followed. Even that was not easy, for the snow disguised the edge of it and often the ground beyond was too soft to walk upon.

At length even the path became too sodden but ancient hands had fashioned a crude walkway which led across the water. This causeway, as it was called, was like a long, snaking bridge but was barely wide enough to walk along even in single file. It stood just clear of the surface and was carried on posts driven deep into the mud to which planks had been secured. It looked very unsteady and, in places, had deep water on either side, but it was not this that troubled most of the men. Each of them would gladly have run the full length of the causeway a dozen times rather than face the charms which had been set to guard it.

These are pagan charms of which I speak – animal skulls and the bones of stillborn children which had been suspended from one of the posts. They were such a fearful sign that no one would pass them in case his sleeve or the hem of his cloak brushed against them, for the touch of such relics was said to burn a mark upon a man's soul which Satan himself would recognise in order to claim it for his own. They were set there to bar the way, all the more potent for being the work of ancient peoples who, for reasons of their own, sought to keep the marshes to themselves. Only Alfred, who had been to Athelney before, seemed unconcerned by them. The rest of us were hesitant as if waiting for some sort of sign. Seeing this, Brother Felix went and stood beside the relics then sank to his knees and prayed. When he had finished he stood up and looked at each of the men in turn as though shaming them for their lack of faith. Then he began plucking the relics from the post one by one, spitting on them and hurling them into the water. Several of the men crossed themselves when they saw this but, when he had finished, the monk opened his hands and held them up to show there were no marks upon them. Finally he took the Bible from his back, held it in both hands high above his head and led the way along the causeway.

At this point Ethelnorth and his men turned back, taking all the horses with them as there was no way they could be led across the narrow walkway. Alfred and the rest of us then followed Brother Felix for some distance, keeping to the causeway until we came to a jetty jutting out into a vast stretch of open water. There a woman waited with a raft, a crude vessel built of reeds heaped upon each other and lashed to a simple wooden frame, looking more like the handiwork of a thatcher than a skilled ferryman.

This woman was one of the few to have escaped from the terror at Chippenham. As the men arrived she peered at each of them in turn as though searching for someone among the ragged band of survivors. Disappointed, she began to ferry us across to a small island which lay within the open water perhaps fifty paces from the shore. She could take no more than three or four at a time so, with other women waiting anxiously on the far side, those men who had reason to think their wives or loved ones might be among them went first. The joy of the few who were reunited was enough to cheer even the saddest heart though, for the rest, arriving at Athelney was a bitter blow as they were forced to confront the stark and terrible truth that their loved ones might not have survived or, worse still, had been taken by the Vikings.

* * * * *

It did not do to think of what the women who had been at Chippenham at the time of the attack had each endured. If captured they would have been ill used for certain and then, if still alive, taken for whores or to be sold as slaves. Some would surely have taken their own lives rather than endure the dishonour of being passed among the Viking warriors like so much baggage, but it was not known whether any had managed to escape and find shelter with friends or kin nearby. All those who reached Athelney had travelled with the good Bishop having been met on the road by Ethelnorth's men. That is not to say they had not been harmed, for many had suffered during their escape in ways they would not mention. We were told that Alfred's wife, the Lady Elswith, had fared better than most. She and her children with a few loyal attendants escaped with Alfred from the Vill at Chippenham and had then been sent under armed escort to meet Ethelnorth. He personally saw them safe to Exeter where she had gone into hiding with a trusted and loyal household. It was said her courage during the escape had been an example to all, but in truth I doubt she endured but a fraction of the abuse meted out to those less fortunate women who had been forced to fend for themselves.

* * * * *

With no kin to greet us, Edwin and I busied ourselves by inspecting the defences.

The island was partly man made as was the causeway leading to it, both of which had been formed and originally occupied long before Roman times. The Vill was a more recent addition and comprised a large rounded building made of timber and reeds, together with a small forge and various stores and outbuildings. The ground was too wet for a ditch or an earthen rampart but, being surrounded by water, the island was easy to defend. In fact the raft was the only viable way to reach it.

'We could hold such a place for ever,' said Edwin cheerfully. 'We'll need to improve the defences but we have water, so if we stockpile food and firewood it will see us safe till spring.'

'What about the ice?' said Cedric who, like us, had no one to greet him. 'In places it's thick enough for the whole of Guthrum's army to walk across with ease.'

It was an exaggeration but Edwin took his point. The still water of the marshes had frozen hard around the edges and in places the ice stretched almost to the island. 'We'll break it,' he said at last. 'Daily if we must. And we'll keep the raft on the island with us so it can't be used by any who would reach us. If needs be we can set up hides along the water's edge to provide cover for the men to keep watch and—'

'Pah, we could build a new island in the time it takes to do all that!' said Cedric dismissively.

Edwin was not dismayed. 'Food first,' he said. 'Four men must be sent to stock our larder. There are fish and eels in plenty and some game. Others shall work with me to strengthen the defences and improve the Vill.'

'With what?' sneered Cedric.

He knew the answer to that. 'Good Saxon craft,' he said proudly. 'We'll charge Ethelnorth to have his men bring us withies cut from saplings of ash taken from the forests beyond the marsh. The stouter ones we set in the ground, the others we split to weave between them like a basket. They'll stop a spear or even an arrow at this distance. For the shelter we must add mud mixed with straw to seal the gaps and thereby keep out the weather. There's not a man here who hasn't done this a hundred times before.'

'And what then?' demanded Cedric.

'Then we shall make ourselves stronger, mend our weapons and wait till spring. Beyond that there's nothing we can do but pray.

Chapter Eleven

Settling into the Vill required everyone to lend a hand with work needed to improve the defences and accommodation. Most of the men within our band were thanes and therefore used to having others attend them, but there were also a number of ceorls and several slaves. Alfred decreed that all should contribute according to their skills and ability which, although resented by some, was the only practical way we would survive the winter. Nonetheless he was careful in the allocation of duties so as not to cause undue offence. Small groups were also sent out as Edwin had suggested, some to hunt or fish and others to gather the firewood we would need if we were to keep a fire burning at all times. As it was necessary for some of these groups to travel far beyond the marshes they were gone for several days. Meanwhile, Lord Ethelnorth sent his own slaves under armed escort to cut the withies and carry them to Athelney in large bundles together with any provisions which could be spared from nearby settlements. All this meant a great number of people coming and going, so Edwin and I were sent across on the raft to check the condition of the causeway and the jetty. Being both a warrior and of noble birth Edwin could have refused such menial work but he saw it as a chance to lead by example. It was also a chance for him to speak with me in private.

'So he was adamant that the gates at Chippenham were not opened from within,' mused Edwin when I recounted the conversation I'd had with Osric during the retreat to Athelney. Edwin was lying flat on his stomach and peering down at the posts supporting the jetty whilst I steadied the raft.

'That's right,' I agreed. 'He claimed the Vikings had forced them open.'

Edwin looked up at me. 'But that's impossible. The cross beam used to secure them was weathered oak and so heavy it took two good men just to lift it. The gates must have been left open for some reason.'

'Osric nearly bit my head off when I suggested that,' I said dismissively.

Still on his stomach, Edwin shuffled across to look at the timbers on the opposite side. Finding them coated with a thick green slime he was concerned that rot was setting in. It was not yet an imminent problem so he returned his attention to the question of Osric. 'How can he be so sure? Perhaps there was an "arrangement" to allow someone to enter or leave the settlement that night,' he suggested. 'It wouldn't be the first time guards have been bribed to look the other way.'

'But why should anyone need to come or go in secret?' I asked. 'There was no curfew in place. They had only to ask and the gates would have been opened for them.'

Edwin looked up at me and grinned. 'Sometimes men have meetings they prefer to conduct in private...'

I thought for a moment then realised what he meant. 'Oh...you mean with a woman... I see. Yes, that's possible I suppose but why leave the settlement for that? And anyway, if the guards had been bribed, surely they'd have been even more careful to secure the gates afterwards if only to ensure they were not found out?'

Edwin sat up and dried his hands on his cloak. 'All of which convinces me I'm right. Someone opened those gates to let the Vikings in. And whoever that traitor is he could yet be among us.'

'Most likely it was someone from the settlement,' I suggested. 'Or what about the tinker we met on the way here? We don't know where he was at the time of the attack. Could it be that he was sent to Chippenham by the Vikings for that very purpose? That would explain why they gave him so much silver.'

Edwin considered this. 'That's possible. But if so, would he have been so foolish as to set up camp so close by? I'd have abandoned the cart and got as far away as I could whatever the weather.' Having finished checking the posts Edwin got up and stepped onto the jetty to test the boards. Finding them sound enough, he walked a little way along the causeway where we already knew some of the planks would need renewing. 'Anyway, the guards would surely have replaced the bar after he'd gone.'

'It's a pity none of them survived to tell us what happened,' I said.

Edwin carefully stepped back onto the raft so as not to rock it too hard. 'The poor bastards wouldn't have stood much chance,' he observed. 'Being at the forefront of the battle they were probably killed in the first wave of the attack. What I don't understand is what Osric was doing there. Normally he won't leave Alfred's side even for a moment. Why would he do so at a time like that?'

'Perhaps he went to see whether there was any means of getting Alfred and his family out that way. He said that when he reached the southern gates all the guards were dead and the Vikings swarming through the breach.'

Edwin used his hands to ease the raft around the end of the jetty, making one final inspection of the underside of the boards.

'None of this makes much sense,' I continued. 'Unless…'

'Unless what?' prompted Edwin

'Well what if the guards were dead before the Vikings launched their attack?'

Edwin stopped what he was doing and looked up, clearly startled. 'What are you saying? That someone killed the guards then opened the gates?'

'It's possible,' I ventured.

'Yes, but who would do that?'

'Well, Goda for a start. He could have killed the guards, opened the gates and been gone before anyone knew anything about it, collecting his silver on the way.'

Edwin shook his head. 'He was a treacherous knave I'll grant you that, but not man enough to kill the guards single-handed. If what you say is right the man we're looking for is a warrior; and a good one. Yet as Osric said, everyone there could be trusted.'

'Osric,' I mused. 'Always it comes back to him. As you say, he had no business even being there yet he's the only one who refutes that the gates were opened.'

'You're not suggesting it was him!' said Edwin incredulous at the very thought of it.

'I wasn't accusing anyone,' I replied hastily, but even as I said it I realised the thought was now there.

'No, the traitor can't be him,' reasoned Edwin. 'Osric's loyalty is beyond question. He's both friend and kin to Alfred. He holds lands from him and has been honoured above others. What possible cause had he to betray him?'

'I confess I can make no sense of it,' I agreed. 'But why was he at such pains to deny any suggestion that the gates were opened? Also, if the fighting was so fierce how come he returned without a scratch?'

Edwin stared at me in bewilderment. 'All right, I agree there are questions to be answered but none of this means Osric opened the gates. Or that he murdered the guards!'

I stopped to think carefully before saying more. 'No, but perhaps he knows who did and is lying to protect them.'

'Hold on little brother! These are very serious allegations and as yet you've no proof there was any treachery whether by Osric or by anyone else for that matter!' He hesitated as though considering what to do next then picked up the long pole used to punt the raft across the water. 'Here you'd best take this and get us back to the island. Perhaps some hard work will divert you from so much idle speculation!'

I took the pole and pushed the end of it down into the mud. The water was deep and it took a lot of effort to start the raft moving. 'But you agree it is a possibility?' I asked, leaning on the pole and straining with all my might.

'There are grounds for doubt, I'll grant you that,' conceded Edwin. 'And I'm convinced there was a traitor, whether now living or dead. If we knew who stood to gain from the Viking attack it might all become clear, but for now we must keep our suspicions to ourselves.'

I knew he was right. To even suggest that the head of the King's personal guard was involved in the treachery which had virtually wiped out the Saxon army was not an accusation to be banded lightly. 'So what do we do?' I asked.

'We watch points,' said Edwin. 'And if proof exists, we find it.'

'And then what?'

Edwin looked at me intently. 'If Osric is a traitor then friend or not, he shall pay for his treachery with every drop of blood that flows within his veins. That much I swear upon our father's grave. In fact I swear it upon everything which I hold sacred.'

* * * * *

One task to which all the men willingly set their hands was the building of a place in which to worship. It was a crude structure, open at the sides but with a pitched roof thatched with reeds. We intended that walls would be added later when time allowed but felt that even as it was it would suffice for our immediate needs. Among our number was a man skilled enough to carve an elaborate cross which we set upon a table and placed alongside it the Bible which belonged to Brother Felix. Being such a fine volume it warranted pride of place, having a wooden cover which was inset with small brightly coloured jewels, albeit some were missing.

When the church was finished, each of us took turns to kneel and place one hand on the precious Bible so that Bishop Eahlstan might at last hear our confessions. Despite being frail and forgetful, the old Bishop was much revered and respected by all, not least because although used to finer surroundings, he was willing to tend to our spiritual needs whilst sharing our hardship and discomfort in that wretched swamp.

Brother Felix attended Bishop Eahlstan throughout these proceedings, seeing to his person and being on hand to prompt and remind him when the need arose. The monk stood behind the Bishop's chair gently combing out his fine white hair as the old man listened to the list of sins each of the men recited. Strictly speaking the presence of Brother Felix was an intrusion on the privacy of the confession but none saw it as such because he was a Holy man and also because he had sworn a vow of silence. In any event, most men sought only to repent that which had been done in the heat of battle or in the dreadful hours which followed when no quarter was asked or given. Needless to say, absolution for such crimes was readily awarded with only a nominal penance.

When it was my turn to make confession I recounted my remorse at having killed the unarmed man so brutally during the battle, which I freely admitted was against my calling and my conscience. I then confessed the doubts I was having about my commitment to the Church and how I feared my faith had several times been tested and found wanting.

The old Bishop listened in silence before asking me to rise and sit beside him as there was much we needed to debate. I unburdened myself of so many things – small things I thought I had forgotten but which came suddenly to mind as well as the sins which troubled me daily. I finished by telling Bishop Eahlstan of the monks we had met along the way, explaining how they had taught me it was better to play a small part of something worthy than a large part of something which is false. I added that I had been tempted to stay with them and aid the founding of the new church dedicated to the Holy Splinter but, at the very last minute, felt that God intended me to follow the course I was now on.

'God will surely guide your steps,' agreed the Bishop when he had considered all this. 'And it's not for us to question what in his infinite mercy he has planned for each of us. He needs warriors as much as he needs priests, but he also needs farmers and blacksmiths and foresters for his great purpose to unfold. As for your sins during the battle, remember there are some warriors, like your brother and your King, whose duty it is to uphold and protect the Holy Church. Such men are good men though daily they perform the very acts for which you seek forgiveness. The difference between one who kills for good and one who kills for evil is not in the way in which they take a life but in their purpose. So look to what was in your heart. As to your commitment to the Church, I say this young Matthew, open up your life to God, give him room and you'll know what it is he wants of you when the time comes.'

I left feeling encouraged by this even if still unsure of exactly what it was I was supposed to do.

As for Edwin, he was the only one who sought absolution for a man he had not killed. He explained to the Bishop how our old family friend Aelwyn had suffered for his weakness that night after the battle. The good Bishop thought it curious that Edwin should be troubled by the death of just one man when he had brutally slaughtered so many without the slightest sign of contrition. 'But as you acted out of compassion no blame is set upon your soul,' he assured him.

Edwin seemed much comforted by this but insisted on being given penance as, to his simple warrior's logic, he could not expect redemption without it.

Meanwhile Brother Felix watched all this whilst observing his customary silence. Considering that he spoke to no one except as part of his calling it was surprising how quickly the men took him to their hearts. I think we all saw how truly committed he was to the service of God. As if to prove his devotion, he slept each night on a bed of dried rushes which he laid directly on the cold, damp ground beside the altar, too far from the fire to feel its warmth. He ate and drank in modest amounts so as not to exceed his share and he seemed content with little more than his Bible and a candle by which to read it. This fortitude earned him the respect of all, for none could say he trod an easy path. Also, because of his vow of silence, there came no complaint from him about his lot nor boast about his piety compared to ours.

* * * * *

Edwin had hoped that Bishop Eahlstan might bless the sword he had taken from the Viking but, when he asked, the good Bishop refused without giving any cause. Edwin decided not to press him knowing the old man was still unwell and probably had other more urgent matters to attend to. It was left to me to try to explain the logic.

'Many priests regard weapons as tools of the Devil's trade and thus they cannot be sanctified,' I said.

Edwin seemed bewildered by this. 'But it will be used to fight the enemies of the Church and thereby thwart the Devil's work,' he reasoned, though he knew it would change nothing. In the end he dedicated the sword to the service of Lord Alfred who kissed the blade in recognition of that pledge. The question then was who should wield it.

Despite all my misgivings, I had agreed I would bear arms to defend my faith and my King if called upon to do so. After making such a poor fist of killing the unarmed man at Chippenham I was anxious to learn how to fight properly. Thus Edwin gave me the sword and, keeping his promise to Alfred, began to teach me how to use it.

Normally as the son of a noble family I would have been schooled in the rudiments of sword craft from an early age, but having two older brothers meant I was marked out for a life in the Church almost at birth and therefore never fully taught those skills. Edwin had me practise first with a wooden replica with which I learned to slash, cut and thrust. When at last he let me try those moves with a real sword the sheer weight of it quickly tired my hand.

'Your arm must grow used to it,' explained Edwin who, keen that I should master the finer points, spent much time in training me and showing me the skills for which he was renowned. Edwin could make a sword come to life. The speed of his arm and the way his wrist would flex and twist were devastating. He could use the blade to sweep aside any attempt to block his blow, his own weapon then ending up a hair's breath from his opponent's throat. 'Force fear into the heart of your enemy,' he urged me. 'That's a weapon as deadly as any sword, for your foe is beaten from the very moment he thinks he'll lose. So, look directly into his eyes and remember he is your target, not his sword or his shield. To simply clash your weapon against his serves no purpose except to spoil the blades. Let the metals touch only when you have no option except to block his blow.'

I tried this and managed well enough.

'Good,' said Edwin. 'Now aim for his face or his legs, not his body which is too easily protected by his shield. A wound to the legs will fell him quickest leaving him at your mercy but blows aimed directly to the face are more cunning for his eyes will follow the blade leaving him exposed.' He demonstrated this by cutting his sword through the air right in front of my nose. Sure enough, I watched the blade sweep past leaving myself wide open to a feigned blow from the boss of his shield. Such advice came thick and fast and I learned quickly, though the exertion left me so weary that my sword strokes became sloppy. Despite this it was soon apparent that I had something of my brother's skill and I began testing Edwin as though I were a trained warrior.

Sometimes we swapped swords so that Edwin got the chance to try the one we had taken from the Viking. He had the skill to use such a fine weapon to its full effect and on one occasion managed to disarm me by twisting my sword from my grasp. Those who saw the stroke laughed but Cedric, who was also watching, was not impressed.

'You rely upon his inexperience,' he claimed. 'With a true warrior you couldn't do such a thing.'

Edwin was quick to see the challenge. 'Then take up the sword yourself,' he offered.

Those around us stopped whatever they were doing. It had long been felt that the rivalry between the two men could not be contained on such a small island for long.

In all good conscience Cedric could not back down, but then neither did he seem to want to. He stepped forward, slipped the great fur cloak from his shoulders and flexed his arms. Picking up my sword, he tried the weight of it in his hand then borrowed my shield. Without another word, he and Edwin began to circle each other as though in a slow dance, crouching low behind their shields.

Cedric was the first to strike. Wielding his sword like an axe – the weapon he was more used to – he roared as he hammered it down upon Edwin with such force he was lucky the blade did not become embedded in Edwin's shield. Then he struck again, this time sweeping his sword from the side and shouting his defiance. Again Edwin used his shield to block the blow, heaving Cedric aside in the process.

By this time all had gathered to see the fight, forming a circle around the two men. I feared for Edwin's safety not through any lack of faith in his skill but because Cedric towered above him and seemed to be able to use that height and power to full effect. The force of his blows was awesome as he advanced again, still shouting but this time hacking from left to right, every stroke crashing into Edwin's shield like a hammer. Then he committed all his strength to a single blow, heaving the blade in from the side with enough power to cut a man in two. But Edwin's eyes did not follow the blade as they were meant to. Instead he did just as he had taught me: he leaned back and let it sweep past him before bringing the edge of his shield up under it so hard that it splintered on impact. Both men were thrown off balance and fell backwards. Although dazed, Edwin recovered first. Casting aside what was left of the broken shield he rounded on Cedric but found the giant on the ground, still not sure what had hit him.

Edwin pressed the blade of his sword against Cedric's throat so that the giant hardly dared to breathe. Having made his point, he stepped back, sheathed his weapon and turned to walk away.

But Cedric was not done. He struggled to his feet, grabbed his sword and made a cowardly charge at Edwin's back, swinging the blade wildly. Edwin barely had time to duck as one of the blows came close to slicing off the top of his head.

There followed a moment in which time seemed to stop. Then Edwin rose up like a beast wakened from sleep. Anger clouded his eyes as he drew his sword once more, this time gripping it in both hands.

No man would have wished to stand against the awful onslaught that followed. It was as though Edwin was possessed by Devils. With a chilling cry he went straight at Cedric, cutting blow after blow so close and quick the giant could do nothing but retreat to avoid them. He put up his shield in defence but it was shattered with the first two blows. Helpless, he was then driven back under a hail of sword strokes until he stood right on the water's edge.

There Edwin stopped. With his sword poised above his shoulder ready to strike he looked deep into Cedric's eyes where he saw the man's fear. 'Enough?' he demanded, raising his sword a little higher.

All could see that Cedric was beaten. With the very next stroke he would have to decide between death and an undignified soaking.

The giant made a frantic thrust with his own sword, lunging forward as he tried to push past Edwin to escape.

Edwin was ready for him. Their swords crashed together; steel on steel with such force it was a miracle they didn't shatter. As they clashed, Edwin twisted his in his hand and so plucked Cedric's weapon cleanly from his grasp. As it fell to the ground it left the giant defenceless.

Edwin looked at the discarded sword. 'For once you were right,' he said calmly, his voice loud enough for all to hear. 'With a true warrior I couldn't do such a thing.' Then he sheathed his sword, secured the peace tie and walked away.

Chapter Twelve

All at the camp knew that the fight between Edwin and Cedric had not pleased Alfred.

Privately, many spoke of Edwin's skill, but as the punishment for drawing a sword in anger in the presence of the King was so severe the matter was not discussed openly.

Meanwhile work on fortifying the island progressed well with interwoven panels being erected at all points where the bank was judged close enough to present a danger from arrows or spears. Also the Vill itself was extended, making it large enough to house everyone. The good Bishop blessed these endeavours and the mood within the camp improved. With food in their bellies and their wounds beginning to heal Alfred turned his mind to the men's baser needs.

Edwin suggested asking Ethelnorth to bring in female slaves to act as whores, but the risk of them trying to escape once on the island was too great given that they could then easily betray its location to the Vikings in return for their freedom. All the women in the camp of a suitable age were married even though most had no idea whether their husbands were still alive. That left Alfred with only one option.

As the daughter of a traitor Emelda had no rights. All she owned was forfeited to Alfred and that included both her life and her honour. In many ways she was still a child so, fearing she might not fully understand what was required of her, he had two of the women present when he, Edwin and Cedric told her of her fate. In reality she was older than her years suggested and seemed to understand all too well. At first she listened in silence, stunned by what he had to say. Then, when Alfred had finished, she looked at each of the two women in turn as though expecting them to intervene. When it was clear neither they nor even Edwin had anything to say in her defence, she fell to her knees.

'My Lords I beg you,' she implored them. 'I'm but a simple girl, pure and as yet untainted by the touch of man. You've already taken me from my family. Now you would make a whore of me to bear the bastards your men will disown from the moment they're conceived. What cruel and heartless fate is this for one who's done nothing save to serve you as best she may?'

'You'll do as you're ordered,' stormed Cedric. 'You know the punishment for dissent.'

Emelda was quiet for a moment and simply shook her head in despair. 'My Lord, why should I fear death at the edge of your sword?' she managed at last. ''Twould be better to die thus than riddled with the pox and my soul burdened with so much sin that I sink into the very depths of hell—'

'Be silent!' commanded Alfred sternly. 'Nothing you can say will change this course. I regret what must become of you but you carry the guilt of your father for which your rights and your freedom are forfeit. I cannot spare you from your lot within this world but as to your soul, I will have Bishop Eahlstan offer prayers for its salvation.'

With that she was led away by the two women, weeping and wailing uncontrollably. Once it was known what she was to become none of the other women would have anything to do with her even though it was reported that, despite her years, the girl had spoken up well for herself. Nonetheless she was taken to a small hut which had been hastily erected on the far side of the island where she was to receive the men, then left to await her fate.

As in all things, we Saxons had a strict code when it came to whores. The privilege of being first to visit Emelda belonged to Alfred, Edwin and then Cedric, with the other men then taking turns according to their rank. Both Alfred and Edwin declined their rights but for very different reasons. Alfred was greatly troubled by an inflammation of the gut which flared up from time to time producing a dull ache which sometimes became so acute he could barely stand. The priests had told him it was God's punishment for having lived so wilfully during his younger days, bedding servants and slaves with an almost legendary zeal. He had since sworn to put those days behind him and, though sorely tempted, feared the pains would return if he transgressed. Edwin on the other hand had never shown much interest in women having devoted himself instead to his skills as a warrior. If questioned he would have said he feared any distraction which might weaken his resolve and he therefore avoided women but, in truth, I think it was a sacrifice he found easy enough to make. Thus it was left to Cedric to be the first to take the girl; and he showed no restraint.

As soon as it was dark he turned to one of the men and handed him his huge axe. 'Here, mind this for me,' he said grinning. 'I've another weapon more suited for this particular quarry.'

'Ah, but is it a sword or merely a dagger?' jibed one of the men.

Cedric made a lewd gesture with his arm then laughed as he strode towards the hut and, without a moment's hesitation, went inside. He took the girl so savagely that her cries could be heard by all. When he was done with her three others were waiting for their turn outside.

By the end of that week there were few men who had not visited the hut and many had been there more than once. In that short time Emelda changed visibly. Not surprisingly, she no longer took any interest in her clothes or appearance and seldom washed herself even between visits from the men. When her services were not needed she would sit on the bank with her feet in the slimy waters of the marsh talking aloud to herself, though no one could understand her ravings. Her face had changed as well. Though never pretty, her cheeks had become blotchy and her skin speckled with boils and pus-ridden spots. Her eyes were filled with such madness that they seemed to stare into the distance as if trying to look beyond her immediate plight.

One day when I was alone she came to sit beside me. I confess that having spent my boyhood in an Abbey I felt awkward in her presence and was not sure what to say.

'I'm told that you and your brother...that you returned to aid my father,' she said simply, breaking the silence. Her voice was still and quiet, which surprised me for since her downfall she seemed to take no care about what she said and to whom. Also I was not sure whether she knew that the true purpose of our mission had been to kill Goda.

'Don't worry, I know why you really went,' she said as though sensing my disquiet. 'I only wish you'd got there in time. He was nothing but a fool and deserved to die.'

'He did what he had to in order to protect his family,' I chided. 'Which of us would not have done the same?'

'Protect us!' she sniped, the softness now gone from her voice. 'Is this what you mean by protection? That I'm to be used by every man in this camp? To lay with them and suffer their pawing and their beatings as they fill me with their filthy seed? Is that the protection my father earned for his daughter? To be a whore even before I'm a woman?'

I could not bring myself to look at her. Then having said more than I think she intended, she got up and began to walk away.

'Will you come again?' I asked, not sure why I said it.

When she turned to look back at me some of the softness seemed to return. I think the girl in her wanted to say 'yes' but the whore she had been forced to become would answer differently. ''Tis for you to come to me,' she said flatly. 'That's my lot in life. The men come to me when they will and I'm to pleasure them and receive them. You're welcome, Matthew; more welcome than most. Perhaps one day soon I can thank you and your brother properly. For if I'm to lie with strangers then why not with the men who were wont to serve me by ridding me of my worthless, wretched father.'

* * * * *

Following several brighter days everyone seemed cheered and set about their tasks with renewed enthusiasm. On one such morning a group of men working by the water's edge disturbed a thin green snake of which there were many living within the reeds. Despite the warmth, the snake was still sleepy and the men trapped it easily enough by placing a basket over its coiled body. Edwin lifted the basket and quickly grasped the snake around its neck with his fingers and picked it up. The snake writhed and twisted until he took hold of its tail with his other hand and stretched it out. Those around him laughed as he toyed with it. He offered it to Osric who, seeming confused, entreated him to kill it lest it bite someone. Instead Edwin tossed the snake into the water and we watched it swim away.

'This was an aimless serpent,' he said loudly. 'I wouldn't kill one of God's creatures without good cause. But were it a viper I discovered in our camp I would have as soon cut off its head as look at it.'

Osric clearly did not understand what Edwin was implying; nor did anyone else for that matter. Afterwards Edwin asked me whether I had noticed any sign of guilt on Osric's face at the mention of 'a viper in our camp'. I had to admit that Osric had seemed merely concerned lest someone should be bitten and perhaps a little confused. Edwin was disappointed but resolved to say nothing more on the subject until he had grounds to support an accusation. As he had told me when we first discussed the question of there being a traitor, it was not a charge to be levelled lightly.

* * * * *

All the men were required to take turns at standing guard at night. It was usually a long and thankless duty and, with Ethelnorth and his men still watching the roads, not

154

considered by most to be essential. Usually the guards were therefore positioned only at the places which were regarded as a viable crossing.

One night when it was my turn for guard duty I had taken my place beside a small willow, the roots of which barely managed to hold in the wet soil so that it leaned over like an old man, bent and twisted. It provided a small measure of shelter yet still left a clear view across the open water. Like others, I much preferred sitting there rather than spending the night huddled behind the wicker panel which had been erected to provide cover.

Having kept my place through much of the night without falling asleep, I was watching two otters playing on the far bank. A light mist had formed on the water and seemed to be drifting towards me eerily when I heard movement behind me. Not sure what it was, I eased myself behind the tree and waited.

A figure appeared through the darkness. Only as it drew nearer did I realise it was Lord Alfred himself.

'Ah, there you are,' said Alfred. 'I swear you could hide in an open field. How goes it young Matthew?'

I was flustered by this sudden intimacy but knew that Alfred often took the time to speak with his subjects, particularly at night as it was known that he was a poor sleeper. 'All quiet, my Lord,' I stammered. 'Except the otters which play noisily tonight.'

'It's surely a night to be restless,' he observed staring across the water. 'Do you not feel that? It seems that some nights even honest men find it hard to sleep.'

Having spent the whole night trying to stay awake I was not sure what to say.

'I gather from your brother that you now have doubts about your Holy calling?'

'That's true, sire. Though I intend no disrespect to my abbot who is a good man and to whom I'm truly grateful for all I've learned.'

'It's your right to question your path in life, though not all of us have the chance to choose. But tell me, what do your studies of the Holy Scriptures tell you about spirits and such like?'

I shivered at the very thought of such fearful beings, recalling the stories I had heard about the demons said to lurk within those very marshes.

'No, I don't mean here,' laughed Alfred seeing my disquiet. 'No man alive or dead would linger in such a place as this for longer than he must. But do you believe there are such things?'

Of course I had to answer yes for our faith relied upon it. Did not the Lord Jesus himself rise from the dead?

Alfred seemed reluctant to go on.

'My Lord, are you troubled by such things?' I asked. 'I know there's much talk of demons and such like but I've seen nothing, not even whilst keeping watch in the dead of night...'

'I've no fear of demons,' replied Alfred. 'But there are spirits abroad this night and they've shown me things I would I hadn't seen.'

'Sire?' I queried, now confused.

'Fear not,' said Alfred. 'The spirits of which I speak come from the Lord. They are his messengers and mean us no harm. I don't even fear the sight of them for they came not as flesh and blood but as a vision in a dream.'

'A dream?' I queried. 'Surely if it was just a dream...'

'Perhaps,' admitted Alfred. 'But it seemed so real. Have you never been troubled by a dream?'

I had to say I had, especially since the death of my parents. There were many nights when I felt I saw them, sometimes even waking to find myself speaking to them as if they were still with me.

Alfred touched my arm. 'You must miss them,' he said seeming concerned. 'And I'm sorry if I've worried you. But in whom may a King confide? Not in men like your brother for although I trust his counsel in matters of war, I dare not trouble him with dreams.'

'Sire, it's not my place to...'

'Why do you say that? Are not all men equal in the eyes of God – King and ceorl alike?'

'Yes, sire.'

'And all men have dreams, Matthew. All men dream and must interpret for themselves the meaning of their dreams.'

'Sire, that's true,' I said still confused. 'And your dream tonight has troubled you, I can see that.'

'In truth it has.'

'The dreams of Kings are a worry for us all,' I said quietly. 'For when a King is guided by a dream are not the consequences shared by all?'

'You have your father's wisdom,' observed Alfred. 'I well remember how he always gave good counsel.'

'Do you wish to tell me of your dream, sire? I would not presume to pry but...'

Again Alfred smiled. 'The question is as innocent as any that was ever asked. And I will tell you but first you must swear to be my confidant in this.'

'I so swear,' I said solemnly, crossing myself to seal the oath.

Alfred sat down, perching on a fallen tree rather than on the cold, damp ground. He hesitated for a moment as though not sure what it was he wanted to say or how to begin. 'I dreamed this night that St Cuthbert himself came to me,' he said, struggling to make himself comfortable. 'I saw him as clearly as I see you now...' He then looked at me in the dull half light of the coming dawn with the mist swirling about us and corrected himself. 'No, clearer than I see you now.'

St Cuthbert was a saint much revered by all Saxons. So much so that his bones had been exhumed and moved to a secret grave to ensure they did not fall into Viking hands. Many were unhappy at this for it was said that having been disturbed he was no longer at rest.

'You saw his ghost!' I said, alarmed at the prospect.

'Aye lad, if you will. The ghost of St Cuthbert or St Cuthbert in a dream, for I know not which it was; only that he stood before me. He came to show me that which I needed to see but feared to know.' At that point Alfred sensed he had unnerved me. 'The Holy saint then returned from whence he came. As indeed must we all,' he added, struggling to his feet. 'You have your duty to complete and I would return to my bed.'

As I helped him up I realised I had understood nothing of what Alfred had said. 'Sire, I am certain we need have no fear,' I suggested as much to reassure myself as anything. 'For St Cuthbert was ever a goodly saint whose purpose was our own. Surely no Saxon need worry about guidance you receive from him.'

'Then perhaps it was he who guided me to speak with you,' said Alfred. 'For you've helped me much in this and I'm grateful. I fear that if the path you choose leads you from the Mother Church she will have lost a good and wise servant. Now, one last thing. Pray tell your brother I would speak with him. And Matthew, think no more upon these things. Sometimes a King must confide in others though the burden he would share must always rest with him. Now keep your eyes open.'

'Why? Do you think St Cuthbert may return?'

Alfred laughed. 'No lad. It's the Vikings who would harm you, not the Holy saint. Save your young eyes for them and I may at least sleep sound on that account.'

* * * * *

The following morning Edwin went to see the King as ordered and then returned looking very worried. 'When you spoke with Alfred last night what did he tell you?' he asked.

'Not much,' I said remembering my oath to keep silent.

'Well was he troubled by a dream?' asked Edwin pointedly.

I avoided answering by saying that I had not really understood what Alfred was concerned about.

'Then listen to me, Matthew,' said Edwin firmly. 'You must not speak of what he told you to anyone. Is that clear?'

'But why?' I asked.

Edwin gripped me by the shoulders and looked hard into my eyes. 'You're my brother and I must answer true but you must swear it shall remain a secret between us.' When I agreed Edwin continued. 'St Cuthbert visited Alfred in a dream last night and told him he must defeat those who have defiled the Holy Church. He is to attack Guthrum in the spring.'

It was the last part Alfred had not mentioned to me but I realised its significance at once. 'In the spring!' I protested. 'But he can't hope to be ready to fight Guthrum by then! Why, they've fifty men at least to every one of ours! If we go against him too soon...'

'I know,' said Edwin. 'And I've told him that it can't be done. He's called a council for tonight – a full Witan to which all are summoned, including Ethelnorth. We shall each have our say, but I fear he'll not be swayed.'

'Then should we not speak to others and give them cause to back us?' I suggested.

'I would not lobby men against my King,' said Edwin firmly. 'Besides, don't forget there may be one among us who is traitor to us all. If so, we dare not give him fuel to stir up dissent. So until tonight remember you've sworn to keep silent on all you've heard.'

I readily agreed not just because of my oath, but also because I was afraid. We Saxons lived by such simple truths which, albeit welded to our Christian faith, were such that even a dream was enough to compel a King, particularly if it told him what he wanted to hear. If by that dream Alfred was persuaded to attack the Vikings too soon I knew we would all pay a fearful price.

* * * * *

As we gathered around the fire that night to form the Witan, Alfred was seated at one end, with Osric and his men behind him. Brother Felix stood at his side as representative for Bishop Eahlstan who was not well enough to attend in person. Being both of senior rank, Ethelnorth and Edwin sat together, with the rest of the men and women then sitting where they chose but with the more senior thanes and warriors nearest the front. Among them was Cedric who, though not from Wessex, was permitted to attend and even speak if any matters were of concern to him.

At first Alfred dealt with various sundry items – Edwin was rewarded for his loyal service by being promoted to the rank of Ealdorman in our late father's stead. That was not unexpected for whilst the rank was not inherited as of right, it was often passed from father to son, particularly within a family with such a noble pedigree as ours. Alfred next attended to the routine business of settling some disputes, the transfer of some land and other matters all of which were written down by me acting as scribe. In particular, several men were judged to have fled abroad and had therefore deserted Alfred's cause. It was a serious charge and they were dispossessed of their land, which then reverted to the King as forfeit for the crime.

One such man had apparently come from a family who, though not Saxons by blood, had lived among the people of Southern Wessex and prospered. He was not present to defend himself but had sent word pleading that, although he wished us well, our fight was not his fight and his lands should not therefore be forfeited. His nephew, a young man named Dudwine, had also sent word via Ethelnorth swearing his allegiance to Alfred and pledging military support if the rights to his uncle's land could be transferred to him. With little prospect of a battle the oath of allegiance seemed almost futile and most urged Alfred to ignore it. He did not agree.

'We need all the support we can muster and shouldn't discourage those who would be loyal to our cause,' he said firmly. 'I shall charge Dudwine to attend me when the time comes to march against Guthrum and he may then prove his loyalty with some special duty. If he acquits himself well he shall have his reward, but his uncle is hereby banished and declared to be our foe.'

I dutifully recorded the decision and the two senior men present – Ethelnorth and Edwin – were required to attest it. Others then signed or made their mark beneath those names to confirm they had witnessed it as well, including Cedric. We then reached the main business of the Witan.

Ethelnorth rose to make his report. 'Sire, I would that I could say that all is well beyond this camp,' the old warrior said slowly. 'But 'tis not so. As I must speak truly I am bound to report that we suffer cruelly under Viking rule. No man is safe, not even in his own home, those of them who still have homes that is. Many have fled abroad or taken refuge in the hills and forests. Sire, Guthrum holds your Vill at Chippenham and rules from there. He has sacked the settlement itself and killed those who would resist him. Others have been cast as slaves. My men have watched the roads to protect you as best they can and we've harried any Viking band left unguarded, burned the homes of those who have aided our enemies and robbed traders and merchants who would supply their needs. Yet I fear our cause is lost and there's nothing more that we can do.'

Alfred got to his feet when Lord Ethelnorth had finished. 'My heart grieves when I hear how my people suffer,' he said solemnly. 'I would have you tell them I live only for the day I shall avenge them. When the weather breaks so shall come

162

that chance for I plan to wrest Chippenham from Guthrum's hand come spring. Then we shall drive the Vikings back into the sea!'

A general murmur of surprise arose when Alfred outlined his objective even though the rumours had been rife. In truth, Alfred had never made any secret of this plan even in those dreadful days immediately after the battle, but most had thought it an impossible dream and certainly not something he would seek to accomplish quite so soon.

Edwin seemed to speak for many. 'Sire, I count myself as both your loyal subject and your friend. I know you well enough to speak freely and my blood and my heritage compel you to listen.'

Alfred acknowledged the point, so Edwin continued.

'Sire, I want nothing more than to avenge the death of so many friends. I can scarce keep my sword in its scabbard when ere I think of it. But I fear you go too far.'

There was a gasp from those around him, for even Edwin had no right to be so bold, but Alfred did not reproach him.

'Sire, we cannot hope to take on Guthrum's force so soon. He has an army still and his men are well fed and rested. For us the work has been hard just to survive this winter. We can trouble him if you will; help Lord Ethelnorth with his raids. We can steal their cattle and attack any Vikings who would venture from the safety of the Vill, but even to think of taking on his army—'

Alfred waved him aside. 'One small victory is all we need,' he said. 'One small triumph for every true Saxon in this land to rise and take up arms. Then let Guthrum taste the true power of Saxon might! Remember Lord Edwin, it was you who reminded me after the battle at Chippenham that we lost but a fraction of our men in that dreadful fray. The others had returned to their homes and farms long before Guthrum struck and they wait there still. We need only give a sign for them to follow, a single spark which shall ignite a fire to sweep across this land.' He paused and looked at Ethelnorth. 'Is that not so?'

Ethelnorth remained seated and considered his words carefully. 'The men will follow where you lead sire, as they are sworn to do. Yet I fear that after all these years of war there are many who now crave for peace above all else.'

'What, at the price of freedom?' stormed Alfred.

'You must be patient, sire. All of us have lost friends and family and we mourn those losses still. And the winter has been hard; you're in no fit state even to think of fighting. I would counsel that you leave this place and venture south where I may furnish ships to carry you abroad.'

'You mean desert my people now!' said Alfred clearly incredulous that the old warrior should even suggest such a thing.

Edwin rose again. 'Sire, there is sense in this. Guthrum has sworn to take you alive. He boasts of how he'll cut out your heart and eat it before your very eyes! And remember, if you're slain our cause dies with you, for what hope is there for us without a King? Are you not the last of your father's sons?'

'And not so easily killed as my brothers!' said Alfred defiantly. 'There are many Viking warriors in Valhalla who may testify to that!'

Ethelnorth got to his feet. 'Sire, daily we patrol the roads which lead here. Every path is covered but if Guthrum were to come with even half his army we could not hope to hold them back. You must let us take you to a place of safety.

Perhaps to Rome where the Mother Church would receive you and protect you?'

Edwin, still standing, readily agreed. 'Aye, you've been her faithful servant; would she not help to restore you?'

Alfred walked over to the fire and warmed himself beside it before speaking. 'Restore me you say? Restore me to what? To this muddy isle in the corner of the kingdom which my father and my brothers ruled?'

'My Lord, you are King in all our hearts,' said Edwin. 'That's a love which knows no frontier.'

'As you say, Edwin. But does a good farmer not plough all his fields? Does a good shepherd tend only half his flock? What would you have me do? Rest here while Guthrum drinks the last drop of Saxon blood? Watch from Rome whilst his men rape our women and destroy our land? No! Whilst there are Saxons left for me to lead my place is here!'

There was a silence as all considered what had been said. Then Cedric spoke. 'Where are these Saxons of which I hear you speak? Are they hiding and afraid to fight?' he called.

Edwin shot to his feet and glared at him. 'Don't dare to speak of our warriors and fear in the same breath!' he warned.

Slowly Cedric looked around at those gathered for the Witan. 'I say again, where are they?' he demanded. 'Warming their fat arses by their fires and filling their bellies whilst we endure their hardship for them, that's where! Their place is here! With their King!'

Alfred raised his right hand for silence then motioned for both men to be seated. 'I've listened to all that's been said but will not flee this land whilst there are Saxons left who would support me. On this my mind is set. As to how I mean to defeat Guthrum I will answer only this. St Cuthbert himself appeared before me and urged me to that course which my heart would have me follow. He assured me that if I call upon him all will be well.' He paused for a moment, letting his words sink in. 'Lord Ethelnorth, I charge you to go from here and carry word to the Ealdormen of all the surrounding Shires. Tell them to have warriors ready to assemble at Egbert's Stone when I give the sign.'

Edwin shook his head in dismay. 'But sire, if Guthrum has even the slightest inkling of our coming we shall all be slaughtered! Have not enough Saxons died already?'

Alfred calmed him. 'If you would speak of our dead then remember they live on only through us,' he said. 'So let their graves be our stepping stones to a great victory. And as for Guthrum's spies, they shall not hear of what it is we intend. Our message will be whispered on the wind. Not one word must be heard by anyone whose loyalty cannot be trusted and if any man should breathe a word out of turn he shall answer with his blood.'

Silence descended on the camp. Then Alfred continued softly. 'Saxon shall summon Saxon just as they did in our forefathers' time. And when that call is answered we shall have an army as fit for battle as any that has ever marched. Then shall we return to Chippenham and take back all that was taken from us. In this I shall not be deterred, for I was told it in a dream.'

Chapter Thirteen

The following day Alfred summoned Edwin, Ethelnorth and Cedric to speak with him in private. As these four most senior men stood together at the far end of the island, the rest of us could only watch and wait expectantly, curious to know what was being said. It was soon clear to everyone that the three Ealdormen were arguing. Cedric's voice could be heard raised above the rest and at one point Edwin turned away as though displeased. Then Ethelnorth bowed half-heartedly to Alfred and left. He spoke not a word to anyone as he stormed through the camp and went directly to the raft where one of his men waited. Some said Alfred had given him orders so urgent they allowed no time for him to bid farewell, others that he was angry. In truth it was all idle speculation for Lord Ethelnorth was a man who would impart nothing by word or gesture except that which he intended. Even Wilfred who had punted the raft across to the causeway could not enlighten us. Apart from a token word of thanks neither Ethelnorth nor his guard spoke a single word during the crossing. Meanwhile, all kept their distance leaving Edwin and Cedric to continue to argue before Alfred. Then I was sent for and knew at once that none of the three men were in good humour. It was Alfred himself who addressed me.

'Matthew, I would have you go with Cedric,' he ordered bluntly. 'He's to return to Chippenham tomorrow for I must know all I can of the defences there. You are to assess what repairs have been completed and what improvements have been made. Most important of all, I must know how many men Guthrum can muster.'

'And I'm to go with him?' I asked, my mind racing back to the last time I was detailed to accompany Cedric.

'That is my will. 'Twill be dangerous work and if discovered you know the consequences.'

On that I needed no elaboration. It was known that the Vikings had a deep hatred of spies. They reasoned that whereas a murderer might take a single life a spy could be responsible for the slaughter of many. Thus they meted out the most dreadful penance they could devise in the hope of dissuading any who were tempted to betray them. I had heard tales of men being boiled alive and having their skin peeled from their bodies, others who had been tortured with red-hot swords or had been roasted on a spit. Despite this it was not from fear that I questioned the order. 'Sire, is my place not here with my brother...?'

'Edwin has other duties,' replied Alfred curtly. 'He's also argued you're not suited to this task, but you must answer for yourself.'

I looked at my brother but he wouldn't meet my gaze. In truth, I had been given an order by my King. Being of high birth I was entitled to some say in the matter but I was not expected to refuse even though the prospect of going with Cedric was something I dreaded. 'If it is your will, sire, then I'm bound to obey,' I acknowledged. 'How soon before we leave?'

Alfred looked to Cedric to answer.

'In the morning, boy. And be ready to leave at first light for we've a hard march ahead of us. I would be there and back within the week.'

There was something about Cedric's tone which unsettled me. I hardly expected to be made welcome on the mission, but I sensed it went deeper than that. Somehow the thought of travelling with this surly giant from Northumbria frightened me almost as much as the prospect of coming face to face with the Vikings.

* * * * *

'This whole plan is ill conceived,' complained Edwin bitterly when we were alone. 'It's not Cedric's place to go to Chippenham, nor yours to go with him!' In reality I think his anger stemmed from the fact that the duty he had been given was not to his liking rather than out of any concern for me. He had been detailed to help Ethelnorth set up the chain which would be used to summon the Saxons to battle when the time came. He had been chosen for this because many of the Ealdormen would know him personally, or at least know of his lineage and reputation. Therefore they would trust him whereas had that task been left to Cedric they would have been suspicious because he was not from Wessex.

Needless to say Edwin would have much preferred the more dangerous task assigned to Cedric and myself and regarded what was being asked of him as a slight upon his ability as a warrior. Yet I saw that Alfred's logic was sound. He had allocated the tasks to those most suited to perform them, though that pleased no one. Ethelnorth was offended when Edwin was reluctant to work with him on what was clearly a vital part of their King's plan; Cedric, who was chosen for his role because he looked more like a Viking than most Vikings, was displeased at being saddled with a novice monk, particularly after the incident with the dogs during the retreat from Chippenham. As for me, I had no idea why Alfred had chosen me for such dangerous work but would have much preferred to stay with my brother.

'So why am I to go with him?' I asked Edwin.

He had not given the matter much thought. 'Who can say?' he shrugged. 'Like I said, the whole plan is riddled with fault.' Taking out a small knife, he offered it to me. 'Here, you'd best have this. There'll be many dangers in Guthrum's camp so keep it with you at all times.'

It was a plain knife with a single edge, more suited to skinning hares than for use as a weapon. I looked at it disdainfully. 'I'd prefer to take the sword,' I said boldly. 'I'm growing used to it now and have been practising as you showed me.'

'Oh, so you'd take a Viking sword into a Viking camp would you? Will you also boast how you killed the man who owned it?'

I saw my mistake at once and felt very foolish.

Edwin offered the knife again. 'Remember, the blade is as sharp whether the handle is made of ivory or of wood,' he advised. 'Your disguise is to be that of a lowly houseboy so none will think it strange that you carry such a common blade.'

I took the knife and tucked it into my belt. 'But why will I need it?' I asked. 'It can hardly be of use against an axe or a sword!'

'Just do as I say,' warned Edwin. 'It's not only the Vikings you need to be wary of. Keep one eye on Cedric at all times, do you hear me? And keep your wits about you. He's not to be trusted, so watch him like a hawk.'

* * * * *

I began to feel that my life was changing faster than I could manage. I was now almost certain that I would not return to the Abbey, yet the path ahead of me remained far from clear. With such thoughts as these and of the dangerous mission I was about to undertake, I wandered alone beside the water's edge. I was idly snapping off small twigs from a bush and tossing them into the water when Emelda came and stood beside me.

'You look troubled,' she ventured.

I was not sure what to say. She was the only person in the camp of about my age and I would have liked to speak with her but somehow the words I wanted were tangled in my head.

'Do I embarrass you?' she asked mistaking my silence for rejection.

'No,' I said quickly. 'No it's just that I've a lot to think about.'

'These are harsh times for us all,' she sighed. 'I'm told you lost both your parents. Do you still grieve for them?'

'Yes of course. And for my dear brother and sister who were taken at the same time, not to mention their families as well. I fear for what will become of them, especially my sister who—' I stopped myself when I realised that my sister's fate was the same as that which Emelda already endured.

She said nothing.

'What will you do when these dark days are over?' I managed, changing the subject.

'They'll never end for me!' she snapped. 'Now that I'm spoiled no man would think of taking me to wife. I'm a whore and shall stay one till I die. I pray only that my life is now short and passes without too much pain, for when these men grow tired of me or return to the wives I'll be left with nothing...except perhaps the pox. For all I know I may already be with child and—' She stopped when she realised she had said too much.

It had not occurred to me to think of anything beyond Emelda's immediate plight but her sudden outburst reminded me all too clearly of the fate which awaited her. 'Are you with child?' I asked, knowing nothing of such matters.

Emelda shrugged. 'I don't think so. Not yet, anyway. But I probably will be sooner or later. Then what will become of me?'

'You could go to a convent,' I suggested. 'They'd take you in and care for you and for the child, though I grant it's a hard life for which not everyone is suited.'

'Were you happy at the Abbey?' she asked.

I had to think before I could answer. 'Happy enough at the time,' I said at last. 'Or at least content. The life was chosen for me by my father and I have known little else.'

'And now?'

'So much has happened now that I'm no longer sure where my future lies. One half of me feels I've betrayed my Holy vows, yet I believe my life has greater purpose here, with my King and with the men who serve him.'

'I think you'd make a fine warrior,' she said. 'For you're very brave.'

Her words took me by surprise.

'No it's true. I recall how bold you were when you were sent into those trees to see whether Vikings were waiting there to ambush us. You marched in with your head held high as though afraid of nothing.'

'But I was terrified!' I admitted.

'Well, you didn't show it,' she said but was then suddenly distracted by one of the men who was standing nearby clearly intent upon her services. She had no option but to go. 'I'm glad we spoke,' she said turning to leave.

When I realised what was taking her away from me my heart was saddened. 'We'll speak again when I get back,' I offered.

'You're going away?'

'I also have duties I wish were not my own,' I explained. 'But, God willing, I shall be back within a week. Perhaps we can speak some more then?'

She smiled at me. 'Perhaps,' she said. 'Or maybe we'll do more than talk?' With that she walked away.

* * * * *

That night as everyone at the camp gathered round the fire, Rufus was called upon to entertain us. He was an accomplished musician, as nimble with the strings of the lyre as he was with the bow, but had no instrument to play. Instead he elected to recite one of his tales.

'I'll tell you the story of Cynewulf,' he offered. Of course we all knew the story well enough having heard it many times before, but the magic was always in the telling and Rufus had that gift. It was said he derived this skill from having spent so much of his time listening to sagas whilst sitting with other hunters around a camp fire at night. Thus he readily took his place in the centre of our circle, working his way around it so that each of us in turn could see him; for to tell a story well he had to be part actor as well as muse. The story he told went thus:

'In the times when our forefathers dwelt in the lands beyond the sea there was a man named Cynewulf who was the eldest of ten brothers. Their father was a poor but honest man who toiled upon the land to earn his living. One day he called all his sons to him and told them that their humble farmstead could no longer support them all. It was time for them to go off and seek their fortunes and, if they were so minded, to take a wife. To each he gave a small gift – to one a knife, to another a pin, whilst another received a belt of leather until everyone save Cynewulf had been given something. "You are my eldest son," he said to Cynewulf. "And I would have you take this small farmstead as your own but first you must see all your brothers safe across the sea where they may each start a new life. To that end you must build a boat big enough to carry four men and all their belongings, yet one which you'll be able to sail back alone."

'"But why only four?" asked Cynewulf. "I have nine brothers and can easily build a boat big enough to carry all. With ten of us to row the voyage will be three times faster and…"

'His father explained that he was worried that if they sailed together and met foul weather they might all be lost and thus their blood line would perish at a stroke. He wanted Cynewulf to take just three brothers at a time.

'"But that means I must brave the sea three times there and three times back!" complained Cynewulf.

'Well his father knew this but he was a wise man and would not be swayed. He reminded Cynewulf that the prize for his labour would be to claim the farmstead for his own. "Also," he said, "I have consulted with the priests and they have assured me that if you offer prayers before each trip the Gods will not see you drown."

'So it was that Cynewulf built a boat big enough to carry four but light enough for him to sail back on his own. When he had finished all agreed it was a fine craft and he prepared to make the first voyage. Before he left he prayed to the Gods for good weather and a safe passage just as the priests had told him to do. Sure enough, to his great relief those prayers were answered. Within a week he had returned having seen his first three brothers safe across the sea.

'Once back he was anxious to set off again without delay for fear that the winter, which was a time for rough seas and storms, would soon be upon them. Having said his prayers, he set off again with all speed. Although not as smooth as the first crossing he was able to return safely and almost at once decided to set off for the last time.

'"Wait for the spring," warned his father. "Now is the time for storms and you run the gravest risk."

'But Cynewulf would not wait. Instead he left in haste, not even stopping to pray but saying he would offer prayers enough whilst on the voyage.

'No sooner had he lost sight of land than a dreadful storm blew up and his small boat was rocked from side to side in the wind and waves. Cynewulf and his three brothers were afraid and each called out to the Gods imploring them to be merciful.

'"Protect us," pleaded Cynewulf. "See us safe to land and I swear I'll never set sail upon the sea again."

'Sure enough the Gods were merciful. The little boat landed safely and no sooner had Cynewulf helped his brothers ashore than he prepared to return home.

'"You can't!" warned one of his brothers. "You promised the Gods you would not set sail again and…"

'But Cynewulf wouldn't listen. "I meant after I returned home," he claimed. "The Gods will understand that I can't stay here. I have to return to claim my inheritance."

'With that he set sail, this time remembering to pray as he went. Once again a huge storm blew up and the little boat was tossed about until it seemed certain to sink. Cynewulf cried out to the Gods. "I'm sorry," he said. "I didn't mean to go back on my word and…" With that a huge wave swamped the boat and tore the mast from its housing, snapping it in half. Another wave ripped the oars from their ports and washed them overboard.

'"Spare me!" cried Cynewulf falling to his knees on the deck. "Spare me! Don't let me drown, for you promised I should never perish thus!"

'The Gods heard his prayers and the storm abated. For three days Cynewulf drifted in the boat. With no sail and no oars he was at the mercy of the tides. As he had no food and nothing but rainwater to drink, each day he grew weaker. Then on the fourth day he saw what seemed to him like a gift from the Gods – a huge grey fish bigger than the boat itself swimming in the water alongside him. Cynewulf took his harpoon and tied a length of rope to one end of it, lashing the other end to what was left of the mast. Standing on the prow, he speared the fish, driving the harpoon deep into its back. But as he tried to pull the fish alongside he found he had not the strength to do it. Instead the fish began to swim away from him, dragging the boat with it. Frantically Cynewulf tried to loosen the rope but it was pulled much too taut and he had no knife with which to cut it. The fish swam faster and faster, dragging Cynewulf's boat behind it, ploughing through the waters for day after day after day. Those days became weeks and the weeks became months and still poor Cynewulf clung to the boat as it was dragged past lands he had never seen or even heard of. Strange lands capped with snow, islands which smoked and smouldered as if on fire and places so distant that even the peoples there were of a different hue.

'No one can say how long Cynewulf was pulled along in his boat by the giant fish but eventually he died of hunger and of thirst in a place many leagues from home. But he never drowned. For the Gods at least knew how to keep their promise.'

When Rufus had finished he sat down. At first there was silence as men considered the story then slowly began to discuss it. Had the good Bishop been well enough to speak I think he would have berated us about the perils of trusting the old Gods but, in his absence, most seemed to think the moral of Rufus's tale was that fate could not be cheated.

Others argued it was nothing more than a reminder to offer prayers even when it was thought none were needed. Alfred, who had also listened to the story and was thought wise in such matters, said these were all true but that the tale reminded him that even when we think the course of our lives is set fair things will change – often in ways not readily foreseen.

For my part I struggled with its meaning, trying to wring from it some simple message which would guide me. It so perplexed me that I could barely sleep that night, particularly knowing that with the dawn my own destiny could well be revealed.

Chapter Fourteen

The next morning I rose early, dreading the prospect of all that lay ahead. I knelt beside my cot to pray and, when I had finished, I humbly kissed the crucifix I normally wore around my neck and laid it down beside my sword. Next I took off my habit and folded it, placing it and my undershirt to one side for the women to wash whilst I was away. For a moment I stood there, naked and shivering slightly, thinking how strangely symbolic it all seemed: as though in removing my robes I was also shedding my commitment to the Church. The sight of my crucifix and sword lying together was even more poignant as if they represented the two great dilemmas in my life, so close yet so widely divided.

Suddenly aware how cold I was, I turned and started to put on the tunic, leggings and cloak I had been given to wear as part of my disguise. These were rough, ill-fitting garments, so coarse they itched dreadfully where the fabric scratched my skin. The plan was for Cedric to pass as a warrior intent on joining Guthrum's army. The Vikings would expect to recruit mercenaries and would see nothing strange in a man offering his battle skills in return for patronage and a share of any booty. As such the giant from Northumbria would certainly look the part whilst I, who was to pass as his servant, would not warrant so much as a second glance. Once inside the Vill it would be easy to inspect the fortifications closely. Getting out again would be more difficult but we would not be prisoners and could therefore take our chances. At worst we would join one of their many raids and then desert.

Cedric was already waiting to set off complete with all his war gear, such as it was. He had a shield slung across his back and was dressed in a mail vest and his long fur cloak. The vest, which he had borrowed from one of Ethelnorth's men, was a light tabard draped across his shoulders and open at the sides where it was secured with leather straps, albeit these could not be fastened properly because of his giant frame. Although not proof against every blow, it offered some protection yet allowed freedom of movement and was light enough to be worn whilst marching. He also had his axe and a helmet, both of which he gave to me to carry.

Before leaving, Cedric and I went to the altar and knelt before Bishop Eahlstan for a blessing as we each placed one hand upon the precious Bible. The good Bishop was not much recovered from whatever ills had prevented him attending the Witan and was too frail to stand over us as was the custom. Also his mind seemed to wander from its purpose so that he needed prompting by Brother Felix even when reciting a passage from the Bible he would normally have known by heart. I feared even then that the old man was not long for this world and might not live to see us return.

Once we had finished our prayers Edwin took us across to the causeway on the raft. 'Remember, keep your wits about you and don't trust Cedric,' he whispered when he and I embraced to say farewell.

I took off my birth ring and gave it to Edwin to hold. The gesture was a significant one for to hold a man's birth ring was to hold all that he possessed. It meant also that he could speak for me and act in my stead, thus it was never given lightly. Edwin was clearly touched by the gesture and we embraced once more before I knelt and kissed the ring. I then set off behind Cedric as we made our way along the narrow causeway and through the swamp.

Our route to Chippenham would be more direct than that which Alfred had followed during the retreat as he had needed to avoid as many of the settlements as possible lest he was recognised and betrayed. We would go via Glastonbury, although skirting around the settlement itself before meeting the road which would then lead us eventually to the Vill.

Initially we made good progress but our pace slowed as heavy rain began to fall. By late afternoon we had barely left the marshes before we were forced to stop, well short of the place Cedric had hoped to reach that first day. Reluctantly he agreed we should set camp just inside the forest and make up the time lost by starting early the next morning the better for the rest.

We sheltered from the rain as best we could but had to do without a fire for all the wood we could find was too wet to burn. Instead we sat with our backs against a large oak and huddled beneath our cloaks trying to keep the rain from finding its way beneath our clothes. I realised we had set no guard but dared not mention it for fear it would be left to me. Besides, with the weather as it was we would be safe enough, for surely no man in his right mind would venture forth in such foul weather. Having not slept much the night before and then risen early, I soon gave way to a fitful sleep but was much disturbed by a fearsome dream which seemed all too real.

'*He's not to be trusted… Keep your wits about you.*' Edwin's words echoed through my dream. '*Watch him like a hawk…*' Then it felt as if someone had hold of me, gripping me by the shoulder and pulling at me as though trying to turn me on my side. Instinctively I reached out to free myself.

'Stop wriggling boy or I'll gut you like a fish!' roared a gruff voice I recognised at once.

As I opened my eyes I realised it was not a dream. Cedric was towering over me with the blade of his huge axe pressed against my chest. 'But…but what… Why are you doing this?' I protested still half asleep.

'Why? Because I didn't want you coming with me you little runt, that's why.'

'But you asked for me! I thought…' My words trailed off as I caught sight of the hatred burning in Cedric's eyes. I could almost feel it scorching my skin.

'You know my secret, don't you?' said Cedric sourly, raising his axe so the blade was right in front of my face. 'That's why I asked for you. So that I could put an end to all your questions. Now you'll not live long enough to tell a single soul, especially not that bastard brother of yours! Or does he know already?'

'What secret? I don't know anything about a—'

'Don't play the innocent with me, boy. You told Osric you suspected someone had opened the gates at Chippenham. I knew it wouldn't take you long to fathom who it was.'

It took a moment or two for me to realise what he was saying. 'You!' I blurted out. 'It was you! You're the traitor!'

'Not a traitor. A mercenary. I wield my axe for silver not some pious dream. And Guthrum pays better than you miserly Saxons. That's right, I fight for money. And that's why I slew the guards then opened the gates – for a sack full of silver so heavy I could barely lift it! And when I tell Guthrum where Alfred is he'll give me another just like it!'

'Edwin will kill you if he learns of this!' I threatened. 'You wait till I tell him. He'll...'

But Cedric just scoffed. 'Ah! So he doesn't yet know? That's what I needed to hear. And now he never will. When I get back I'll tell him how you ran off when the Vikings attacked us. I'll say how I searched until I found your wretched body all bloody and broken. If only you'd kept your head and stayed with me. If only you hadn't run like the little craven brat that you are.'

I could almost hear him saying that to Edwin; almost see the smug satisfaction he would get from telling him his brother had died a coward. As anger swept through me I knew I had to act, but how? Then I remembered the knife Edwin had given me and pulled it from my belt. It was too far for me to reach up and stab Cedric. Besides, the giant was wearing the mail vest and I could never hope to cut through that with such a simple blade. So keeping my eyes on the axe still poised above my head, I placed the edge of the knife against the back of Cedric's knee and pressed as hard as I could before slicing deep into his flesh.

'Aaargh! You bastard!' screamed Cedric as he reeled away, limping and clutching the wound. But the knife had cut through muscle and sinew so the leg just buckled beneath him. He sank to his knees, cursing and groaning. 'You little runt! You bast...aargh!'

I scrambled to my feet and rushed at Cedric, grabbing him round the neck and trying to wrestle him to the ground. But it was like fighting a rock. Whatever I tried I could not move the giant one way or the other as he was just too strong for me. Worse still, Cedric seemed able to fight back despite his wound, rearing up and sending me sprawling to the ground. I got up and charged again, this time driving into Cedric as though trying to knock him down by sheer force. The two of us locked together, twisting and writhing as we each struggled to secure our grip. Then I saw that Cedric's ill-fitting mail vest gaped open at the sides and knew that was my only chance.

Pulling myself free, I picked up the knife and lunged at the giant again. As we came together I drove the blade home, burying it deep into Cedric's side and twisting it, just as Edwin had taught me.

The giant looked as though he could scarcely believe what had happened, glancing first at the handle of the knife still buried in his side, then at me.

I could afford to waste no time. With my eyes now accustomed to the dark I could see Cedric's axe on the ground where it had fallen. Seizing it, I turned to confront the giant, rain streaming down my face.

Cedric was up on his knees, swaying as the blood oozed from both wounds. The knife was in deep and he clutched the handle of it, not daring to pull it free. 'G-go on! F-finish it!' he challenged through laboured breaths, his voice almost hissing the words. 'Str-strike and be d-done with it! Or have you…have you not the gr-gravel f-for it boy!'

I remembered how much I regretted killing the unarmed man during the battle at Chippenham. This time would be different. 'Face me!' I challenged. 'Come on! Get up and fight me, man to man!'

The strength was draining from Cedric's body and he must have known that even if he managed to stand his leg would not support him long. 'F-finish it!' he demanded. 'Go on b-boy! Strike and be d-done with it!'

'No! You'll face me like a warrior and then I'll kill you. You've only to pull that blade from your side to have the same chance you offered me – a knife against this axe. And that's more than you deserve, you traitor!'

Cedric grumbled as he looked at the blood on his hands from where he had nursed his wounds. The cut behind his knee was bleeding most, the rain washing the blood so that his whole lower leg was covered in it. 'I t-told you,' he gasped still struggling against the pain. 'I am...tr-traitor...to... to...no man... I serve...o-only...my purse... I was true... t-to that.'

'Tell it to all the poor wretches who perished at Chippenham!' I said. 'I should take you back to Alfred and let those who lost friends and kin there decree your fate.'

That prospect clearly worried Cedric for he shook his head. 'No! No I... I am done... I will...d-die here...b-but at my own...ha-hand.' With that he pulled the knife from his side and held it up for me to see. Blood pulsed from the wound, dripping to form pools in the mud beside him. He tried to staunch it with his hand but it was a hopeless task for it flowed much too freely. He looked first at me then down at the blood. 'Now d-do your worst b-boy,' he sneered. 'I'm d-dead e-either way.' Feebly, he tossed the knife towards me.

I knew then I would be denied the satisfaction of killing Cedric in combat. The next best thing was to let him die slowly but my pride demanded more. If the traitor's life was forfeit it was neither for having tried to murder me nor for the insults he had traded with my brother. It was for his treachery at Chippenham which had claimed the lives of so many innocent people. For that he had to die at the hands of a Saxon; nothing else would do. Slowly I moved closer to the giant, picked up the knife and wiped the blade on the grass before tucking it into my belt. Then I took the axe in both hands and raised it above him.

'N-not so e-easy...b-boy...is it? To k-kill a man.'

I smiled at him. 'No,' I said. 'But it's easy to kill vermin.' With that I brought the axe down upon his neck.

* * * * *

When it was done I could scarce bring myself to look at Cedric's mangled body. The blow had taken the giant across the neck with enough force to all but sever his head completely. The sight of it made me want to vomit but instead, seized with a sudden panic, I just dropped the axe and ran.

At that moment I cared nothing for the darkness or for the dangers of the forest, I just ran and ran, tears and rain streaming down my face. As I went the thoughts of what I had just done seemed to tumble around inside my head. At first I reproached myself but then gradually I began to justify my actions as if explaining them to others. Cedric had been a traitor to us all, a serpent in our midst – the image of Edwin holding the twisting and writhing snake in his hands kept coming to mind. Still I ran, clawing my way through the trees and foliage, crashing through the undergrowth like a startled pig. And still the rain beat down soaking me to the skin, but I cared no more about that than about where I was going.

I woke at dawn the next day shivering with the cold and unable to remember how or why I had chosen that place to sleep, knowing only that I was somewhere deep inside the forest. I had never felt so desolate and alone as I did that morning, wishing for all the world Edwin was nearby to tell me what I should do. I fingered the small knife he had given me. Having discarded Cedric's axe it was now my only weapon.

After so much rain the forest seemed full of small streams and I chose one of them at which to drink. The water was muddy and gritty but served to quench my thirst. When I had bathed my face and refreshed myself, I stripped off all my rain-soaked clothes and wrung the water from them. I would have liked to light a fire to dry them but all the wood was so wet it would have filled the forest with smoke, even if I actually managed to get it to light. Others would quickly be drawn to the smoke and in such a place as that it was unlikely that any I should meet would be friends.

Lost and alone, I had no provisions and no proper weapons with which to hunt or defend myself. As such my plight seemed hopeless. I sat down and began to dress myself in the still damp clothes and, as I did so, noticed that my cloak was stained with Cedric's blood, which even the rain had not been enough to wash away. Seeing the blood stirred memories of the night before and I struggled to confront the bitter reality of what had happened.

First I had killed Cedric. I could barely grasp the truth of that. I had slain the fearsome giant in unequal combat with the advantage against me. Why did I not feel proud of that? I knew the answer. It was because I had run from the act like a coward, lacking the courage even to bury him as was my Christian duty. But Cedric was a traitor. I saw again the image of Edwin and the snake and remembered his words – *'were it a viper in our camp I would have as soon cut off its head as look at it'*. There was the justification if any were needed, for what else was I to do but avenge Saxon honour? It occurred to me then that if Cedric was the traitor that meant that Osric was not. That thought pleased me as I knew it would surely please Edwin.

Amid all this I was reminded of my duty. I had been charged by Lord Alfred himself to go to Chippenham to gather as much information as I could about the defences and the number of men there. Whatever danger waited in my path I knew that duty should not be denied. As I had killed Cedric before the traitor had time to pass any information to Guthrum my purpose was still clear and I could ill afford to squander any more time in self-pity.

Gathering up my few belongings, I set off in the hope of intercepting the road again. In fact that proved not as difficult as I feared as it seemed I had not strayed as far from it as I thought. Also I found the going easier than on the march from Chippenham, not just because the snow was gone, but also because I was now a warrior in all but name. What's more I was proud of it, having been tested in open combat and in the service of my liege. Perhaps God was now showing me the course he truly wanted me to follow.

All the tiredness seemed to have gone and I travelled fast through that day and much of the one that followed. At one point I considered whether I should visit some of the nearby settlements and seek assistance, but before leaving we had been expressly ordered not to speak to anyone for fear of word reaching the Vikings of our coming.

Thus I continued and, as I went, I thought again of Cedric. Whilst my faith reproached me for having offered no prayer for the giant's soul, as a warrior I felt it was right to leave his worthless body to the mercy of the wolves. It was not worth burying.

* * * * *

I recalled that the settlement at Chippenham was set within a loop in the river and thus had water on three sides. The open end to the south was protected by earthen ramparts and a ditch plus a low palisade of sharpened stakes. The only gap was where the old Roman road entered Chippenham, which was guarded by a timber gatehouse – the place where the Vikings had first broken through. Alfred's Vill was in the western corner where there was another gatehouse and a narrow bridge carrying the road across the river to join the one I was now following. This western gatehouse had also been breached during the battle and was the scene of much of the fiercest fighting. It was this I came to first.

Taking advantage of whatever cover I could find, I lay flat on my belly to crawl as close as I dared so that I could assess the defences. The gatehouse itself looked to be intact and the bridge seemed to have suffered little during the battle save for signs of where it had been set afire – many of the timbers were charred and one section of the rail was missing. Two guards had been stationed on the far side but the gates were flung wide open. Beyond them I could see Alfred's Vill.

It included a huge timbered hall, big enough to quarter his personal retinue and standing on the foundations of what was once a Roman villa, sharing part of its original stone walls. These were scorched and the roof of the Great Hall had been newly thatched, something which Guthrum must have ordered for I recalled seeing it burning fiercely. This was confirmed by the fact that all the stores and workshops serving the Vill had been destroyed. Being built of thatch and timber this was not surprising but gone also were the stables, the kennels and even the cages used for housing Alfred's treasured gyrfalcons.

I let my eyes follow the line of the river but could see little of the southern defences or of the main settlement itself. To view these properly I would need to get much closer, which would mean crossing the river. With no other bridge for several miles that was out of the question and I knew I would have to rely on what I could see from there.

The first thing I noted was that the Vikings lacked any skills of husbandry. Having foolishly allowed their cattle to eat all the grass in the rich water meadows which lay directly beside the river, they had driven them to graze in new pastures some way off. These herds were tended by boys no older than myself, something Ethelnorth would be pleased to learn of as they would make an easy target.

It was also apparent that the southern ramparts had been repaired but poorly so, with fresh earth heaped up to close gaps in the fortifications. I could see that sharpened stakes were missing from the palisade in many places and the ditch was filled with so much debris that it would be easy to cross.

The southern gatehouse looked to be still guarded but had been badly damaged. Behind it lay the buildings that made up the settlement itself: the homes and workshops of the ordinary people who had lived and worked in the shadow of the Vill. They had numbered perhaps 200 households within the ramparts, most built on the higher ground but with the poorer dwellings closest to the river. Even from where I lay I could see that many had been reduced to charred and blackened ruins. It was hard to believe so much destruction had been caused in a single day.

I knew then I would have to venture inside the Vill itself to make a proper judgement as to the number of men Guthrum commanded, something which I was certain Edwin would not have approved had he been there for, as I have said, a Viking camp was no place for a Saxon spy. But I was a warrior now and had orders from my King. That was reason enough for the lamb to enter the den of the lion. Besides, I had a plan.

Chapter Fifteen

Rather than starve, there were some Saxons who would eke out a meagre existence by trading with the Vikings. This uneasy commerce was a weakness those who had not yet given up the fight for freedom despised. Nonetheless it was a common trait and one upon which the Vikings depended for their day-to-day essentials. As well as these 'traders' the guards would be used to seeing orphans who, with no kin willing or able to support them, would offer to do menial work in return for food. These poor wretches were treated little better than slaves but their presence was accepted and, like the traders, they were free to come and go, albeit watched constantly. I was sure that if I was bold enough this might be one way of getting into the Vill. The question was whether once inside I could observe things without being noticed and, more importantly, get out again alive.

I decided to approach the western gates. The ones to the south would have been easier because the Vikings would have seen no need to guard them too closely, but it would have meant first fording the river. Also, once inside the settlement there were bound to be more guards stationed at the entrance to the Vill itself and so I would still have to find a way to get past them.

Having waited till it was dark, I discarded my cloak in case the blood stains aroused suspicion, then plucked up enough courage to approach the gatehouse. I was so nervous that I wanted to retch, my fear not helped by the thought of the Saxons who had been slaughtered within the shadow of the Vill, many of whom perished at that very spot. But I had little time to dwell upon such matters. No sooner had I started across the bridge than two men armed with spears stepped forward to bar my path.

With my face dirty and my tunic soiled from the journey I knew I looked a wretched sight, but that was to the good, for I needed the Viking guards to see me as just another bedraggled orphan come to beg for food. As I crossed towards them I pointed to my mouth but could sense their disdain at once. They waved me off, making it plain they were not one bit interested in the plight of yet another young beggar.

I shrugged and, looking as dejected as I could, walked back a few steps before turning and starting to sing a few lines from an old Saxon ballad I had learned from my father. I hoped they wouldn't realise that I was singing about their deaths or, at least, about the deaths of warriors just like them! When I had finished the first few lines of the song I pointed to my mouth again. They just laughed but I was not deterred. Having spent many long hours standing guard at Athelney I knew they would welcome even the smallest distraction to relieve their boredom. So I started to sing again, this time a whole verse. Sure enough they seemed amused and called me over. I managed several songs which I sang as loud and as best I could, sometimes even keeping the rhythm with my hands and feet. Then, when I did a little dance, they laughed and clapped me on the shoulders. I knew they derided me and took me for a fool, but the deception served my purpose.

It was not long before the guards stationed on the other side of the gatehouse came to watch as well.

At length it seemed I had done enough and was taken in through the gates and escorted across the courtyard towards the Great Hall where I assumed I would be given food. As we went I kept turning and pointing to my mouth whilst using the opportunity to look more closely at the defences. For the most part these were much as I had seen from the outside except that I realised why the gates had been left open: the timbers had split so badly they had become unhinged. Huge beams had been found which would be used to prop them shut if the need arose but otherwise it was simpler for them to remain ajar. It was also evident how lazy the Vikings had been in other ways, for little had been done to repair the buildings beyond that needed to keep out wind and rain. More importantly, there were many more men than I expected, mostly gathered in small groups sheltering beside the walls or huddled together around their fires. They watched intently as we passed and I could feel their eyes follow me but was careful not to return their gaze.

It was at this point that my plan first began to go awry. They clearly meant to take me into the Great Hall itself, a place to which normally only the favoured few would be admitted. My heart sank when I realised this for I knew that once inside it would be very difficult to get out. Two more guards had been stationed at the entrance and one of them muttered something as we approached. Although I had no idea what they said, the others all laughed heartily at the quip. Apart from this they said nothing and were obviously well used to boys being taken there to work.

As we waited outside the Great Hall I heard many voices within. When at last the huge doors were opened the noise was even worse. It seemed the Vikings could not speak without shouting and their voices boomed even deeper than the bitterns I had heard in the marshes. A fire burned fiercely in the hearth in the centre of the Hall and men were seated all around it on benches or on the floor. They were as quarrelsome as they were noisy, with much drinking and fighting as scuffles broke out between them.

Although it had been many years since I last visited the Great Hall it seemed darker and gloomier than I remembered and, looking up, I could see why. The roof timbers were still blackened from when the building had been on fire even though the thatch had been replaced. The only light came from a few smoky torches set in brackets on the wall but left untended.

The last time I had been there I recalled seeing a beautiful fresco depicting scenes from some of the many Saxon tales which had been painted on all four walls so that it seemed to run all around the room. This had been defaced and spoiled, as had the finely woven tapestries which had once hung from the gables. On the floor there was also much litter in the form of broken pots or beakers which no one seemed inclined to pick up and in every corner rats picked through the leavings of discarded food.

At one end of the Great Hall was the tall chair where Alfred used to sit, a large wooden seat set up on a platform so that it appeared slightly higher than all the other chairs and benches. It also had elaborately carved posts holding up a canopy of the finest green silk. Although I had never seen Guthrum I was certain he was the huge bear of a man seated in Alfred's place. He was swathed in furs and had a thick yellow beard that almost covered his face.

Men were seated on either side of him on the benches Alfred would have reserved for his Ealdormen. The one to Guthrum's right was bent forward with his arms rested upon his knees and his head hung low. He looked up as I was led over to them, showing a toothless grin and eyes so round they were like little amber stones. His hair, which was almost the colour of copper, was worn long and tied back with a silver ring and his face was pale and almost sallow. But it was the man on Guthrum's left who frightened me most. He was at least as big as Cedric and, like Guthrum, had a vast beard. His face bore a scar so long it cut right across the bridge of his nose and the socket of his left eye. That eye socket was empty and his nose crooked to one side making it the most vicious scar I had ever seen on the face of any man, living or dead. In fact it was a miracle he had survived the blow that caused it. At first I thought the man was smiling but soon realised it was only because the skin was stretched at his mouth, pulling the flesh up at the corner.

The guard led me forward to stand before this trio and forced me to my knees in homage. As he told Guthrum why I had been brought I am certain he was implying that I was some sort of simpleton. Guthrum seemed faintly amused by this, so I was pulled to my feet and slapped hard on the back to indicate it was time to sing and dance some more.

At first my throat was too dry. I coughed to clear it but even so the words came out at a higher pitch than I intended. The few Vikings who bothered to listen were unimpressed. Some jeered and pelted me with half-eaten legs of poultry or crusts of stale bread and such like, but most simply turned away and ignored me. I quickly composed myself and, once started, made a reasonable fist of singing the first few verses of a song, then finished with a little dance. This time I made a more careful selection by choosing a song which made no reference to slaying Vikings, only to the glory of battle itself.

Having caught their attention, I sang a more rousing song which was a chant our warriors used for keeping time whilst rowing and which required the last line to be shouted in unison. I indicated this by shouting myself and punching my fist into the air with such vigour that almost every man joined in.

It was a glorious song but my rendition of it was lost under so much shouting. No one except Guthrum seemed to know when I had finished, but he eventually nodded his approval and I was led to a table on one side of the Hall and allowed to take food from the remnants of their feast.

I helped myself to oat cakes and boiled mutton, then worked my way to the back of the room. From there I could see Guthrum more clearly. He was talking avidly to the man with the scar but I could not hear their words. I noticed they kept pointing to a piece of parchment which had been unrolled and was rested on Guthrum's knee. As all three of them studied it so intently I knew I had to see what it was.

Still gnawing the last scraps from the leg of boiled mutton, I began to edge nearer by easing a path between those seated on the floor. Many of the Vikings were drunk, some so much so they were asleep. Gingerly I stepped over them making my way as carefully as I could but, in such poor light and with so many men sprawled upon the floor, I was almost bound to disturb someone. Sure enough, there was a yelp of pain when I stepped on someone's hand followed by what sounded like an oath. A huge arm reached out and pulled me down until I was staring into a pair of bloodshot eyes with the man's putrid breath filling my nostrils. Then, with an almighty roar, I was heaved backwards.

I landed amid others who, laughing riotously, gathered me up, set me on my feet again and then thrust me back, clearly expecting me to make a fight of it. The Viking was already up by then but being so full of sleep and mead was unsteady on his feet. I cowered, waiting for the blow I was sure would follow, but was distracted by a commotion behind me. When I turned to see what it was one of the men held up my knife – the one Edwin had given me. It had obviously come out when I fell and, from the look on their faces, they had assumed the worst.

* * * * *

One of the Vikings came towards me holding up the knife for all to see. I smiled weakly but, when I reached out to take it back, it was snatched away from me. I shrugged trying to pretend I could see no reason why I shouldn't have it, but I knew that was not convincing.

Two others came forward and, leaning on each other for support, seemed to be riling the man who had found the knife. He was a simple soul, somewhat wary at first until a faint smile appeared on his face. With that the three of them grabbed me and although I protested, they tied my hands together in front and looped a rope around my neck. I was then led around the Great Hall like a bear on a lead with Vikings slapping me on the back and baiting me as we passed. By this time I was so frightened I could scarce place one foot in front of the other. Yet I had no choice but to go where I was led, for if I so much as stumbled the rope was jerked roughly and I was pulled almost to my knees.

Certain that with every step I was moving closer to a terrible death, I was dragged and goaded into the centre of the Hall to stand beside the fire. There I shuddered, vividly recalling some of the dreadful stories I had heard about how they dealt with spies. With my hands so securely tied there was nothing I could do except die well – and if not in combat then at least in prayer. So, sinking to my knees, I raised my tethered hands to God.

At this the Vikings roared with laughter. The rope was then jerked again so that it tightened even more about my neck and two men stepped forward to hold me whilst a third untied my bonds. Then pelts and hides left drying beside the fire were roughly swept aside as I was dragged backwards until my arms could be lashed securely to one of the frames.

All through this I kept praying, reciting the words over and over again under my breath. I prayed for mercy, I prayed for forgiveness for my sins and I prayed for courage but, most of all, I prayed that death would come swiftly.

By this time all around me men were on their feet jeering and yelling as if baying for blood. A dwarf, who stood no more than half height, appeared from their midst and began skipping round and round the fire brandishing my knife like some sort of trophy. Then he began walking slowly towards me, each step exaggerated as though he were stalking his prey. Holding the knife out in front of him, he squinted along the blade, grinning as if relishing what he was about to do.

This dwarf was like a miniature Viking. He was dressed in a sleeveless fleece coat that he wore over a short tunic which revealed his puny arms. His hair and beard were long and unkempt, his teeth like little black pegs most of which were missing. But it was his eyes which frightened me. They had a wild almost manic look about them as though they thirsted to avenge nature's cruel trick of robbing him of his stature.

As the blade of the knife was laid across my stomach I fought hard to control myself. I desperately didn't want to let myself down by pissing myself or pleading for mercy but I was already weak with fear. I flinched as I felt a line being traced across my belly but there came no pain. When I looked down I could see why. The dwarf had used the unsharpened edge of the blade thereby not cutting into me at all.

The other Vikings roared their encouragement, howling and whooping like demented dogs as the dwarf then licked the blade and pretended to savour the taste of my imaginary blood. At this the horde began chanting and stamping their feet, the noise growing louder and louder until all I wanted to do was scream. As I twisted and strained at my bonds I was suddenly aware that the Great Hall had gone quiet and that all eyes were upon me.

The dwarf had moved away to stand beside the fire where he was heating the knife in the flames. I could only imagine what he intended to do with a red-hot blade! The possibilities were too terrible to think of but all I could do was watch and wait, helpless to defend myself.

When he had heated it to his satisfaction the little man came skipping towards me again, this time dancing round me brandishing the still smoking knife in the air before reaching up as though to stab it into my eyes. The crowd mocked the dwarf cruelly when they saw he could barely reach that high, but he called the man who had first taken the knife from me and ordered him to kneel on all fours so that he could climb onto his back. In this the dwarf was a true jester. At first he pretended to ride the man, sitting astride him as though on a horse, facing first one way and then the other. Every so often he would rise up and fart, causing the Vikings to laugh so much they could scarce contain themselves.

Determined not to give up without a fight, I did the only thing I could think of. I kicked out hard, burying my foot deep into the man's belly and causing him to rear up and send his little 'rider' tumbling to the floor.

Everyone roared their approval as the dwarf got up, dusted himself down then proceeded to scold the man for having tipped him off! I could make no sense of this but the whole episode was then repeated with everyone laughing even more as the little man was sent sprawling once again. By this time the man on the floor seemed to have tired of playing the fool. He started to get up but the dwarf took a running leap onto his back and together they careered round and round, turning this way and that until they both collapsed in a heap. In the frantic chase which followed, the dwarf dashed back and forth, diving between the man's legs or skipping round him but always keeping just out of reach. At one point when they found themselves face to face on the floor, he kissed the man full on the lips before turning to the crowd to make a lewd gesture with his arm. With that he was off. Stopping only to fart again, he scuttled into the crowd and disappeared.

It was only then that I realised the whole thing was a game! They were not torturing me; they were taunting the man who had taken my knife, berating him for having disarmed such a fearsome 'warrior' as the boy who came to sing songs to them!

With their fun over I was left still tied to the frame and ignored for what seemed like hours. How my arms ached as the evening wore on, the heat from the fire becoming almost unbearable. Yet I had no choice but to watch in silence as the Vikings continued drinking and fighting. Every so often the revelries were interrupted when one or other of them stood up to speak aloud. Some, I think, were boasting of their exploits whilst others recited poems or sagas all of which ended with more toasting and shouting. Then Guthrum called for some sort of order and began to give out shares of booty to three men for some service they had rendered. The first received a fine pewter chalice which I guessed had been looted from a church whilst the other two were each given silver arm rings to add to those they already wore. All three then bowed and kissed Guthrum's ring as a sign of their continued allegiance.

After this Guthrum and his two henchmen left taking the parchment with them. By that time most of the Vikings had become too drunk to stand or too tired to care and, one by one, they settled down to sleep where they lay. Those who did remain awake gathered in small groups about the Great Hall. In one corner three men were baiting a small dog, tugging at its tail and placing bets on how long it would be before it bit someone. In another they had one of Alfred's gyrfalcons which they were teasing with morsels of food, encouraging it to fan out its wings and screech at them. Others were either playing dice or telling more tales of their feats and conquests much as the Saxons might have done.

In fact it struck me then that the Viking camp was so like our own that even understanding nothing of what they said, I could still follow what was going on.

'You was lucky,' whispered a voice to the right of me. I looked round to see a woman standing beside me dressed in rags, her hair uncovered and loose about her shoulders, her face dirty and one eye so badly bruised it was only half open. At first I was not sure what to make of her but was glad of someone who at least spoke my own tongue.

'Who are you?' I asked.

She hesitated to answer. 'You know me, boy,' she said at last. 'Leastways you should do right enough.'

I looked at her again but still couldn't place her.

'You was with them, you was,' she said accusingly. 'Not like the rest, I'll grant you. But you was there when those bastards cut off my Goda's hand and left us both to starve.'

'Mildrith!' I said, shocked at her transformation. Even as I said it my heart sank for I realised I had as much to fear from her as from the Vikings. Worse still, she had retrieved my knife from the floor and was holding it up for me to see.

'Aye, Mildrith, though it's been many weeks since I answered to my name.' With that she raised the blade as if to threaten me. 'So tell me boy, what's become of my girl?'

I swallowed hard not sure how to answer. 'She was well when I left,' I managed. 'Though they work her hard. She and I are friends and...'

'I can guess what sort of friend you'd be,' said Mildrith sourly. Then she pressed the knife hard against my ribs. 'I should bleed you, boy. Bleed you for all I've suffered from you and your kind.'

203

'Do it then,' I challenged, not sure where my courage came from but keen to end the nightmare. I had suffered enough that night and was beyond caring. 'Do it and have done with it. Either that or cut me free and then come with me. Your daughter needs you and...'

'Why, what have they done with her? Made a whore of her? They will in time. Her fate will be the same as mine, you mark my words.'

I didn't answer for there was nothing I could say.

'I'll set you free all right,' said Mildrith at last. 'Free as a bird if you want it. But you must promise me something first.'

'What?' I asked.

'Look out for her, do you hear me? She's no one left to help her now, so I'll set you free if you swear to do as much for her.'

I thought for a moment then agreed. 'I'll do my best,' I promised guardedly.

Satisfied with that, Mildrith reached up and began to cut through the bonds so that my hands were free at last.

'So how came you to this wretched end?' I asked, nursing my wrists which were raw and bleeding from where the ropes had chaffed the skin.

'We come here of our own accord, Goda and me,' she said ruefully. 'We'd no place else to go and thought to earn something for telling Guthrum which way you was all headed. 'Cept the bastards slew him where he stood. After all a tinker with just one hand was no use to them, not even as a slave, particularly as he was full of the fever from his wound. As for me, they set me to working as a slave and a whore serving their vile needs.'

I considered the cruel irony of a mother and daughter sharing such a dreadful fate, both punished for a crime neither had committed. 'Come with me,' I offered. 'I'm sure Alfred would be merciful if I tell him Goda's dead.'

Mildrith shook her head. 'What for, boy? There's nothing I can do to help Emelda. Her life will be hard enough without another mouth to feed. No, I wait only for the comfort of my grave to which end I would keep this blade.'

I was not sure what she meant at first. When I realised I was shocked. 'But you can't...your soul will be damned forever if...'

She looked at me sternly. 'You know nothing of what I've endured, so save your pious tongue. With this I've the means to end my misery when my need is most. So take what food you will from the table and go whilst they're still too drunk to care. Come morning your chance will be wasted!'

I turned to take her advice but a thought struck me. 'Just tell me one thing,' I asked. 'Was that Guthrum at the front? The one seated in the middle?'

'Aye that was him. And I've cause to know him right enough.'

'Then did you see the parchment he was looking at?'

'Much good would it do if I had. I can't read in my own words never mind theirs.'

'You don't have to have read it, not like a book. I just need to know what it was.'

She stared at me as if I was mad. 'Why do you ask this?' she demanded.

'Have you seen it or not?' I pressed.

With her thin hand she reached out and grasped my arm. 'What are you come for, boy? Not to sing for your supper, that's for sure.'

I returned her gaze but made no attempt to answer.

After a few moments she gently nodded her head as though she understood. 'You're a bold one to come in here like this,' she said. 'You saw the one with the scar? I've heard them call him Ubba. He arrived but a few days since and as far as I can tell they're planning to use his men for some sort of raid.'

'Do you know where?'

She shook her head. 'That's all I know. I think he has some of them longships and perhaps the parchment is some sort of map. Anyways, they're all in awe of him, that's for certain.'

'I'm not surprised. That scar is enough to frighten anyone!'

She smiled, revealing a face in which, fleetingly, I could see the likeness of Emelda. 'I've heard it said that he kills the women who lay with him, and them that won't. They're all animals but he's far worse than the rest put together.'

'Are there many of you here?' I asked.

'A few,' she said.

'Enough to help if we—' I stopped, realising I should say no more.

She looked at me sadly. 'There are no Saxon warriors if that's what you ask. And God be thanked for that. Them that was taken was tortured till they died, most wishing they hadn't lived quite so long as they did. Just be grateful they grew tired of you, for you was sport for them, that's all. Now they've done with you and as like as not will kill you come the morning. So be gone from here and don't come back. Do you hear me? If you stay you'll die for certain.'

As she turned away I began to edge towards the doors, creeping past the sleeping Vikings or carefully stepping over them. I was almost there when I felt a heavy hand on my shoulder. I turned to find myself staring at a man who was clearly very drunk, so much so he was swaying from side to side. He gripped me roughly, his eyes struggling to focus as he tried to recall my face, then belched.

Thinking quickly, I pointed to between my legs to indicate that I wanted to relieve myself outside but the drunk did not seem to understand. Then Mildrith appeared again, leaned on the man's shoulder and whispered something in his ear. She took his hands and guided them to her breasts and, as he fondled them, his face broke into a broad smile. Taking his arm, she led him out of the Great Hall like a lamb. I followed, slipping past the guards on the pretence of helping to steady the man's uncertain steps. Once we were safely outside I dipped away into the shadows from where I watched as she led the Viking off, her arm wrapped around his waist to support him. She turned briefly as if to say something but was then lost to the darkness.

For a while I wandered about the Vill in the hope of learning more about the defences whilst most of the Vikings were asleep or too drunk to notice me. Although nearly dawn, it was still too dark to see my way clearly and there were just a few torches which flickered lamely to light my path. As I went I tried to get a better idea of the number of men there and even managed to venture out of the Vill and into the settlement itself where I wandered among what was left of the Saxon homes. Few were left standing and even those that were had been burned or damaged. Some of the pens had been repaired and now held sheep or pigs but otherwise everything had been destroyed. In fact it was hard to believe it had once been such a thriving settlement. Yet even having been reduced to ruins it was far from deserted. Everywhere I looked there were men and women sleeping, some stretched out on the ground and others propped up against the ruined walls. A few were probably Saxon survivors from the attack who were now slaves or prisoners but most, I was sure, were Vikings. It was as if Guthrum's victory had summoned every Norseman in the land to join him. I had never seen so many men in one place and knew I had to get word of this to Alfred as soon as possible. Thus I began to retrace my steps towards the western gates.

As I went I had the eerie feeling of being followed but whenever I looked I saw only shadows. Even so I could not dispel the thought of someone watching me and grew anxious to get away as quickly as I could.

The same guards were sitting outside the gates as were there when I arrived, talking intently as they waited for the dawn to end their long shift. Praying they would recognise me and let me pass, I strode towards them as boldly as I dared, smiling and rubbing my belly to show it was now full. They greeted me without getting up, perhaps thinking I had come to sing to them again.

As calmly as I could I went and stood beside them, warming my hands over their brazier. One of the men said something but I just smiled and nodded. Then I started towards the bridge, ambling slowly so as not to cause alarm. I was aware of both men watching me but gambled on the fact they would not be sure whether they should stop me or not. After all, they had no cause to detain me as I had entered of my own free will, yet I knew they would still feel uneasy about letting me pass. Therefore instead of rushing to make my escape, I turned and began to recite a short verse from an epic poem. Though clearly the words meant nothing to them they both nodded appreciatively. Having thus put them at their ease I bade them farewell and, with my heart beating furiously, simply strolled back across the bridge.

At every step I half expected to be summoned back or for them to come after me, but nothing happened. Only once I was safe on the far bank did I give in to the temptation to look behind me. When I did I saw someone else in the shadows – a small boy standing beside the gatehouse in the half-light of dawn. I recognised who it was at once.

Chapter Sixteen

I was almost certain that the boy watching me from the gates was Edmund, the young orphan Edwin and I had befriended and who I was supposed to have looked after during the battle at Chippenham.

My first thought was to go back for him and thereby make amends for having lost him during the battle, but I knew I had been lucky to escape from the Viking stronghold in the first place. Also, my duty was to return to Alfred in haste with all the information I now had, that duty ranking above whatever personal concerns I had for my young friend. Besides, he seemed to be in no danger having already endured whatever harm was likely to befall him.

What worried me was that it would be all too easy for him to betray me. He would not do so intentionally, I was sure of that, but he was still only a boy and could not possibly understand that even to acknowledge me could put both our lives in danger. I was not sure what to do but remembered something my father had taught me:

> To count his flock the shepherd had best stand still and let the sheep run past him. To chase after them serves only to spoil the count.

It was sound advice and, to heed it, I realised I needed to take a few moments to consider all my options one by one rather than rush headlong into whatever thoughts came first into my head. After all it was not just my life which was at stake but possibly those of Alfred and Edwin, not to mention all those who sheltered with them at Athelney.

First, if indeed it had been Edmund at the Vill – and in such poor light and at such a distance I could not be absolutely certain that it was – had he recognised me? After all some months had passed and in that time much would have happened in the boy's life. Second, even if he had recognised me, had he yet recovered his voice or would his silence be my shield?

These were, I decided, questions without answers. All I could do was to assume the worst and that meant I had to distance myself from Chippenham as swiftly as I could.

If the Vikings did come after me I knew that by keeping to the open road I would be all too quickly overtaken. Therefore I decided to risk finding my way through the forest, travelling in a wide arc until rejoining the road a safe distance from the Vill. At least that way anyone trying to follow me would have to do so on foot, for the trees would be too dense for them to use their horses.

Many would have thought the plan too dangerous or even reckless. Yet Edwin had taught me that it was sometimes safer to travel through even the thickest forests as these offered a slower but more secure route than many of the roads where bands of thieves were always a threat to travellers, especially those who, like me, journeyed alone and unarmed.

My real concern was wild beasts. As if to make the point I heard the piercing screech of an owl and, somewhere behind me, something scurried into the undergrowth. I told myself these were only God's creatures, most of them more frightened of me than I should be of them. The only ones I needed to fear were the larger ones such as wolves and bears. The chances of meeting the latter were very slight for they kept mainly to areas far to the north of Wessex and even then it was rare to actually see one. As for wolves, they were common enough, with packs roaming freely in all the forests, but they were cautious creatures and would only trouble man if they were hungry or sensed an easy kill. All the same, I regretted having gifted my knife to Mildrith even though it was a small price to pay for my liberty and, in all likelihood, my life.

The sun was already rising so, taking my bearings from that, I recovered the blood-stained cloak I had discarded before going into the Vill, then set off at once. There were no paths to follow once I reached the forest so, being forced to weave my way between the trees, I needed to check my position often in case I got lost. Even so I seemed to make good progress and began to feel I had indeed made the right decision. If the Vikings did follow they would have no advantage in the forest and even if they guessed my plan and sought to intercept me once I rejoined the road, they would have no way of knowing where to set their ambush. Thus comforted, I reasoned that I had only to maintain my course and to keep moving in order to make good my escape.

Desperate to make as much haste as possible, I pushed on hard through the day and to speed the journey did not even stop to rest that night. Although tired from not having slept the night before, I was beginning to feel much surer of myself. I should have known better. For is it not true that from confidence comes the quickest fall?

It was in the early hours of the morning when for some strange reason I was quite suddenly overwhelmed with panic. Perhaps it was because of the image I had formed in my tired mind of the Vikings hacking their way through the forest in pursuit of me; or perhaps it was the thought of unseen eyes watching from the dark. Either way my anxiety began feeding upon those fears and my imagination did the rest. My pace quickened until, seized by a madness I could not control, I began crashing through the foliage like a man possessed. It was as if I was trying to tear a path through the trees with my bare hands, stopping at nothing. With branches and thorns scratching my face and arms I thrashed about wildly, oblivious to the noise I created or to the injury I might do to myself.

In the end I was saved not by my own good sense but by a sapling tree which sprang back at me as I pushed past it. The pain as it swiped across my face sent me reeling backwards leaving me sprawled on the ground. With the spell which had caused such madness broken so abruptly, I sat up and wiped the blood from my brow. Relieved it was only a minor cut, I was about to get up when I realised how quiet the forest had become.

My first thought was that everything around me had been frightened by the noise of my approach, but I realised it was more than that. Not only was the forest silent, it was strangely still as though holding its breath waiting for something to happen.

Then to my left something stirred. It was nothing more than a rustle in the undergrowth but there was no mistaking it. Then there was more movement, this time behind me. Whilst I knew that even the slightest sound might give away my position, every instinct I had was willing me to get up and run.

Warily, I began to look about me, peering into the gloom. Then I saw them – a pair of eyes staring at me from the foliage like two amber lights glowing in the dark. I knew at once what it was.

They had come as silent as death itself: a pack of wolves working their way around me no doubt summoned by all the noise I had made. To them it would have sounded like a wounded animal thrashing through the undergrowth and now they were closing in for their kill.

Under my breath I cursed myself for being so stupid. If they smelled my fear the wolves would attack, of that I was certain. Looking around I spotted a tree not far off that looked possible to climb quickly if I could but reach it, but the wolves were getting closer all the time. They were also noisier, growing excited and careless of their position as they sensed an easy kill.

I knew that wolves worked together so that when one moved the others followed in order to keep their prey surrounded. Thus they would not close on me until they could do so as one. That was my only chance of survival. With no time to waste, I crossed myself then reached out and picked up two large stones from the ground. With one swift movement, I leaped to my feet and charged headlong towards where I thought the nearest wolf to be, screaming at the top of my voice. Sure enough the beast was up in an instant and bounding away, yelping in surprise at such a direct assault. All around me was the sound of movement as others from the pack adjusted their position. I allowed them no time for that; I just turned and ran as fast as I could towards the tree. I was almost there when one of the beasts appeared to my left, snarling and growling like a fiend from hell.

Courage was now my only hope. That and the wolf's natural reluctance to close on such large and dangerous prey as a man without the rest of the pack in support. Screaming again, I challenged the beast and hurled the stones at it as hard as I could. As the wolf bounded back into the undergrowth I made a desperate lunge for the tree. Grabbing it, I hung there for a moment before hauling myself up into the safety of its branches.

Almost at once the rest of the pack closed in, howling and baying for blood as they circled beneath me. I knew they would not readily give up the hunt so climbed to the next branch to make certain I was safe.

Briefly I considered trying to outwit them by scrambling through the branches and across to the next tree but knew that if I slipped or if one of the boughs snapped I would be torn apart as soon as I hit the ground. Thus I had no option but to sit it out hoping the wolves would soon tire of waiting.

To make myself as comfortable as possible, I sat astride the branch and leaned back against the trunk for support. Though desperately tired, I dared not let myself sleep for fear of falling so took off my belt and passed it around one of the branches and then around my waist to keep myself secure. Next I tried to think of things to keep myself awake. My first thought was of how foolish I had been. So much so that my stupidity had nearly cost me my life. I wondered what Edwin would say about a noble Saxon cowering in a tree! Yet I felt I could excuse myself given how much I had achieved. I had discharged my orders well, of that I was certain, and I had gathered the information Alfred would need. For that my brother would be proud of me when I returned to Athelney. I longed to tell him of my battle with Cedric, of how I could now clear Osric's name and of all that had befallen me whilst in the Vikings' camp but, as I rehearsed what I would say, it occurred to me that not everyone would readily believe that Cedric had been the traitor or indeed that I, a novice monk and would-be warrior, had actually slain him. I would need to find something to take back as proof – but first I had to escape the wolves.

I had originally counted seven or possibly eight in the pack. Most were sitting in the undergrowth panting and yawning as they waited for me to come down but one, a particularly large animal with a very dark coat and no lighter markings, paced back and forth impatiently, stopping only to cock its leg against the tree every so often and to look up at me expectantly. At first I tried shouting in the hope of driving him and the others off, but in the end they sloped away of their own accord as soon as it began to get light. I could hear them howling in the distance as they went but decided to wait until it was fully light before climbing down.

Before continuing, I found a large stick which, once stripped of twigs, made a good, stout staff which I hoped would serve as a makeshift weapon if the need arose again. It wasn't much but it was better than nothing, for I knew that my encounter with the wolves had been a very close call. How often had Edwin told me that warriors do not rely on luck? Yet it was that and nothing more which had saved me from being torn to pieces. I realised then it was one thing to be bold enough to brave the dangers of the forest alone but to ignore those dangers was the mark of a fool. I resolved not to make the same mistake again but such is the arrogance of youth. As I was about to learn, trouble, like misfortune, seldom comes alone.

Chapter Seventeen

As soon as I was sure the wolves had gone I changed my plan. Wary of continuing through the forest, I decided to strike out for the road from there. Given that I was already tired and it would mean travelling for another day without sleep it was perhaps a lot to ask of myself to push on so hard, but the fact was it felt safer to keep moving.

As it turned out I reached the road well before midday. From there I continued westwards, travelling as quickly and as quietly as I could for fear of drawing unwelcome attention to myself. It was not that I was worried about meeting any local Saxons for they would pay little mind to a bedraggled boy, and with nothing obvious worth stealing, robbers were unlikely to trouble me. No, what really worried me was the prospect of being overtaken by the Vikings. That or worse still, walking straight into their trap.

Thus I was suspicious when I came upon a horse, still saddled, grazing idly beside the road. It had all the makings of an ambush, particularly when I noticed that the saddle was the type favoured by the Vikings. The question was what should I do? To go round would mean re-entering the forest, which was probably what they expected me do, whereas to continue along the road seemed almost suicidal. In the end I decided to do what Edwin would have done and try to get close enough to assess the situation fully. Using the edge of the forest for cover, I crawled forward on my hands and knees, creeping carefully towards the horse. The first thing I noticed was that it was not tethered. Not sure whether that was a good sign or not, I crept nearer still. It was only then that I realised there was a man there as well, lying in a clearing a little way away from the horse and half hidden by the undergrowth. He seemed to lie so still that he might be dead. The obvious assumption was that he had fallen from the horse. Or was that what I was supposed to think?

Although I found it difficult to ignore the plight of someone in need my instinct was to withdraw. In fact, all things considered, that was the only safe option. I began to edge away slowly but, by then, the man had seen me. He called out in a strange tongue whilst beckoning for help. When he realised I could not understand what he said, he spoke in English.

'I have a wound to my leg,' he called patting his left thigh. 'Will you help me, please?'

'Is that your horse?' I asked, still suspicious.

'It is,' insisted the man.

'Then you probably stole it and this is God's punishment,' I said rather uncharitably. 'If so I should leave you here to die.'

'No. No, the horse is my own,' the man assured me.

'But you're a Viking?' I said, not certain that he was. The man's demeanour was unlike the Vikings I had seen at the Vill, but judging by his clothes he was not a Saxon either.

'No,' said the man firmly. 'I come from the northlands, yes. But I am not a Viking.'

'If you come from the northlands then you are a Viking. And if you're a Viking you're my enemy and I should kill you,' I reasoned, getting to my feet then frantically looking around in case there were others. I realised that if there were I would have been taken by then but knew better than to relax my guard.

The man shook his head. 'No, no I am not your enemy.'

'You're a Viking yet you're not my enemy? How can this be?'

'Not all men from the northlands are Vikings,' he explained. 'I come to this cursed land to trade not fight. But if you think I am your enemy then kill me and be done with it. I would rather that than lie here helpless waiting to be eaten by wild beasts. There's a body on the road ahead of you on which they have already feasted. The crows have pecked out his eyes and…'

'I know,' I said, realising he was referring to Cedric. 'It was I who killed him.' By this time I had moved closer to the man but still kept a few paces between us.

Cautiously he looked up at me. 'You do a lot of killing for one so young. In my land you would be a great warrior, I think.'

'Perhaps I'm a great warrior here in Wessex,' I replied rather boastfully.

'Well, then I can't say I'm pleased to meet with you but I would like it if you would decide whether to help me or to kill me.'

'What's your name and if you are from the northlands, how come you speak my language?' I asked still unsure of him.

'My name is Sweyn. I am a trader come to find routes for goods to be traded with your peoples and mine. I speak your language because a trader must know these things.'

'Well Sweyn, I have a trade for you. If I help you will you give me your horse?'

He thought about it for a moment. 'Do I have a choice? You will take it anyway. How could I stop you?'

'I wouldn't steal it!' I said quickly.

'Do you know I believe you? All right I agree. If you help me I will give you my horse but if you kill me, I will not.'

We both laughed when we realised what an odd bargain had been struck. 'My name is Matthew, son of Edwulf, and I will do what I can for you,' I said feeling confident enough to move closer. 'But at first light I must be gone from here for I have urgent duties I could not neglect even if my own brother were lying here in your stead.' I knelt down and looked at Sweyn's leg. There was an arrow lodged in his thigh, the shaft of which had broken off. 'How did this happen?' I asked.

Sweyn grimaced. 'I was set upon by robbers. I managed to ride free but was struck by the arrow as I made my escape.'

'And they didn't follow?' I asked suspiciously.

'No, they were too busy with my pack horse which carried all my wares.'

The story was feasible but unlikely. Robbers would not have given up so easily when there was a chance of stealing another good horse and saddle, but I said nothing. Instead I began to examine the wound more closely. Undoing the strap Sweyn used to bind his leggings seemed to cause too much pain so in the end I took Sweyn's knife and cut it, slicing through the coarse woollen leggings as well to expose the wound more fully. The flesh around it was livid and very swollen. It was also beginning to blacken and dried blood had crusted where the shaft still protruded. 'You need more help than I can give,' I said wincing. 'Does it pain you much?'

He shook his head. 'The leg is numb and I can hardly feel it. But it throbs so. Already I fear the poison seeps into my body. You must release the arrow and drain the bad blood or I shall die.'

I hesitated. It would mean digging out the arrowhead with a knife then, with no leeches or maggots to cleanse the wound, bleeding it until all the poison was gone.

'You have done this before?' asked Sweyn anxiously.

In truth the answer was no. I had once seen my abbot perform the operation on a man following a hunting accident but had never actually done it myself. I decided not to say as much to Sweyn. 'The knife will first need to be cleansed,' I said remembering how Edwin had done this when he nursed Aelwyn after the battle at Chippenham. I set about lighting a fire then whilst we waited for the flames to become hot enough, I attended to Sweyn's horse. It seemed a placid beast as I took it to a stream to let it drink then led it back nearer to where Sweyn lay and tethered it to a tree. There I removed the saddle together with a large leather bag which was strapped to one side. I took the saddle across to Sweyn, setting it on the ground so that he could rest against it. I then fetched the bag and gave that to him as well. From this the Norseman produced some stale bread and a cheese which we shared. When we had finished eating I took Sweyn's knife and honed it on a stone to make the point as sharp as possible before placing it in the flames to cleanse it.

'You are a good man,' said Sweyn as he watched over my ministrations. 'It is a pity you see only the worst of my people. It is the desperate and the greedy who come here;

second sons who have nothing to inherit or those banished for crimes they have committed. These are the ones who you call Vikings who come to plunder your shores.'

'You mean you send the dregs of your people here,' I teased.

Sweyn looked offended. 'No,' he insisted. 'We lose many good men to your lands for it takes great courage to journey across the sea. Adventurers and warriors come here, men who I grant you would live and die by their sword, but their strength and courage is not to be denied.'

'And these are the Vikings?'

'Yes. These are Vikings. And for every one of them there are ten like me – traders and merchants, farmers and hunters; skilled craftsmen who work with silver, or poets who write songs to stir your heart. These are the people with whom I think you might be friends if things were different.'

'So why did you come?' I asked.

'As I said, I come to trade. To open up routes to bring in goods you would have and take back those things you have which we do not. Behind all warriors should come the merchants and the traders, I think.'

This was not a side of the Vikings I had ever seen or even heard of and I was intrigued. 'Do you know Guthrum?' I asked.

Sweyn shook his head. 'I need his permission to trade and was on my way there when this happened.'

It suddenly dawned on me that assuming Edmund had not already given me away, if this man survived my ministrations and then went to Chippenham there was a real danger that Guthrum would then realise I had been a spy. If so, he would know I had seen the poor state of the defences at the Vill and the huge number of men there. I could not risk forsaking whatever small advantage that information would give the Saxons and so decided there and then to take Sweyn with me as a prisoner – if he survived the night. I said nothing of this as I lifted the knife from the fire and examined the blackened blade.

Sweyn sat up and watched me intently but showed little sign of fear. 'If the blood flows too much you lay the blade across the wound. Yes?'

I nodded. 'Have you a God to pray to?' I asked.

'Such things are decreed by fate not by prayer,' explained Sweyn. 'We cannot choose when to die but we can sometimes choose how. Our warriors, for example, would choose a glorious death rather than life. That is a good creed for a warrior for it makes them fearless. I am not such a man but if now is my time of death then I would as soon meet it as they would: with courage and with pride.'

'I think you and my brother would have much to discuss,' I observed.

'Then I hope I shall live long enough to meet with him,' replied Sweyn, lying back against the saddle. 'But hear me in this my friend. If I die you will not think badly of yourself, no? My life was forfeit from the moment the arrow struck. You have tried to give it back, which is all I could ask of you.'

My hand was trembling as I gripped Sweyn's leg then pushed the point of the knife deep into the wound to find the arrowhead. As I did so the blood welled up around the blade and began to flow in a small rivulet, dripping onto the ground.

Even though Sweyn cried out I probed deeper and deeper, enlarging the wound as I tried to prise the arrowhead free.

At last I managed to dislodge it and held it up for Sweyn to see. Unfortunately it was made of bone, which we both knew might have splintered on entry. If so there was the risk of small slithers remaining in the wound which would then fester unless the flow of blood could cleanse it.

Arching his back, Sweyn strained himself against the pain as I squeezed the leg above and below the wound, pressing hard to help the blood to flow more freely. 'A little more, I think,' he said sounding weaker. 'All the fever must come out.'

When it was done I took the knife from the fire once more and touched the wound with the red-hot blade to seal it.

Relieved, Sweyn lay back with eyes half closed, breathing deeply. I offered him some water but the poor man was so weak and distant he could barely lift his head to drink.

I examined the wound and knew there was no question of Sweyn walking without help for several days. I knew also that come the morning I would have some difficult choices to make, for Sweyn had been wrong about one thing: it was not always up to fate to decide when it was time for a man to die. Sometimes it was left to mere mortals like myself.

*   *   *   *   *

Although I slept heavily, I awoke during the night when I heard Sweyn groaning. At first I feared I had taken too much blood thereby making the merchant's heart so weak it would stop beating. Then, as the night wore on, I began to think I had not taken enough.

By morning Sweyn was worse. His whole body shook and shivered even though I tended him as best I could, wiping the sweat from his face and trying to cool the fever which burned within. Sweyn was delirious by then and would not lie still. Like a man racked with pain, he tossed and turned, moaning and crying out aloud. Although I knew there was a chance the fever would break I had no way of knowing when. My duty was to return to Athelney with all haste, but that would mean leaving Sweyn knowing that, come nightfall, his fevered body would be torn apart by wolves. The only other option was to lay him across the saddle of his horse and hope he was strong enough to survive the journey. There seemed little chance of that and besides, with him on the horse and myself on foot we would travel much too slowly.

Although I had come to like Sweyn I knew then what I had to do. I recalled how much Edwin had regretted his compassion when we tended Aelwyn after the battle at Chippenham and was not about to make the same mistake. I therefore resolved to act swiftly before I changed my mind, though dreaded the very thought of what I was about to do. It was sin in anyone's eyes and although I had strayed far from my religious convictions, I knew that this one act would render me beyond redemption.

Lifting Sweyn so that he was sitting up, I comforted him as best I could by trying to find the words to explain what I was about to do. In truth I knew the merchant was beyond hearing anything I said, lost in some deep recess of his fevered mind and barely conscious. Yet the sound of my voice seemed to soothe him. I uttered a short prayer then, with my hand trembling, I reached for his knife and without letting him see it, swept the blade across Sweyn's throat.

'God have mercy on us both,' I whispered to myself as I sat there shaking, both arms wrapped around the Norseman, cradling him as I watched the life flow from him.

Chapter Eighteen

I confess that I wept as I watched Sweyn die. Then, as my sorrow and my urge for repentance merged, I felt nothing but a deep-seated rage which made me cry out against the injustice of it all.

I cannot say how long I stayed with Sweyn but once roused from my sorrow I became aware of two men edging towards me from the forest. They came like shadows, silent and menacing, one of them already untying Sweyn's horse which he clearly meant to steal and the other eyeing up the saddle against which the Norseman's body still rested.

These were ragged men, brutish and dirty from living rough. I guessed at once they were part of the band which had robbed Sweyn now come to claim the rest of their prize.

The one now leading the horse looked a simple fellow. He held his head to one side and his face twitched so that his eye seemed to flicker. Although he carried a spear I sensed that he posed little danger. The other man was a different matter. He was older and taller, with long straight hair and a string of animal claws which he wore about his neck. He held a sword which looked old and tarnished but which I had no doubt that he meant to use.

Being in no mood for them to try me, I gently released Sweyn's body then reached for the staff I had picked up after hiding from the wolves. 'What do you want of me?'

I demanded, rising to my feet then picking up Sweyn's knife as well and tucking it into my belt.

The one with the sword grinned. 'What have you got?' he asked.

'Nothing for you!' I shouted disdainfully. 'Unless you've a liking for the feel of my staff across your back.'

The man laughed then glanced at his companion. 'Two against one, boy,' he said coldly. 'You can give me that knife then leave or you can take your chances. Which is it to be?'

I hurriedly assessed the odds. These men were not alone of that I was certain for Sweyn had been hit by an arrow, yet neither carried a bow. But where were the others? I guessed these two had been sent on ahead to retrieve the horse leaving the others to follow. If so, time was not on my side.

All Edwin had taught me came to mind; I could almost hear his words: *Show no fear. Pick your ground then make them come to you.*

Instinctively I stepped away from Sweyn's body to give myself more room. 'You're lucky,' I said boldly. 'I never kill more than one man in a single day and this one got here first. Mind, I could make an exception for the likes of you.'

The man with the sword began to circle around me. 'Oh, the likes of us, is it?' he mocked. 'And what would that be coming from a wretch like you?'

Then I remembered the ragged clothes I was wearing as a disguise, none the better for all I had endured during the previous few days. 'Don't be fooled,' I warned. 'I'm a Saxon warrior and I serve my King. If you have business with me then let's be done with it. If not stand aside, for I have a duty to perform and will not be detained.'

The man made a mock bow. 'Oh, don't let us hinder you, good sir. I mean it's not for the likes of us to stand between a great Saxon warrior and his duty, now is it?' He was creeping closer as he spoke, edging nearer step by step hoping it would not be noticed. Every so often he glanced back at his friend, but I was not fooled; I knew the rogue would strike as soon as he was close enough.

I judged him to be strong but unmannered with the sword. In fact without it he would have been a dangerous man to confront but with it he seemed unbalanced and ill at ease. Even so, when he did strike he almost took me by surprise, lurching forward and trying to bring the sword down upon my head. It was so sudden that I barely had time to react but did so by stepping aside and jabbing the end of my staff hard into the man's side. These were the skills I had practised with Edwin so often they had become second nature – *avoid and strike, strike and prevail.* Thus I followed through quickly with another jab into the small of the man's back then struck him hard across the shoulders. The wretch gave out a stifled groan then folded forwards, dropping the sword as he sank to his knees. Within moments I was standing behind him with the knife pressed against his throat.

'We meant no harm,' he pleaded, swallowing hard against the pressure of the blade. 'We're just—'

'Hold your tongue!' I ordered, secretly surprised at my own skill. But Edwin's words were still there: *The fight is not done until all the swords are sheathed.* Out of the corner of my eye I had seen the other man drop the reins of the horse and take up his spear with both hands.

'Come on!' I challenged him. 'Try me if you've the stomach for it!'

He was a simple soul and looked uncertain.

'What's it to be?' I pressed. 'Are we done or shall I slit this rogue's throat then treat with you?'

The man kept circling, eyeing his friend's sword, which lay on the ground between us but was well beyond his reach.

'Go on,' I dared him. 'Make your move and I shan't need to find anyone to kill tomorrow or the day after.'

At last the wretch seemed to accept the fight was done. He lowered the spear and began to back away. 'All right, but for the love of God spare my friend!' he pleaded. 'He meant no harm.'

I lowered the knife then half pushed, half kicked my hostage so that he fell face down onto the ground. 'Like I said, you're lucky. I've already killed a man today. Besides I save my killing for the Vikings. Now who are you and what's your business here?'

Neither of them seemed inclined to speak, so I prodded the man on the ground with my foot. 'So you meant no harm. You wanted only to kill me and steal my horse!' I scoffed, picking up the sword and examining it. It was indeed an old weapon, the blade being pitted and rusted and the hilt broken. I guessed he had probably found it on a battlefield where it had been either lost or discarded. 'I say again who are you? And where are you from?'

Still they were silent.

'You must live somewhere!' I demanded angrily. Then I raised the sword and pointed the blade at each of them in turn. 'Well if you have no names and live nowhere I'll offend no one even if I kill you both, will I? And if that's so I might just as well do so if only for the practice!'

At this the one on the ground spoke up. 'We live here, in the forest,' he managed. 'He was a slave sold at birth because of the affliction to his face which they feared was a spirit trapped within his head. I'm a convicted man. Innocent, but convicted just the same.'

I laughed. 'Convicted for what? Stealing?'

'I never stole!' he protested. 'I would have paid if I could but I was hungry and...' His words faltered when he could see I was unimpressed. 'Now we live as best we can but answer to no name so that none shall know us or our kin.'

Many good men had taken to living rough, some as refugees from the Vikings, others to escape punishment or slavery. As for those two, I felt sorry for them both. I tucked the sword into my belt making it plain that I intended to keep it. 'Get up and go in peace,' I said quietly. 'We all of us have a right to live as best we may.'

The hostage did not need telling twice and quickly scrambled to his feet. 'You're letting us go?' he asked suspiciously as he brushed the twigs and grass from his clothes.

'Is it not the Christian way to forgive?' I said. 'And we're all good Christians here are we not?'

Both men hurriedly crossed themselves.

'So we are, brother, but...'

'But what?' I asked. 'You expect no mercy in this world?'

'Nor the next,' he said, shaking his head in disbelief. 'At least, not for the likes of us.'

I laughed. 'Ah! The likes of you! Well let me tell you this, you and I are subjects of the same King.'

The man thought for a moment. 'Which King is that?' he asked.

'Why Lord Alfred of course,' I replied thinking it strange he needed to ask. 'Who else?'

The man shrugged. 'Kings come and go. First we are subject to one then to another. In the end it makes no difference to us, Viking or Saxon. Anyway we heard Alfred had fled abroad.'

'Alfred will not leave this land until he has driven the Vikings from our shores!' I boasted. 'On that you may depend. And when he has there'll be justice for all, you mark my words. Now I must be gone for I have my duty to attend to.'

One of them fetched the horse and re-saddled it for me then tied Sweyn's bag to its back. It occurred to me that perhaps I had no right to take the horse, for in killing Sweyn I had broken my part of our bargain even though I had acted from compassion, not malice or greed. After all, the merchant had pleaded not to be left to the mercy of wild beasts. Besides, I knew that if I left the horse the two robbers would take it readily enough, so in a way I was stealing it from them. That said, I could not bring myself to leave Sweyn's body untended.

'I've spared your lives,' I said to the two men. 'Now you can repay me. Take time and bury this man as best you can. He died well and I saw in him a courage any Saxon should admire. He wears a ring which you may keep for your trouble. Do I have your word you'll complete the task for I've not the time to do it myself?'

They both nodded so I left them to it, intent on riding to Athelney as quickly as I could, stopping only to retrieve

Cedric's axe along the way, which I hoped would suffice as proof that I had indeed slain the traitor.

* * * * *

Like all Saxons of noble birth, I was trained to ride almost from the moment I could stand. However most of my riding had been bareback on sturdy farm animals and certainly I wasn't used to a Viking saddle. Thus I walked the beast slowly at first until feeling confident enough to urge him on until we came to the place I recognised as that where Cedric's body lay.

It was all much as I had left it except that as Sweyn had said, the corpse had been badly mauled and half eaten. The mail vest had offered little protection against teeth and claws, having been simply ripped aside to allow Cedric's innards to be pulled from his gut. His eyes had also been pecked out by crows and one arm now lay gnawed on the ground a few paces off. It was an awful sight, as bad as any I had seen on the battlefield. My only thought was how this man who had seemed such a giant when alive now looked so small in death. Yet I felt no pity. Instead I busied myself searching for the axe. All I could remember was dropping it and running in a blind panic, yet it was nowhere to be seen.

In the end I assumed that perhaps Sweyn had taken it and that it was among his things stolen by the robbers. Either way I could ill afford to waste more time searching, so considered whether I should cut off Cedric's head and take that as my proof instead. In the end I decided to leave things as they were. If anyone needed proof they could view Cedric's body for themselves. With that I remounted and rode with all speed to Athelney.

* * * * *

I was not surprised when two of Ethelnorth's men intercepted me just before I entered the marshes, riding down hard on me and forcing me to stop. One of them seized the reins of my horse whilst the other held out a spear to threaten me.

'Who are you and what's your cause?' demanded the one with the spear.

'I am Matthew, son of Edwulf,' I said proudly. 'I have urgent news for Lord Alfred and must pass.'

The guard settled back in his saddle but kept the spear levelled at my chest. He was at once suspicious, for few Saxons of high birth would be given a name not derived from that of his father. 'What is this news?' he challenged.

'What I have to report is for Lord Alfred's ears alone,' I protested indignantly. 'Now let me pass.'

With his companion still holding the reins he felt safe enough to lower the spear a little. 'We do not know you, Matthew, son of Edwulf. And our orders are to let no man pass.'

The other man laughed. 'And no boy either, however bold he holds himself to be!'

'Then I shall tell Alfred that Lord Ethelnorth's orders have delayed the news he charged me to bring with all speed.'

'How do you know the name of Lord Ethelnorth?' asked the man with the spear.

'I'm known to him,' I explained. 'And to other noble Saxons. Would you still detain me?'

The guard seemed less sure of himself at this but was still not convinced. 'What else should we do with a "noble Saxon" who's dressed in rags and rides a horse with a Viking saddle? We shall take you to Lord Ethelnorth and see whether he knows you or not. And if he doesn't, boy, I'll skewer your weedy frame and pin you to a tree!'

I leaned forward to look him in the eye. 'If you would spill Saxon blood with a Saxon spear then I must doubt that you serve Lord Ethelnorth at all.'

The guard's horse backed away a little and he urged it forward so that its flanks rubbed against those of my mount. It was the other man who then spoke. 'The boy's defiant enough to be a Saxon.'

'Of course I'm a Saxon. Would a Viking ride into Alfred's camp alone? How far off is Ethelnorth?'

'Do you think we'd tell you that?'

I yanked the reins of my horse free from the man's grasp and spurred the beast with my heels, kicking its flanks as hard as I could. Startled, it reared up putting both men off balance as their own horses shied away. As they struggled to control their mounts I rode between them then turned and drew the sword from my belt.

'Hold!' I screamed at them. 'I am Matthew, Christened Edward and I serve Lord Alfred. Even now I return to his camp in haste and cannot be detained. If you doubt me then come with me. There my brother Lord Edwin shall answer for me.'

Once they had calmed their horses they turned them to face me.

'I'm Matthew,' I repeated defiantly. 'Son of—'

'You spoke of your brother Lord Edwin,' said one of the men.

'Yes.'

'Then the matter's easily resolved.'

'How so?' I asked.

He produced a horn which he carried on a lanyard across his back and held it up. 'Because Lord Edwin rides with us and can be summoned by this horn.' It was the sort used in battle rather than hunting, offering a shrill note that could be heard more easily above the din of combat. He put it to his lips and sounded two long notes.

The other Saxon, becoming more amiable, started towards me. 'But we'd best hold your weapon till he arrives. As a token.'

I knew better than to give away my sword. 'I will lower it but no man shall take it from me,' I said.

The man understood that and nodded his agreement. 'You're a true Saxon, I see that plain enough. And a brave one.'

I laid the sword across my lap and smiled. 'And I shall sleep better when I reach Athelney knowing the road is so well guarded.'

Almost at once we heard the sound of a horn some way off and so waited until Edwin eventually appeared with three riders. He could scarce believe his eyes when he saw me. We both dismounted and rushed to greet each other.

'You're safe!' said Edwin, almost crushing me as he clasped both arms about my shoulders. He released me then stood back as if to check that I was all in one piece. Satisfied, he slipped off the birth ring and gave it back to me, pressing it into my hand. 'It's good to have you back,' he said. 'But where's Cedric? Is he not with you?'

'Cedric's dead,' I said. 'I killed him. I would have brought his axe as proof but couldn't find it.'

I felt Edwin relax his grasp as he stared at me, clearly astonished.

I gave him no time to press more questions. 'He was a traitor,' I explained excitedly. 'He tried to kill me the first night after we left here.'

'This cannot be!' said Edwin.

The others had all drawn closer now and were hanging on my every word.

'Cedric was a mercenary in Guthrum's employ,' I continued quickly. 'It was he who killed the guards and opened the gates at Chippenham. He was intent upon telling Guthrum about our plans but he knew I'd prevent him so tried to murder me as I slept.'

'You slew Cedric?' said one of the two guards who had detained me.

'I used the knife you gave me,' I explained looking at Edwin. 'His body or what the wolves have not yet eaten lies but a few hours ride from here.'

'And what of this horse?' said the man who held the reins, his hand now stroking the beast's neck. 'How came you by this? It's a sturdy beast but has a Viking saddle. Did you kill its owner as well?'

I hesitated. 'I did. Though I wish I hadn't. But that's a long story and must wait for I have urgent news I must take at once to Lord Alfred in person.'

Chapter Nineteen

'Are you saying that you actually ventured into the Great Hall itself?' inquired Alfred as I made my report. The King was seated at a table in the open reading various documents which Ethelnorth had brought for him to construe but seemed much more interested in what I had to say.

'I did, sire. I pretended I was hungry and sang and danced for food to get past the guards at the gates.'

'And they couldn't see that you're the son of a noble Saxon Ealdorman?' he asked looking askance at the state of my clothes. There was more than a trace of irony in his voice but I knew he meant no offence. In fact I am certain he much admired the sheer audacity of my ploy.

'No, sire. After my fight with Cedric and my time in the forest I must have looked a wretched sight, but that was to my good. They eventually took me into the Great Hall where Guthrum was seated in your place. He had a map but I couldn't get close enough to read it.'

'Guthrum himself?' said Edwin, clearly impressed. 'You stood before him in person?'

'And dined from his table,' I boasted. 'I even sang to him about our great Saxon heroes! In truth I was more afraid of his two companions than of him. One of them had a dreadful scar which cut across his face. The other had fearsome eyes and hair almost the colour of copper. I wouldn't want to meet either one of them again.'

'The one with the scar, did you hear his name?' asked Ethelnorth.

'No, but at one point I thought they were going to kill me and Mildrith, the wife of that tinker who betrayed us, helped me to escape. She told me she thought his name was "Ubba" and that he had a band of men and several longships. He—'

Alfred didn't let me finish. 'Ubba! God save us if it's truly him! He's a butcher who even the Vikings fear to cross!'

'His men are berserkers,' explained Ethelnorth solemnly. 'They kill without mercy. Men, women or children; it makes no difference to them. Believe me, I've fought against these warriors and know how terrible they can be. They strip themselves to the waist to reveal heathen symbols drawn on their bare chests. Emboldened by the vapours of some foul fungus which they imbibe, they come down upon you wailing and screeching like wild animals. With neither mail vest nor helmet you'd think they'd be easy to slay but I tell you this, they fight like men possessed. It's as though whilst their bodies labour with sword or axe their minds are in another place making them impossible to fight. God alone knows who this other man is that Matthew saw but if Guthrum is keeping such company as Ubba we'll all be sorely tested!'

They were all silent for a moment then Alfred spoke to me again. 'What of the defences at Chippenham?' he asked.

'They've repaired some of the breaches to the ramparts, sire,' I replied. 'But poorly so. The southern gates are so badly damaged they've nailed them shut. A few repairs have also been carried out to the Vill itself but otherwise they've not troubled to make good much of the damage from the battle. As for the western gates, they could be closed against an attack but they would need a buttress to secure them properly. There were only a few guards there and they hardly cared who came or went. Most of the other men were either drunk or asleep and all are grown fat and lazy. They whore and drink and pay little mind to fighting save to boast to each other of their deeds. Also they must now take the cattle beyond the river if they are to feed them properly. With a few men even I could drive off the whole herd and...'

'But could you say how many men there were?' pressed Edwin.

I shook my head. 'I'm sorry my Lords. I dared not risk staying long enough to count them, but there were many more than I expected. It seemed as though every Viking in the land has gathered there. So many that they were forced to spread out into the settlement itself just to find a place to sleep!'

'You did well to learn as much as you did,' conceded Alfred. 'But you're certain Cedric didn't have time to betray us?'

'Yes, sire. He revealed his treachery the first night after we left. He told me himself he had yet to inform Guthrum of our plans and I killed him before he could do so.'

'Then you did well,' said Alfred. 'At least we now know what we're up against.'

Edwin looked thoughtful. 'Sire, is it not strange that Guthrum has done so little? He's had all winter to put the defences into good repair and ready his men. Does he not fear an attack from us?'

'Why should he?' queried Alfred. 'He knows we're too few to risk attacking the Vill so does not think to fight us there. Instead I fear he'll send Ubba and his berserkers to root us out.'

'Then he'll have to get past my men first!' said Ethelnorth proudly. 'All the roads are being watched. We'll see him coming long before he gets here.'

'But what about the rivers?' suggested Alfred. 'Are you guarding them as well? There are many which are wide enough and deep enough for Ubba's ships. That way he could easily slip past you and get close enough to strike right into the heart of this swamp.'

We could all see at once that Alfred was right. Also, because the causeway was the only way in or out, Ubba had only to secure that for us to be trapped.

'But why would he pay Ubba and his horde to do what he could so easily do himself?' asked Ethelnorth. 'From what Matthew's said, once Guthrum knows where we are he has more than enough men to surround and overwhelm us.'

'Because he means to keep his army intact,' explained Alfred. 'If Ubba finds and destroys us the lands Guthrum will have promised him will be a cheap price to pay for victory over all Wessex. Besides, he has nothing to lose. If we prevail he'll not have to pay Ubba anything and will know exactly where to find us.'

Osric spoke next. 'Then I say we should strike camp and be gone from here. Someone's bound to betray us sooner or later and—'

'If we run now we're beaten,' mused Edwin. 'We'll be pursued and must eventually be run to ground. Besides, none of the Ealdormen will rally their men to join an army in retreat.'

'I didn't say we should run!' said Osric sharply. 'Only that we should pick our ground and ready ourselves before we face an enemy such as this!'

'This is our ground,' said Edwin firmly. 'And if he does come here at least it can be defended.'

Osric shook his head. 'Defended for how long? A week? A month? Sooner or later we'll have to surrender. It's said these berserkers drink the blood of their enemies then roast their bodies on a spit and eat them. Is that how you would meet your maker, Edwin? With a Viking chewing on your roasted bones?'

Alfred raised his hands to stem the argument. 'Ethelnorth, how long would it take to raise enough men to fight Ubba?'

It was a difficult question and Ethelnorth stroked his beard thoughtfully before he answered. It was the sworn responsibility of the Ealdormen to each levy men to serve the King from those thanes within their charge, so the answer depended on their loyalty as much as anything else. 'Not soon enough,' he replied at last. 'As I've said before, there are few who still believe you can win this war. Most of the Ealdormen remain loyal but many would now rather make peace with the Vikings as those in Mercia and Northumbria have done. Those who could be persuaded are spread far and wide, so unless we can be sure of victory I fear we're on our own. And if word gets out that you plan to fight Ubba...'

'Then we keep that to ourselves,' said Alfred coldly. 'That would be an unholy alliance: Guthrum and Ubba. And you're right, the men are nervous enough about fighting Guthrum again. If they learn of Ubba's hand in this we'll be lost before we start.'

'Could we not buy them off again?' suggested Osric. 'Surely we have only to better Guthrum's offer and Ubba would be less inclined to fight.'

'With what?' asked Alfred. 'Guthrum has our lands and our cattle. Have you enough gold? Besides Guthrum will have promised Ubba more lands than he can farm. Every man with him will be rich beyond their wildest dreams. All they have to do is find us and it's theirs for the taking. We could not begin to compete with an offer such as that.'

'So what's to be done?' I asked, worried by all this talk of what seemed to be a hopeless situation.

'We die in glory!' said Edwin proudly. 'We dig in here and fight to the last man. As Saxons should!'

Alfred put his hand on Edwin's shoulder. 'And I know you would,' he said fondly. 'And if it comes to that we shall stand together you and I, shoulder to shoulder. But there is another way. I am convinced that Ubba will use his longships to attack us; it is his only viable option. He will seek to close upon us quietly, thinking to take us by surprise. We should therefore attack his forces as they sail up the river. He will not be expecting that.'

The words stunned everyone into silence.

'He would then be at his weakest,' continued Alfred carefully, knowing not everyone would approve of what he was about to suggest. 'Whilst his vessels are unable to manoeuvre in the narrow waters and his men are committed to their oars to row upstream, that's when we should strike. There are places we could set our trap and as they row past we could fill their ships with arrows. With God's will we might prevail.'

'What!' exclaimed Osric. 'Are we reduced to setting traps to fight our foes?'

'Does it matter how he dies?' asked Edwin. 'For if we do slay Ubba, every Saxon in this realm would rise behind us like a storm.'

'Exactly!' agreed Alfred. 'We can use Guthrum's plan against him. Not only will victory over Ubba serve to swell our ranks, it will unite our spirits. And think of Guthrum ill prepared and expecting others to fight his battle for him. When they see Ubba has been defeated his troops will be despondent. When he's weak and we are strong, that will be our best chance for victory!'

None of the others present much liked the plan for it went against their Saxon creed, yet all could see they had no choice.

'What numbers can we count on?' asked Edwin.

Ethelnorth did some hurried calculations. 'As we stand there are now but thirty men here who could be called upon to fight, with perhaps one or two of the women who would stand with us.'

'Not enough,' observed Alfred ruefully. 'Ubba will have three times that number at least.'

Then an idea came to me. 'There are other bands who, like us, have taken shelter in these marshes and in the forests beyond,' I suggested. 'I met two such men earlier today. Not warriors I grant you, but with training they could swell our ranks.'

'Yes, Matthew,' said Ethelnorth. 'I've met some of them myself. They're desperate souls, mostly runaway slaves and outcasts or men with a price upon their head. As such I doubt they could be trusted.'

Edwin considered this. 'Perhaps. But they might join us if promised freedom or a pardon in return. With them we would number what? Perhaps fifty or more?'

'And my men,' said Ethelnorth. 'They'll want to be a part of this.'

'The courage of your men is beyond question but I have other work for them,' explained Alfred. 'Some must watch our back in case Guthrum is planning to double-cross Ubba. He might take the chance to attack whilst we're locked in combat. That way he's rid of us and has to pay Ubba nothing. Believe me, such treachery is not beyond him. Thus I would have you send two men to Chippenham. Bid them ride like the wind to warn us should Guthrum leave the Vill. Also send others to watch the coast for sight of Ubba's longships. We must know which river he takes if we're to set our ambush. With the rest of your men you must continue to raid and harry the Vikings just as you've been doing, for if you cease Guthrum will surely suspect something. Also build upon the chain that will summon all the Saxons to my side the moment we've beaten Ubba. That will be the time to strike at Guthrum and I shall need every man that can be mustered.'

'So it comes down to just fifty warriors,' said Edwin. 'Fifty men to fight more than twice their number of the most dreadful heathens ever to set foot upon this land.'

Alfred nodded. 'Ah yes, Edwin, but you're forgetting one thing. These are fifty Saxon warriors. And what's more, they're fifty Saxon warriors with nothing left to lose!'

* * * * *

'You gave a good account of yourself,' admitted Edwin proudly when he and I were alone.

We were seated on the ground as I examined the leather bag which had been strapped to Sweyn's saddle. Having untied it, I emptied out the contents but they did not amount

245

to very much – a blanket, some utensils, a touchstone for testing gold and, wrapped in a soft leather cloth, a small pair of scales which Sweyn would have used in his trade. 'I'm sure it was Edmund at the gates,' I said, sifting through the items one by one. 'He was watching as I left but I didn't dare go back for him.'

'And you were right not to,' Edwin assured me. 'Your first duty was to your King and to the rest of us. The information you brought back is vital to our cause. In fact without it we might all have been taken by surprise and quickly overwhelmed.'

I felt the weight of the bag and realised it contained something more. When I looked inside I found another section at the bottom which had been loosely stitched. I borrowed Edwin's knife and gently cut the stitching then tipped up the bag. When I saw what tumbled out I could scarce believe my eyes.

In all it amounted to a small fortune in gems and fine jewellery. This included several valuable rings and cloak pins. One item in particular was a brooch delicately fashioned from ivory traced with silver in the pattern of a flower. Meanwhile Edwin picked up a leather pouch crammed full of precious stones. They were mostly small emeralds and pieces of jet but included some amber beads, all of which had probably been prised from the covers of books looted from various churches during Viking raids. We also found some thin ingots of silver which Sweyn would have used instead of coin and that were probably melted down from yet more booty.

'He was a trader,' I explained, unable to believe the size of the hoard.

'Then he was a good one!' exclaimed Edwin. 'You said he was on his way to see Guthrum?'

'So he said. He needed his permission to trade. Do you think this treasure was intended as a gift?'

'As like as not some of it was,' agreed Edwin examining a handful of gems and letting them trickle through his fingers. 'But now it's rightfully yours.'

I was not so sure. 'Having taken Sweyn's life it doesn't seem fitting I should profit from his death,' I ventured.

'Better that than leaving this treasure to waste. Besides you killed him out of duty not greed.'

'But supposing he has family who are in need?'

'Well even if he does you can't hope to find them now. If you hadn't taken these things those two rogues you met would have done so soon enough. Besides, most of this has been looted from Saxon homes and churches so who's to say to whom it rightfully belongs? What I can't understand is why anyone would carry this much treasure when travelling alone. Was he not afraid of being robbed?'

I had to agree it did seem strange. 'Perhaps he had an escort when he started out,' I suggested.

'Perhaps,' said Edwin. 'But I sense there's more to this than meets the eye. Did he wear a ring?'

I remembered that he did and described it as best I could, recalling that it had a cross, though not a Christian emblem, in the centre of which was a single stone.

Edwin seemed intrigued. 'I think that ring was like a passport,' he concluded. 'A symbol which ensured no Viking would ever raise a sword against him.'

'Then it's a pity for him that the robbers didn't know that!'

'He was obviously used to travelling alone and knew how to do so quietly. You say he had no sword but I suspect he was a skilled warrior. I have known men who have learned skills which mean they need no weapons in order to defend themselves.'

'That still doesn't explain why he carried so much treasure.'

'Why to buy information of course,' said Edwin as though it were obvious. 'These gems are all small stones, each enough to loosen someone's tongue.'

I was astonished. 'You mean Sweyn was a spy?'

'Of sorts,' agreed Edwin. 'Perhaps he was sent by Guthrum to discover what he could of Alfred's plans. It would be the perfect cover to travel under the guise of being a trader who could venture into settlements without arousing suspicion, particularly as he could speak our language.'

I recalled how the traitor Goda had been paid handsomely for the information he gave and had to admit it made more sense than Sweyn being a simple trader who just happened to have a small fortune stashed in his saddle bag. 'I still liked him,' I managed weakly.

'And why not? He was just like us in that he served his liege. After all, you went to Chippenham to find out about Guthrum's plans and we saw no disgrace in that. But if Sweyn was a spy, then in killing him you've done service to our cause. So just be thankful, for now you're not only a warrior but a rich one at that. You have a sword and a horse and all this treasure. What more could you want?'

I hesitated before I answered. 'Am I a warrior?' I asked.

'You are. And you could be a good one if you put your mind to it and keep that righteous streak of yours in check.'

Suddenly my path in life seemed clear. 'Then perhaps that's the road I'm meant to travel. But what about my vows, I'll need to renounce them.'

Edwin picked up another handful of gems. 'Some of these may help to persuade the good abbot to release you. I never met one yet who could resist a generous donation!'

'I shall also give some to Emelda,' I said. 'Her plight is something which has worried me and I would ease it if I could.'

Edwin looked at me clearly stunned by the suggestion. 'There's nothing you can do to help her,' he said flatly.

'I could buy her freedom. I promised her mother I would try and am obliged to keep my word, not least because she saved my life. I'm sure that if I spoke to Alfred he would...'

Edwin was looking at me strangely. 'There are some things you cannot buy even with this much wealth. You may give Emelda her freedom but having now laid with almost every man in this camp you can never buy back her honour. She's fit for nothing but to remain as a slave and a whore and you'll never change that whatever price you pay.'

* * * * *

Despite Edwin's counsel, I felt compelled to see Emelda. I was not sure what I would say to her but felt I should at least tell her what had become of her parents. When I reached her small hut on the far edge of the island I was grateful to find she was alone. Nervously I went inside as, having not visited her there before, I was not quite sure what to expect.

'So you've come at last,' said Emelda. She was in her bed, naked but for a blanket draped across her body.

'N-no,' I stammered. 'At least not for...'

She grinned. 'Not for what, Matthew?' she said teasing me cruelly.

'I came to give you news for I saw your mother when I went to Chippenham.'

Emelda's expression changed. 'So?' she shrugged.

I was surprised at her reaction. 'Do you not want to know how she fares?'

Emelda turned her head away from me. 'Why should I care?' she said. 'She's nothing to me now.'

'But she's still your mother. She—'

'She abandoned me. Is that what a mother is supposed to do? Abandon her daughter to a life as a whore.'

Anxious to comfort the girl, I knelt beside the cot. 'She wanted only what she hoped would be a better life for you.'

'And this is what she calls a better life?'

I did not answer at first. 'Her fate is much the same as yours,' I managed at last. 'Except the Vikings treat her badly.'

As Emelda turned to face me again I noticed that one of her eyes was red and only half open. When I looked closer, I saw bruises to her arm and to the side of her face. Embarrassed, I said nothing.

'Are you saying my mother is also a whore?' said Emelda, laughing.

I nodded.

'Then there's justice in that. And what of my father?'

Again I hesitated, not sure how to tell her he was dead.

'They killed him, didn't they?' she said sounding almost pleased. 'So the old fool got what he deserved as well!'

'You mustn't say such things! Whatever wrong he did he was still your father. Remember these are cruel times and we each manage as best we can.'

Emelda was smiling again. 'Yes Matthew, we each do what we can.' As she spoke the blanket slipped revealing her naked breast. When she saw me staring at it she pulled the blanket down to reveal the other one then reached out and drew me to her.

Although I protested weakly I was lost from the moment I felt the closeness of her body. I had not been held by a woman since my mother died and even then, it was not like that.

* * * * *

Word of my new-found wealth spread quickly and many came to congratulate me. Yet despite all their good wishes the camp suddenly seemed so very small to me that I had to get away. Without a word to Edwin, I persuaded the guard at the water's edge to take me across to the causeway on the pretext that I wanted to speak with the man to whom I had lent Sweyn's horse.

In reality so much had happened that my thoughts simply swamped my head; thoughts I needed to confront but dared hardly admit existed, even to myself. The issues which had previously troubled me – leaving the Church and becoming a warrior – were now even more complicated because of my wealth and because of what had happened between me and Emelda.

Of course I should have known better but with my mind in such turmoil I mistakenly wandered further from the causeway than I intended. As was almost bound to happen, I soon found myself in great difficulty as the ground became too soft to bear my weight. With every step my feet sank deeper and deeper until I was up to my knees in soft, stinking mud.

When I tried to turn and go back the mud seemed to suck me in still further, as though drawing me down into the very bowels of the earth. Reaching out, I managed to grab a clump of reeds with which to pull myself free but they came away in my hand. Before I knew it I was buried up to the waist and unable to move my legs at all. By turning onto my back I almost managed to lift one leg free but the mud still pulled and sucked at me until, in panic, I called out hoping someone might hear.

Although I knew there was little chance of there being anyone close enough to help I called again and again, my voice getting more desperate as the mud began to press so hard upon my chest that I could barely breathe. It was as though the bog was trying to devour me, sucking me into its putrid guts like a snake swallowing a frog. I knew I would quickly reach the point beyond which there was any hope of survival, for once my arms were covered I would be unable to help myself at all. Instinctively I pulled them clear and held them above my head, then looked around. My only chance lay with a large log which floated just beyond my reach, albeit it half submerged. Using all my strength, I heaved myself around to face it then leaned forward desperately stretching out to grasp it. I managed to ease myself closer but was still sinking so that only my head and arms were clear of the mire. It needed all the strength I had but at last I did manage to touch the log with just the tips of my fingers.

Clawing at it, I eased it closer until I could drape my arm around it, then hung there for a moment, gratefully gulping air into my lungs. Relieved, I put the other arm over the log as well and tried to haul myself up. Although my shoulders were clear the rest of me was still stuck fast. All I could do was cling to the log and push it, bit by bit, until I could at last feel something solid beneath my feet. From there I managed to ease myself from the bog until I lay on the bank exhausted.

It had been a sharp lesson. I had heard men speak of the dangers of the marsh and how those who ventured in alone were often never seen again. The stories all told of spirits and demons, but I knew then the marsh needed no such tenants, for it had enough power of its own to swallow a man complete.

The light was beginning to fail and I was wet to the skin, my clothes caked in stinking mud and slime. Unable to face the prospect of a cold night in the open I decided that whatever the dangers I would retrace my steps to the causeway.

I was blessed with a full moon which greatly helped to light my path and, although it was not easy to find the way, I managed well enough. As I went I began to rehearse the words I would say to Edwin to excuse myself for having behaved so foolishly but, when I reached the causeway, no explanations were needed. I was greeted by men carrying torches but they were not out searching for me. They had been sent to find Lord Ethelnorth and to summon him to the camp, for our beloved Bishop Eahlstan had been taken unto God.

Chapter Twenty

I was anxious to offer my apology to Edwin for having been so foolish but, when I arrived back at camp, my brother was just relieved to see me safe.

'You needed time to yourself,' he acknowledged as he embraced me. 'I take it you've heard the news about Bishop Eahlstan?'

'I have,' I said. 'Those I met on the causeway could speak of nothing else. I gather he passed peacefully from this world.'

'Aye. And there's not a man or woman in the camp not saddened by the news. Alfred has decreed that his body shall be taken to the Abbey at Exeter for burial and Ethelnorth has been summoned to escort it there.'

'But what of our preparations for the attack on Ubba?' I asked. 'Surely we dare not delay that however much we grieve?'

Edwin shook his head. 'You're right but it seems no one has the stomach for such matters at a time like this.'

Even as we spoke the women were lovingly preparing the old man's body, washing it ready for burial. When they were finished it would be dressed and laid out on a trestle so that everyone could pay their last respects.

Meanwhile Edwin and I walked together to the Vill where I stripped off my muddy tunic. When I had dried myself I pulled a cloak about my shoulders and settled down beside the fire hoping my clothes would dry by morning. I was tempted to put on my old habit but somehow it no longer seemed right to wear it.

The next morning we each took our turn to kneel at the Bishop's feet and offer prayers. As I bent to kiss the gold crucifix which had been placed in the Bishop's hands I fleetingly touched the dead man's skin and was instantly shocked that one who had exuded so much warmth in life could quickly grow so cold. I was also surprised to see how peacefully he seemed to rest, for although in my short life I had witnessed death in many guises I had never before seen one who had died of old age.

Brother Felix had, with others, kept vigil through the night and saw it as his duty to escort the good Bishop safely to his grave. He thus went with the solemn procession led by Ethelnorth which carried the body from our camp. As it was taken across the water on the raft all the Saxons stood in silent prayer until the column disappeared from view.

Once his body had been taken the spirit of the good Bishop seemed to leave us all as well. The camp became very subdued and all talk of fighting the Vikings was abandoned. Many saw the death as a bad omen whilst others felt it was a timely reminder from God that death waited for us all.

Realising how despondent we were, Alfred addressed us hoping to revive our flagging spirits. 'I feel the sorrow of our loss as much as any man,' he said. 'The good Bishop was a friend to me when I was young. He brought me here, to the fringes of these very marshes to hunt and I'm bound to say that I learned from him as much about the ways of man as I did about the ways of God. His was an inspiration which has served me well in these times of such great worry and we're bound to mourn our loss; it's only fitting that we should. But remember, he lived to a good age doing that which he loved best – serving God and the Holy Church. That was his duty and we best show our love and respect for him by doing ours. Thus we must continue with our efforts to defeat the Vikings. That pressing need was ever in his thoughts and for his sake if not our own we must not squander the chance we now have. So do not waste your tears. Instead work with me to honour this good man by avenging the Church he loved and served so well and by bringing peace to this troubled land.'

As ever they were fine, well-chosen words but many still seemed less than eager to rally to Alfred's cause. It was as though with the good Bishop dead and Brother Felix absent we were left hollow and empty, with all the fight gone out of us. Given that death was such a frequent visitor in all our lives it was touching that the loss of a single man could mean so much to so many.

* * * * *

The next day Edwin set about making preparations for the attack on Ubba's fleet. Men who were at first disinterested soon found solace in hard work and training. Others arrived at the camp to join us; some were men who had fought before and had good cause to fight again but most had been rounded up by Ethelnorth's men who, in his absence, had scoured the marshes and surrounding forests passing word that a pardon would be given to all who came to fight at Alfred's side. Better than the pardon was the prospect of plunder and booty, for the rumours had it we were to attack the rich merchants and traders who were supplying Guthrum's Vill at Chippenham. These rumours were no doubt fuelled by talk of the hoard I had taken from Sweyn. Only Edwin, Ethelnorth, Osric and I knew the truth – that Alfred was to fight Ubba and his feared army of berserkers!

Men drifted into the camp two or three at a time, most bringing their own weapons, albeit these were often crude items they had fashioned for themselves – spears, axes, bows, even pitchforks – until within three days we numbered sixty strong. Among them was Eadred, the warrior we had left in the care of the monks during the retreat from Chippenham so that his wound could be treated. His shoulder seemed to have healed but his arm was now immobile, making it impossible for him to wield a weapon, but still his return did much to lift our spirits.

Those who joined us also included many rogues who were either wanted men or runaway slaves. Whereas some among the original band seemed to feel they should not fight alongside such people, Alfred greeted each of these recruits personally, repeating to them face to face his promise of a pardon or freedom without ever asking the nature of their crime. To keep their spirits up he set them busy joining Ethelnorth's men on small raids so they would become used to fighting together and also so their strengths and weaknesses could be assessed. This they all relished for it brought small items of plunder which they saw as a taste of things to come.

* * * * *

It was Edwin who first suggested I should offer Sweyn's treasure to Alfred. 'Either that or you must find a place to hide it,' he warned. 'For there are now many strangers in this camp and not all are of noble worth.'

He was right and I knew it. Almost everyone had heard about my treasure and I couldn't possibly keep watch on it all the time. Alfred would need funds if and when the Vikings were defeated and if they weren't, all the treasure in the world would be of little use to me or anyone.

Having kept the brooch plus enough silver to secure the release of my vows, I handed the bag to Alfred.

The King was visibly moved when he looked inside. 'This is very generous,' he said. 'I've yet to thank you properly for having avenged our people for Cedric's treachery. Your courage does you great credit for in slaying him you may well have saved us all. Thus you've served me well in fighting for the peace we all crave so dearly. These trinkets shall hasten that end and as such are a welcome addition to our cause. I can never repay what you and your brother have given of yourselves, but for this treasure I will ensure you receive lands of even greater value once my realm is restored.'

As we walked away Edwin put his hand on my shoulder. 'A fool might say you gave your treasure to a wasted cause,' he observed. 'But I say this, Matthew. You've bought the favour of a King. Not only that, you've bought the favour of a King who may one day rule this land complete. A King who I firmly believe is destined to become the greatest Saxon King of all.'

* * * * *

During the days that followed few men in the camp seemed inclined to visit Emelda, either because it seemed wrong whilst they mourned the loss of the Bishop or because they were busy training or away on raids. I, however, went to see her every day. If Edwin disapproved he said nothing at that time, though I know there were many who commented aloud that having taken those few steps to reach Emelda's hut I had strayed a very long way from my Holy vows.

'What will become of me?' she asked one night as we lay together in the hut. Whilst I knew she welcomed my attentions she had not yet accepted her lot in life and probably never would. Yet she seemed more settled and less inclined to the erratic outbursts and ravings she had once been prone to.

I said nothing. My mind was still troubled by what I saw as yet another of my failings, this time one of the flesh. I knew it was a sin but I seemed unable to help myself. In fact I seemed to desire this girl more than I had ever desired anything before and the more I saw of her the more that desire grew strong. Yet I despised her as well. I despised her for the weakness she brought out in me and for the way the pleasures of her body had turned me even further from the ways of the Church. The guilt I felt at having decided to renounce my vows was heightened by the thought that with the death of Bishop Eahlstan and the absence of Brother Felix I should have been doing something to tend the men's spiritual needs. Instead I was revelling in the joys of the flesh.

Emelda sensed my disdain but seemed to understand. 'If your soul is troubled you should not come to me,' she said. Then her arm slid across my chest to draw me closer. 'But I find no sin in this. Out there, in the minds of men who would kill and rob each other is where you'll find true sin. Not here in the warmth of my embrace.'

I knew she was not beautiful; not like my sister had been or my mother. They both had a serene grace which somehow seemed pure and strong whereas Emelda was wild and wanton, careless with her favours. Yet she was all I wanted in a woman. 'I can never return to the Church now,' I complained as if that were all her fault.

'You were lost to the Church long before you lay with me. You said yourself that you wanted God to show you the path he intended you should follow. Well then, open your eyes, Matthew, for its clear enough for all to see that you were meant to be a warrior not a monk.'

And I knew she was right. Something inside me had indeed changed. The boy in me had become a man and the man in me knew exactly what I wanted as I pulled her towards me and took her yet again.

* * * * *

When Ethelnorth returned from escorting Bishop Eahlstan's body he brought with him a farmer named Ulbrecht who was a ceorl accused of having paid tax and homage to the Vikings, serving them as he should have served his Lord. The poor man was dragged before Alfred and forced to his knees then told to beg for mercy.

The punishment for such treachery was death and so although the evidence against the farmer was damning, Alfred gave him the chance to speak up for himself before passing sentence. Many who witnessed this thought it was more than he deserved, but he spoke well, seemingly unafraid as he stood up proudly and addressed us.

'My Lord, you speak of loyalty,' he said. 'Well I'm no Saxon. My father was a slave who earned his freedom fighting for your brother though he never called your cause his own. That has not changed and it matters not to me whether it be the Vikings or you Saxons who come to collect my levy for I pay it just the same. I give what's due to him that demands it and continue to scratch a meagre living from the soil. In my eyes one master is as bad as any other. Either way I pay and still my family starves.'

Ethelnorth, who was obliged to prosecute his charge against Ulbrecht, argued that the prisoner's execution would send a clear message to all who would aid our enemies. 'We must find those who will stand with us and those who will not,' he reasoned. 'For any man who prefers to keep the middle ground is as much our enemy as those who raise their swords against us. Whilst I would that you could pardon this man, if you set him free the life of every loyal Saxon may be forfeit for we can be betrayed by any who would profit from the Vikings' favour.'

Ulbrecht did not protest at this but seemed to accept that he was to be made an example of. Alfred thought long and hard before passing sentence but eventually ordained that the execution should proceed. 'If justice were the only issue here you would be punished severely but allowed to live,' he said wisely. 'But I do not yet command the hearts of my people and must use fear if I'm to rule at all. I wish it were not so but for now I have no choice but to let the people see that my authority is not to be rebuked nor my mercy taken for granted.'

Then he ordered Ulbrecht to be taken away for execution, which was a sign that he was troubled by the sentence he had passed as he wanted to spare the farmer the dishonour of being beheaded in front of his King.

For a moment Ulbrecht stared at Alfred scornfully, then he spat at the ground. 'That's for your Saxon justice,' he said bitterly. Then he spat again. 'And that's for your cursed Saxon cause! You bleed the people of this land to pay for your wars; you seize the crops we've laboured all year to grow; you drive off the stock we've reared and you take the stores we've set aside to see us through the winter. You seize them and pay us what you will, if you pay anything at all. And you expect us to be grateful. Now you'll take my life as well. And for what? Because I paid tax to a man who held a sword to my throat?'

At first no one knew quite what to say. Then Ethelnorth himself stepped forward and cuffed Ulbrecht across the face, striking him so hard that the farmer was knocked to the ground. 'You deserve to die for your insolence never mind your crime!' he said angrily. With that he drew his sword and raised it, waiting for Alfred's permission to strike.

Perhaps the farmer expected no mercy or perhaps he knew his guilt was even deeper than that for which he was charged; either way he faced death so bravely that it made an impression on us all. He was still on his knees but raised himself up so that his back was straight and his head held high, looking directly into Ethelnorth's eyes as he awaited the death blow.

Because of this courage there were many who might then have pleaded his cause, but he had gone too far. We all knew this, as did Alfred, and though it pained him, he nodded his approval for Ethelnorth to proceed.

'Prepare yourself!' ordered Ethelnorth but Ulbrecht just glared at him then spat at the ground once more.

'I'll not send you to your maker unresolved! I said prepare yourself!'

Still Ulbrecht did nothing.

Ethelnorth looked for guidance but no one knew what to do. 'Then may God forgive your sins,' he said aloud and, with that, swept the sword into the back of Ulbrecht's neck.

Mercifully Ethelnorth made a clean cut which severed the farmer's head at a single stroke. The body slumped to the ground and everyone stared at it in silence before two men dragged it away to be buried in a lonely grave somewhere in the dank marshes.

This small incident was only one of many, yet it marked the point at which every man in Wessex was forced to decide where he stood and, for those already committed to Alfred's cause, the point from which there could be no turning back.

Chapter Twenty-One

The crux of Alfred's plan was simple: he would line his men along both banks of the river and rain arrows down upon Ubba and his berserkers as they laboured at the oars of their longships. The problem was that there were only half a dozen bows in the camp at that time, which was hardly enough to produce the storm of arrows he had in mind.

'I'll furnish more from the settlements nearby,' Ethelnorth assured him. 'Almost every household will have one. But how will you persuade the men to use them as you intend?'

He and Edwin had been much concerned with this aspect of Alfred's plan for we Saxons were taught to look our enemy in the eye as we slew him, not cut him down with an arrow from behind a tree.

'We'll tell the men nothing until the time comes,' said Alfred. 'Just as we shall keep secret who it is they are to fight.'

'But they'll need to practise,' advised Edwin. 'Most will not have lifted a bow in months.'

Alfred was ahead of him on that. 'Rufus can provide whatever training is needed, for he has the skill. The men will work with him just as they'll work under you to practise with whatever hand weapons they have, be it sword, axe or spear. That way they'll suspect nothing.'

With that Rufus arrived looking tired and dishevelled having only just returned from a night spent hunting.

'Ah!' said Alfred greeting him. 'Have you secured enough food for our supper? And pray don't mention eels when you answer!'

We all laughed for with so little game on hand eels had become our staple diet to the point where we had all grown heartily tired of them.

'Sire, I've taken a deer from the forest and snared a good hare from the fields beyond the marsh. These will serve tonight but with now so many mouths to feed I fear that come tomorrow...'

Alfred waved away the suggestion. 'Well then eels it shall be tomorrow and I fear for many days yet to come as I now have other duties for you which will keep you here with us.'

Having been up all night Rufus was clearly tired, yet he still looked less than happy at the prospect of being confined to camp.

'I need you to train the men to handle a bow as a weapon. They'll each be compelled to spend some time with you to learn those skills. Teach them as best you can.'

'But, sire, we have but a handful of bows and few arrows...'

'Ethelnorth will provide more bows. As for the arrows, we shall set the women busy making more.'

Rufus still looked uncertain. 'But why?' he asked simply.

'That I cannot tell you at this time, but think that no slight upon yourself. Just oblige me in this for it's crucial to our cause.'

'Sire, I will. Of course I will but—'

'But what?' challenged Osric.

'Well, for a start, what will the women use to make the arrows?'

It was Ethelnorth who answered. 'The day after tomorrow my men will bring a supply of freshly cut shafts. They can set about fitting flights made from the feathers of a swan and arrowheads carved from bone.'

Rufus seemed satisfied with that. Although not as durable as arrowheads cast from metal they would suffice for a single shot, which was all that was needed in battle. In fact it was better if the arrows did blunt on impact for it meant they could not then be reused against us to any real effect. 'Such crude arrows will not be accurate,' he warned. 'Shafts cut at this time of the year will prove too green for that.'

Alfred just laughed. 'Even I cannot command the sap to stop rising in the trees!' he said. 'But it matters not, so long as the arrows are correctly flighted. They'll be loosed at such short range they'll not have time to pass astray and when they strike their mark will kill a Viking just as easily whether the shaft be seasoned or not.'

'Perhaps,' agreed Rufus. 'But bone will be of no use against mail vests or shields.'

'The Vikings will have neither when we attack,' Alfred assured him. 'But enough of this. The training must commence for we must be ready. All our lives depend upon it.'

* * * * *

True to his word, Ethelnorth provided the bows and three baskets full of freshly cut shafts for the arrows. Those who were not given a bow made slings from strips of leather, forging shot from the metal gained by melting down old tools. Casting the shot was a simple process by which a man pushed his thumb into the mud to make a small hole into which the molten metal was then poured. When set this produced a near perfect shot which in skilled hands was accurate enough even at some distance.

In addition to the bow or sling, each man would carry either an axe or a spear into battle, with those who had them also carrying a shield. Having fled from Chippenham in such haste only a few had helmets or mail vests.

For training they were divided into two groups, each with broadly the same number of men. Alfred himself commanded one group and Edwin the other. I was ordered to fight beside my brother and Ethelnorth was to remain in charge of his own levy with the various duties already assigned to them beyond the camp. The old warrior would have much preferred to take part in the battle itself but Alfred clearly considered his role as our protector much too important.

So it was just a question of waiting for Ubba to collect his longships and sail along the Severn. When he did he would keep close inshore to avoid any risk of heavy weather and thus Ethelnorth's men would be able to spot them and watch until it was clear which river they would take. Riders would then swiftly bring word so that we could prepare our ambush. Until then all at the camp continued daily to practise with their weapons whilst Ethelnorth harried the Vikings wherever he could find them. The women also did their bit by making yet more arrows and the men's spirits rose as the store of these grew higher. Our skills with the bow also improved with so much practice under the supervision of Rufus. He showed us that whilst it was true the arrows were not well made, their accuracy would suffice to wound or maim even at some distance if shot properly. In particular, he showed us how to hold four arrows in the hand and deftly slip them up into position one after the other so they could be loosed with barely a heartbeat between each shot. Whilst only a few men fully mastered that particular skill, all improved to the point where we could produce a storm of arrows almost at will.

Meanwhile, Edwin developed our fighting skills with whatever weapon each of us had.

'You've done well,' he said to me after one very arduous practice with the sword. Although I never once managed to disarm him I believe I tested him well enough. 'I think now you understand the science of it,' he praised. 'You've learned much from all your adventures.'

'I learned most from you,' I said, grateful for a rest.

Edwin smiled. 'No, I taught you how to fight, that's all. You taught yourself how to kill. That's something we learn only for ourselves.'

'Killing Cedric was easy,' I replied recalling the incident. 'But I'm not well disposed to the slaughter of men without good cause and only hope I shall find the courage again when the time comes.'

Edwin put his hand upon my shoulder. 'Courage will find you if you let it,' he assured me. 'You killed Cedric with pride, not because of it. That's the difference. What's more you learned mercy and compassion from that merchant or spy or whatever he really was.'

'You mean Sweyn?' I said thoughtfully. 'He was a good man. How strange I should willingly slay the one I thought to be my friend yet wish I could have spared the one who should have been my enemy.'

'God grant we may always know the difference,' mused Edwin. 'I wonder how many men I've killed who might have been my friend had I met them on different terms.'

'Like Edmund?' I suggested, for some reason calling the boy to mind. 'When I saw him at the gates of Chippenham he seemed to have made friends with the Vikings for he showed no sign of wanting to escape with me.'

'Then we should be pleased for him for we all need the company of friends and none more so than him, poor lad.' With that Edwin seemed to have something more to say but looked very uneasy. 'Speaking of friends, little brother, there's something I've been meaning to mention.'

I half sensed it would concern Emelda. 'What is it?' I asked.

'You're spending a lot of time with that girl. I can understand why but you must take care. There's much talk in the camp and I fear you're making a fool of yourself.'

'That's my business,' I snapped.

Edwin was shocked at my response. 'You carry our family name. That makes it my concern as well,' he said curtly. 'Tup her if you will, it's only natural that you should, but just remember she's both a whore and the daughter of a traitor…'

'If she's a whore it's because we made her one. And as for her father being a traitor, you said yourself that he had no choice.'

Edwin sensed he was on difficult ground. 'Perhaps,' he acknowledged. 'But the men are saying you're drawn to her like a bee to the flower.'

'That's nonsense!' I insisted. 'She's the only one here my age and—'

'And what?' demanded Edwin. 'Would you risk the good name of our father and that of our family for a whore? She thinks you're rich and knows you're of good stock so will do anything she can to snare you. Besides, remember you're still in Holy Orders.'

The last point touched a nerve and I was not sure what to say. I was about to argue that I was simply keeping my promise to Mildrith when I was interrupted by a man on the causeway shouting to be ferried across. As soon as he was fetched he went straight to Alfred where he knelt then spoke aloud of the news for which we all waited. Then it was as if all the furies of hell had been set loose at once.

* * * * *

'We travel north!' Alfred announced loudly, spurring all into action. 'Be ready to march within the hour! Edwin, I must speak with you.'

Men hurried to gather what they needed, made their farewells to loved ones and formed up ready to leave. There was an urgency about them that did them great credit, yet no panic.

'We march to Combwich,' Alfred told Edwin, though many others heard it as indeed he intended they should. 'We shall meet a small group of Vikings as they ford the river there.'

He made no mention of the fact that the 'small group of Vikings' was over a hundred strong and led by Ubba. Nor did Edwin; he just acknowledged the orders and set about hustling men into position.

I hurriedly sought out Emelda and gave her the brooch I had kept from Sweyn's hoard, pressing it into her hand. 'Take it,' I urged. 'If I fall in this battle take it to Alfred and use it to buy your freedom.'

As I turned to walk away she caught my arm. 'Keep the brooch,' she insisted, giving it back to me. 'Bring it to me again when you return safe and sound. My freedom's worth nothing to me unless you do.'

As we embraced, tears formed in my eyes. 'If only things had been different,' I whispered, hearing Edwin's words still ringing in my ears.

'They will be,' Emelda assured me. 'They will be, you'll see.'

With that Alfred's voice sounded above the commotion commanding silence.

'The Vikings are coming,' he announced. 'They have but three longships which they've sailed into the mouth of the river Parrett. That means a hundred men, no more. And they've rowed all day and will be weary from their labours. We shall meet them as they cross the ford at Combwich.'

There was a murmur from among the men for few knew of the place and none had actually been there.

'It's but a few hours march from here,' continued Alfred. 'We shall take up positions either side of the river: Edwin and his men on one bank, my own command on the other. We shall strike as the longships are carried across the shallows.' He stopped and pointed to the baskets crammed full of arrows. 'These shall rain down upon them like hail!'

Edwin nodded approvingly. 'From both sides at once! That means they'll have no shelter!'

'Exactly!' agreed Alfred. 'And if we can we'll wait until the second boat is being dragged across so the ford divides their fleet. Those upstream will toil to prevent their boat drifting back onto the shallows and those not already across will have to work hard against the current lest they drift away.'

'They'll be easy targets for our bows,' exclaimed Edwin. 'Like ducks on a pond!'

Pleased to have Edwin's support, Alfred continued heartily. 'As each one dies so the task of those remaining in the longships will grow harder. Eventually those not already across will not be able to hold against the current and will be swept back into the Severn. We shall then charge down upon those who are left and put them to the sword. This will be a great Saxon victory of which our children will tell their children for generations to come!'

There was an uneasy silence at first as the men absorbed what he had told them. He sensed their disquiet at once and knew it stemmed from the tactics he proposed but, as always, he found the words needed to lift their spirits. 'I will speak for any man here who feels the manner of this plan goes against his creed,' he assured us. 'I know this is not the Saxon way. Nor is it the way our fathers would approve. But remember we're fighting not for glory or for gold but for the right to live as Saxons. We're fighting for our freedom, for our homes, for our Holy Church and for all that we hold dear. If we meet on equal terms and trade with our enemy 'a life for a life' we shall surely fail, for there are at least two of them for every one of us. No, we must learn new ways if we're to win this war, for the old ways have brought us nothing but defeat. And pray don't tell me there's honour in defeat for I've tasted little else. I grow so tired of the flavour of it I would spit it from my mouth rather than swallow more. Instead I'm ready to drink the blood of the Vikings and chew upon their flesh! I so crave to savour the taste of victory that I care not how that feast is set upon the table!'

There was a murmur of what he took to be assent. 'Remember,' he continued pressing them still harder. 'We fight to win. How long has it been since Vikings fled before a Saxon army?'

This seemed to rouse them and they began to shout out their support.

'I say kill the Vikings!'

'Yes, slay them! Let's put them to the sword!'

'Kill them!'

'Kill them all; soak our spear points in their heathen blood!'

Alfred raised his hand. 'Aye kill them. Let none survive. And when we are done the river shall have their bones as surely as the Devil in hell shall have their souls!'

* * * * *

A Saxon army on the move was something to behold. Our warriors would march quickly, half running, half walking to sustain a pace which would have left others trailing in their wake. Each man – or woman, for they sometimes fought beside the men if they were so minded – carried their own weapons and enough food for the march. It was our practice to permit women to fight in battle for our creed was such that each person contributed according to their skill, regardless of their sex. We thought no less of a man who was of a gentler persuasion and wished to follow a life within the Church or as a poet and, by the same token, were happy to fight alongside a woman if she had the notion and the skill. On that day a few were so inclined, each having cause to fight or at least no reason not to. The others were to go with Ethelnorth to help him where they could but now waited on the bank as we were ferried across to the causeway, waving as the small Saxon army marched away in single file.

Once clear of the causeway, we followed a track which led us towards Combwich. I walked beside Osric who, as usual, kept his eye on Alfred at all times. It was difficult to converse with him for he was always nervously looking this way and that as if expecting an attack at any moment.

'I've not thanked you for clearing my name,' said Osric quietly. 'It seems there were many who suspected it was me or one of my men who opened the gates at Chippenham.'

'None of us wanted to believe that,' I assured him.

He seemed to accept this. 'I was a fool not to see there had been a traitor. Believe me, had I known of Cedric's treachery I'd have cut out his heart and fed it to the crows.'

'As would any true Saxon,' I agreed. 'But take comfort from the fact that he died as he deserved and I left his body to be torn apart by wolves.'

'A fitting end. And I hear you also killed a Viking spy.'

'We don't know he was a spy,' I replied carefully. 'Edwin thinks as much but I'm not so sure.'

'Well one thing's certain, you're quickly earning a reputation as a warrior,' added Osric. 'I hope you'll forgive me for having doubted your intentions that day we spoke whilst on the way to Athelney.'

Without stopping I offered my hand. 'Only if you can forgive me for ever having doubted you.'

Osric clasped my hand and shook it firmly, even briefly looking me in the eye rather than watching his charge. 'I do so willingly,' he said. 'And shall now be as proud to fight beside you as I am to stand beside your brother.'

* * * * *

It took a little longer than expected for us to reach Combwich but we still had time to spare. Ubba's longships had yet to negotiate the lower reaches of the river having been forced to wait upon the tide. The settlement there was little more than a few weathered huts plus several outbuildings and a smoke house, all enclosed within a low stockade. It was set on higher ground some distance from the ford itself but overlooking the dunes which stretched as far as the sea. The river at Combwich was wide and had steep, sandy banks through which the water flowed slowly. The ford was barely ankle deep but beyond it there was deeper water which would carry ships quickly to the sea, making it an ideal place for fishermen to shelter on an otherwise inhospitable coast. When he saw all this Alfred looked concerned.

'The current's not strong,' he said to Edwin. 'It won't trouble them much even if there's only a few left to man each ship. We must attack when the first vessel is being carried across the ford.'

Edwin agreed and offered to take up his position on the far bank.

Alfred looked at the sun which was already falling towards the west. 'Are there any people in the settlement?' he asked.

'No, sire,' replied Edwin. 'These were fisher folk and must have received word of the Vikings coming. They've taken their belongings and fled.'

Alfred did not seem satisfied at this. 'Either that or they heard us coming,' he warned. 'Fisher folk live in both camps as must any man who makes his living from the sea.'

He was right. Those who lived close to the sea often had strong ties with the Vikings. Many fishermen were descended from traders who had sailed across from the northlands and settled near the coast. The ancestral bonds between them were still strong, enabling the Vikings to rely on certain coastal settlements for fresh water and supplies. In return the people were spared the savage raids others endured and left to live their lives in peace. This was not treachery; it was simply a question of survival for, without such an arrangement, it would not have been possible for anyone to make a living there. But Ubba's men were not traders and few men, if any, would count them as either friend or kin. Still, Alfred was right to be cautious.

'Post three men within the stockade,' he ordered. 'Have them watch in case the fisher folk return. Tell them to hold the stockade at all costs, for if things don't go well we shall need to fall back there in retreat.'

Even as he spoke a rider appeared galloping at full pelt towards us. He went directly to Alfred and dismounted even before his horse had stopped. 'One hour,' he said struggling for breath. 'Three longships, sire. Already you can see their masts!'

Alfred acknowledged the information and turned to address his troops all of whom had gathered round anticipating this news. But the rider was not finished. 'Sire, there's more!'

Alfred turned back to him.

'These are not just Vikings, my Lord,' he said gravely. 'These are Ubba's men. Berserkers every one of them! The hulls of their ships are as black as hell, each with a fiendish beast carved upon the prow. The sails are stained blood red and a black raven standard flies from their masts!'

Silence descended on the whole group like a mist sweeping down from the hills. Then the name of Ubba was repeated many times as the news was shared.

'So?' demanded Alfred. 'What of it?'

The rider looked surprised. 'Sire, have you not heard of this man Ubba? He's no ordinary warrior for he's not human! They say...'

'I know what they say,' said Alfred calmly. 'But ask those who've actually met him. Matthew, you've come face to face with this butcher. What say you?'

I had to think quickly as to how I should respond. 'He's as any other man,' I managed. 'Not so pretty as most but he's of human flesh and has a scar that proves it.'

'But are you afraid to fight him?' asked Alfred looking at me directly.

I shook my head emphatically. 'No, sire.'

Alfred turned again to the rest of the men. 'There, even our youngest warrior has no fear of this man. He has looked him in the eyes and—'

'Eye, my Lord,' I corrected. 'For he has but one. The other is an empty socket.'

Alfred laughed. 'I stand corrected. Matthew has looked him in the eye and is not afraid. Are you?'

A murmur went around the group but no one spoke up.

'Good, then conceal yourselves well.' He took an arrow from the man nearest him, a small round fellow with fierce blue eyes. 'Eagbert here shall stand beside me,' he said placing his hand on the man's shoulder. Then he kissed the head of Eagbert's arrow. 'He will shoot this arrow when I sound three times upon my horn to summon St Cuthbert to our cause. Let no man shoot before Eagbert, but once he does I would see fifty arrows in the air before this one finds its mark. Then after that another fifty. Then fifty more until there are no arrows left to shoot.'

'What then?' asked one of the warriors.

'Then we fight in the old way – the Saxon way with sword, axe and spear.'

'What if Eagbert misses?' called someone from the back of the group. His quip was rewarded by a laugh from all who heard it.

'He'll not miss,' said Alfred.

'No man can be sure of that,' said another from the group. 'Not even Rufus. Besides, Eagbert is near as blind as a bat!'

There was a roar of laughter.

Alfred looked at Eagbert, smiling. 'Is this true, Eagbert,' he asked. 'Or is your aim as good as I've said?'

In truth Eagbert looked very unsure of himself, but he straightened his back proudly. 'I'm not one to boast, sire, but my aim is as good as any man here.'

There was another peel of laughter at which Eagbert looked hurt. Alfred would not see him mocked and so held the arrow aloft. 'He has spoken as an honest Saxon and I've chosen him on merit. He says this arrow will strike its mark. Does any man doubt it?' There was no reply as Alfred looked about the group. 'Then his word is good enough for me. Your task is to loose your arrows before his hits home.' He stopped speaking and clapped Eagbert on the back light-heartedly. 'And perhaps Eagbert, you had best then loose another arrow after that…just in case!'

They all roared with laughter and Alfred seemed much pleased by the fact that our spirits were so high despite now knowing who it was we were to face. He then raised his hands to signal that all should kneel to offer prayers.

When that was done Edwin rose to his feet and, holding his sword aloft, led the way towards the far bank, beckoning his group to follow. We waded across at the ford then took up our positions behind whatever cover we could find. Then we settled down to wait in silence for what we knew would be the fiercest foes we were ever likely to encounter.

Chapter Twenty-Two

The longships looked very large as they sailed into view. These were the sleek ships the Vikings used for coastal raids, not the larger flat-bottomed vessels we tended to see most often and which were designed for making short sea journeys ferrying stock and supplies. Built for war, the longships served their purpose well, their shallow draught making them ideal for navigating rivers and therefore enabling them to strike deep inland. They were powered by a dozen men on either side as they were rowed upstream, their sails still loosely furled from their time at sea, their gunwales hung with the shields of the warriors who laboured at the oars.

As the Vikings drew closer we could hear them calling to men on the bank who were hauling on long ropes to help pull the ships along. These men had seen the settlement by then and clearly thought to plunder it when they reached the ford, but one man was too impatient. Discarding his rope, he drew a small hand axe from his belt and, with two others, ran towards the stockade.

'They'll see us from there!' I whispered to Edwin, realising that once the Vikings were inside the settlement all those stationed between it and the river would be in full view.

Edwin cursed then gave the order to withdraw knowing it would take us out of bow range. Instead of shooting our arrows from the cover of the dunes we would now have to move up first, giving the Vikings vital moments to ready themselves.

He need not have worried. The three Vikings had barely reached the edge of the stockade when one of them cried out then reeled back with an arrow in his chest. The other two Vikings were out of view but their screams confirmed that the Saxons stationed within the stockade had dealt with them as well.

On hearing this commotion those still working the ropes paused briefly. Unable to see what had happened, they could only assume the three warriors had met resistance, probably from a few fisher folk intent on defending their homes. Their comrades had either perished or prevailed; it made little difference either way for if they had taken the settlement then the booty was spoken for and, if not, the slaughter of a few fisher folk could wait. More important at that point was to secure their ships ready to be hauled across the ford.

All three vessels had reached the ford by then and men began leaping ashore. They secured the first two by taking them to Alfred's side of the river and mooring them with the port rail nearest the bank. This was to ensure that the steering oar, which was on the starboard side, was protected in the deeper water.

The Vikings then set about preparing the first vessel to be dragged across the shallows as soon as the tide allowed. Some emptied the ballast from the hull to lighten it, manhandling the large flat stones and setting them down in a line on the sand, whilst others lowered the sail and unstepped the mast. The oars were then taken out and reversed before being pushed back through the ports in the side of the ship to provide leverage. Others removed a dozen heavy logs which had been stowed aboard one of the vessels, greased them in a thick coat of oil and fish guts then, in what seemed a well-practised manoeuvre, placed them under the bow so that the ship could be pulled onto them. With the tide rising, the water even at the ford was, by then, near thigh deep and the Vikings had stripped naked to avoid getting their clothes wet as they strained at the ropes and oars, heaving with all their might.

At first the longship would not budge. Then they started to rock it back and forth until, once securely located on the first log, it seemed to slide more easily. As it was dragged, the logs were taken from the rear and placed at the bow until the vessel was well nigh across. It was then that Alfred gave the order for three shrill blasts to be sounded on the horn to summon St Cuthbert.

'Nooooow!' he cried, and Eagbert loosed his arrow. It was followed by what looked like a huge swarm of black bees hissing through the air from both sides of the river. Those Vikings who were clustered around the ship stood bolt upright in shock, then fell back as the arrows struck home. Many screamed in pain as first one wave of arrows hit them then the next. Edwin ordered me back to check that all three Vikings who had attacked the settlement had indeed been slain. I protested, certain the men posted there could deal with them, but Edwin insisted, reminding me of Alfred's orders to secure our retreat at all costs. By the time I got there the Saxon guards were outside the stockade and rushing to join the main fight. Heeding my brother's words, I ordered them back but, as I turned to rejoin Edwin, I could scarce believe my eyes. Never had I dreamed such carnage could exist!

The Vikings in the water were defenceless. Many were still stripped naked and with no helmet, mail vest or even a shield there was nothing they could do to escape the arrows and shot being rained down upon them. Most just lay in the water, their bodies drifting as the blood washed from their wounds, whilst others were cut down as they struggled for the bank. Those few who had remained in the two moored longships took what cover they could but the arrows fell on them as well. At one point they even thought to row one of the longships away against the tide, but those sent to cut the mooring ropes were killed trying.

The Saxons would not let up the torrent until the supply of arrows and shot was exhausted. Only then did Alfred give the signal to attack. Every man at once threw aside his bow, grabbed whatever weapon he had, then charged down to the water. The women were supposed to hold back at this point but joined the charge as well, picking up weapons where they could and wielding them with a terrible ferocity.

Alfred was at the head of his group, slashing with his sword as he waded towards the stranded longships with Osric at his side. Edwin led the other group but slipped on the bank so that others were soon ahead of him. They all charged like demons, stabbing and cutting even at those who were already slain.

Any Vikings who had managed to struggle to their feet were quickly overwhelmed by the assault. Whilst most of the men in Edwin's group were busy hacking at those in the water, five or six of Alfred's men had boarded the longships and were throwing the survivors over the sides to be butchered. A few Vikings tried wading upstream in an attempt to get away but once past the ford they found the water too deep. They were quickly caught and slain. Then, even seeing the day was won, Alfred gave an order most thought never to hear from a Saxon King. 'Take no prisoners!' he shouted. 'Show no mercy!'

Vengeance stored over a long, hard winter was suddenly vented. The wounded were hauled from the river and butchered as the Saxons laughed and toyed with them. Limbs were hacked off and bellies sliced open. One poor soul had his arms and legs cut off and was writhing in agony as he was shown his own severed limbs, one by one. As his body convulsed the Saxons laughed saying that was why they were called berserkers.

I stood on the river bank with a few other men and watched in horror, helpless to stem the blood lust which seemed to have engulfed our men. Even Alfred made no attempt to stop them as they found ever more ways to torment and torture the few Vikings they found still alive. Many had their tongues cut out or their noses sliced off, others had their manhood severed and pushed into their mouth before being disembowelled. Even the corpses were mutilated then discarded into the river or laid on the bank to be butchered.

The women were even more cruel. One of them seized an axe and used it to hack a wounded man to pieces, raining blow after blow upon him in a mad frenzy. Later she was seen kneeling in the shallower water near the bank covered in blood as she offered up parts of his severed body as if showing them to the spirit of her dead son who was among those who had perished at Chippenham. Tears were streaming down her face and she was wailing uncontrollably as though her grief was finally vented.

Throughout all these dreadful acts the Saxons cheered and cried out in sheer excitement, scouring the river for more bodies to desecrate. Not one single Viking survived that day. Our losses were small – three dead and six wounded – and our souls rejoiced at that, though looking at the carnage we had inflicted some might say they would be damned for ever.

* * * * *

Alfred called for Ubba's head to be brought, offering silver to the man who could find it. The Saxons searched among the dead until, at last, someone discovered the body aboard one of the longships. It bristled with arrows, having been struck during the first wave and fallen back and lodged below the deck. His head was quickly cut off and carried back to Alfred who examined it in silence.

'Place it in a sack,' he ordered at last. 'Then sever the heads from the other dead Vikings and put them in the baskets in which we brought the arrows.'

Edwin protested but Alfred's mind was set. 'I have need of them, you'll see,' was all he would say. Then suddenly aware that all eyes were upon him, he spoke again. 'You've fought as Saxons should,' he announced, carefully avoiding any reference to the way in which the battle was conducted, knowing many would still feel it was against our Saxon creed to fight as we had done. 'I promised freedom for those who were slaves and a pardon for those convicted of crimes. I hereby keep my word. You are all free men and may go in peace with your lawful share of the booty and my thanks.' He paused for a moment then continued. 'Or you may come with us to even greater glory.'

'Where to?' asked one of them, his face still streaked with blood.

'To avenge our dead,' said Alfred. 'To fight Guthrum and retake Chippenham.'

'We few?' asked another as though incredulous that Alfred should even think of such an ambitious plan.

'We may be few in numbers,' replied Alfred. 'But are we not the ones who have defeated and slain the most feared Viking of them all?' He held up the sack he was still holding. 'Is this not the head of Ubba who, but a few hours since, you were afraid to even think of fighting?'

As ever he was beginning to talk them round. 'Men will speak of those who were here this day,' he continued. 'They'll tell how a few Saxons fought more than twice their number of berserkers and won a great victory. They'll tell how the river ran with blood and how not a single Viking was spared.' He paused to look about him. 'Besides, others will join us now. Edwin and his brother shall ride from here to tell Ethelnorth the news of our great victory. He'll then summon every able Saxon to our cause. They shall rise up and meet us at Egbert's Stone where we shall form an army such as Guthrum has never seen.'

There was a clamour of voices but Alfred raised his hand to quieten them. 'So who will come with me to Egbert's Stone? Who will come and see a great Saxon army crush the Vikings once and for ever?'

This time he was answered by an even louder cheer.

* * * * *

Despite their good spirits there were many who regretted what had been done in the heat of battle and in the carnage afterwards. The women sat in a circle near the stockade, their hands joined together and their eyes closed tight as they whispered prayers. They had sought vengeance as a cure, but like a remedy to purge the bowel it had left them hollow and empty. As for the men, some wandered from place to place talking endlessly of the battle whilst others were strangely quiet. I was tempted to join a small group who had gathered near the river to pray, asking for forgiveness for themselves and for the souls of those who had done such dreadful things. Even Edwin, not normally a pious man, seemed inclined to join them, but we stood instead and watched as they knelt at their devotions.

'Why would Alfred take no prisoners?' I asked quietly.

'So none were left who might carry word to Guthrum,' he explained.

Alfred was standing alone, also watching those at prayer. 'If it troubles them they should not have come,' he said when Edwin and I joined him. 'I would have them risk their lives for me but not their souls.'

Beyond us many bodies still lay strewn in the river. On the banks a party of men was piling up the booty taken from the ships and from the dead so that Alfred could distribute it as was the custom. It was mostly weapons but there was also jewellery and silver which had been stripped from the bodies. Once all had been collected they began destroying the longships by breaking through the hulls to allow the water in, then setting fire to the sails.

'Such a waste,' said Alfred, almost to himself.

'Sire, do you mean the men we've slain or the ships?' asked Edwin.

But Alfred didn't answer. He just shook his head and said again, 'Such a dreadful waste.'

Chapter Twenty-Three

Alfred and his small army began the long march to Egbert's Stone carrying with them the baskets heaped full of severed Viking heads. All who were travelling with him were now free men and most had earned a small quantity of jewellery or silver taken from the dead Vikings. More importantly, every one of them was now fully armed.

Meanwhile, Edwin and I borrowed horses and rode as though the Devil himself was at our heels.

'Take with you Ubba's head,' Alfred had urged us. 'It may serve to stir the resolve of those who are of thinner blood.'

Thus with the head still in the sack which was strapped to Edwin's saddle, we headed south, following the river before striking out westwards in search of the Vill belonging to a man named Aethelred. There Ethelnorth would be waiting ready to pass the word for the Saxons to unite.

Aethelred was an Ealdorman in those parts, a big man who was as round as a basket and as strong as an ox. When we reached his Vill we found others there, too, anxiously waiting for the news we carried.

'Victory is ours!' shouted Edwin as he reined back his horse and prepared to dismount.

But Aethelred could not contain himself long enough for that. 'Victory you say? Then the day was won?'

'And what news of Alfred?' pressed Ethelnorth.

'Alfred is safe,' Edwin assured them after drinking deeply from a horn that was offered by one of Aethelred's men. 'We lost a few men but the river ran red with Viking blood. None asked for quarter nor was any given. Every man who sailed with Ubba has been slain!'

'God be praised!' said Ethelnorth excitedly.

'Aye,' said Edwin. 'And we shall give thanks. But first we've work to do. Lord Alfred would have every loyal Ealdorman meet him at Egbert's Stone within two days, each bringing with him whatever force he can muster.'

A group of Saxon thanes had gathered round who, in anticipation of the news, had lodged with their Lord overnight. 'You mentioned Ubba,' complained one of them. 'We were not told Alfred was to fight with him. It was just a band of renegade Vikings he went to meet, not that bastard Ubba!'

'It was Ubba,' confirmed Edwin proudly. 'And a hundred of his men; berserkers every one of them!'

'Ubba slain! This is providence indeed!' said Aethelred, turning as though to share the news with the others.

'Have you proof of this?' demanded one of the men who was clearly not convinced. 'Not that I would doubt you Lord Edwin but there have been more rumours of Ubba's death than I can count.'

Edwin delved into the sack and pulled out Ubba's head by the hair, holding it aloft for all to see. 'Then why don't you ask him?' he said laughing. 'For behold the face of your most feared enemy!'

* * * * *

Edwin had planned for us to work our way to Egbert's Stone passing the word as we went. As it turned out there was little need for at every settlement or farmstead men were preparing to leave or had already done so. It seemed Ethelnorth's chain had passed the word like a fire spreading through a forest and there was little to be done except to fan the flames. My brother and I were greeted with cheers as we rode through each settlement, Edwin often showing Ubba's head as we passed, gripping it by the hair and waving it like a banner. Seldom was it even necessary to stop except for fresh horses and for food and drink, which was always offered freely. A few tried to follow us but Edwin turned them away lest they slowed our progress.

'Go to Egbert's Stone,' he shouted. 'Your King and victory await.'

'Tell others,' I would call. 'Pass the word to any Saxon who's fit for battle. Tell them to don their war gear and come armed and ready!'

By the time we reached Egbert's Stone Alfred's army was already more than 800 strong. Men had gathered in groups, some seated on the ground and others milling about renewing old acquaintances. Many had brought food and several large fires burned over which venison and wild boar were being roasted.

'Welcome,' called Alfred once we had dismounted. 'I can greet you now as a King should, with an army at his command.'

'You were ever King to us, sire,' acknowledged Edwin as Alfred embraced us each in turn.

'And it shall not be forgotten,' said Alfred sincerely. 'You've both served me well in my time of need and shall reap your reward when my kingdom is restored.'

Edwin looked around at the faces of the men, many of whom he recognised. 'We have our reward, my Lord. To see this Saxon army gathered where most of us thought none could ever rise again. What more could any loyal Saxon ask?'

'True, but there's still much to be done,' said Alfred leading us both aside. 'Guthrum will soon learn of Ubba's fate. When he does he must come out to meet us. His honour and his reputation depend upon it.'

'And he has more than enough troops with which to make a fight of it,' I added. 'I saw them for myself.'

'Yes, Matthew, many in number. But as you said they've wintered foolishly, feasting and whoring. They're not fit for battle, so he'll take his time hoping our men will grow weary of waiting and disperse.'

'But your ranks swell by the hour and our confidence grows as quickly!' I protested.

'Exactly,' replied Alfred. 'Which is why we shall carry the battle to him. When he learns we're on the move he'll have no choice. He cannot stay at Chippenham for the defences there could not withstand an army of this size. I've sent men to find a place where we can meet him on our own terms.'

'Then what?' asked Edwin.

'Very simple,' said Alfred. 'I defeat Guthrum and retake Chippenham.'

'No, sire, I meant—'

Alfred raised his hand. 'I know what you meant, Edwin. But I'm not yet ready to tell anyone of my plan. Not even you.'

'Do you mean you've yet to form one?' suggested Edwin. 'Would you tempt the bear into the trap before you've set it?'

'No, I have a plan,' Alfred assured him. 'But I'm troubled because last night I saw again the spirit of St Cuthbert.

He came to me in a dream and told me once more that I must avenge the Holy Church.'

'But he didn't deign to tell you how?' asked Edwin somewhat sourly.

'He assured me I shall know when the time comes. If I call upon him he'll bless our endeavours and show me what I need to do, just as he did at Combwich. Beyond that I can say no more.'

Edwin considered this, then chose his words carefully. 'Then all is well. For with St Cuthbert's Holy guidance and an army such as this are we not assured of victory?' But something in his voice suggested he was not convinced.

* * * * *

There were many rumours as to how Alfred planned to beat Guthrum, most of which involved the heads of Ubba's men. The more macabre among us said Alfred would boil them and eat the flesh the night before the battle to strike fear into the hearts of Guthrum's army, others that he would hurl them into the Viking ranks as they advanced and thereby deter their warriors' resolve.

That evening Alfred summoned all to form a Witan. Whilst he knew he had everyone's support, he needed to make his intentions clear so there was no misunderstanding about the nature of the war he was about to wage. As he took his place beside the ancient Stone there were six Ealdormen beside him, including Ethelnorth, Aethelred and Edwin. Osric and his men stood behind him together with various senior members of the Church. The rest of the men were grouped together in front, mostly seated on the ground or leaning on their weapons for support.

'The time has come to avenge the Saxon blood which has been spilled so freely in this land,' announced Alfred. 'I will not say that what lies ahead of us is easy; Guthrum has many men to command and they're well rested if ill prepared to fight. I therefore call upon you to follow me to meet him in open battle to retake Chippenham and then drive his horde back beyond the borders of my realm. I do this as your liege and Bretwalda. Indeed I command it as your King.'

No one spoke as Alfred continued. 'Remember these heathens would take your daughters as whores and your sons as slaves. They've already ravaged the land and burned our homes, destroying all that once was part of our Saxon way. The question is, will you stand with me and fight or have you come here to watch as they make free with all that we hold dear?'

A voice rose up from the ranks, but Alfred could not see who was speaking. 'But sire, if we fight them, can we win? Guthrum has many troops who have spent a warm winter. As you've said, they're well fed and rested.'

Alfred considered the question carefully. 'Those who were with me at Combwich had best answer that. They were also outnumbered and faced the most fearsome men Guthrum could find to set against us.'

'What if we lose?' asked another.

Alfred shrugged. 'Then we shall die. For my part I would as soon die as a Saxon than live as a slave.'

'Perhaps,' said another voice. 'But we have fought before. And bled. And suffered. Yet still the Vikings come. Wave after wave of them, sire – more than we can count. If we fight them now who's to say they'll not come again?'

'Not I,' answered Alfred simply. 'Yet we are Saxons. Our forefathers fought for this land as did their fathers and their fathers before them. Are we not the sons of those great men? Does not their blood flow in our veins?' At that Alfred drew his dagger. Baring his arm, he ran the blade across his forearm until the blood trickled down. 'This is Saxon blood,' he declared holding up his arm for all to see whilst allowing a few drops to fall onto Egbert's Stone itself. 'My line goes back beyond the memory of any man alive and deep into our history. Witness how I've spilled that pure and untainted blood here before you today as it drains from my arm onto this Holy Stone. And I shall spill yet more of it if that's what it takes to drive the Vikings from my realm. In fact I would offer every drop to see this land safe and my people restored. Thus I ask only this of you: Who will stand with me?'

The answer was a cheer which echoed through the Saxon ranks stirring even the more doubtful souls to join him. At this Alfred was more than satisfied. He had his army; he had a mandate to lead that army into battle; and he had the blessing of our most Holy saint, St Cuthbert. More important than all of this, he had the support of his men and knew full well that once roused the spirit of the Saxons would not now be denied the freedom we all so dearly craved.

* * * * *

Alfred summoned the Ealdormen to hear his plan in private. They all seemed very pleased with their status now that such a large army had assembled, but it was they who would need to press the men within their charge to follow him, thus he needed their full support. This was the balance Saxon Kings had always to maintain, for they ruled by consent and not by right.

'Tomorrow we march to Eley where we shall spend the night,' said Alfred addressing the group. 'From there we go to Edington where I intend that we shall make our stand. It's a place I know well because I went there once with my brother to witness the signing of a charter. I recall that it may suit our purpose being too close to Chippenham for Guthrum to ignore our presence yet too far for him to make an orderly retreat once he's beaten. But we must move fast for I would hold the ridge there and thus the advantage of the field. Once in position we'll form three ranks to stand one behind the other, each with runners to carry orders along the line. When the Vikings advance towards the ridge we shall loose such a volley of arrows that they'll stagger beneath its weight. Even before the arrows have struck home we'll close up, shield to shield.'

'A shield wall! Like the old days!' said Aethelred. 'Now that's what I call proper fighting!'

'Exactly,' agreed Alfred. 'We advance down the hill with the slope in our favour and a solid mass of shields to cover us from the maelstrom of javelins, spears, axes and arrows the Vikings will surely rain down upon us. The second rank shall then follow the first but keeping always twenty paces back.'

'Then why three ranks?' asked Ethelnorth.

'The first is to break their assault. The second shall put to the sword any Vikings who come through the first, for we cannot risk letting them regroup behind us. The third shall stay back and move only to fill the gaps if our ranks are breached.'

All seemed satisfied with the plan except Edwin. 'They'll still outnumber us,' he warned. 'If they spread their lines thin they may envelop us from either side.'

'The terrain will not allow that,' explained Alfred. 'The slope is steep enough but almost sheer on either flank. Not until we are on level ground can they use their numbers to any real advantage. By then, God willing, we shall have put them to flight.'

As always Alfred had been thorough and no one had any reservations; at least, not until he announced his chain of command. 'Edwin shall command the first rank, Ethelnorth the second and Matthew here the third,' he said simply, then waited for the response.

It was a great honour for me but I knew it would stir resentment from the Ealdormen. 'What does a novice monk know about the ways of war?' they demanded. 'We mean no offence to the boy but he should serve his time in the shield wall as did we all!'

Alfred listened to their grumbles before he replied. 'This "boy" as you call him has served me well. Twice I've asked him to face death on my account and he's not been found wanting. He's shown both skill and courage and I'll not risk having him needlessly slaughtered in the shield wall.'

Aethelred was first to reply. 'If he's earned your favour who are we to argue, but is it not our place to lead our own men into battle? Have you summoned us here to die in the ranks?'

'It was your place to support your liege when his need was most,' replied Alfred accusingly. 'You'll each answer to the command of those I've chosen until the Vikings' lines are broken. Then you'll have your chance to lead, for you must then call your men to you. This is vital. You must keep your men close for Guthrum will divide us if he can.'

He waited to see if this would be acceptable, knowing what each of the Ealdormen was thinking. Commanding their own men at that point in the battle – when the Vikings were retreating – offered a chance for personal glory, plunder and revenge. Alfred had gambled on their greed and lust for blood. He was not disappointed.

'Aethelred, there is a bridge a few miles south of Chippenham. I would have you take twenty men and hold it,' he continued. 'With so much booty stored in the Vill Guthrum is bound to go back there even in retreat.'

Aethelred knew he and his men were being given the honour of having one of the most important tasks, for by holding the bridge the Vikings would be prevented from reaching the safety of the Vill. It also meant certain death if they were not relieved in time, for they would be crushed as the Vikings fought to escape the advancing Saxon army. He looked at Alfred and nodded his agreement.

'But can you hold it with just twenty men?' asked Edwin.

Aethelred seemed uncertain. 'How wide is the bridge?' he asked.

'Not near as wide as you!' joked one of the other Ealdormen.

Aethelred puffed up his huge chest. 'Then no man shall pass save with your leave, sire. I shall go tonight and send word when Guthrum advances. Once he's crossed the bridge my men and I will secure it and hold it till you get there. Or we shall die trying.'

For a moment everyone was quiet whilst they considered all the other aspects of Alfred's plan. There was no doubt it could work, but the prospect of meeting Guthrum in battle now loomed large in all our thoughts.

'Fear not,' said Alfred. 'When Guthrum's men learn that Ubba has been defeated the day will be ours. The reputation of the berserkers was as fearsome to them as it was to us. To see them slain will strike fear into their hearts and I have a plan to ensure we feast upon that fear just as the falcon feeds upon the dove.'

* * * * *

As we marched first to Eley and then on to Edington the next day our ranks swelled still further. Men came from every corner of Wessex. Some were seasoned warriors sent by Ealdormen who, though they would not come themselves, were anxious to be seen to support Alfred; others were young thanes who had come of their own accord hoping for the chance of advancement, but there were also a few farmers and tradesmen pressed into service by the fyrd, who brought with them crude weapons taken from their barns but carried with pride.

With the ranks now filled, most of the women who had fought at Combwich said they would not fight again, though all volunteered to stay and tend the wounded. Having proved their Saxon courage as much as any man – perhaps even more than most – what they feared now was not the Vikings but the lust for blood and vengeance they had each unleashed within themselves.

No sooner had we arrived at Edington than word came from Aethelred that Guthrum's army was getting ready to move and would arrive at daybreak. We settled down to await its arrival, seated in small groups, each around a fire on which we cooked whatever food we had. That night we witnessed a sunset of such a vivid hue that all who saw it thought it was an omen. As the sky turned red some said it was awash with blood to herald that which would be shed come the dawn, but Rufus said it was surely a good sign, for red sky at night tended to sign fair weather. 'And which of us would wish to die in the rain?' he added. His was a bleak humour yet strangely cheering just the same.

* * * * *

As we waited for the dawn men sharpened their weapons and readied themselves for battle. Many spoke of freedom and of returning to the Saxon ways of farming and hunting, sharing stories of loved ones and of kin they had left behind. Others boasted of the battles they had fought, vying with each other to tell of the bloodiest contest though, on that account, few could match the tales of those of us who were at Combwich.

I sat with Edwin and noticed how he said very little. The quarrel between us over Emelda now seemed a long way off and neither of us had mentioned it. With us was a young warrior called Dudwine who was perhaps five or six years older than me. He was not a Saxon by birth but his family had lived among us for many years. He was a tall man, thin and dark skinned with long black hair that hung loose and straight. Using his fingers, he was spreading ochre across his face in large stripes as he told us how his uncle had brought shame upon his family by refusing to support Alfred's cause. According to Saxon law his family's lands were now forfeit to the King, indeed I recalled how Alfred had dispossessed them that night at Athelney just before he stunned us all by announcing his intention to regain Chippenham so soon.

'He's told me that if I serve him well they'll be restored,' said Dudwine cheerfully. 'I've special orders for I must take the raven banner.'

Edwin looked surprised. 'That is dangerous work! They'll not give it up except you kill them all!'

'I know it,' acknowledged Dudwine. 'But I have no choice. If I fall trying, Alfred has said he'll restore my uncle's lands to my son who is yet a year old.'

I picked a taper from the fire and toyed with it, watching the end smoulder. 'I think your son might rather have a father than the lands of his uncle,' I suggested, thinking of when my own dear parents were so cruelly taken from me.

Dudwine looked at me as though unable to understand what I meant. 'Without lands we're nothing,' he reasoned. 'My future and his depend upon me regaining what was once our birthright.'

'Under whose command have you been placed?' asked Edwin.

Dudwine smiled. 'Under yours,' he said looking at me. 'But I'm to remain mounted, ready to seize the chance if and when it comes.'

It was news to me yet I saw at once what Alfred had in mind. The battle would be closely fought with men trading a blow for a blow, a life for a life. Victory would hang in the balance and rest upon the slightest advantage which could be gained by one side or the other. Seizing their sacred banner might well be enough to break the Vikings, causing them to scatter like leaves on the wind. Yet to gamble the life of one as young as Dudwine on that small chance seemed most unlike the man I called King. 'Then you shall wait for my signal,' I said, not relishing the responsibility of giving it.

Dudwine shook his head. 'I will obey your command, Matthew, for I much respect all I've heard of you, but in this I answer directly to Alfred. I go at his word and no other's.'

In a way I was relieved but I also began to see that I had been honoured with command of the third rank to make a point to the other Ealdormen, nothing more. Alfred would be close by commanding me as I commanded those beneath me. It was then I realised that Edwin had been aware of this from the start. Sensing my disappointment, he tried to console me. 'You're trusted with command but must prove yourself,' he explained. 'The honour is the greater for that.'

I took comfort from his words knowing that with the dawn would come the chance for me to prove my worth, as would we all.

Chapter Twenty-Four

Guthrum's men arrived looking more like a rabble than an army. Shouting abuse at us, they pushed and shoved themselves into position at the foot of the slope, each vying for a favoured place.

Alfred watched them as he walked among our men knowing that their sheer numbers would be enough to weaken the resolve of even his most steadfast warriors. 'They look angry at being roused from their beds too soon,' he quipped. 'I fear they've come looking for breakfast, not a fight.'

He got little response from anyone as we shivered in the crisp early morning air. All had risen well before dawn in order to attend a special Mass held in the open, but the time for prayer was past. Having taken up our positions on the ridge we were, for the most part, ready. The Ealdormen had strapped on their mail vests and helmets, the warriors had braided their hair, and all who were so minded had painted their faces just as our forefathers had done before a battle. Some took the horses and baggage to the rear whilst others were busy setting spears into the ground along the edge of the ridge where Alfred planned we should make our stand. Although crude, this line of spears would help check the Viking charge but, as every warrior knew, only dogged determination and blood would halt it.

Many men still whispered prayers as they were ushered into position. All knew only too well that the shield wall was a dreadful place in which to serve, particularly the first rank commanded by Edwin which would take the full brunt of the attack. In the front row of that rank were those trying to prove themselves as warriors. They were armed with spear and shield plus a seax – a short sword which could be drawn once the spear was thrown, lost or broken and used where there was little room to wield anything longer. It would be cruel and bloody work, hacking and cutting with short, vicious stabs trying to slay a foe pressed up hard against them, shield to shield. Behind the front row stood men with long-handled spears, the points of which would form a barrier to keep the Vikings at bay. These were trained men who also carried a hand weapon as well. The veteran warriors would stand behind these two rows armed with whatever they chose to carry. Most relied on an axe, though the wealthier ones had swords. Some also had special weapons such as clubs, hammers or even spikes they could wield according to their own particular skill and preference. Most important of all, every man carried a shield needed as part of the protective shell that would guard the whole rank from the arrows, spears, throwing axes and javelins which would be rained down mercilessly upon them. Once the rows were combined the shields would be locked together and the whole unit would then move as one, a manoeuvre Saxon warriors practised to perfection.

The rank commanded by Ethelnorth was similarly formed and they too would advance as a single unit, following Edwin's men down the slope. My own rank was made up of less-experienced men all of whom carried at least one throwing spear, some form of hand weapon, plus a bow which was needed to provide a hail of arrows which it was hoped would slow the Viking advance. They would also remain loosely bound so they could move quickly to fill any gaps, thereby replacing those who had fallen. Such gaps provided the chance for advancement or for a greater share of any booty for those who had the nerve.

* * * * *

From his position at the foot of the slope Guthrum would have seen at once that we Saxons had seized the advantage. His warriors would have to charge up the steep hill and, because of the severe fall of the ground on either side, could not spread out and use their superior numbers to any effect, just as Alfred had predicted. Guthrum started to assemble his men under their resplendent banners such as the bear, the hawk, the eagle and the boar ready to form the armed 'wedge' needed to punch a hole through the Saxon shield wall. They were a fearsome sight. Those with no mail or leather vests had stripped to the waist, their bodies painted and their cloaks cast aside. Almost all wore helmets of one form or another and each carried a sword, spear or some form of axe, including the brutal dane axe which was a dreadful weapon to come against, for it could be used to haul aside a shield and leave an opponent hopelessly exposed. The blade of one of those axes was heavy and sharp enough to rip through flesh and bone, thereby inflicting a terrible wound. It could just as easily be used to hack off limbs or to split a man's skull and was thus a favoured weapon for the Vikings and the one all Saxon warriors feared most.

Although anxious to start the battle whilst his men were still eager, Guthrum needed to wait until they had all arrived. Alfred on the other hand was keen to draw the Vikings before they were ready, to which end he had a simple plan. He ordered Ethelnorth to take four men and to ride down the slope carrying the large baskets containing the heads of Ubba's men, but covered over so the Vikings could not see what was inside.

Thinking he was about to be offered tribute to spare the Saxon army, Guthrum's heart must have leaped when he saw the baskets. He would not have cared much what was in them; for even if they were brim full of silver or gold it was nothing compared to the real prize of all Wessex at his feet and Alfred himself at his mercy. Securing victory without having to fight would be an added bonus and so straight away he sent two of his senior Jarls forward to receive what he hoped would be his due – Alfred's unconditional surrender.

Ethelnorth waited until the Viking horsemen were closer before ordering his men to upend the baskets. As they did so the heads of Ubba's men spilled out then rolled and bounced down the slope towards the Viking lines like fruit from an upturned stall. Feeling they had been made to look like fools, the two Jarls drew their weapons and charged.

'Back!' ordered Ethelnorth. Then, as the men who had carried the baskets made good their escape, he wheeled his own horse around to face the angry Jarls.

The two Vikings were good but no match for such a seasoned warrior. Ethelnorth rode straight at them and, as they split to pass either side of him, he hacked at first one then the other with his sword. Pulling up his horse, he then turned and rode back to admire his handiwork. Neither blow

305

had been fatal but both men had been wounded as much by the fall as anything. He quickly dismounted and finished them off. Satisfied, he then turned to face the Viking horde. Holding up his sword he made great play of licking the blood from its blade.

The Vikings were furious. They screamed for vengeance but Ethelnorth was not yet done. He remounted and pulled Ubba's head from the sack strapped to his saddle then rode the full length of their lines waving it in the air to insult them still further.

Although some of the Vikings tried to shoot him with arrows or hurl javelins at him as he passed, Ethelnorth skilfully avoided these with a fine display of horsemanship. To the cheers of the Saxons, he turned to make another pass but by then dozens of Viking warriors had broken rank and were swarming up the slope towards him. Stopping only to hurl Ubba's head at those nearest him, Ethelnorth rode hard for the safety of our lines.

At this all semblance of order within the Viking army seemed to dissolve. Guthrum had planned to try the slope just once and make it count, but with some of his men still not arrived, some already charging up the slope in pursuit of Ethelnorth and others staying back, his force was in chaos. He therefore had no choice. With a wave of his sword he tried to unite his men by leading them in a desperate charge.

Alfred was delighted to see his ruse work so well. In fact thanks to Ethelnorth's bravado it had worked even better than expected. As the Viking rabble started up the slope they had not even formed into a proper wedge, which meant they had virtually no hope of breaching our shield wall once they reached it.

As they watched the Vikings come, my bowmen loosed first one wave of arrows then another. The arrows were easily deflected but served to slow their advance so much that our warriors began shouting our war cry of 'OUT! OUT! OUT!' whilst others started beating the backs of their shields in a steady, taunting rhythm which soon became as loud as twenty drums.

Still the Viking horde surged forward. The slope and the arrows were enough to take the pace out of their assault but not enough to stop them. Screaming and shouting, they swarmed nearer, furiously wielding their weapons as they closed.

We Saxons held our ranks waiting on Alfred's orders. Only when he judged the time to be right did he give his signal for three shrill blasts to be sounded on the horn to summon St Cuthbert. In truth, St Cuthbert would have been lucky to have heard it above the noise of men beating their shields and shouting, but Edwin had orders enough. From his position behind his men he bellowed out his command.

'Close up!' he ordered and the Saxon wall moved as one, bracing itself for the impact just as the Vikings slammed into it; a solid mass of men and shields crashed into their ranks like a battering ram.

It was a miracle that the line held, absorbing that terrible impact like a bale of straw.

The fray that followed was as fierce as any even the most seasoned warriors had ever seen. At first neither side would give ground as swords clashed on shields and javelins and arrows flew through the air. For the most part those in the first wave of the Viking assault were quickly killed, either skewered by spears or butchered with the short-bladed swords.

The ground quickly became so slippery with blood and gore that those Vikings who followed struggled to scramble over their own dead and wounded to reach us. But the longhandled spears were useless once the Vikings got between them and began hacking at the legs and feet of the Saxons in the front line hoping to bring a man down and thus open up the wall. Their efforts were wasted as, already tired, they could not hope to hold against the slope and with one last push from the Saxons, their whole rank gave way. Still screaming and yelling they began retreating down the hill.

Edwin's men were tempted to go after them but were quickly checked. He ordered them to wait, to hold rank and to keep their shields locked together.

He was wise to do so, for Guthrum sent bowmen to cover his retreating army and their arrows clattered on the Saxons' upturned shields like hail. More arrows and javelins followed but the shield wall would not give. Instead, at Edwin's command, it began to advance down the slope, its progress carefully controlled by him so that no part of it was left exposed.

Some Vikings sought to stand against the advance but were simply trampled underfoot. Then Ethelnorth also moved up but keeping his rank twenty paces behind Edwin's just as Alfred had ordered. Loosely bound, this second rank swept up the wounded and dying Vikings left behind. They caught one man bawling his challenge as Edwin and his men marched away, seemingly unaware of the next rank bearing down upon him. When at last he turned and saw them he must have known his fate was sealed. In a brave but futile gesture he let out a cry of defiance then charged headlong onto their shields to be slain.

Both ranks advanced steadily down the slope but the Vikings were not yet done. They began to regroup at the bottom, forming into a rough line. Edwin saw the danger as that line began to spread wider and wider, knowing it could engulf his men once they reached it, particularly if he allowed the Vikings time to form a shield wall of their own. Raising his sword, he ordered a charge that slammed into them, his men breaking free and spreading out as they made contact.

The Vikings took this onslaught bravely and fought back hard, the cries of the wounded and the dying ringing out as the two armies locked once more.

At one point Guthrum managed to split Edwin's force and break through his lines. Alfred's heart must have sunk when he saw this. With Edwin's men divided, the Vikings were able to exact a terrible toll, hacking with their swords and axes at those who were exposed. Thankfully Ethelnorth spotted the breach and with his long silver hair trailing behind him, led his men in a desperate charge to close it. Screaming like wild beasts, they swarmed into the gap and drove the Vikings back.

Meanwhile, I steadied my men and held them ready. With Ethelnorth and Edwin having joined ranks and now pressing the Vikings hard, I was desperate to join the fray. Then Alfred gave the signal for me to move up and, at last, I had a part to play.

'Advance!' I shouted, then urged my rank down the slope picking a path through the dead and dying. Ahead was a melee of axes and spears, of arrows and javelins – and anything else which could be thrown as both armies fought in what had become a deadly hand-to-hand brawl. My men joined it, pushing their way to the sides to reinforce both flanks. Having split them, half to one side and half to the other, I kept back a dozen as a reserve then took my position at the rear from where I could best read Alfred's signals.

Looking back towards the ridge I could see the dead and wounded on the slope. The turf was streaked with their blood and littered with discarded weapons like a scene from hell. Beyond that, Alfred still occupied the ridge itself, guarded by Osric and a few hand-picked men. Dudwine was also with them. He was wearing a helmet and a vest of mail but carried no shield so that he could keep one hand free to grasp the banner when his chance came whilst still controlling his horse with the other. His was a dangerous task. Being one of the few men mounted during the battle would make him an obvious target. If he fell or was taken he could expect no mercy and would be hacked to pieces at once.

* * * * *

Several times the Vikings rallied. Mostly small groups formed together and mounted a counter-attack whilst others kept up a hail of arrows. With the shield wall now abandoned it was bloody work. Men were hacking and cutting with barely enough room between them to wield a sword and both sides took heavy casualties.

As I worked my way along the lines I looked at the faces of those who had fallen, noting with horror the many good men among them.

It was then that Dudwine made his move. The banner was being held where the fighting was most fierce and I watched as he, accompanied by Rufus, rode hard towards it

310

then pushed his way through the lines, desperately urging his horse to ignore the battle. Up it reared, bringing its hooves crashing down upon those beneath it. Again and again Dudwine wheeled the beast from side to side or reined it back hard, clearing a path through the already terrified men. Vikings tried to tear him from his mount but he would not be stopped. Even when wounded he pushed on. Then, when the time was right, Rufus loosed an arrow that was aimed directly at the man holding the banner. As ever, his shot was near perfect and the man pitched forward, giving Dudwine the chance to grasp the banner. He reached forward until he could touch the tip of it then tried to pluck it free. Even though dying from his wound, the man holding it would not let go so Dudwine lashed out with his axe, hacking at the hands that grasped it. Then with a frantic cry, he grabbed the banner and hurled it back towards our ranks.

From where I was I could not see who received it but it was soon held aloft in triumph. Unfortunately Dudwine was lost. With the Vikings packed so tight about him he was unable to turn his horse and so had no option but to push on through their ranks. As he did so men clawed at him, struck him, hurled their weapons at him but still he rode on. He was all but through when, struck by another arrow, they managed to pull him from his saddle and he disappeared into a sea of very angry men.

At the loss of the banner much of Guthrum's army began to lose heart knowing they were beaten. One by one they began to flee for the safety of Chippenham but enough remained to make a fight of it. Alfred saw through their plan. Those few were buying time for their comrades to escape, so he and Osric rode down the slope urging us to despatch those that were left as quickly as we could. This we did in a last violent clash.

Alfred knew that if Aethelred and his men still lived they would be hard pressed at the bridge. 'Follow!' he screamed, charging with his men. 'Give chase!'

Ethelnorth also urged the men on. 'To the bridge!' he ordered. 'To the bridge! Don't let them find the safety of the Vill!'

In the chaos of the battle some of my men had not managed to find their Ealdormen and so remained with me. They had surrounded a group of prisoners who, having thrown down their weapons, looked terrified, some even falling to their knees to beg for mercy. Not sure what to do I looked to Ethelnorth for help.

'Strike them down!' the old warrior ordered coldly. 'Put them to the sword and be done with it! You're needed at the bridge!'

The men did not need telling twice. They quickly butchered the prisoners then went with Ethelnorth to relieve Aethelred. I went as well, not sure what else I should do. By then my voice was hoarse from shouting and my throat was parched but at least I was otherwise unscathed. I knew I should be thankful for that when I saw how the road to Chippenham was strewn with fallen men. Many Saxons had stopped to plunder the dead and wounded, seizing weapons and any jewellery which they could strip or cut from the bodies. Ethelnorth rebuked these men harshly, forcing them to abandon their booty as he drove them on. 'Aethelred still holds the bridge!' he shouted. 'Would you trade his life and that of his men for a handful of trinkets?'

When at last I arrived at the bridge I was shocked by the sight that greeted me. Aethelred and his men had tried to destroy it in order to stop the Vikings crossing but had been overrun before they could finish the job. In the fierce fighting which followed, Aethelred had been taken alive and, as expected, had been shown no mercy. His huge body had been hoisted onto a crude gantry made from timbers taken from the bridge itself then, with his wrists and legs securely tied, he had been cruelly tortured. The 'blood eagle' was perhaps the most brutal death the Vikings ever devised. His ribcage had been cracked open and his lungs lifted out so he could watch them inflate with his last desperate breaths, the taunts of his tormentors ringing in his ears. His broken body was a clear message to us all but the Vikings had left another one as well. Every Saxon warrior killed defending the bridge had been beheaded to imitate that which had been done to Ubba and his troops. The heads had been stacked in a neat pile on the bridge itself like a macabre sign to mark the path. The only consolation was that Aethelred and his men had clearly sold themselves dearly, for all around were the bodies of the Vikings they had slain.

'These were great Saxons,' said Alfred as he watched Aethelred's body being taken down. 'They shall be buried with honour and their names carried forward as an example to our children.' He then turned his attention to Chippenham where the Vikings were now ensconced. The gates had been closed with perhaps a third of Guthrum's force safe inside.

'We could easily take the Vill,' I suggested. 'The defences are weak and they're now too few to defend it.'

'I'll not destroy that which I came to save,' said Alfred wisely. 'If we're patient God will deliver our foe into our hands. Guthrum has not prepared himself for a siege and will come out when his men are hungry. Surround the Vill and let none escape. In the meantime we shall tend to our wounded, bury our dead and give thanks for this great victory.'

'Don't count your victory too soon,' warned Ethelnorth who had taken a wound to his arm. Even as he spoke he was trying to bind it to staunch the bleeding. 'Guthrum has been in tight corners before. He'll not readily give up what he's fought for all these years.'

Alfred knew he was right. 'Then bring the raven banner which Dudwine took so bravely,' he ordered.

Whilst they fetched it Alfred inquired after Edwin.

'I saw him hit across the head,' admitted Ethelnorth. 'He went down hard but I couldn't reach him.'

'Is he wounded, then?' I asked, stunned at the news.

'All I can say is that he was alive when I last saw him,' assured Ethelnorth.

Apart from that no one seemed to know what had become of my brother, so Alfred intervened. 'Send someone to bring us word,' he ordered.

With that a group of men appeared carrying the raven banner. On Alfred's orders it was taken to an area of open ground in front of the Vill and laid out on the turf just beyond the range of even an expert bowman. One by one the Saxons used it to wipe the blood from their blades in full view of those within the Vill. Others pissed on it or pretended to wipe their arses with it whilst the rest of us jeered. The Vikings who witnessed this were incensed and insulted, for the banner was as sacred to them as was the cross of Christ to us.

'Now we must have patience,' said Alfred. 'They'll come to us in time. Tend our wounded then bring all prisoners here to me. We shall spare those who are prepared to turn to God but the rest shall be put to the sword here upon this field where so many good Saxons died the day they took this place from me.'

Chapter Twenty-Five

I t was Ethelnorth who broke the news to me. He took
me to one side so we could speak in private, then told me
how badly Edwin had been wounded.

'The blow all but slew him,' he said quietly. 'We can offer
him nothing but our prayers.'

'But...but he will get well,' I protested.

Ethelnorth tried to reassure me. 'We shall pray that's so,'
he offered. 'For now go to him and let him see you. What
few words he has uttered have all been to ask for you.'

I hurried back to Edington where I found Edwin laid
out with the many others who were wounded. A group of
women were tending them, binding wounds, giving water
and offering some comfort where, in reality, there was little
to be found, for even the smallest wounds received in battle
tended to fester quickly.

Edwin's head had been bound with cloth soaked in
vinegar but, apart from that, there was little that could be
done to help him. Although barely conscious, his eyes looked
wild and were staring in a way I wished never to see again
in any man, least of all my brother. A small wooden bowl
containing fresh water had been left beside him, which I used
to bathe his head and wash the blood from his matted hair.
That done, I tried to make him as comfortable as I could by
wrapping him in a cloak to keep him warm.

Ethelnorth joined me for a while, sitting beside me on the ground. His own wound had been dressed and did not seem to trouble him beyond making it difficult to use his left arm.

'If you have other duties...' I offered. 'Edwin would not wish that I detain you.'

Ethelnorth made no attempt to move. 'My work is done,' he said sorrowfully. 'What remains is more suited to these women and the priests. Sometimes I wonder why we think such carnage can ever lead to peace.'

I could see how weary he was, not just from the battle but from the heavy burden of his duty. It was something which seemed to cut to the very core of his being and, for the first time, the old warrior truly looked his age.

'Surely it's not for you to worry about such things,' I assured him, hoping it would be of some comfort. 'You've done your duty; all that was asked of you and more.'

He nodded. 'We've all done our duty. Our swords are soaked in blood and Alfred has his great victory. Yet I fear the killing is not yet over for, though we bury friends and foe alike, it will still go on.'

I sensed that a great weight preyed upon his soul. I knew Ethelnorth had lived his life by the sword, yet he seemed to take no pleasure from it. 'Did you always want to be a warrior?' I asked whilst still cradling Edwin's head in my lap.

Ethelnorth gave a little laugh and stared at the ground. 'I never wanted to be a warrior,' he confided. 'I'm proud to have served my King but wish I could have done so as a musician. That was always my first love even as a boy.'

'What you, a musician?' I said, incredulous at the very thought of it.

'Is that so strange?' he asked.

'No. No it's just that I never thought of you as anything but a warrior.'

Ethelnorth nodded as though resigned to that. 'When I was a boy we were all expected to fight,' he mused. 'And when it was found I had some talent for it I was made to put away my lyre and to practise with the sword instead. Strange how easily we are persuaded to follow the course of our duty and not the way of our hearts.'

'Do you now regret that course?' I asked. 'After all, your reputation is now more famous than any man in Wessex. You're honoured by your King, loved by your men...'

'There are many things about my life I'd change,' he reasoned. 'But I believe the path we must follow is set at birth, determined by a force far greater than any we can ever know.'

'You mean the Holy Power of God's Great Purpose,' I acknowledged, recalling my religious training.

Ethelnorth laughed. 'Now you sound like a priest again!' he scoffed. 'No, God is forgiving, or at least I hope he is! But I don't believe he plans our daily lives. Instead he simply moves our hearts and minds to know right from wrong. That's why each of us must answer for our own sins and omissions. No, the power of which I speak is destiny itself. That's the force which shapes the pattern of our lives. And if your destiny sits well with what is in your heart then you're truly blessed, for if not there's nothing you can do to change it.'

'With all this talk of "fate" and "destiny", you remind me of my own decisions,' I said looking down at Edwin's troubled face as his head rested in my hands.

'So you've not yet finally decided to abandon your precious Church?' asked Ethelnorth.

'I thought I had,' I said. 'I was truly beginning to feel that God wanted me to serve him as a warrior but now as I look at my brother I'm not so sure.'

'Pah! All warriors feel the same when the killing is done. We lament the shedding of so much blood and are full of remorse for the friends we've lost and sometimes even for the men we've killed. Yet when the call comes again we all take up arms readily enough.'

'Is that what you'll do?' I asked.

The old warrior shrugged. 'What other option do I have? But it's not too late for you. Make your choice and pray that your destiny then fulfils your dreams. That's the path to happiness.'

I smiled at him, grateful for the advice. 'I pray that it will,' I said, stroking Edwin's brow softly. 'As indeed I pray that Edwin's final destiny is not about to be revealed.'

* * * * *

That first night after the battle the Saxons thought to celebrate their victory, but with so many friends dead or wounded and with Guthrum still inside the Vill, most of us were in no mood for a feast. I preferred to sit with Edwin thereby remaining close at hand in case there was any change in his being. Those who did celebrate sat together around a huge fire drinking and exchanging tales of the battle and of the deeds they had witnessed or performed. Some composed or recited poems but otherwise it was a sombre occasion, most unlike the Saxon feasts which usually followed a great triumph.

The next day men began to recover the bodies of our dead and laid them out for burial. Some 300 of our men had been killed outright and the wounds they had suffered testified to the ferocity of the battle. Alfred decreed they should be buried together at Edington and that a burial pit should be dug at the foot of the slope where most had perished. On this it was planned to build a mound with a large cross set at the eastern corner to mark the spot.

Dudwine's body was singled out for the honour of being placed nearest the cross for it was judged that his bravery had tipped the balance of the fighting in our favour. There was great praise for him and many spoke of how they had seen the young warrior turning this way and that, striking at the enemy whilst soaking up their arrows and their blows but never yielding. Yet when his tangled body was fetched Alfred shed tears of remorse for what he had asked of one so young. Indeed no man who saw it could help but wonder whether all the glory Dudwine had achieved could ever be worth the price he paid.

As the burials began a priest was summoned to lead our prayers. He was a thin lipped, rather pious little man, much given to citing the law of the Church rather than extending the warmth of its embrace. As such he was not well liked, but his task was to absolve the dead before they were committed to their graves. For this purpose the bodies were laid out in rows within the pit. The priest worked his way along each row in turn insisting that if he did not know any of the men personally someone should speak for them before he granted absolution. Only then were they sprinkled with lime before being covered over and laid to rest. Our haste stemmed from the fact that the bodies were already beginning to reek and though they were guarded day and night, we could not risk them being disturbed by wild beasts.

The mound could not be finally topped out whilst there were still so many wounded who, as like as not, would join their comrades when God chose to take their souls. I prayed that Edwin would not be counted among their number but although I dared not admit as much to myself, my brother was showing no sign of getting better.

The bodies of the Vikings were easier for us to deal with. They were stripped and heaped in a great pile on the edge of the battlefield. This was plagued with rats and vermin and many of the corpses were dragged off by wolves during the night to be left half devoured come morning. Eventually a number of huge fires were built onto which they were thrown one by one.

That left only the prisoners to be dealt with and, as Alfred had decreed, these were given a simple choice: they could embrace the Christian faith or else be slain.

'I never saw such willing converts!' declared Osric, laughing as they were led out and made to form a line in full view of the Vill with their hands tied behind their backs. The priest walked along the line with three Saxon warriors beside him. He stopped at each prisoner in turn and if they knelt before him and kissed his Holy crucifix they were led away to be prepared for baptism. If they refused they were seized by the three warriors, wrestled to the ground and put to the sword at once. Their bodies were then loaded onto a cart to be taken to join their comrades in the fires.

Despite all this Guthrum showed no sign of giving in. Lacking enough men to hold the whole of Chippenham, he had been forced to yield the settlement and withdrawn into the Vill itself where he sought to make his stand. Whilst their stock of food was low they could at least rely upon fresh water and fish from the river and so Alfred knew it might be several weeks before they would at last surrender.

'They'll eat their horses first,' said Ethelnorth.

'They would eat each other rather than die of hunger,' observed Alfred whose real concern was to keep his army together whilst we waited. Given that all were now free to leave this was no easy task, which is why Alfred had yet to distribute the booty, carefully holding it back as an incentive for men to stay. Many had secretly taken enough personal plunder from those they had killed and would have preferred to return with their spoil to their homes and farmsteads if they could. To keep them busy, Alfred set them tasks: some hunting, some to stand guard and some to work on the burial mound. He also had others start to dig a large ditch in front of the Vill to serve as protection in case Viking reinforcements arrived, though no one truly believed they would.

It was early on the third day that I was summoned to see Alfred who had taken up residence in one of the houses in Chippenham which had been hastily repaired. I found Ethelnorth was there when I arrived and Osric also. Alfred bade me sit then waited for me to settle before speaking.

'Matthew, the time has come for us to speak plainly,' said Alfred at last. 'You must have seen for yourself how Edwin suffers. You know what must be done.'

It was indeed a black moment, one which I feared even to think of but knew would come. At first I just shook my head as if I could somehow change their words. Then I looked across at Alfred, desperately trying to hold back the tears which were welling in my eyes. Why it worried me for them to see me cry I cannot say. Perhaps because I had striven so hard for them to regard me as a warrior but, in truth, I was not much more than a boy and, what's more, a boy who was about to lose not just his brother but also the last surviving member of his family.

'But he may yet be well!' I reasoned.

'No,' insisted Ethelnorth kindly. 'And if he does survive the blow he'll not be right for his brain is addled. Also he's in much pain and there's only one thing which we who love him best can do to help him now.'

'No!' I protested. 'We must wait. Things change, you know they do!'

Alfred and Ethelnorth looked at each other but said nothing.

'One more day,' I pleaded. 'Wait one more day to see if...'

Alfred was shaking his head. 'One more day; one more hour; one more moment – it'll make no difference except to prolong his pain. Edwin is lost to us now and though every true Saxon in this land shall mourn that loss, there's only one thing to be done. We must set his great spirit free.' He paused, looking at me kindly. 'Matthew, you're a warrior now and the right is yours. But Ethelnorth who is both friend and equal to Edwin has offered to perform this as a last act of kindness for your brother in your stead.'

Ethelnorth did not wait for my answer. 'Though it may test my courage more than any Viking ever did, I am prepared and will somehow find the strength to do what's needed,' he said sadly. 'The question is, will you stand beside me? Will you comfort your brother in his last moments or would you rather play no part in this? No man will think the less of you for that.'

In my heart I knew that what they said was right, just as I knew it was my duty to be there even if I lacked the courage to take my brother's life with my own hand. I nodded my agreement.

'And I shall attend as well,' declared Alfred. 'For no man has served me better and I would wish that he should pass knowing the great regard and love I have for him.'

With that the matter was settled. As was the Saxon way it was to be done at once, so Alfred got up and walked towards the door. I followed but Osric had to steady me for I was almost too dazed to stand unaided.

Once outside it seemed that the whole camp had anticipated the news and gathered expectantly but, despite their number, they waited in silence. The men just stood and stared at the small party, grimly parting as we walked towards them.

Edwin had been brought into the settlement and lay on a litter amid the ruins with many of the Saxons he had commanded gathered about him. He was, I am certain, completely unaware of what was about to happen but I was grateful that the priest had attended him and given the last rites. Alfred stood beside the litter and addressed us all. 'This man, Lord Edwin, son of Edwulf, is a great Saxon warrior worthy of the name and the heritage we all hold so dear. He has served me as he has served you all. Now, through wounds received on our account, he is in pain and waits upon the threshold of death. We would prefer to take his life in love and respect rather than see him suffer more. His brother Matthew and Lord Ethelnorth have decreed this course and I as King and Bretwalda of all Wessex say let it be so.'

Others then stepped forward in turn to speak in praise of Edwin's life, some simply recounting tales of his courage or recalling past events. Greatly moved by the love and respect shown by all, I sat down beside my brother and took his hand. Then Alfred and the whole assembly knelt in prayer. When they had finished the men gradually rose to their feet one by one. As they did so, they began to beat the backs of their shields just as they did before a battle. It was during this that Ethelnorth moved in behind Edwin and, without a word, reached forward and gently but swiftly slid the blade of his knife across his throat.

I held Edwin as the life ebbed from him. With tears welling in my eyes, I gently kissed his forehead and stroked his brow. Thus my brother died as he had lived, with courage and without complaint. Every man who watched him die knew we had indeed set free a great and noble spirit.

Chapter Twenty-Six

I kept vigil over Edwin's body all that day and through the night. I sat with him, talking to him as if he were alive and recalling many of the things we had been through together. Most of the memories saddened me for we seemed to have shared little that was not tinged with death, sorrow or loss. It was as though Alfred's plight had overshadowed our own.

Come morning Ethelnorth persuaded me to let him take my place. 'Others also have a right to pay their respects,' he reasoned. 'Besides, you've arrangements to make. The funeral is to be tomorrow and Alfred would speak with you about what's to be done.'

In truth I was grateful for the chance to leave. I felt a need to grieve for my brother in private and so accepted the offer, trusting Ethelnorth to guard Edwin's precious body well.

Solemnly I made my way to see Alfred but went first to stand beside the river. There, where none could see me, I shed my tears freely, sobbing bitterly for nearly an hour. Afterwards, as I tried to compose myself, I noticed Brother Felix had arrived bringing with him the women from Athelney and my heart soared when I realised Emelda was among them. Then I reproached myself, recalling how much Edwin had disapproved of my seeing her.

As she joined me she threw her arms around me but must have noticed a change in me. I felt awkward and distant, as though trying to keep a space between us. 'I was so sorry to hear the news,' she whispered with genuine sadness.

Out of respect for Edwin I tried to resist Emelda but, when it came to it, I could not help myself. As she drew me close her tears mingled with my own.

'He was a great man,' she said as I tried to pull myself together. 'And you should be proud for word even reached us as we travelled here yesterday.'

'But I killed him,' I protested, still tearful. 'I didn't wield the knife myself but the responsibility was mine.'

She gently brushed a few strands of her hair from my face. 'No, the Vikings killed him,' she said soothingly. 'You merely helped him to die as he would have wished, with pride and dignity. Imagine if he'd lived with his mind gone to be regarded as a fool. Edwin would not have endured that, not for anything.'

'So what's left for me now?' I asked. 'My whole family have been taken from me and...'

'You may yet find your brother and sister alive, perhaps even here at Chippenham.'

I had long since abandoned any hope of that. 'No, Edwin said they would've been taken across the sea to be sold abroad,' I explained. 'They're lost to me now and I must accept it.'

'Well you still have me,' suggested Emelda. Her voice was shy and tentative as though not sure what I would say to that.

My response was to pull away from her embrace. 'Yes, but you know we can't ever... Not now... I'll soon take my father's lands and may even become an Ealdorman in Edwin's stead.

I am now also a warrior and Alfred would never allow one of his warriors to take a wife so...'

Emelda looked hurt and disappointed. 'When first we met you were set to become a monk,' she reminded me. 'As such you were forbidden the pleasures of the flesh yet came willingly and often to my bed. Somewhere between then and now you've changed your mind and would now be a warrior but I see no cause for that to alter anything between us.'

'You mean you'll be my whore?' I said almost accusingly.

'I'll be your woman,' corrected Emelda. 'Whether we're wed or not.'

I still yearned for her, there was no denying that. I wanted her with all my being, perhaps even more now that I needed someone to comfort and console me. Yet to acknowledge that need would have been to betray my brother's dying wish. 'This is not the time to speak of such things,' I said. 'It's not fitting and, besides, there's much to be done. Even now I'm summoned by Lord Alfred himself to discuss Edwin's funeral and...'

With great sadness she turned and began to walk away from me.

'I'm just not sure of anything at the moment,' I called after her.

Emelda turned her head and smiled weakly. She looked lost and dejected.

Unable to watch her leave like that, I went after her. Taking her by the shoulders more roughly than I meant to, I turned her to face me. 'Look, you must understand that I've much on my mind,' I explained. 'I need some time to think, that's all. We'll speak again after the funeral. Perhaps then things will be different and—'

328

Emelda put her finger to my lips to stop me saying more. I know now that she had expected little from me but had hoped for more than that.

* * * * *

As an honour, Edwin was to be buried next to Dudwine with the cross set between them. Almost every man and woman in the camp wanted to attend his funeral which, if it was to be held at the graveside as was the Saxon way, would have meant leaving the Vill unguarded. To avoid this Alfred decreed that a special Mass would be said in the open so that all could attend. Then Edwin's body would be taken back to Edington borne on the shoulders of the most senior Ealdormen who would then witness his interment in the burial pit on behalf of all.

During the Mass all within the camp knelt as a sign of their respect, even those who remained on duty. I was told later that even some Vikings stood on the walls with their heads bowed and their weapons lowered. Then, as the funeral procession left, there was complete silence until it passed from view.

At the burial pit Brother Felix stood beside the cross and the priest led our prayers as, in sombre mood, we committed my brother's body to the ground.

* * * * *

A few days later Alfred and I stood together looking back at the Vill which Guthrum still refused to surrender.

'Matthew, I would speak with you on a matter of some weight,' said Alfred as if broaching a subject he was reluctant to raise. 'I know that much has happened in your life since that fateful day when the Vikings first took this place. You were then a novice monk anxious to return to your abbot. Now by all that is right you should look to become an Ealdorman in your father's and your brother's stead, and a wealthy one at that. You have your father's lands and I shall not forget my promise to give you more in return for the treasure you so generously donated to our cause. Also, you are now an accomplished warrior and I see in you a worthy replacement for your dear brother, but I must know first that you've given up all thoughts of returning to the Church, for my conscience would not let me tempt you from your calling.'

'I have my Lord, though am mindful that my father wisely sought a path for each of his sons to follow and sometimes feel I should respect his wish.'

'I'm certain your father would be pleased to find such respect in you,' said Alfred. 'Indeed he would have been proud of you just as he was proud of Edwin.'

'Thank you, sire. The truth is that whilst I love the Church, I fear I was never truly committed to a life in Holy Orders. Now, after all that's happened, I cannot go back to it. I shall of course do penance and offer recompense to my abbot but...'

Alfred put his hand on my shoulder. 'From what I've seen of you that's a wise decision and one of which I'm certain your dear father would approve. I'm mindful that he chose Edwin's path before ever choosing yours. Does that not mean that he wanted a warrior for a son before a priest?'

I was grateful for the comfort of that remark and said so.

'So, you'll become a warrior?' asked Alfred.

I bowed my head but said nothing.

'What, has all this blood swayed you from that course as well? Or is it the loss of your brother which has sown these seeds of doubt?'

I thought very carefully before I answered, not sure how much I dared say to my King. 'Sire, there's something else which troubles me but I must speak plainly if I'm to tell you what's in my heart,' I said at last.

'I trust you know me well enough by now to have no fear of doing that,' replied Alfred.

The trouble was I was not sure where to start. 'Sire, for generations my family have prospered and served with honour,' I tried. 'I cannot betray their endeavours and achievements.'

'That's true,' said Alfred. 'But that heritage is founded on many of your family being great warriors. How would you betray it by becoming one yourself? You've already shown you have the courage and the skill.'

'Sire, I have to assume that my older brother and my sister are also killed, which means I'm all that's left of our family,' I explained. 'Therefore if I'm to preserve my line I should look to take a wife.'

Alfred laughed aloud. 'Ah! Now I understand,' he acknowledged. 'If you become a warrior you cannot marry. Is that what troubles you?'

'Exactly, sire. I fear that our blood line might end here and all that my father and my forebears strived to achieve would be wasted.'

'Some warriors marry later in life,' suggested Alfred. 'Indeed I recall that your father and his father before him did as much.'

'But if I was to fall in battle there would then be no one left to carry on our name. Thus I'm minded to put all thoughts of being a warrior aside and to return to my lands to raise a family instead.'

'Which would be a great loss to me,' admitted Alfred. He considered this carefully then seemed to have an idea. 'You've earned a place beside your King,' he said thoughtfully. 'But whilst a warrior is free to take a woman where he may – and many do – their first loyalty must always be to me. That I cannot change. But what if I were to welcome you at Court as a trusted adviser, would that not answer your problem?'

'Edwin never received such an honour,' I reminded him, surprised and more than a little flattered by the suggestion. 'He was content to serve you with his sword and did so faithfully for years.'

'Ah, but then Edwin never sought to take a wife,' explained Alfred. 'And I shall need men at my Court I can trust. Who better than one who's risked everything for me without question? As a courtier you would be free to wed and if you were minded to choose a lady of good Saxon stock you could rise to high office.'

When I fell silent again Alfred sensed there was something more which troubled me. 'What is it, Matthew?' he pressed.

'Sire, I must tell you that I've chosen the girl I wish to take as my wife but I know that neither you nor Edwin would approve.'

Alfred thought for a moment then realised who I was referring to. 'Dear God, you cannot mean…!'

I nodded but said nothing.

'But she's a whore! She lay with near every man in the camp at Athelney and worse still, she's the daughter of a traitor! You can't possibly mean to marry her!'

Still I kept my silence.

'Look, take her,' said Alfred. 'I'll give her to you as a slave. Tup her every night for all I care but pray don't even think of marrying her!'

'But, sire, you don't know her as I do. She is wise well beyond her years and her station and has been a true friend to me. If she's sinned it's only because she had no choice. She's a whore because we made her one and why must she answer for the crimes of her father? Inside her heart is pure and...'

Alfred shook his head. 'Inside she's a scheming witch who's snared you with her charms! You're her one chance to save herself, don't you see that? She'd do anything she can to keep that prospect alive. You must see that's so.'

I could hear Edwin's words in this but my mind was made up. 'Sire, nothing would please me more than to serve you but in this I must follow my heart.'

Although shocked, Alfred calmed himself before he answered. 'Matthew, I would remind you that your blood line is almost as noble as my own. For generations your family have married to preserve the purity of that blood and thus you may count among your forebears many great men. If you break that line you betray that heritage and all those who have gone before you.'

'If I marry Emelda do I break that line? Is the blood she was born with any less pure because her father became a traitor? When he gave that blood to flow through her veins it was pure enough, for he was not a traitor then.'

'But her reputation is tainted by her father's treachery and by what she's become.'

'Are you saying there's a place for me at Court but not if I marry the girl I love? If so I might as well return to my lands and live my life as best I please.'

We walked on for a few yards each keeping our silence. Then I spoke, saying something which went far beyond anything I had a right to say. 'Why after all the Saxon blood that's been spilled are we still bound to a creed which places duty over choice? I've served you, sire. I've willingly risked my life for your cause and I've watched as every member of my family has been taken or slain. Now I must do what my heart demands. I say that my line must endure and that whether the blood be pure or tainted the fruit of my marriage should be able to hold their heads up high for what I and my forebears have achieved.'

Alfred looked stunned for a moment. Then he gently nodded his head as if resigned to the force of the argument. 'Your blood entitles you to speak so freely,' he acknowledged. 'And you're right. There's nothing you need to prove and no man alive may question your loyalty, your courage or your honour. The truth is that I have great plans for this realm for which I shall need men of ability not just those of good blood. So take Emelda to be your wife if you must. For your father's sake I shall not approve, but in recognition of all that you and your family have done for me I will offer you your place at Court and swear never to hold back any advancement or promotion that is rightfully yours on that account alone.'

I could scarce believe my ears. 'Sire, I—'

'There is but one condition,' said Alfred as though to stem my enthusiasm. 'Marriage is a matter of some consequence and this one more than most. You've much sorrow in your heart and I would urge you to think carefully before you decide, that's all. I shall devise an errand which will take you from here and thereby give you a chance to consider all we've said. When you return I shall respect whatever decision you've made. Until then, give me your word that you'll say nothing of this to Emelda or to anyone else. Are we agreed on that?'

* * * * *

Word was sent to Guthrum entreating him to surrender but the messengers were always turned away. It seemed the Vikings were intent upon dying within the walls rather than give themselves up. Whilst we waited we completed the ditch in front of the Vill and fortified the houses which we occupied within the settlement itself. Still desperate to keep his force together, Alfred set about repairing the chapel and as many of the other houses as he could. Many men complained at this saying that if they were to spend their time mending roofs they had homes of their own they had neglected for too long.

Alfred, Ethelnorth and I were inspecting their work when Ethelnorth expressed the view that if Guthrum did not surrender soon our army would disperse.

'We need to attack the Vill,' he urged. 'The prospect of so much plunder will then be incentive enough to keep the men here.'

Alfred would not even consider it. 'We've already paid the price for peace,' he argued. 'I would not risk another Saxon life without good cause.'

'But, sire—'

Alfred held up his hand. 'I am resolved to wait. Besides, there are many things which must be done even once I have Guthrum's sword. You who have helped me to win this war will need to help me keep the peace. To that end I would have you and Matthew work together to assemble an army that will answer to me direct without the need for me first to persuade the Ealdormen to back me every time I need to defend my realm.'

It was a great honour for both of us, for few men were trusted more than those charged to build an army for a King. Yet what Alfred proposed would shock many for it meant a change in the very balance of the power with which he was entrusted. Even so, with such a great victory to his credit there were those who would openly welcome such a change. Indeed rumours that Alfred meant to go forth and conquer all the surrounding lands had been rife and many boasted how they would march with him. It was this prospect which had kept many of the men there, not the menial tasks he had set for them to do.

'To defend the land, not to extend it?' asked Ethelnorth pointedly. 'Will you not seek to stretch the boundaries of your kingdom? With your victories you could rule in all the lands after Wessex and beyond!'

'Yes, I would extend my boundaries as any ruler should,' agreed Alfred. 'But I would rule in peace and that comes only from strength, but not that which stems from force or from subjection. I want other lands to see our Saxon justice and the protection we can offer and so flock to join us of their own accord. That way we shall grow ever stronger and not weaker as the realm grows bigger. We shall build prosperity through peaceful trade and farming safe from plunder and attack, and the stronger and the more prosperous we grow so shall others wish to be a part of a great kingdom united under Saxon law.'

They were fine words and I wanted desperately to believe them. Was this the road which God had planned for me all along? To build an army that would fight for peace? If so, I would welcome it wholeheartedly for it seemed to bring the paths of my life together. What's more, it was something I could truly believe in for I had never known a time of peace. To live in a land where I might raise a family safe and free from war seemed an almost impossible dream, yet for the first time there was hope – for if anyone could make that dream come true it was surely Alfred.

Chapter Twenty-Seven

Although Guthrum still refused to surrender, his men began to come out one or two at a time, usually trying to steal past our guards under the cover of darkness. Those who were caught were put to the sword at first light in full view of their comrades. Unlike the other prisoners they were not offered the chance of baptism, for Alfred wanted to make an example of them to weaken the resolve of those still within the Vill.

'We would have them stay inside,' he explained. 'The more mouths they have to feed the quicker they'll exhaust their supplies.'

And so it went on until the gates were opened at last and a party of about twenty men emerged on foot. They were led by Guthrum in person.

Rightfully distrustful, Osric drew his sword and positioned his men between this group and the King. Even though the Vikings were unarmed he was taking no chances and formed a line to keep them at a safe distance.

Alfred greeted Guthrum and his Jarls, though not in their language. For a moment it looked as though the Vikings' long-awaited surrender would be thwarted on the grounds that neither party could properly understand the other!

'I thought you could speak their tongue?' whispered Ethelnorth who stood beside him.

'I can,' said Alfred. 'But sometimes it's better to negotiate when they don't know that you understand what they say. Besides, they'll have someone who can interpret for us.'

With that Guthrum turned and spoke to one of his group, an elderly and dishevelled man who walked with a limp and relied upon a stick tucked beneath his arm for support. It was he who then addressed us.

'Lord Guthrum is wishing for peace,' he said. 'If you will have it so.'

Alfred indicated that Guthrum and the translator should step forward and stand before the Ealdormen who had, by that time, assembled themselves behind their King. The remaining Vikings were made to stay where they were with Osric's men guarding them with their swords still drawn.

'I am Ulf and will speak for you,' said the translator studying Alfred carefully. 'You I think are Lord Alfred for who we are with much respect. Your reputation carries far. Lord Guthrum says you are a brave and a valiant warrior and a wise King.'

Alfred acknowledged the compliment but did not reciprocate as was expected. Ulf made an aside to Guthrum.

'He says we're discourteous dogs,' Alfred whispered to us, smiling. Then he put his hand on Ethelnorth's arm lest he draw his sword and show we had understood what was said. Alfred then spoke aloud. 'Tell Lord Guthrum that I call upon him to surrender,' he declared. 'I require him and his men to hand us their weapons and offer back the Vill of Chippenham with all booty intact. Also all Saxons taken as slaves shall be freed and given to our care.'

The words were repeated to Guthrum who feigned surprise at the severity of the terms.

'I've not come to negotiate,' said Alfred firmly. 'You're beaten and will accept what's offered. Either that or you starve; the choice is yours.' With that he turned and began to walk away.

Ulf started after him. 'If Lord Guthrum will leave the Vill, you will spare the lives of his men?'

'Does he offer them as slaves?' asked Alfred.

Again Ulf conferred with Guthrum whose reply was obvious. 'My Lord demands they leave as free men,' he replied.

'Your Lord can demand nothing!' stormed Alfred. 'If they prefer they can join their comrades on the funeral pyre. I offer them a quick and honourable death, nothing more!'

Guthrum, who expected no quarter, seemed resigned to that and nodded his agreement knowing that his men would all prefer death at the point of a sword rather than starve or become slaves.

It was then that I noticed a small boy among the group Osric's men were guarding.

'Edmund!' I called, surprised and delighted to see him there.

The boy looked apprehensive at first then started towards me. He was quickly grabbed and restrained by Osric but shouted something to Ulf who began to translate.

'He can speak!' I said, cutting him short.

Ulf nodded. 'Of course. But not your tongue,' he said. 'He asks after the sword you carry and would claim it for his own.'

'As well he might,' I replied, recalling how much the boy had coveted it at the time. 'But the sword was a gift from my brother who took it from a Viking warrior.'

Ulf nodded. 'Then your brother had much courage, for it belonged to a great warrior – a man much respected by our people. He was also this boy's father.'

I stared in disbelief but suddenly all was clear. Edmund had pretended to be mute so that Edwin and I would think he was a poor orphan and the sole survivor of the slaughter at the settlement, whereas in fact he was a Viking! I laughed aloud at the boy's impudence. Then a thought occurred to me. 'His father!?' I said. 'But we—' I stopped myself when I recalled how cruelly Edwin had extracted the information about the whereabouts of Guthrum's army.

Edmund then spoke to Ulf who solemnly translated for him. 'He says his father was dying. That the wound was too deep. He thanks your brother for allowing his father to die with honour and asks you to return the sword which should, by rights, be his. In exchange he will give another of great beauty and of equal worth.'

This explained much. Edmund had stayed with his dying father waiting to claim the sword for himself. It was no wonder he had preferred to walk beside me rather than Edwin for I carried the one thing the boy wanted most in all the world. Although I knew I should be angry at this deceit I also felt very sorry for the lad. Part of me was ready to accede to his request but I was aware I was delaying Alfred's negotiations. I turned to apologise for this but Alfred would have none of it.

'These are matters of some weight,' he said. 'And I see they're not unconnected with our purpose here. I think Edwin would have seen the return of the sword as a noble gesture and approved it, provided the exchange is fair. But you must ask how this boy intends to provide such a weapon

341

when all he owns is forfeit to me. Besides, he's about to be put to death along with the rest of Guthrum's men.'

As he spoke Alfred winked at me to ensure I did not overreact to the last point. He clearly had no intention of killing so many men.

Ulf listened to all this then spoke to Edmund. 'The boy says he will offer himself as a slave to recover the sword,' he announced. 'He will work until he is able to pay a fair price.'

'Ah, but only if I agree to spare him,' observed Alfred.

I was wary lest my response should come from my heart and not my head. In the end I said I would think upon the matter but if Alfred chose not to spare the boy, Edmund could choose to die by his father's sword if he wished.

Alfred seemed amused by all this and suddenly raised his hand. 'This boy reminds me that there's been enough bloodshed, both Saxon and Viking,' he announced. 'As a Christian, I'm minded to spare what remains of your army but the Vill and the booty will be mine, together with all slaves. Your men will surrender their weapons and if they turn to God and swear allegiance to me they may then depart these lands in peace, but the lives of Guthrum and all his Jarls of senior rank shall be forfeit.'

Ulf explained the terms to Guthrum who seemed unperturbed by what was said. He replied to Ulf in no more than a few words.

'Lord Guthrum says you are a great leader. He will offer his life but not that of any other.'

Alfred thought about this then went across to Guthrum and led him aside, speaking to him in his native tongue. Although Ulf looked astonished at this he said nothing.

Instead he watched with the rest of us as the two most powerful men in the land spoke together in private. It was some time before they came to rejoin us.

'Guthrum has agreed to accept baptism,' announced Alfred. 'He and twelve men of senior rank shall take instruction at our Holy Church at Bath and I shall stand sponsor for them at the font. Their lives will be spared as will those of all others who convert to our faith and offer me allegiance. To this end Guthrum has offered to swear an oath upon his Holy ring dipped in blood, but I shall accept his word, for I believe him to be in earnest.'

'And after that?' asked Ethelnorth.

'After that Guthrum shall take lands which he may govern in my name. He's free to distribute these to those of his men who wish to live in peace. The others must depart this place unarmed and swear never to return to Wessex.'

'We cannot allow this!' protested one of the Ealdormen. 'Slay them now and be done with it! Destroy them while you can!'

Alfred shook his head. 'There's been enough killing,' he said.

The Ealdorman looked stunned. 'Why have we fought to take back lands we then give away to the very people who took them from us in the first place?'

Alfred raised his hand again. 'Because we're so few and they are many, that's why. And because most of them want peace as much as we do. They came in search of land not blood and if we give them the means to support themselves they'll have no cause to rise against us. Remember, it's better we govern by consent than try to rule by force. Besides, we've tried to fight back the invasion without success. Now it's time to try a new road in the hope that it will lead to peace.'

* * * * *

The next day Alfred was preparing to go to Bath where Guthrum and his Jarls would be baptised. Ethelnorth was to go with him together with a large force of men. In the meantime, a line of Viking warriors was leaving the Vill, each of them tossing his weapons onto a growing pile of swords, shields, axes and spears before filing past Alfred and kneeling in homage to swear their allegiance. They also knelt before the priest and kissed his crucifix.

'This is nonsense!' warned Ethelnorth. 'These are treacherous heathen bastards. They'll kill us all the moment our backs are turned!'

'They're beaten,' Alfred assured him as we watched the Vikings file past. 'Some will fight again but not here. And as our boundaries extend so shall we push them further from us until they're closer to the lands from which they came than to Wessex.'

Ethelnorth was not convinced. 'I still say they're not to be trusted,' he warned.

With that I saw Edmund in the line and called him over.

'So what of this boy?' asked Alfred. 'Will you take him as a slave that he might earn the right to buy back his father's sword?'

'That could take him a lifetime to achieve,' I replied. 'Thus I would like to know whether he has other kin who'll take him in.'

Alfred asked Ulf who spoke with Edmund. The boy shook his head.

It seemed his fate like that of all orphans now rested on the goodwill of others.

'Then say this to him,' I said. 'I've lost all my family in this cursed war. Most recent was the brother I held very dear. Both he and I were fond of this lad and so whilst I would not take him as a slave, I would have him as a brother. He shall grow to manhood in my care and after proper instruction, be baptised as "Edmund", the name my brother and I gave him when first we met. As a token, I shall give him back his father's sword and take Edwin's as my own instead, for that once belonged to my own father and thus I understand the importance of such things.'

'Are you saying you wish to adopt him?' asked one of the Ealdormen, sounding incredulous. 'The son of a dead Viking! The man your brother slew!'

'Yes, if Alfred will permit me. I shall be baptised again, taking back my old name of Edward, which is the one my father gave me. As such I mean to make a new life so why not start with a new brother as well?'

Alfred again intervened. 'It's fitting that the son of a noble Viking should join a noble Saxon family,' he said simply. 'Let it signify the new bond between our two peoples.'

The proposal was explained to Edmund who readily agreed and came to stand beside me. As he did so, I unbuckled the sword and gave it to him.

'Take care,' warned Ethelnorth. 'He's not some simple farm lad who may be schooled and tutored. His young eyes have seen much slaughter and his mind must be like a fog through which the ways of normal lads his age can scarce be seen.'

Alfred overheard Ethelnorth's warning but chose to ignore it. He was much pleased with my suggestion which he saw as an inspired political gesture. 'This is to the good,' he said. 'For I know you'll raise him in the ways of God. But you'll recall I mentioned an errand you might perform for me. It's one which may also serve to help Edmund learn something of our Saxon ways.'

'I had hoped to come with you to Bath,' I said.

'No, I'm reminded that I also have a family I've not seen for many months. I would have you ride ahead to Exeter and make arrangements there for a glorious reception for us all. One such that it will swell the pride of our men as they march in as heroes. I hope this will help persuade them to remain in my service and form the core of the standing army which you and Ethelnorth are to assemble. Can you arrange that for me?'

I was certain I could. Indeed I was proud of being given such an honour, my first mission as a courtier to a great and very noble King.

* * * * *

That night with the Vikings gone and Guthrum and his remaining Jarls safely under guard, the Saxons celebrated their victory in the Great Hall at Chippenham. Alfred took his place on the carved chair from where he watched as they drank and feasted. During the course of the evening many men recounted their exploits, standing in the centre by the fire close to the very spot where I had been so cruelly tormented that night I spied on the Viking camp. Some repeated a saga or recited poems which proudly boasted of epic and heroic deeds, others simply sang songs or drank to their newly restored King. Alfred watched all this good naturedly, enjoying every moment. Earlier, before all were too drunk to hear properly, he had distributed booty to the men according to that which they each deserved. It meant almost every one of them was rewarded well beyond their expectations, for the Vikings had stored a great deal of plunder within the Vill for safekeeping. Alfred also attended to various sundry matters. He settled a dispute which had arisen between two men and, most important of all, decreed that Dudwine's lands should be restored to his infant son. A Witan would be called at which all these items would be formally recorded and witnessed, but the announcements themselves did much to encourage the revelries.

Being so soon after Edwin's death, I was in no mood to celebrate. I left the feast early and strolled beside the river with Emelda, listening to the sounds of merriment drifting towards us from the Great Hall. It was the first time we had been alone together since Edwin's funeral and, having been reunited with her mother, she seemed more like a maid as she walked beside me – as though what she had been forced to become was now somehow forgotten. Certainly she had not been asked to provide her favours for anyone since she arrived for, with so many women freed from Chippenham, the men were now spoilt for choice.

'Before I left to go to battle I offered you this brooch,' I said, holding it out for her to see. 'I now offer it again.'

Emelda was confused. 'I thought you'd changed your feelings towards me?' she said.

'Nothing's changed,' I assured her. 'Yet everything is about to.'

She looked at me strangely, understanding nothing of what I said, which was not surprising as I meant to keep my word to Alfred and not mention marriage until after I returned from my mission.

'I have a duty to perform but when I get back things will be different, you'll see. So take this brooch and, if anything should happen to me, show it to Lord Alfred and tell him I gave it to you before I left. Use it to buy your freedom.'

'What could possibly happen to you? The war's over now and—'

'Take it and keep it safe until I return. Also look out for your mother for I've not forgotten that she saved my life.'

Emelda looked even more confused. 'You speak as though you may not come back,' she ventured.

'I will, just trust me in this,' I promised. 'I cannot say more at this stage for I've given my word, but all will yet be well between us.' I kissed her, then we walked back together arm in arm towards the settlement where, without anything being said between us, it was understood she would share my lodgings.

On the way I should have felt happier than I had for a very long time. My future seemed clearer than before and I was eagerly looking forward to my new life. Yet still I had my doubts. Perhaps there was something in all that Alfred had said that gave me cause to question whether in taking Emelda to wife I was following my conscience rather than my heart. I needed her right enough, or rather I believed I did, yet if that was the case I had to ask myself why I so welcomed the short respite from her presence that my mission would allow me. Of course I was also concerned that my new responsibilities might find me wanting, for all that Alfred proposed was indeed a very great honour and carried with it many responsibilities. I was, after all, still young and had much to learn. Similarly, having dispelled all thoughts of returning to the Church meant I had strayed far from my convictions and I felt that my soul needed consolation for that. Thus I easily convinced myself that I had good cause for whatever misgivings played upon my mind that night but, in reality, I knew there was something more which troubled me, something which cut to the very core of my being. It was only later as I lay in Emelda's arms that I realised what it was.

Having been filled with sadness, danger and uncertainty, my short and turbulent life had reached a point where, suddenly, everything seemed to be going too well...

To be continued...

Glossary

Whilst not all universally accepted, the following is an explanation of some of the terms as used in this story:

BERSERKERS Feared Viking warriors who were said to work themselves up into frenzy prior to fighting, often by imbibing some form of hallucinogen. They sometimes fought bare chested or wearing a symbolic bear skin and were said not to feel pain or fear anything, even death.

BRETWALDA A mainly honorary title given to a recognised overlord.

CEORL The lowest rank of freemen.

EALDORMAN A high-ranking nobleman usually appointed by the king to oversee a shire or group of shires.

FYRD A group of able-bodied freemen who could be mobilised for military service when required.

JARL A Viking nobleman or chieftain.

SEAX A short single-edged sword.

THANE A freeman holding land granted by the King or by an Ealdorman to whom he owed allegiance and for whom he provided military support when needed.

WITAN An assembly whose duty was to advise the King and with whom he could consult.

Acknowledgements

Although woven around recognised historical events, *Blood and Destiny* remains primarily a work of fiction and most characters, including Matthew and Edwin, have emerged from my own imagination rather than from the pages of history. Also, the story is largely my own interpretation of events, albeit based on a good deal of detailed research. For that I must thank the many very knowledgeable historians, too numerous to mention, whose work has provided both information and inspiration. Similarly, I am indebted to several re-enactment groups who, through their commitment and attention to detail, share my enthusiasm for bringing history to life. The more I have seen of what they do the more I admire and respect their craft.

That said, any mistakes, errors or omissions are all mine, including the many 'liberties' I have taken throughout the story.

It would not be right to miss this opportunity to acknowledge the support of my wife and family in writing this novel – they were so often deprived of my full attention whilst I was away with Matthew on his many adventures.

I should also like to thank the team at my publishers, RedDoor – particularly Clare, Heather and Anna – not just for their professionalism in producing this book but for believing in me when many others didn't.

In memory of David Kevin Bishop
1949–2017

About the Author

Chris Bishop was born in London in 1951. After a successful career as a chartered surveyor, he retired to concentrate on writing, combining this with his lifelong interest in history. *Blood and Destiny* is his first novel and is part of a series entitled *The Shadow of the Raven*.